BEG FOR ME
HAWKEYE VOLUME TWO

SIERRA CARTWRIGHT

Beg For Me

Copyright @ 2021 Sierra Cartwright

Editing by Jennifer Barker

Proofing by Bev Albin

Layout Design by Once Upon An Alpha, Shannon Hunt

Cover Design by Once Upon An Alpha, Shannon Hunt

Cover Model: Josh Gibson

Photographer: Dxpert Image, Daniel Xaysongkham

Promotion by Once Upon An Alpha, Shannon Hunt

All rights reserved. Except for use in a review, no part of this publication may be reproduced, distributed, or transmitted in any form, or by any means, electronic or mechanical, including photocopying, recording, or by any information storage and retrieval system, without prior written permission of the author.

This is a work of fiction. Names, characters, places, brands, media, and incidents are either the products of the author's imagination or are used fictitiously, and any resemblance to any actual persons, living or dead, is entirely coincidental.

The author acknowledges the trademarked status and trademark owners of various products referenced in this work of fiction. The publication/use of these trademarks is not authorized, associated with, or sponsored by the trademark owners.

Adult Reading Material

Disclaimer: This work of fiction is for mature (18+) audiences only and contains strong sexual content and situations.

It is a standalone with my guarantee of satisfying, happily ever after.

All rights reserved.

DEDICATION

For YOU.

HAWKEYE

MEANT FOR
me

USA TODAY BESTSELLING AUTHOR
SIERRA CARTWRIGHT

PROLOGUE

HAWKEYE

"What do you think?"

From his place on the raised platform that had once served as a fire outlook post, Torin Carter glanced at Hawkeye, his boss and mentor. The man owned the security firm Torin worked for, as well as this eight-hundred-acre outpost in the remote part of the West. "Think of what? The class?"

Six times a year, recruits new to the VIP protection program cycled through the Aiken Training Facility. It wasn't Torin's job to get them through. It was his job to make sure that everyone, except the very best, washed out.

"That recruit in specific. Going through the bog." Aviator glasses shaded Hawkeye's eyes as well as his thoughts.

"Mira Araceli?" Torin asked.

"That's the one."

Carrying a thirty-pound pack, face smeared with mud, her training uniform soaked, Mira Araceli dashed at full-out speed toward the next obstacle. She grabbed the rope and began to pull herself up the ten-foot wall as if she hadn't just navigated a killer course designed to destroy her energy reserves.

Today, her long-black hair with its deep fiery highlights was not only in a ponytail, it was tucked inside her jacket. She concentrated on the task in front of her, never looking away from her goal.

Torin had been running the training program for several years. During that time, only a few recruits stood out. "She's…" He searched for words to convey his conflict. Brave. Relentless. Driven, by something she'd never talked about during the admission process.

On a couple of occasions, he'd studied her file. Hawkeye's comprehensive background check had turned up nothing out of the ordinary. Youngest of three kids. Her father was a congressman and former military. Both of her brothers had followed his legacy—and expectations?—into the service.

Araceli's academic scores were excellent. She'd graduated in the top of her college class but had opted not to put her skills to use in a safe corporate environment. Instead, she'd applied to be part of Hawkeye Security, even though she knew the scope of their work, from protecting people and things, to operating in some of the most difficult places on the planet. *Why does she want to put her life at risk?*

Fuck. Why did anyone?

Hawkeye cleared his throat.

Torin glanced back at his boss. "She's one of the most determined I've ever seen. Works harder than anyone. Longer hours." Yesterday he'd hit the gym at five a.m. She was already there, wearing a sports bra beneath a sheer gray tank top. Rather than workout pants, she opted for formfitting shorts that showed off her toned legs and well-formed rear. They exchanged polite greetings, and she'd wandered over to be his spotter for his bench presses, then offered a hand up when he was done.

MEANT FOR ME

He shouldn't have accepted. But he had. A sensation, dormant for years, had sparked. Raw sexual attraction for Mira Araceli had shot straight to his cock, a violation of his personal ethics.

She hadn't pulled away like she should have. Her palms were callused, and so much smaller than his. Torin was smart enough to recognize her danger, though. He'd honed her strength himself. She would have him flat on his back anytime she wanted.

In the distance, a door slammed, and they moved away from each other. From across the room, he saw her looking at her hand.

No doubt she'd experienced the same electric pulse as he did.

Since that morning, he'd been damn sure she wasn't in the gym before he entered. Relationships among Hawkeye operatives weren't expressly forbidden. Hawkeye was smart enough to know that close quarters, adrenaline, fear, and survival instincts were a powerful cocktail. But the relationship between a recruit and instructors was sacred.

Having sex with Araceli wouldn't just be stupid—it would border on insane.

In addition to the fact that he was responsible for her safety, Araceli was far too young for his carnal demands. And it wasn't just in terms of age. Life had dealt him a vicious blow, leaving parts of him in jagged pieces.

He no longer even pretended to be relationship material.

When he could, he went to a BDSM club. There, he found women who wanted the same things he did. Extreme. Extreme enough to round the edges off the memories, the past.

There was no way he would subject a recruit to the danger that he represented, even if she was tempting as hell.

SIERRA CARTWRIGHT

Hawkeye was still waiting, and Torin settled for a nonanswer. "Her potential is unlimited."

"But?" Hawkeye folded his arms. Despite the thirty-seven-degree temperature, he'd skipped a coat and opted for a sweatshirt to go with his customary black khakis. Combined with his aviator glasses and black ball cap embroidered with the Hawkeye logo, the company owner was incognito.

Torin looked at her again. "She does best in situations where she is by herself." And that wasn't how Hawkeye Security operated. They believed no person was better alone than as part of a team. Certainly there were times when an agent had no backup and was left with no choice but to take individual action. But the ability to work with others was crucial to success.

"What do you think of her chances?"

Torin shrugged. When she first joined Hawkeye a year ago, she'd trained at the Tactical Operations Center. She could pump thirty-seven out of forty shots into a target's heart and was first through the door during hostage rescue exercises. Though she'd excelled, she took unnecessary risks. At times, she calculatingly ignored superiors' commands. So far it had worked well for her, much to the annoyance of her numerous instructors.

On her application to the program that Torin headed, she'd indicated she had too much downtime during her assignments. She wanted something more demanding. VIP protection could provide that. If she made it.

Araceli summited a second wall, then leaped off and kept moving, dropping down to crawl through a tunnel, then back up to navigate the ridiculously tough agility course.

Hawkeye watched her progress. "There's something about her."

At the end of the course, she doubled over to catch her

breath; then she checked her time on a fitness watch. Only then did she shrug off the pack.

"Lots of potential," Torin agreed.

"Either hone it or get her out of here." Hawkeye adjusted his ball cap. "They'd be glad to have her back in tactical. And with her IQ scores, she'd do well in a support role. Strategy."

She was a little young for that.

Then again, age wasn't always a factor. He knew that more than most.

"You doing okay?" Hawkeye asked.

Torin twitched. "It's easier."

In his usual way, Hawkeye remained silent, letting time and tension stretch, waiting.

"I think about it every day." Dreams. Nightmares. Second-guessing himself, his reactions, replaying it and never changing the outcome.

"You've accumulated plenty of time off."

"I'd rather work."

"Understood."

Torin and Hawkeye watched a couple more recruits finish the course. Results were fed through to his high-tech tablet. Not surprisingly, Mira had finished in the top three.

In the distance, an old bus lumbered toward them, spewing a cloud of dirt in its wake.

Turning his head to watch it, Hawkeye asked, "You heading to Aiken Junction?"

"Yeah." Torin grinned. Drills in the mock town were one of his favorite parts of being an instructor. And he fully intended to use the opportunity to be sure Araceli learned a valuable lesson. "Want to join us?"

"If I had time." Hawkeye sighed. "Another damn dinner. Another damn meeting with a multinational company." Hawkeye wasn't just the founder and owner of the security firm—he was their best performing salesperson. "And I'm going to get the account."

"Never doubted you, boss."

Hawkeye clapped Torin on the shoulder. "I've taken enough of your day."

After nodding, Torin descended the steps, then jogged over to the finish line where recruits were talking, drinking water, dreaming about a beer or the hot tub. "Listen up!"

Talking ceased.

"You're responsible for protecting the family of an important diplomat. Their youngest daughter is seventeen and just slipped her security detail. And you're going to get her back."

There were groans and resigned sighs. The group had hit the running track at six a.m., had hours of classroom instruction, missed lunch, and been timed on their run through the mud challenge. And their day was just beginning.

He pointed to the approaching vehicle. "Gear up."

Exhausted recruits picked up the packs they'd just shucked.

"The bus will stop for ninety seconds. If you're not on it, you'll be hiking to Aiken Junction."

Mira grabbed a protein bar from her bag then slung it over one shoulder. She made sure she was first on the bus and moved to a seat farthest in the back.

Torin jumped on as the driver dropped the transmission into gear. While others had doubled up and were chatting, Araceli leaned forward and draped a T-shirt over her head. Smart. She was taking time to recover mentally and physically.

"Here's the drill." He stood at the top of the stairwell, holding on to a pole as the ancient vehicle hit every damn rock and pothole, jarring his jaw. "The tattoo parlor denied her because she's underage, and the artist we interviewed said he saw her move over to Thump, the nightclub next to

Bones." The name of their fictitious high-end steakhouse. "She has a fake ID, so it's possible she got past security. Her daddy wants her home, and wants her safe. This isn't the first time she's slipped her detail. You'll stage at the church. Choose a team leader and make a plan. Any questions?"

Most people lapsed into silence, a few engaged in banter and trash talk, and he took a seat behind the driver.

A mind-numbing thirty minutes later, the bus churned through Hell's Acre, the seedy area of town, then crossed the fake railroad tracks that separated the sleazy area of town from the more respectable suburban setting.

The driver braked to a grinding halt in front of the clapboard All Saints Church.

"Not so fast," Torin said when the recruits began to stand. "This isn't your stop."

He jogged down the steps to the sidewalk, and the driver pulled the lever to shut the door, then hit the accelerator fast enough to cause the occupants some whiplash—good training for real-life evasive driving. The recruits would be taken around the town several times in order to give Torin and the role-players time to set up.

Once the bus disappeared from view, he pulled open the door to the restaurant and entered the dining room where he greeted fellow instructors. "Who's playing our principal?"

"That's me, Commander." Charlotte Bixby—four feet eleven, ninety-two pounds, and ferocious as a man twice her size—waved from the back of the room. She wore a black dress and flats that would give her some maneuverability.

"And your gentlemen friends?"

Two agents raised their hands.

Torin went through the rest of the roles, couples, bartenders, cocktail servers, DJ Asylum, partiers on the dance floor. All in all, over two dozen people were assigned to the scene. "Okay, people! Let's head over."

Twenty minutes later, music blared. Charlotte was seated in a booth attached to the far wall. She was wedged between two solid men, a cocktail in front of her. The dance floor in the center of the room was filled with gyrating couples, servers moved around the room, and a bartender was drawing a beer. The surveillance room was being manned by one of the instructors, and he was wearing a polo shirt that identified him as one of Thump's security team. The bouncer, nicknamed Bear, was dressed similarly, but wearing a jacket that emphasized his broad shoulders and beefy biceps. Arms folded, Torin stood behind Bear.

Since a cold front was moving through and the temperature had dropped to just above freezing, a coat check had been set up near the front door, close to the restrooms.

Everything was in place.

A role player sashayed through the front door and gave Bear a once-over and an inviting smile. That didn't stop him from scrutinizing her ID.

"Enjoy your evening, Miss."

After snatching her ID back, she breezed past them and headed straight for the bar.

Several more people entered, and none of them were Hawkeye recruits. Hopefully that meant they were still strategizing. He preferred that to seeing them head in without a plan…like they had last time they ran a similar drill.

He checked his watch.

Fifteen minutes.

Then thirty.

Charlotte was on her second cocktail.

An hour.

Torin left the door to grab a beer at the bar. Then he carried it to the side of the room and stood at a tall round table.

MEANT FOR ME

DJ Asylum turned on pulsing colored strobe lights and cranked up the music. The walls echoed from the bass. People shouted to be heard.

Exactly like an ordinary bar in Anytown, USA.

One of Charlotte's companions signaled for another drink and then draped that arm across her back. She leaned into him.

Within minutes, Araceli strolled in. Her face was clean, and she'd changed into clean clothes—obviously they'd been in her backpack, along with a shiny headband. Nothing could hide her combat boots, though.

Life wasn't a series of perfect opportunities. Blending in mattered, but speed was critical. It did mean that the role players had an advantage, though.

Along with a fellow trainee, Araceli found a table. Instead of waiting for a cocktail waitress, she headed to the bar. She scanned the occupants, saw him, gave no acknowledgment that they'd ever met.

Yeah. Hawkeye was right. She was damn good.

She secured two drinks, then, instead of heading back to the table, walked to the far end of the room and began a search for their principal.

Smart. She wouldn't approach right away, she'd make sweep, assess the situation, all the while looking as if she fit in.

Except for those ridiculous combat boots.

Under the flashing lights, he lost her. Until her headband winked in the light.

He checked out the other recruits and their strategies. Two of them—women—looped arms like besties and pretended to look for men.

DJ Asylum's voice boomed through the room, distorted by some sort of synthesizer. "Get on the floor and show me your moves!"

One of the trainers walked to the table where Charlotte sat and whispered into the ear of the man with his arm draped over her shoulder.

Araceli put down her drink.

The companion nodded and moved his arm to reach into his pocket. Money exchanged hands.

The second guy slid off his seat, effectively blocking the pathway to the booth.

The man Charlotte was cozying up to led her to the dance floor. Araceli stood, looked around for a male agent, grabbed him, then pulled him toward the other couple.

Moments later, fog spilled from machines, clouding the air.

Lights went out, and the music stopped so abruptly that it seemed to thunder off the still-pulsating walls.

It took a few seconds for emergency lighting to kick on. When it did, the fog was thick and surreal, and Charlotte and her dance partner were gone.

Araceli headed toward the exit and shoved her way past Bear and out of the building.

Torin strolled toward the coatroom. He pushed the door most of the way closed, leaving a crack so he could watch the front door.

Moments later, Araceli hurried back in, her winking headband all but a neon sign indicating her position. He eased the door open, then, as she started past, reached out, grabbed her, pulled her in, and caught her in a rear hold, an elbow under her chin, his right arm beneath her breasts.

She was breathing hard, but she grabbed his forearms to try to break free. In response, he tightened the hold to ward off an elbow jab. And he leaned her forward to prevent one of her vicious, calculated stomps. "Knock it off, Araceli," he growled into her ear.

"Commander Carter?" She froze. "It's dark. How did you know it was me?"

"Your headband."

"Shit."

"That's right. You lose." He loosened his grip slightly, but she kept her hands in place. "Your target is gone."

With a deep, frustrated sigh, she tipped her head back, resting it on his chest. And he noticed her. The way she fit with him, and how she trusted him, despite her annoyance at having been bested. And even the way she smelled…wildflowers and innocence, despite the grueling ordeal earlier today. He wanted to reassure her, let her know how proud he was of her efforts.

Jesus. Immediately he released her. He'd held her longer than he need to. Longer than he should have. "Go to Bones. I'll meet you there." Torin took a step back, literal as well as mental.

In the near dark, she faced him. "But I can—"

"Go. I'm one of the bad guys, Araceli." And not just for the role-playing scenario. He was no good for her. "I took you out of the game. You never even noticed me. You didn't make a plan. You rushed forward without assessing the situation. You failed."

After a few seconds of hesitation, she nodded. "It will be the last time, Commander Carter. You underestimate me and my capabilities."

Something he didn't want to name snaked through him.

She had to be talking about the job, nothing more. Araceli couldn't know about his inner turmoil and his dark attraction to her.

Alone in the dark, Torin balled his hand into a fist over and over, opening, closing. Opening. Closing.

By far, Mira Araceli was the most dangerous student he'd ever had.

CHAPTER ONE

HAWKEYE

"You all right, Mira?"

For three years, six months, and twelve days, Torin Carter had haunted Mira Araceli's days and teased her nights.

Jonathan, the personal trainer she worked with when she was staying in New Orleans, snapped his fingers in front of her face. "Mira?"

His proximity, along with the sharp sound, finally broke through her runaway thoughts, and she shook head to clear it of the distraction that was her former Hawkeye instructor.

What the hell was wrong with her? She shouldn't have checked out mentally, even for a fraction of a second. In the wrong circumstances, it could mean the difference between survival and death. "Sorry." With a smile meant to be reassuring, she met his eyes.

For most of her life, she'd practiced yoga. Five years ago, she'd learned to meditate. Yet when it came to Torin, she never remembered to use her skills.

"Something on your mind?"

"*Was.* There was. I'm good to go now." She was almost

SIERRA CARTWRIGHT

done with the final set—squatting over two hundred pounds. She could do this. *Right?* In a couple of minutes, she'd be out of here and headed for the house where she would spend the next nine weeks living with her nemesis.

How the hell had this even happened? Hawkeye required all instructors—even the head of the program—to spend time in the field to keep their skills sharp. But for them to be assigned to the same team…?

"Ready?" Jonathan asked. "You have three more reps."

With single-minded focus, she tucked way thoughts of her demanding and mysterious former instructor.

Jonathan scowled. "You sure everything's okay?"

She got in position, adjusted her grip, then took a breath.

"Hold up." He nudged one of her feet.

"Thanks." After executing the squat, watching her form, breathing correctly, she racked the bar and stepped away. No matter what she wanted to believe, thoughts of Torin had wormed past her defenses to dominate her thoughts. "I'm calling it."

Jonathan nodded. "Good plan." He checked his clipboard. "See you back the day after tomorrow?"

"Six a.m. I won't miss it." She grabbed her water bottle, took a swig, then headed for the locker room. This was the first time in her adult life that she'd cut a workout short.

Mira showered, then took longer than normal with her makeup. Long enough to piss her off. Frustrated, she shoved the cap back onto her lipstick and dropped it in her bag.

Even though she routinely had male partners, she wasn't in the habit of primping. Of course, she'd never had an all-consuming attraction to one of them before.

Torin Carter wasn't just gorgeous. As her VIP Protective Services instructor, he'd been tougher on her than anyone ever had been, demanding her very best, harshly grading her work. It was his job to make her a stellar agent or cut her from the program. He hadn't known that failure was never a possibility.

During her training, he'd never shown anything beyond a hard-ass, impersonal interaction toward her. Except for that night at Thump.

When he'd caught her in that choke hold, she'd struggled, elbowing him, attempting to stomp on his foot. His commanding voice had subdued her, and when she stopped struggling, she noticed his arms around her.

Even though he loosened his hold, Torin didn't release her right away like other instructors had. And in a reaction that was wholly unlike her, she tipped her head back and relaxed into him, seeking comfort, a brief respite from the relentless and grueling training exercises. For a moment, she forgot about her job, stopped noticing the fog and pandemonium around them.

She thought—maybe—that he experienced an echoing flare, but he pushed her away, with a harsh indictment of her skills.

Drowning in rejection and embarrassment, she squared her shoulders and locked away her ridiculous unrequited emotions and vowed never to examine them again.

Even though she'd graduated years ago and hadn't heard his name since, he was never far away. Frustratingly, she thought of him every time she went out on a date. It was as if her subconscious was weighing and measuring all men against him.

The comparisons even happened when she scened at a BDSM club.

Torin was everything she wanted a Dom to be—uncompromising, strong, intelligent...and, at the right time, reassuring. In his arms, in that coatroom, she'd discovered he was capable of tenderness. Maybe if she'd only seen him be an ass, he would have been easier to forget.

Surviving Torin might be her greatest test ever.

Mira dragged her hair back over her shoulder and stared at herself in the mirror. "You." She pointed at her reflection. "You're smarter this time. Wiser. More in control."

A blonde emerged from one of the shower stalls. "Man problems?"

Embarrassed, Mira lifted a shoulder. She hadn't realized her words would be overheard.

"Isn't it always?" the woman asked.

For other people, not her. "That's the thing. It never has been until now."

"I see you here all the time. You're tough. Whatever it is, you can handle it."

Mira hoped so. She smiled at the other woman. "Thank you. I needed that pep talk." After blotting her lipstick, she gathered her belongings, exited the gym, then strode across the parking lot to her car.

She and Torin were scheduled to rendezvous at seven p.m. at Hawkeye's mansion in the Garden District. Since it was equipped with modern security both inside and out, he preferred his high-value clients utilize it when they visited NOLA. In addition to eight bedrooms, there was a spacious carriage house apartment for use by security personnel.

The grounds were spectacular, with a large outdoor swimming pool, a concrete courtyard with plenty of lounge chairs, tables, and umbrellas. Potted plants provided splashes of color, while numerous trees offered privacy as well as shade.

She'd stayed on the property several times, including earlier this year for Mardi Gras while she was working the detail for an A-list actor. She planned to arrive before Torin so she could select her bedroom, get settled, have the upper hand. Any advantage, no matter how small, was a necessity.

Since it was still early afternoon, she managed the traffic

MEANT FOR ME

with only the usual snarls.

After passing the biometric security system at the gate, she drove onto the property.

More confident now, she grabbed her gear, then jogged up the stairs to enter the code on the keypad. A moment later, the lock turned, and she opened the door.

Torin stood in the middle of the main living space, arms folded, damn biceps bulging. His rakishly long black hair was damp, and the atmosphere sizzled with his scent, that of crisp moonlit nights. He swept his gaze over her, and it took all her concentration to remain in place as he assessed her with his shockingly blue eyes.

When he tipped his head to the side, reaction flooded her. Her knees wobbled, and she dropped her duffel bag off her shoulder and lowered her gear to the hardwood floor to disguise her too-real, too-feminine reaction.

His jaw was set, his mouth compressed. There was no way to tell what he was thinking.

How the hell had he arrived before she had? For her not to have seen his car, he must have parked it in the garage. She gave a quick, smart nod, being as stoic as he was. "Commander Carter."

"At present, we're partners. So make it Carter. Or Torin."

Not a chance. No way was she allowing herself to be on intimate terms with him.

Mira turned to close the door and dragged in a deep breath. She was early. Hours and hours early, yet he had the upper hand. As always. Before facing him, she exhaled, focusing on controlling her pulse rate.

"I took the first bedroom."

Not having any other choice, she nodded. "I'll bunk in the back one." Which left an empty one between them

"The fridge is stocked, and so is the pantry, but I figured we'd go to the grocery store together for additional items."

"I'll give you a list of what I need."

"Still not a team player, Araceli?"

Fuck you. "Still critiquing every little thing I do, Carter?" She squared her chin. She'd passed every one of his damn tests.

"Your loss." He shrugged. "I was going to buy you dinner while we were out. There's a place in the French Quarter, on Chartres Street. Their Taste of New Orleans platter is divine."

He was a foodie?

"Crawfish étouffée, gumbo, jambalaya. And a loaf of fresh hot bread."

Damn him, he'd named some of her favorite dishes. Eating was one of the reasons she'd asked to work out of the Southern office. And when she'd received her assignment, she'd bought a house nearby.

"Up to you." He lifted one shoulder in a casual shrug. "Can't starve yourself while you're here."

Eat when you can. Sleep when you can. One of the first things she'd learned as a Hawkeye recruit. Calls for action never arrived when expected. Or convenient. More than once, she'd been up more than twenty-four hours with no food and limited water.

As if on cue, her stomach growled. The protein bar she'd eaten before her workout had long since been metabolized. Logic told her not to be stubborn. After all, she was going to share a majority of her meals with Torin for the foreseeable future.

"Come on, Araceli. I won't bite." His grin was quick and lethal.

Damn him. Part of her wished he would. It might help get rid of the tension crawling through her so she could move on, forget him. There was no way any man could be as hot as she believed he would be.

MEANT FOR ME

"We'll go as coworkers. I promise, no critiques."

"Okay. Fine." She exhaled. "Give me half an hour to get settled." Mira grabbed her belongings and escaped to the back bedroom.

It took her each one of those thirty minutes to regain her composure.

When she rejoined him, he was at the kitchen table, doing something on his computer. "Ready?" he asked, pushing back.

"Yes." It was a total lie, and her half smile was a total fake.

He drove them to the French Quarter in his gloss-white SUV, and he handled traffic without getting frustrated, making her wonder if he ever betrayed ordinary human emotion.

"You don't like me," she said, wanting to get it out of the way.

"Like you?" He slid her a quick glance. "Never thought about it."

She sank a little in her leather seat. This was another time that maybe she should have kept her mouth shut.

"But respect you? Very much. I think you have a lot of talent."

"You were damn tough on me."

He didn't respond.

"In training." It had bothered her. Other recruits didn't receive as much of his attention as she did. It had been difficult not to take it personally.

"You scare me."

She blinked, then stared at him.

"You're a good agent. Great instincts."

"But...?" Mira raked her hair back from her forehead. Why was she doing this to herself?

"You're a maverick. As if you've got something to prove." He was silent for so long, she wondered if he was going to say anything more. "You remind me of someone." He shrugged. "She got herself killed."

Breath rushed out of her lungs. "I'm cautious."

He checked the mirrors before looking at her again. "So was she. And I still fucking buried her."

Though she squirmed beneath the intensity in his gaze, she defended herself. "I'm me, Commander. Don't confuse me with anyone else."

He lifted a shoulder but returned his attention to the road.

Agreeing to go out with him had been stupid. They weren't ordinary coworkers. He was still the trainer who found her lacking.

Maybe what bothered her was that he was at least partially right. She did have something to prove. Her father's voice was always in her head, whispering that she wasn't good enough, that she'd never measure up.

That Torin had seen her determination to prove her dad wrong scared the hell out of her.

She leaned back against the headrest. This assignment promised to be challenging and grueling, maybe the worst of her career.

Two weeks later

Together, Mira and Torin exited the vehicle provided by Hawkeye Security, then checked the surroundings as they walked around to the back of the Maison Sterling hotel.

Passersby continued down the sidewalk, most likely unaware that the door was used only by VIPs and a handful

MEANT FOR ME

of residents of the exclusive building. "I'll let Barstow know we're in position."

Torin nodded, then walked away to check the rest of the perimeter.

After their uncomfortable discussion on the first night, he'd treated her as a trusted partner. They'd worked together well, and they swapped out the lead position, based on what seemed best for the situation at hand. When she was in charge, he never second-guessed her judgment.

The only unfortunate thing was that it was a slow time of the year, which meant they had too much downtime together. He'd been closemouthed about his personal life, avoiding her questions about family and friends. If he ever made personal calls, she was unaware of them. She and her best friend, Hallie, had gone out for happy hour a couple of times, but as far as Mira knew, he hadn't gotten together with anyone.

What he did do was exercise, a lot...to the point of exhaustion. He ran every morning. And he swam lap after lap while wearing a stupidly tight, stupidly small black swimsuit. Most men wore trunks, but not Torin. The constant sight of his tanned, ripped body rocketed her hormones into overdrive. Work and hitting the gym herself were the only distractions she had.

She dialed the phone, and when the team leader answered, she said, "Araceli and Carter are onsite."

"Guessing another half hour?" Barstow replied. "They're waiting for another bottle of tequila to be delivered."

"Roger that." Not a surprise. Celebrity protection came with a lot of delays.

"I'll keep you posted," Barstow promised.

She ended the call and pocketed the phone. "Approximately another thirty minutes," she told Torin when he returned.

SIERRA CARTWRIGHT

Tonight's assignment was backing up the security team for The Crush, a mega-artist. Recognized as one of the biggest mainstream hip-hop artists in the country, he'd recently won a major music award. Because of his popularity, he had numerous endorsements, and had just finished an acting gig on a hit television show. As far as fame profiles went, this man was at the pinnacle.

Right now, he was taking a week off from his three-month-long tour and had decided to spend a night in the French Quarter before catching a flight to the Caribbean. As charismatic as he was generous and gregarious, The Crush wanted to please his fans. As a result, he signed lots of autographs and posed for pictures. When he went out, he sometimes posted his whereabouts on social media. Which meant protecting him was a security headache.

This evening, he had late dinner reservations and planned to take in some live music afterward. Since it was a Friday night, the crowds were going to be thick and boisterous. "But I'm guessing it's going to be closer to an hour."

"I wouldn't bet against you," Torin replied.

Despite the fact that it was only the end of April, the Southern air was thick and clammy. She'd already been in her bed reading when the call for backup came in.

Mira had opted for slacks and boots, along with a light blue button-down shirt. Since she didn't know what to expect tonight, she'd pulled on a blazer that would hold her phone and her stun gun, cleverly disguised as a lipstick container. Though discreet, its four million watts were surprisingly effective.

A droplet of moisture arrowed down her neck, and she lifted her ponytail for a moment.

"We've got plenty of time. You might as well head inside. Find some air-conditioning," Torin suggested.

Not a bad idea. "I'll stay close."

MEANT FOR ME

While Torin remained at his post, she wandered to the front of the hotel. Before entering, she glanced up at the historic brick building with its wrought-iron accents. It didn't take much effort to spot The Crush and several members of his group on a balcony. He held a glass, raised. As usual, he wore a fedora set at a jaunty angle. His white shirt—stark against his ebony skin—was held together by only the bottom two buttons. Maybe it was a trick of the light, but she was certain there was a shine on his muscular, shaved chest.

She pushed through the enormous revolving glass door, then stepped into the old-world—and blessedly cool— elegance of the Maison Sterling.

The front desk had no line, and a few couples were seated in leather chairs, sipping drinks.

An actual bar was farther in, and she walked toward it. Maybe it would be a unique destination on her next happy hour outing with Hallie. Mira scanned the posted menu, looking for her favorite, a hurricane. Of course, the Maison had its own version of the quintessential New Orleans drink. It was called the Cat Five, and featured five different kinds of rum instead of the traditional two. She loved the fruity cocktail, but this one was more than twice the price that she usually paid.

Of course, her favorite haunts didn't cater to Hollywood A-listers, musicians, politicians, or members of a rumored secret society.

"Would you like a table, ma'am?" the hostess asked.

She wished she could take a seat at the bar and enjoy the rest of the evening. Instead, Mira shook her head. "Thanks. No." Now that she'd cooled off, she exited into the wet, blanket-like atmosphere. Somehow, it was worse now than it had been.

25

The Crush was throwing Mardi Gras beads to a small crowd of women who'd gathered on the street.

She strode back to the valet stand. "You need to get the people onto the sidewalk."

"Losing battle."

No doubt. "Doesn't mean it's okay to ignore it." She walked back inside, to the front desk, then rapped her knuckles on the polished wood surface. "I need a manager."

When the man finally arrived, she glanced over her shoulder, indicating the front door. "Get those people out of here before someone gets hurt and you have a damn lawsuit on your hands."

"I'll handle it, ma'am."

Satisfied, but tossing a glare at the valet, she walked to the back of the building.

Of course, Torin was still in place, still as alert as he always was, seemingly impervious to the humidity or the distractions all around them. And as always, she had an all too feminine reaction to him.

Damn it all three ways to hell, why did he have to look so good?

Beneath a casual blazer, he wore his perennial black T-shirt. Because she'd seen him emerge from the bathroom last night after his shower wearing nothing more than a towel around his waist, she knew his muscular body was nicked by scars, some nicely healed, others that looked as if they'd never received attention. Unfortunately for her, they added to his mystique and the power he held over her.

After she went to bed, she'd had disturbing dreams, haunted by images of him—ordering her to her knees, fisting his hand in her hair as he forced her to look up at his darkly brooding face.

In one dream, he'd pinned her on the floor and yanked off

her pants as she'd screamed yes over and over again. She'd awakened, out of breath, shaking, heart racing. Overwhelmed, she'd tossed back the blankets, jumped out of bed, then spent twenty minutes on the exercise bike before standing beneath the shower's hot spray until the water heater had been drained. Still, it had taken another hour to fall asleep again.

When he met her gaze, the phantom memory returned, with a flame threatening to devour her.

She wasn't sure what, but she needed to do something to get this man out of her thoughts.

"All good?"

"He's tossing beads from the balcony." She shrugged. "I talked to a manager."

A car honked, and brakes squealed.

Biting out a curse, she grabbed her phone and called the Hawkeye team leader. "Shut him down," she instructed.

When Barstow agreed, she looked at Torin again. "It's going to be impossible to get The Crush out of the hotel without getting mobbed." Which was probably okay with him.

A couple of minutes later, a small group of women walked around the building to stand near them.

"What are you waiting for?" Mira asked.

"The Crush." A blonde in faded denim shorts that had strategic holes in them held her cell phone in front of her camera ready. "You're with him, right?" the blonde asked.

"Nah. Just hanging out," Torin replied easily, not moving away from the building.

"You're a bodyguard."

"We do this all the time," the tallest of the group added. "There will be a hundred people in the lobby, waiting, but he won't go through there. And they all have people who say the same thing you do."

"You got us, then." Torin smiled. "Could be a long wait. Don't know that he's planning to go out tonight."

"They all say that too," the blonde stated.

Clearly, the fan was an expert.

Local police arrived to usher fans off the streets and onto the sidewalks, and fortunately someone managed to get The Crush back inside his room. Even though an hour ticked past, the women at the back door never budged.

The blonde, however, reapplied her lipstick for the third time. Not believing her friend that it looked fine, she took a selfie to check for herself.

In her pocket, Mira's phone vibrated with a message. As she pulled out the device, Torin was also checking his.

The principal's on the move.

A stretch limo, one meant to accommodate a party of twenty, double-parked near the exit, ignoring honking cars.

Though neither Torin nor Mira spoke, the blonde moved several feet closer to the exit. Mira sidled in, putting herself between the woman and the door.

Torin pushed away from the building.

"That means he's coming!" the brunette exclaimed.

Mira shrugged. Saying anything seemed pointless.

"Oh my God!" The blonde squealed. "He just posted a picture of himself standing near the elevator."

Almost all of the celebrities Mira worked with preferred to go out incognito. They donned ball caps and sunglasses and didn't broadcast their whereabouts.

This man, though, fed off the frenzy.

It promised to be a really long night.

Instead of emerging at a brisk pace like most protectees,

The Crush strolled out, flanked by his entourage, four Hawkeye agents, and what looked to be two of his own bodyguards.

When the blonde screamed out his name and shouted, "I love you!" he stopped and smiled.

"I'll die unless I get a picture with you."

"Sir," Barstow said to The Crush. "We should keep moving."

With an apologetic smile to Barstow, The Crush waved the woman over.

Grinning and chatting, he posed for half a dozen selfies, then a dozen more with the entire group of women.

When a few more spotted them and squealed and broke into a run toward them, Mira and Torin inserted themselves between him and the oncoming group and nodded toward Barstow.

"Let's move, now," Barstow said. "Not a suggestion, sir."

"Sorry, ladies." The Crush smiled and posed with his knees slightly bent and both thumbs up for a few seconds, waiting for the fans to take a few more shots. Then, with obvious reluctance, he allowed his entourage to move him along.

Mira and Torin stood side by side and took up as much room as they could to discourage the women from following.

"That's it!" Torin called when the limo eased away from the curb. "He's gone."

Because the first group of women were starstruck as they walked away from their encounter with The Crush, they provided a barrier to the other fans.

A second car arrived for her and Torin. By prearrangement, The Crush's driver circled the block while she and Torin ensured everything was prepared at the upscale restaurant on Bienville Street.

Inside, Mira took the lead, introducing herself to the maître d' to confirm the private dining room.

"Yes, ma'am," the woman said. "The Vieux Carré Room is prepared, on the upper landing. Last door on the left. You'll have exclusive use of the entire floor."

Torin lifted his index finger, indicating he was going to check it out.

When he returned, he nodded, and she called Barstow to confirm everything was good.

Torin positioned himself at the bottom of the curbed staircase, and she stationed herself midway between him and the restaurant's entrance.

Less than five minutes later, the limousine glided to a stop directly in front of the restaurant. A Hawkeye member was the first out, and he stood sentry while the passengers exited.

The transfer to the second story went without incident.

"Not so bad," she said to Torin as she closed the door behind her.

Without responding, he wandered the mezzanine area, glanced over the wrought-iron railing, then paced back again.

A short time later, a server exited the dining room carrying two paper cups on a silver tray. "Compliments of The Crush."

"What is it?" she asked.

"Café au lait."

No wonder the man was universally liked.

"Thank you." She accepted the gift and took a sip of the steaming chicory-flavored beverage. It was an unexpected and welcome treat when a short-term protectee remembered their bodyguards.

Torin raised his cup toward her. "The good news is, we have tomorrow night off."

MEANT FOR ME

She grinned. "I wouldn't count on that. If the coffee's any indication, we might still be on this assignment."

"This is one time I'm hoping you're wrong."

Dinner lasted much longer than their beverages. She bent over into a couple of yoga stretches not just to stay alert, but also to keep her body fluid in case she needed to act quickly.

Finally, closer to midnight than eleven, and after most of the other patrons had already left the restaurant, Barstow sent a message that the limousine was out front and that their car was behind it. The Crush's destination was Bourbon Street. She'd hoped he'd select Frenchmen's Street where the crowds were smaller and more sober and celebrities were passé, but she wasn't surprised by his pulse-pounding, frenetic choice.

She and Torin jogged down the stairs to prepare the way for their client, and they had him in the vehicle and underway in less than a minute.

They arrived at the Front Door, a live-music venue in a building that had served as a brothel in the late nineteenth century. Since they hadn't called ahead, she and Torin bypassed the line to grab the bouncer's attention. This guy was even bigger than Bear at the training center.

"We need to see a manager," Torin said.

"Don't got one."

"We need to make arrangements for a VIP," she added.

The guy rolled his eyes. No doubt he'd heard every line.

"A manager," she repeated.

He looked them over and scratched his beard. Obviously deciding they didn't look like partygoers, the guy hooked his thumb over his shoulder. "Talk to the owner. Tall dude. Hawaiian shirt. Might be playing with the band."

"Hey!" the man behind them called out. "We got a VIP in our party." Snickers accompanied the proclamation. "Can we get in too?"

As Torin pulled the door open, she blinked. Strobe lights spun and flashed, disorienting her. The thumping bass reverberated, spiking her anxiety. At least a hundred people were packed into the bar, and shot girls wove through the crowd, pouring alcohol down their throats as others cheered them on.

She spotted the owner and pointed him out to Torin.

Since he was only able to make out their general meaning, he ushered them into a tiny room with an uneven wooden desk and ladder-back chair. The walls were painted a deep old-blood red, and much of it had flaked or faded over the years.

Even with the door shut, Torin still had to shout to be heard.

"The Crush?" the manager echoed. "No shit? How many people you got?"

"About twenty."

"We can do that. Gonna take time. Assume you wanna bring him in the back door?"

Torin nodded.

"We got a three-drink minimum for the night."

"Guessing it won't be a problem," Mira assured him.

Once people were moved, tables were shoved together, and stools were rounded up from back rooms, The Crush arrived.

One woman's eyes widened, and she pulled a friend close and pointed. Though they giggled and took photos, they remained where they were.

After the group was settled, she and Torin split up. He stood near the back door in case they needed to extract their client, and she propped her shoulders against a wall next to the group. From her vantage point, Mira had a good view of the venue's occupants.

The entourage ordered a couple of bottles of the propri-

32

etor's finest spirits, and The Crush settled back to listen to the band.

During a set break, the owner came over to introduce himself.

"Mind if I sit in?" The Crush asked.

Shit. That meant he'd be on stage.

The man grinned. "Reckon it can be arranged."

Suddenly the evening had gotten a whole lot more challenging. She grabbed her phone to update Torin.

After a nudge from the barkeep, the band leader wandered over to shake hands, select a song, and confirm the timing.

When the details were set, she sent them to Torin. The third song would be "Your Love Forevermore," one of The Crush's top ten hits, and made popular on a movie soundtrack. It was midtempo, soulful and deep, ending in tragedy. He'd jump on the stage during the first chorus, finish out the track with the band, then run through the refrain an extra time at the end to leave the crowd on an upbeat note. After that, his bodyguards would escort him back to the table.

Which seemed an unlikely scenario to her. Fans would want autographs. He'd want to give them.

When it was time for The Crush to go on, she and Torin accompanied him to the stage. The moment the audience realized they had a star in their midst, the screams began. Almost everyone yanked out their cell phones to take snapshots, which meant the performance would be all over social media within minutes.

Two bodyguards from his personal team flanked the stairs, while a couple of the Hawkeye agents positioned themselves at the corners of the stage. She and Torin stood toward the front of the crowd, right in the middle, poised to move any direction.

Shot girls wiggled between the swaying, screaming people, adding to the mayhem.

As he reached the refrain, a woman began screaming and sobbing. Mira flicked a glance that direction, ensuring there was no threat from her near-hysterical reaction to being so close to The Crush. When the woman's friends consoled her, Mira continued scanning the attendees.

Midway through the song, a man rushed forward, shouting obscenities, screaming that The Crush had no talent.

Mira moved quick, inserting herself between him and the stage. "Step it down," she instructed.

"The fuck out of my way!"

"Back the hell up!" She flattened her palms on his chest and shoved him back. He was huge, immovable, reeking of alcohol, eyes wide, focused on The Crush and nothing else. Torin fought through the crowd toward her.

She leaned toward the heckler. "Last warning."

"I told you to get the fuck out of my way, bitch!"

From her jacket pocket, she pulled out her small stun gun.

Torin nodded.

The crazed man fisted his enormous hand. Before she could act, he clocked her upside of the head. Seeing stars, she swallowed hard and fought through the sudden nausea to press the tip of the stun gun against the asshole's upper hip. Her hand shook as she sought the green button.

On the first try, she missed it and accidentally activated the flashlight feature. But on the second attempt, four million volts surged into him. Even with his amped-up energy from booze and whatever else he was taking, the charge was enough for him to immediately start to shake, then for his limbs to weaken.

Torin was there, behind the guy to catch him.

MEANT FOR ME

Even though her head was still swimming, she grabbed his legs.

"The fuck, man?" one of his buddies demanded.

"Your friend appears drunk," Torin shouted as they carried him to a chair. "Maybe you should get him home."

"What the hell happened to him?"

"Passed out." Torin shrugged. "Good thing I was there to catch him. He should be more careful in the future."

The man opened his mouth to speak, and Torin guided her away. "You okay?"

"I doubt I'll even have a headache later." Which was a straight-out lie.

"You can sit out for a bit. Take a breather."

Oh hell no. "No need."

"Araceli, you got your bell rung. It's okay to admit—"

"I'm okay." She appreciated his concern, but she wouldn't let down any of her teammates. There was a job to do, a client to keep safe. "Really."

Mouth in a tight, disbelieving line, Torin nodded.

Together, they threaded their way back to the front, using a firm, no-nonsense tone.

Instead of heading back to his table after the song ended, The Crush conferred with the band's lead vocalist while the guitarist launched into a riff to keep the crowd occupied.

A few seconds later, the singer took the mic and announced another song with The Crush and signaled to his bandmates.

The audience was captivated by the haunting lyricism of a relationship gone bad. The Crush closed his eyes, as if giving himself over to emotional pain.

Over the years, she'd protected some well-regarded singers. But she'd never been swept away by their talent. This man bled through is voice. She was quickly becoming a fan.

When the song ended, the crowd launched into rapturous

applause, catcalls, screams. More people than was legal had shoved inside the door, and after they had him securely back with his entourage, Torin found the owner to tell him to get rid of some of the patrons before the fire department showed up.

She glanced toward the guy she'd stunned. Though he was still sitting, he was doing well enough to allow one of the shot girls to pour a blue-colored drink into his open mouth.

"I see our friend is okay," she observed when he rejoined her.

"Stupid runs deep."

It was close to four a.m. when the group called it a night.

"Breakfast?" Torin suggested as The Crush's limo's tail-lights faded from view.

Right now, adrenaline was keeping her upright. When it faded, she'd drop on her ass. If she ate now, hunger might not wake her up in a couple of hours.

"Shamrock Grill's a couple blocks down."

Her tummy rumbled.

"I'll take that as a yes." He grinned, easing tension from his features.

When his tone was teasing like that, he became even more irresistible, sneaking beneath her defenses.

They walked down Bourbon Street. Several bars were still open and had plenty of customers. It took some time in the relative quiet for her ears to stop ringing.

All the tables at the Shamrock were filled, so they seated themselves at the counter on red-vinyl-covered stools.

She opted for eggs and toast while Torin dug into a massive pork chop with mashed potatoes and fried okra.

After a drink of his black coffee, he pushed the cup aside. "Hell of a performer, isn't he? The Crush."

"I'd go see him in concert."

He reached forward to feather back her hair.

MEANT FOR ME

She froze, wide-eyed. Heat, long and slow, arced through her. She told herself to pull away. No other partner had ever touched her like that, and she shouldn't allow him to be the first. But her lips parted, and she remained where she was. "What are you doing?"

"Checking the swelling. That guy hit you pretty hard."

"I'm... It's fine."

"Not completely. You've got a bruise to go along with a nasty bump."

"I'll put some ice on it when we're back at the carriage house." But she wouldn't, mostly because it had been so many hours ago that she doubted treating it would do much good.

"Yeah." Slowly, he lowered his hand. "Good plan."

To him, the touch had been perfunctory. It meant nothing. But her pulse was thready. Ever since the beginning, she'd had disturbing reactions to Torin. Being with him was making her reactions more intense, not less.

Trying to ignore him—and failing—Mira concentrated on slathering raspberry jam on a piece of toast that she didn't really plan to eat.

Every bit of her was aware of him, his crisp scent, the shadow of beard on his strong chin. And when she hazarded a glance up, he was staring at her, his electric-blue eyes hooded and brooding. "What?" she asked.

"Nothing."

He drummed his fingers on the hilt of his knife, his body language saying otherwise. But he shifted his focus, to the almost empty coffee cup, making sure she could no longer see his whole face. "You going to keep all of your thoughts to yourself?"

"Not hiding anything."

"Right. You're a regular open book, Commander."

"Eat your toast, Araceli." He snatched up the bill, then strode to the cashier to pay. "I need to get you to bed."

37

CHAPTER TWO

HAWKEYE

"Going somewhere, Commander Carter?" Mira glanced up from the British crime drama she was streaming and muted the television. Just as he had for the past two Monday nights, Torin was leaving the carriage house around nine p.m. If his usual pattern held, he'd return sometime after one. It didn't matter to her where he went, but the fact that he didn't volunteer the information made her curious. And when she'd asked, he'd given a vague half answer, intriguing her further.

"Don't wait up," he responded.

Though they'd been under the same roof, sharing a bathroom, eating most meals together, partnering for over a dozen operations, they kept their private lives as protected as possible. She trained at the gym, met with Hallie for a couple of happy hours, indulged in the occasional café au lait, visited some of New Orleans's best galleries, and tried to ignore the effect her former instructor had on her sex drive.

Tonight, he was wearing a long-sleeved white dress shirt and tailored slacks. His shoes were polished to a high-shine. He smelled of temptation.

"Hot date?"

"Fishing for information?" he countered.

"Nah." Pretending disinterest, she turned the volume back up.

The moment the door sealed behind him, she moved to the window and nudged back the blinds to watch him reverse out of the garage. As if knowing she was there, he stopped near a lamppost and lifted his right index finger in acknowledgment.

Did he miss nothing?

As she'd already planned to, she crossed to the kitchen table, snagged her keys, then waited until the gate closed behind him before jogging down the stairs to her car.

A short time later, she was behind him on the road. Keeping a couple of vehicles between them, she followed him onto Saint Charles Avenue. When he turned onto Loyola, she raised her eyebrows. The French Quarter? Seemed likely since this was the same route he'd traveled when he took her to dinner that first night.

She lost him on a narrow pedestrian-and-vehicle-packed one-way street. Having no other real option, she continued on, then spotted him again entering a parking lot on Iberville. It wasn't the same one he'd used when they went to dinner. She pulled over, parking illegally next to the curb, waiting for him.

Eventually, he emerged to head down Royal Street. Last week, she'd browsed art galleries there, but she was guessing he wasn't interested in paintings or sculptures.

Knowing the risk of a ticket—or worse, getting towed— she slipped out of her car to follow him.

As if suspecting he had a tail, or just taking appropriate precautions, he darted through jammed, honking vehicles and turned onto Toulouse, heading deeper into the heart of the French Quarter.

As quick as she could, she followed him, down a couple of blocks until...

She pressed her back against a nearby building as he opened an unmarked green door. One she knew well. The Quarter, New Orleans's oldest, most vaunted BDSM club.

Holy hell.

Torin Carter was a Dom? And he attended *her* club?

She dragged in a deep breath. Her fantasies about him hadn't been far out of line. Had something deep inside her intuitively responded to his unspoken vibe?

A tourist carrying a camera jostled into her, dragging her back to reality.

Still hardly able to think, she pushed away from the wall and joined the throngs on the sidewalk.

Now what? Even if it meant seeing him there, Mira refused to give up her occasional visit. BDSM scenes weren't just something casual for her. They were much more than a simple, pleasurable release. Inside the construct and rules, she could be free, let go in ways she wasn't able to in the outside world. Participating fed something essential inside her.

In front of her, a reveler lurched to a stop, and she bumped into him. "Sorry." She shook her head as a way to forcibly reel in her thoughts. Allowing Torin's secret and its implications to distract her was a sure way to lose her edge.

Focusing on where she was going, she walked to a corner restaurant and ordered a muffuletta sandwich to go. It was ginormous enough to feed her for two meals.

When she returned to her car, there was a parking ticket on it. *Of course.* At least she hadn't been towed.

The later it got, the more difficult it became to navigate the narrow one-way streets. Many pedestrians didn't even look before stepping into traffic.

The drive back to the mansion took much longer than the

SIERRA CARTWRIGHT

trip to the French Quarter, and her mind was still scattered when she parked on the property.

Because safety was ingrained, she checked the grounds before entering the carriage house and closing the door behind her.

On automatic, she ate part of her sandwich, then wrapped the remainder and stored it in the refrigerator. Restless, she checked email. Still empty. And no notifications on social media. That wasn't a surprise. Because of the nature of her job, she rarely posted her whereabouts or anything personal. She glanced at the latest memes from her friends. A lot of them had to do with parenting or whether it was wine o'clock yet.

It was as if everyone she knew had a totally different experience of being alive than she did.

Mira closed her browser and plopped onto the couch in front of the television to scroll through the programming guide. There were at least a hundred choices, and none of them captured her interest.

With a sigh, she admitted the truth to herself.

She wanted to go to the club.

Action was the only thing that soothed her and allowed her to put her demons to rest.

Mira stood, turned off the television, then picked up her phone to call Hallie. "Are you still planning to go to the Quarter Wednesday night?"

"Oh my God." Silence echoed between them. "Are you serious? Tell me you're coming!"

She and Hallie had attended the same boarding school, then later, college. Even though they couldn't be more different, they'd roomed together and become lifelong friends.

"Earth to Mira."

"Sorry." She shook her head. "Yes...or, well...I'm thinking about it."

"That will make it so much more fun!"

"I'll be on duty, so there's a chance I'll get a last-minute assignment." Since it was a Wednesday night and the schedule was still clear, things looked good.

"It's a Victorian theme night. You have something to wear, right?"

"No."

"Even better! Let's meet tomorrow at the costume store, then go to happy hour at the Maison Sterling. Ever since you mentioned it, I've wanted to try it. Four o'clock?"

After they ended call, Mira turned the television on again. The drama couldn't hold her attention, and neither could a stand-up comedian.

An hour later, she gave up again, she changed into her bathing suit and headed down the stairs to the hot tub.

She sank into the water up to her neck, then tipped her head back and closed her eyes.

Where was Torin now? Sitting in the bar, observing what was happening in the main dungeon? Scening with some lucky sub?

Damnation and fuck it all.

She didn't want to allow her thoughts to go there.

Did he have someone? A sub? If he had a girlfriend, he wouldn't have been able to hide it for the month they'd been assigned together. But it was completely possible for him to have a woman he played with at the Quarter.

Taunted by her own thoughts, she left the tub in favor of making a few laps in the swimming pool.

The water was blessedly cool on her skin, and the within a few minutes, she was able to banish thoughts of him pleasing some unnamed woman...at least until she went to bed to toss and turn.

Around two, she woke up, dragged out of a deep sleep.

SIERRA CARTWRIGHT

She climbed out of bed and grabbed her robe. As she left the bedroom, she tightened the belt.

The front door was closed and locked. Torin's bedroom door stood ajar, and there was no sign of him anywhere in the carriage house. His wallet wasn't on the counter, and the jacket he'd been wearing wasn't hanging from the peg near the door. Obviously, he hadn't returned from his night out.

Without turning on any lights, she walked to a window. The courtyard was empty, and trees swayed in the gentle breeze.

She wandered toward a window on the far side of the carriage house for a different view when a key turned in the lock.

Moments later, Torin entered and flipped on a light switch.

He stood there, completely naked, holding his clothes.

Water droplets shimmered on his smooth, bare chest, and his dick—*massive dick,* some wild part of her thoughts corrected—was pulsingly erect.

She ordered herself to look away, perhaps mumble something as she fled. Instead, she was immobilized.

"Sorry if I disturbed you."

Being a light sleeper was a hazard of the job.

Torin offered no apology for his nakedness, and in fact, seemed completely unconcerned about it.

Of course, she'd seen him in his swimwear and from a distance. This, though, was different. His muscles were clearly delineated, and if she reached out, she could skim her fingers over his taut, gorgeous muscles.

He turned to close the door, giving her a full view of his tight ass. This was the perfect opportunity for her to excuse herself, but instead, she stood where she was, unmoving.

He placed his clothes on a nearby table, then, in silence, faced her again. His cock was scant inches from her.

"You should go back to bed."

He'd given voice to her thoughts. But his prompting didn't make her walk away.

"Final warning, Araceli."

"Or what?" Her words were a whisper, more of an invitation than a challenge.

"Or what?" He swirled his hand into her hair. "I'm going to kiss you."

No. *Yes.*

Smelling of sin and danger, he leaned in, bringing his magnificently erect cock even closer to her. "Tell me not to."

This, inviting him, tempting him, was foolish. He might be able to fuck her and forget her, move on with his life. But to her, it would mean something, no matter how much she tried to pretend it wouldn't. And yet... Even if she might get hurt, she wanted him. "I might die if you don't."

He brushed his lips across hers in a sweet, tender gesture that was completely unexpected. He'd been at the Quarter, so she'd anticipated he would claim her in a much more dominant manner.

Then she recognized his strategic brilliance. The brief touch fed her hunger, rather than sated it. "Carter..."

"You're so fucking desirable, Mira."

At the use of her first name, with a slight, sexy roll to r, her tummy fluttered. She reached up to loop her arms around his neck. His skin was cool and damp, and droplets from his hair dripped onto her forearm.

"That's it." He captured her chin. "Give me what I want."

Responding to him, she lifted onto her toes. Except for that night in training, they'd never been this close. The reality was more overwhelming than she remembered.

She kissed him, then captured his lower lip with her teeth. He groaned, turning her on. The moment she released him, she soothed the tiny bite with a soft kiss.

SIERRA CARTWRIGHT

"You read me right, Araceli."

His approval made her pulse skitter.

"And now…" He seized control, blue eyes darkening with intent.

This time, he sought entrance to her mouth, and she yielded, opening wide for him. He tasted faintly of whiskey. Bourbon, maybe. If so, that meant he hadn't scened at the club, unless he'd headed for the bar after a very brief encounter. That, she couldn't imagine.

He moved a hand to the center of her back and placed the other at the curve of her spine. It was intimate, and yet…not, as if he was holding part of himself back.

With restrained power, he brought her in a little closer. His cock pressed against her, making the world swirl. He deepened the kiss, exploring her responses, finding what she liked and giving her more of that.

Mira met his slow, sensual dance and surrendered to it until she went dizzy. Her body softened, and she tightened her grip on him so that she could remain upright.

For a moment, he ended the kiss, giving her time to inhale a shaky breath. But he never let go. In fact, he spread his fingers farther apart so he could hold her more completely.

"I'm not done with you."

"Good."

With a deep sound of approval, he claimed her again.

This time, he wasn't gentle. He thrust his tongue into her mouth possessively. She liked it every bit as much as the first kiss, and maybe even more.

He consumed her, igniting a flame that had been dormant for more than a year. Since she was focused on her career, she didn't indulge in casual sex. Suddenly, though, she ached, wanting to be filled, to be taken. But not by any man. By Torin.

She moved one of her arms and dug her fingers into his hair.

Slowly, he eased back.

Part of her was grateful, another, not at all.

When he lowered his hands, she unwrapped herself from around him.

She met his gaze and was consumed by the way he looked at her. Longing. And... Regret? "I should go to bed," she said, an echo of his earlier sentiment.

"Agreed."

She took a step back. Her nightclothes were damp from his skin, and a couple of droplets of water clung to her. His turgid cock was pointed her direction, throbbing. Her hand trembled, and she wanted to reach out and explore him. Would he let her?

The answer didn't matter.

She was too smart to find out.

Mira hurried back to her room. She didn't care if she appeared to be fleeing. She was.

She shut the door with a decisive click, more for his benefit than hers.

In the dark, beneath the sheet, she pressed a hand against her swollen lips, reliving his tenderness as well as his urgency.

Whatever it was she felt for him, it disturbed her. She wanted to name it lust, but it was much deeper. Desire? Not deep enough. It was more like recognition. Inevitability. He saw into her, guessed her secrets, and he still wanted her.

She yanked the sheets around her shoulders, like a cocoon.

Torin Carter was a threat to her, not just because of her attraction, but because he had ghosts of his own, ones that weren't at rest.

In the bathroom, the water ran. She envisioned him beneath the spray, soaping his erection.

Moaning, she turned on her side. But she couldn't escape her imagination.

Knowing she'd never get to sleep, she reached for the tiny vibrator tucked beneath a paperback.

She worked her hand inside her panties. Then, with her eyes closed, the sounds from across the hall and the scent of clean, masculine soap on the air, she turned on the toy and pressed the tip against her clit.

Pressing her lips together so she didn't cry out, she nudged the power a little higher.

Then, lost, she moaned as an orgasm built.

Her thoughts ran wild, and she pictured Torin fastening her to a Saint Andrew's cross, or better, taking her upstairs to a private room at the Quarter where he could strip her completely bare. He'd use a flogger on her, one that had long, thick falls that would wrap around her, delivering dozens of simultaneous thuds to sear her nerve endings. He was a fit, powerful man, capable of the force she needed to achieve subspace.

Rationally, she knew she should fantasize about a nameless, faceless Dom, but Torin filled her senses.

So lost beneath his dominance, she screamed out as she orgasmed.

Out of breath, she dropped the still-humming vibrator and dragged in a dozen desperate breaths.

As reality returned, she became aware of a preternatural quiet.

The water was no longer running. The air conditioner was silent.

Seconds later, a footfall echoed outside her room. Shortly thereafter, his bedroom door closed.

Torin had been there? Listening?

MEANT FOR ME

Embarrassed, praying she hadn't called out his name, she turned off the vibrator. How the hell would she face him in the morning?

The remaining weeks loomed larger than ever. And she was less and less certain about her ability to survive.

"ARE YOU KIDDING ME?" HALLIE DEMANDED AS SHE FASTENED the top button of Mira's Victorian gown.

In the dressing room mirror, she met her friend's gaze. As Hallie had helped her into the long red gown, Mira recounted last night's events with Torin.

"So you're sure he was outside your door while you were, ah, polishing your pearl?"

"I'm sure of it."

"Well, at least he didn't walk in on you."

"He's my partner. I would have died for real, if he had."

"You have nothing to be embarrassed about. What the hell could he have expected after he kissed you and flashed you his full-staff dick?"

Because of Hallie's support, Mira was able to laugh.

"He was probably patting himself on the back."

Maybe.

"I bet he beat off in the shower."

"Hallie!"

"Girl, if he wasn't proud of that thing, he wouldn't have walked around in all his naked glory."

Mira didn't point out that he'd probably believed she was asleep.

"What do you think of the dress?"

Mira studied her reflection. "It's a little tight across the chest." But the waist was perfect. "I like it."

"Do you have shoes you can wear?"

SIERRA CARTWRIGHT

She hadn't thought about that. "No."

"I have some you can borrow. Come by around nine, and then we can take a car from my place." Hallie went on for a few more minutes before winding down. "We're going to have fun. You can find someone to take your mind off Mr. Hard Dick."

With a grin, Mira shook her head.

After she changed back into her boring work clothes and paid the rental fee, she hung up the dress in her car. She and Hallie left their vehicles in the lot and caught a taxi to the Maison Sterling.

"Damn," Hallie said as they walked beneath the green awning.

The door was opened by a man dressed in livery, who tipped his top hat as they entered.

"I've driven past, and I knew it was nice, but…" Obviously at a loss for words, she repeated, "Damn."

"My reaction as well." Mira's boots echoed off the polished marble floor.

They found tall stools at the elegant bar. Within moments, the bartender appeared, with a crystal bowl filled with nuts.

"Oh my God." Hallie picked out a cashew. "These are primo. Not even a single peanut among them. Be still my heart!"

Even though the hurricane was outrageously priced, Mira decided to splurge. After all, there was no way she could drink more than one.

Hallie selected the happy hour house wine. It was still more money than almost anywhere else in town, but the ambience was first rate. Lights were dimmed. Candles sat atop each table. Light jazz played, softly enough that it didn't drown out conversation. The chairs appeared to be hand carved, and the others throughout the area were real leather.

50

MEANT FOR ME

At a table across the room, a couple was cozying up, so into each other that they didn't appear to even notice anyone else. At another, away from anyone, their backs at a slight angle to hide their faces, two men conferred over highball glasses.

"Can you ever give the spy stuff a rest?"

"I'm in protection. That's totally different than being a spy," Mira protested.

Hallie rolled her eyes. "Don't tell me you haven't noticed every single detail of what's going on here."

She gave a half smile. Being a good agent meant she needed to be aware of her surroundings. Her life, and that of her principal, might depend on it.

"That couple..." Hallie prompted.

"An affair. She's cheating on her husband."

Hallie frowned.

"Her diamond flashed when she put her left hand on his shoulder."

"They could be on their honeymoon."

"Not with the way she checks her phone." Mira plucked the cherry from her drink and sucked on it before biting into the delicious sweetness. "Those men over there..." She inclined her head. "One's got money. The other's a politician."

"Cash for influence?"

The way of the world.

"I don't care what you say," Hallie proclaimed. "Figuring out all that stuff is spy shit."

"No. It's just a casual observation."

Hallie shook her head. "Not true. I observed two guys having a drink."

"They're in the far corner, away from the other patrons. No one walking through the lobby can see that part of the bar. Oh. And. They moved their candle to another table."

"See?" Hallie demanded. "Freaking spy shit!" She took a drink. "Where as me, a mere mortal, have just *observed* a prime specimen of masculine glory."

Mira glanced over her shoulder. Hallie was definitely right. The gentleman striding confidently across the floor was exceptionally handsome.

"Evening Mr. Sterling," the bartender greeted.

When the tall, striking man was out of earshot, Hallie signaled for the bartender to come over. "Is that him? The owner? Like *the* Mr. Sterling. As in Sterling Hotels?"

"It is."

"Wow."

He pulled up a chair to join the other two men.

"Worth the cost of the wine to sit here and people watch," Hallie observed.

It was. After a few sips of the Cat Five hurricane, Mira pushed the glass aside and ordered a sparkling water. "It's lethal," she told the bartender.

The woman grinned. "There's a reason we list a warning on the menu."

Mira leaned toward Hallie. "Now it's your turn. Tell me what's going on with you."

Hallie fished out a few more nuts before sighing. "What makes you think there's anything?"

"Seriously?" Mira raised eyebrow. "Do-or-die friends know these things."

"Uh-huh."

Mira grinned. "Okay, you've got a tell, like a poker player might. You've said almost nothing the whole time we've been together. You're keeping the conversation all about me and my life, which means you're being evasive. And you avoided my question just this minute. Ergo…" She paused for dramatic effect. "There's something you don't want to tell me"

MEANT FOR ME

"That's spy shit," Hallie protested, looking down at her glass.

"And… There you go again. Start talking. Otherwise the interrogation begins. I might even get out the thumbscrews."

Hallie shook her head. "You would, too."

"Waiting."

Hallie pushed away her wineglass. "So I met a guy."

"Oh?"

"And no, you can't have his full name, and I do not want you to run a background check on him."

Mira remembered, all too well, what happened the last time Hallie had been so secretive. Her anguish, the tears, the hospital visit… Mira put her hand over her friend's. "Hal—"

"If it gets serious, then you can." She pulled away her hand with an exhalation. "This time, I'm smarter. I promise."

Having no other choice, Mira nodded. "I care about you."

"I appreciate it. But I want to find out more on my own. I mean, assuming it goes anywhere."

As she waited, Mira took a sip of her water.

"I met him at the Quarter."

That helped, just a little. The club owner, Mistress Aviana, vetted all members. But she relied on referrals more than extensive background checks.

"He visits periodically. Lives in Baton Rouge."

It was a commute, for sure, but doable.

"We've played twice, and after the last time, we had a drink before he took me home."

"And…?" She took the lime from the rim of her glass and placed it on the napkin.

"He's…" Hallie paused. "Nice."

Mira hated being a skeptic, but she was. Maybe because she'd rarely met nice men. It didn't mean they didn't exist, but in her world, they didn't. "Give me a first name, at least."

"Master Bartholomew."

"A scene name?" she guessed. Plenty of people used them, herself included. Since she didn't want anyone finding her outside of the club, she went by Ember when she was there, and she never shared her phone number or surname. To her, when she was at the club, she was able to be someone else, and she liked the freedom it gave her.

Hallie looked into her glass.

"You don't know for sure." She swallowed back a sigh. Shit. Even though she protected her identity, she would reveal parts of herself if she were interested in someone. That he hadn't done that much concerned her. "He took you home?"

Hallie nodded. "He walked me to the door, like a perfect gentleman."

"And then what?"

"Nothing." She plucked a cashew from the dish, but she didn't eat it. "He kissed my hand and said good night."

"When was that?"

"Last week."

"And you haven't heard from him since?"

"A text message last night. He'll be out of town for a week."

Hurt wove through Hallie's words, making Mira cringe. "But the scenes were good?"

"He was thoughtful, and…" She smiled, vanquishing her former gloom. "Yes. They've been epic."

"Epic? Then concentrate on that."

"I will." Hallie finally popped the nut into her mouth. "It's better than thinking about work. It still sucks. Too damn many unfilled positions. Always trying to do more with less. Any openings at Hawkeye for math geeks like me?"

Hallie was an office manager at an oil and gas firm that was cycling through another downturn. "You should apply,"

Mira encouraged. "Use my name. Or better, let me call HR and recommend you."

"I'll think about it. Vacation time, retirement…"

The realities of leaving a job.

They finished their drinks, and she watched the politician leave the table. A few minutes later, Mr. Sterling followed suit. The businessman lingered, typing lots of notes into his phone before pocketing the device and adjusting his blazer. After checking his watch, he strode from the bar.

"All that power in one place," Hallie said. "We have to come back here again."

"It definitely is a good place to people watch," Mira agreed before relating the story of protecting The Crush.

"Okay, that's it. I'm applying at Hawkeye."

Mira laughed. "I promise, it's not nearly as glamorous as it sounds."

"But you hung out with The Crush."

"I was about as close to him as we were to that politician. And I got a black eye from the overzealous fan who wanted to climb onto the stage."

The man who'd been snuggled up to the woman stood. Then he left, with a couple of sad over-the-shoulder glances.

After refreshing her lipstick, the woman signaled for a server to clear the table, then ordered a glass of white wine.

A few minutes later, another man—presumably her husband this time—joined her.

"You called that one right," Hallie observed, finishing the last of her drink.

Since she had to drive, Mira gave up on the hurricane. "Next time, I'll catch a ride from the house so I can drink the whole thing."

After finalizing the plans for meeting at the Quarter the next evening, they exited. A valet flagged down a cab to take them back to the costume store.

From there, the drive back to the carriage house took less than fifteen minutes.

She grabbed her purse and the costume from the car and wasn't sure whether or not to be relieved when she discovered Torin wasn't in the pool. She didn't have to worry about seeing his naked body, but it also meant he was probably inside where she couldn't avoid him.

He was cycling on the exercise bike when she entered. Thankfully, he was wearing a shirt and shorts. She was starting to fear that spontaneous combustion might be a real thing.

"Need a hand?"

"Thanks. I've got it all." She placed her purse on the counter, then locked the door.

"What have you got?" he asked.

She debated her answer, then stuck to the truth. No doubt he'd noticed the name on the garment bag. "It's a Victorian gown. For an event tomorrow night."

"Ah."

Mira carried the gown down the hall and hung it in her closet. When she returned to the living area, he had a towel draped around his neck, and he'd opened an amber ale from the famous local brewery.

"Can I get you one?"

"Uh. No. I just had a Cat Five hurricane at the Maison Sterling."

"Sounds dangerous."

"It was slightly worse than that. I didn't finish the whole thing."

"How about a pizza?"

That had fast become a once-a-week tradition. "Sounds good." And normal.

"The usual?"

Mira nodded, relieved he was acting as if he hadn't kissed

her or stood outside her door while she moaned and maybe called out his name.

Forty minutes later, the open pizza box on the coffee table, he sat on the couch and turned on the television to an Australian drama about a lawyer who was currently in trouble with the tax collector. She selected a large slice of the double pepperoni, then curled up on a lounge chair.

He raised an eyebrow at her choice but said nothing.

After watching two back-to-back episodes that she'd paid almost no attention to, she stood. "Good night. I'm going to bed to read for a while."

"Already?"

It wasn't even ten. "The aftereffects of the rum," she lied.

He watched her go.

When she reached the end of the hall, he called out, "Araceli."

The soft command in his voice stopped her cold. But she didn't look back at him.

"It happened. All of it. And at some point we're going to stop pretending it didn't and figure out what the hell to do with it."

She was fine with continuing as they were. "Taking it any further would be a mistake."

"One you want to make."

Then she did look back and wished she hadn't. He was so damn handsome, so inviting. Tempting.

The fact that he was right made it worse. "Good night, Commander Carter."

"So that's how it is."

She escaped into the bedroom and closed the door.

The book couldn't hold her interest. When the door to the outside closed with a slight *click*, she moved to the window. As she guessed, he was swimming, and there was no doubt he was naked.

Quickly, she dropped the blinds, determined not to let him, his statement—or his sexy body—get to her.

It took hours to harness her thoughts, and she didn't manage to fall asleep until he was back inside and out of the shower.

For another hour, she tossed and turned, drifting in and out of sleep, looking at the clock every ten minutes or so.

Around three, she awakened hard, alert.

"No!"

Torin?

"Goddamn it! Noooo!" Pain ripped through the word. "Noooo!"

She tossed back the sheet, then jumped out of bed to dash down the hall. She pounded on his closed door. "Commander Carter?" When there was no response, she turned the knob. "I'm fucking coming in!"

CHAPTER THREE

HAWKEYE

In the darkness, broken only by ambient light from outside, she took in the scene. Wearing only a pair of boxer briefs, Torin was thrashing on the bed, the sheet tangled around his ankles. "Commander Carter!" She took a step into the room, then another. "Torin."

When he didn't respond, she sat on the edge of the mattress, near him, but far enough away that she could stand get away if he reacted badly. "Torin. Wake up!" She gently shook his shoulder.

He opened his eyes in a wide, unseeing stare.

"It's okay," she said, the words instinctive rather than genuine. She had no idea what the hell was going on, other than a nightmare…or closer to a terror. Whatever it was, he was deep in its horrid grips.

Mira reached out again, placing a reassuring hand on his heated skin. "You're safe."

Torin balled his hands at his sides.

"You're in the carriage house. New Orleans."

After a ragged exhalation, he blinked. Then, after a few

steadying breaths, he struggled out of the sheet and worked himself up onto his elbows.

Now that he was awake, she eased her hand back. She'd known he kept secrets, but she'd had no idea they were so destructive.

"Everything's fine," he said.

"I…" She shook her head. "Want to talk about it?"

He sat the rest of the way up. His breathing had returned to normal, and his steely eyes were focused. But the sheen was still on his skin, and his hair was wildly mussed.

"Everything's fine," he repeated, as if on automatic.

"No. It's not." She hated to think about him being alone when this happened, with no one around to anchor him to reality. "Have you seen someone about it?"

"Listen, Araceli…" He captured her wrist, not tightly, but in a loose circle. Then, studying his action, he feathered his thumb across her pulse point. "You never have bad dreams?"

"Of course." She should pull away from him. Instead, she, too, looked down, mesmerized by his long, gentle strokes, in contrast to his raw strength. After what had just happened, she appreciated the reassurance of their connection.

When he stilled, she glanced up to find him staring at her.

"That was beyond a bad dream."

"It's over now. You did your good deed."

"But—"

"Go back to your own room now, Araceli."

He was back to being himself, and he'd made it abundantly clear that staying wasn't an option.

In his place, she wouldn't want anyone to glimpse her vulnerabilities. She had to respect that, even if she didn't like it. She had questions that needed answers.

With a sigh, she stood. "Commander…"

"Thank you, Araceli."

On the threshold, she stopped.

MEANT FOR ME

"Close the door on your way out."

"You can be a total jerk, Carter." To see if her words stung, she glanced back.

Shocking her, he was smiling. There was nothing charming about it. Rather, it was feral, sending a deep shiver through her.

"Believe me, Araceli, you don't want me to invite you into my bed."

Oh God. *Jesus.* That was exactly what she wanted.

"I wouldn't be responsible for my actions."

He'd meant to warn her, no doubt. But her reaction was immediate. Sexual hunger crashed into her. Torin was a flame, and she yearned to touch it.

"I appreciate you coming to my rescue. Sleep well."

Remembering his torment, all mixed up with her craving to be with him, she was unable to settle.

Eventually she tossed back the covers and climbed out of bed to bend into a long yoga stretch that did nothing to center her.

She headed for the living room and the exercise bike, needing a grueling aerobic workout to exhaust her.

Torin Carter was troubled, far more than she'd realized.

She wanted to know why, even if he didn't want to tell her.

MIRA'S HEELS CLICKED ON THE CARRIAGE HOUSE'S HARDWOOD floor, little stabby points of sexy noise. Torin glanced up from his computer.

His eyes widened.

She wore a long gown, bloodred and stunning.

"What do you think?" Without waiting for his response,

she twirled, so slow that he had the opportunity to admire her from every angle.

Her long black hair—alive with flamelike highlights—was pinned back, and a few tendrils had escaped their delicate confines to curl alluringly across her cheeks and at her nape.

Belatedly, he recalled her saying she'd rented a gown. This one was cut fairly low, in a way he was pretty damn sure would have been scandalous when Queen Victoria sat on the British throne. The style of the dress emphasized the alluring swell of Mira's breasts.

Enticing vixen. "Going somewhere?"

"Don't wait up." She checked her phone, presumably to verify the arrival of her ride, then lifted her hand on the way out the door.

The fact that she repeated his words from earlier this week was a barb, and it found its mark.

He drummed his fingers on the table, wondering where the hell she was going. No wonder she followed him the other night. Because of their personality, no mystery remained unsolved.

Where was she going at nine o'clock on a Wednesday evening?

Doesn't matter. Or at least that was what he reminded himself. There were no ties between them. Soon enough, they'd go their separate ways. Perhaps their paths would never cross again.

That thought clouded his brain, getting in the way of rational thought.

Araceli meant something to him. Pure male lust, no doubt. But a whole sweet fuck more. She was fearless. That bothered him as much as the glimpses of her sweet, caring nature.

Last night, she should have tried to wake him from the far side of the room, if at all. Instead, she'd sat on the bed,

MEANT FOR ME

touched him, despite the fact that she hadn't known what to expect.

Hell, *he* hadn't known what to expect.

It'd been over a year since his last episode. He'd thought, believed, they'd gone away.

He'd seen a shrink after Ekaterina had died on his watch. Talking about it had helped, at least enough for him to sleep four hours at a stretch. Still, on rare occasions, something would happen to trigger the memories.

No doubt, it was Araceli herself.

She worried him.

The fearlessness that he admired was the thing that scared him the most, as it had since she stepped foot into his classroom.

Restless, he headed outside for a swim.

When he was worn out, no longer obsessing over her, he headed back inside to shower.

The scent of wildflowers lingered on the air, exceptional because she generally didn't use anything more than an ordinary soap.

When he exited the shower, he noticed her garment bag, hanging from a hook on the back of the door.

With a towel wrapped around his waist, he read the inscription. Masquerade Costume Shop. *Original.* Then he plucked the receipt from the small plastic window on the front of the bag.

Victorian dress. Seventy-nine dollars.

More intrigued than ever, he strode back to the living room, powered up his computer, then opened the web browser. He typed in the little information he knew. Date, approximate time, costume, Victorian.

A fraction of a second later, his screen filled with results. At the top was an announcement of the Quarter's annual theme night.

SIERRA CARTWRIGHT

He pushed the laptop away. Not much surprised him, but this left him shocked.

Mira Araceli, his partner, was on her way to the Quarter? *Fuck.*

How the hell had he not known they were members of the same club? Or that she was a submissive?

He shucked water from his still-damp hair. For a moment, he considered the idea she might be a Domme. It took him no time to dismiss that idea. When he kissed her, her response had been sweet. Instead of protesting his aggressiveness, she gave herself over to him.

There was no doubt she was a sub, and if she was going to the Quarter, she was looking for a Dom.

Torin shouldn't want to be that man.

The primal beast in him said *fuck that.* If she wanted to scene, she would do it with him.

Driven by urgency, he used an app on his phone to summon a ride. He didn't have the patience to take his own car, find parking, then walk a couple of blocks, even if the exercise might calm his temper.

Not giving a damn about the club's theme night, he locked up before jogging down the steps to wait for the driver.

A couple of blocks away from his destination, traffic snarled. Knowing he'd be faster on foot, he paid for the ride, then headed for the unobtrusive door on Toulouse Street.

The closer he got to finding her, the more impatient he became.

"You're supposed to be in costume, Master Torin," Trinity, the hostess, said by way of greeting.

"So it seems." The gentleman in front of him had been wearing an elegant frock coat and a top hat, and he'd been carrying a cane. Torin glanced down at his black jeans and scuffed boots. To complete his attire, he also had on a black bomber jacket. He couldn't be more inappropriate if he'd tried. "I didn't get the memo in time." After signing in, he pushed through the frosted glass door and strode into the main dungeon.

The place was packed, and he didn't immediately see Mira.

He checked the bar, where he'd spent the last three Monday nights, observing, but not participating. Tonight, though, would be different, from the moment he got his hands on her delectable body to the moment he took her home.

Caging his restless energy, he circled the entire dungeon, annoyed not to find her, but damn happy not to see her strapped to one of the Saint Andrew's crosses.

He pushed through the door that led to a quieter part of the club and gave cursory glances at the subs—male as well as female—who were attached to the spanking benches.

At the end of the row, he saw a woman kneeling astride one. She had the same long, strong muscles as Araceli, and her hair was a dark, tumultuous mess, with fiery highlights.

He kept moving, but faster.

It was her.

From the distance, he hadn't seen the color of the gown because of the stupid number of layers of muslin petticoats that were tossed over her waist. But now... Not only were her beautiful round butt cheeks exposed and highlighted by her choice of black stockings and a garter belt, but she was being flogged by Arthur Wilson. Thank God she was wearing a very modern thong. Otherwise Torin's temper might have unraveled entirely.

He had nothing personal against the man—besides the fact that he was wielding leather that was turning Mira's ass red.

Arthur caught her full-on with the flogger, and she

swayed her hips from side to side, not trying to escape, and instead, asking for more.

Right now Torin Carter was a dangerous man.

"Only a few more, pet," Arthur said. He drew back his arm again and soundly smacked Mira with the falls.

Mira rose up as much as the restraints allowed and arched her back.

"Next one. Ready?"

She nodded, wiggling, offering him more of her flesh, clearly loving every moment.

Even from a few feet away, Torin had heard the difference in the intensity of Arthur's next stroke. The man was taking Mira to more extreme pain levels. From her reaction, the blow had clearly stung as it was meant to.

Fury overcame reason.

Through the years, he'd played with dozens of women, many of them at this club. He'd enjoyed showing up and having a new woman kneel at his feet each time. But this was different.

A feeling of possession walloped him, squeezing his lungs as if a weight had been dropped on him. He'd never experienced anything like it before, and he fucking wasn't enjoying it now.

The woman on the bench was his partner. He'd kissed her. Last night, she'd braved the unknown to drag him from the throes of a night terror.

Despite the Quarter's rules, despite the fact that his partner was obviously a willing participant, Torin acted.

He grabbed hold of the smaller man. If Torin exerted a bit more downward pressure, the man would be on his knees. Part of Torin wished the other man would give him the excuse. "Playtime's over, Arthur."

Mira obviously recognized the sound of his voice. With a fierce scowl, she looked over her shoulder. A dental gag was

MEANT FOR ME

shoved in her mouth, making it impossible for her to speak, but she was able to make frantic, desperate noises.

Torin glanced at the gathering crowd. There were plenty of Doms and subs captivated by the scene he was creating. Aviana's most trusted dungeon monitor stopped nearby and folded his arms across his chest.

Torin's focus was totally on the woman immobilized on the spanking bench. "Move along, boys and girls," he said to the Doms and the couple of Dommes who were still staring.

"Trouble?" Aviana, legendary owner of the Quarter, strode toward them with her usual willow grace. In keeping with the theme, she was dressed in Victorian wear, with her expected flair. Her gown was startling white with bright diamante accents. While she generally sported pink- or purple-colored hair, this evening the long tresses were silver. No doubt she wore her customary high heels, because she was looking him straight in the eye. Judging by her scowl, she was not pleased.

"Damn Carter interrupted my scene." Arthur all but sputtered the words as he struggled to pull away. "It's against club rules."

Aviana studied Torin. "By 'Carter,' I presume you mean Master Torin?" Aviana asked, maintaining decorum. Despite the tension, no matter what kind of situation, Aviana never raised her voice. Trouble in the club was handled professionally, defused by the power of the woman's mystery and magnetism.

Torin struggled to maintain his own composure. He was accustomed to being in charge, alpha even in a pack of alphas. But here, Aviana's word was law. Torin met the more controlled woman's eyes.

Arthur—Torin wasn't one to extend the courtesy of addressing the man as Master Arthur, no matter what Aviana insisted—had to tip back his head to look at them both.

"The woman Arthur's flogging—"

"Sub," Arthur interrupted. "At the Quarter, she's a submissive."

"The *woman*," Torin corrected, tightening his grip inexorably, "is my partner. As such, she is under my care and protection." More than anyone, Aviana would understand what that meant. She knew what he did for a living. More than once, he'd provided extra security for the club.

"Well, you're clearly not giving her what she wants, are you?"

Torin clamped his teeth together and exerted a bit more pressure on Arthur's wrist. "No one, *no one*, but me will be touching her."

Mira struggled against her bonds and made tiny mewing sounds.

With his free hand, Torin flipped the material of her dress back down to preserve her modesty.

"Perhaps we should ask the sub what she wants," Arthur suggested.

Aviana inclined her head. "Excellent idea."

Torin wanted to loosen Mira's bonds. Perhaps reading his intent, Aviana held her hand up, her palm toward him. "Stay where you are." She flicked a glance between the two men. "Both of you. Understand?"

He didn't nod until after Arthur did.

"Tore?" Aviana signaled to the massive, bearded dungeon monitor.

With a nod to acknowledge the order, the man closed the distance to Mira, then crouched next to her.

"Unfasten Ember," Aviana instructed.

Ember? It took him a moment to realize Mira must have used a scene name. But he liked it. A play on fire, for the highlights in her hair?

Tore unbuckled her first bond, and she flexed her wrist.

MEANT FOR ME

Torin struggled against the instinctive caveman act. He wanted to be the one to detach her, and ensure she was okay. Then he wanted to toss her over his shoulder, drag her up to one of the private rooms, and give her exactly what she wanted. Talking could come afterward.

Having no choice but to follow the club's protocol, he watched as the dungeon monitor unhooked the clips.

"Drop your flogger," Torin instructed Arthur.

"I—"

"If you don't," he said with a quick smile, "you'll be giving me a reason to break your fucking wrist."

"Master Torin!" Aviana rebuked. "That's quite enough. And Master Arthur, give that flogger to our DM."

Glaring, Arthur did as he was told, then Torin slowly released his grip.

Now that all of Mira's bonds were loosened, the dungeon monitor helped Mira from the bench and held on to her arm for a few seconds, obviously giving her time to catch her bearings and get her circulation back. Torin scowled. He'd meant it when he said he didn't want *anyone* touching her.

For a second she looked at Torin. Her brown eyes were wide, focused on him. She blinked, and then, seeming to recognize her error in staring at him, she dropped her gaze.

Jesus God.

How could he not have really seen her before now, not known what she wanted?

Tore secured her hands behind her back and then exerted pressure on her shoulders so that she knelt before them.

"Take out the gag," Aviana ordered.

The dungeon monitor unbuckled the dental dam and slowly drew it away and handed it back to Arthur. Mira swallowed several times, and Torin couldn't take his gaze off her.

SIERRA CARTWRIGHT

On her knees, her head bowed, she was exquisite. And he was nearly undone.

"Quite the commotion you've caused, Ember."

"My apologies, Milady. That was never my intent."

Aviana's lips twitched. "Well, it seems you have two of our Doms very much interested in you."

"Yes, Ma'am."

"I take it, Ember, that you were willingly engaged in a scene with Master Arthur?"

Torin snapped his back teeth together. The Quarter might be Aviana's club, but Mira was Torin's partner. "Aviana—"

Mira interrupted Torin's protest, saying, "I was. Yes, Milady."

Fuck it to hell, Mira had just given Torin another reason to punish her.

"Go on."

"I approached Master Arthur when I arrived." She looked at Torin, then back at Mistress Aviana. Then, she went on, either not noticing or, more likely, ignoring Torin's clenched jaw, and he attempted to ignore the fact that Aviana cleared her throat to hide her smile. "He asked if I was alone."

"Goddamn it!"

"Last warning, Master Torin."

"Throw him out," Arthur encouraged.

"Stop goading him," Aviana snapped back. She returned her attention to Mira. "Master Torin states you're under his protection."

He figured he had another, oh, forty-five seconds of patience left. A minute, tops.

"Ember?" Aviana prompted.

"Well…"

"A yes or no will suffice."

Torin silently counted to ten, waiting for Mira's answer.

70

MEANT FOR ME

"I—" She looked at Torin. She swallowed. "We—"

"Choose wisely," Torin warned. He had no claim on her, and they both knew it.

But after that kiss, he had no doubt he wanted her as much as she wanted him. The question was, how much emotional risk she was willing to take. Scening together would bond them as nothing else could.

Despite his earlier demand that people move away, several couples had gathered closer to better hear what was being said.

Finally, after swallowing, she reached the right choice and said, "Yes, Milady. We're partners."

"Then the decision to engage in a scene with Master Arthur was not yours to make?"

Any other time he might have acknowledged Aviana's skill at defusing the volatile situation. As it was, with Arthur standing there, onlookers greedily drinking in the scene, and Mira on her knees, Torin wanted the drama to be finished and wanted her alone.

"Ember?" Aviana prompted.

"Technically he—"

"*Damn it!*" Torin snapped. "Answer the question."

She swallowed and then licked her lower lip. She tipped back her head and looked directly at Mistress Aviana, avoiding all contact with Torin. "No, Milady. As you said, the decision to give myself to Master Arthur was not mine to make." She bowed her head. "I'm sorry, Ma'am." She then looked at Arthur. "I apologize, Master Arthur."

Apologizing to the whiny bastard who'd been beating her? Torin closed the distance between them and dug his hand in her hair. Pins scattered across the ceramic-tiled floor.

Always the professional, no matter how much it pissed off Torin, Aviana crouched in front of Mira. Only the three

SIERRA CARTWRIGHT

of them could hear what was being said. Beneath his hand, Mira trembled.

"I'm going to give you a choice. I can turn you over to Master Torin, or I can call for a ride."

Torin tightened his fist in her hair and she rose up a little, as if to ease the pressure.

"Thank you, Milady." She drew in a shaky breath. "I was disobedient to Master Torin."

Master Torin. Goddamn, her words made his cock throb.

"I imagine he'll want to punish you."

She shivered. "Yes, Ma'am."

"You're fortunate I don't do so myself. I don't care for this kind of upset at the Quarter."

"I'll deal with her privately," Torin said.

"In that case, I believe it's settled?" With grace, Aviana stood.

"I'd like a private room. If you'll excuse us?"

"Of course. We'll ensure one is ready." She signaled to Tore. "Give us about ten minutes."

"Thank you." He nodded toward Aviana, then Arthur. Torin kept his fist in Mira's hair and exerted a small amount of pressure, ensuring her continued contrition. "I'd like a collar and a leash, also. Add it to my tab."

Mira gasped. He tightened his grip, silently warning her to keep quiet.

"It can most certainly be arranged."

Tore called over another DM while Aviana swept her arm wide and gave a smile befitting a monarch. "Please, everyone. Enjoy your evening!"

Loud, thumping music suddenly rocked the entire area. Tension eased and conversation around them resumed as people went about their business.

"No hard feelings," Torin said to Arthur.

MEANT FOR ME

"Fuck off." Arthur snarled. "How the hell was anyone supposed to know she was yours?"

How indeed?

Arthur rubbed his wrist. "Next time, claim your subs." He looked at the kneeling Mira. "And when you're done with this asshole, look me up."

Torin took a step forward.

Arthur glared at Torin before moving away.

"He's right," Aviana said. "Claim her. If this happens again, I will back whoever she is scening with. I did you a favor, out of respect for our relationship, but I consider us even. Don't cross me again."

With a tight nod, Torin acknowledged Aviana's order.

Within seconds the blond dungeon monitor returned with a collar and leash. "I'll take it from here," Torin said.

"Yes, sir," the man said, handing over the leather pieces.

Then it was just the two of them. She was still on her knees, and he liked that. "After tonight, we will still be partners, unless you request a transfer."

She nodded.

"Let's get a few things straight. I'm here now, and I sure as hell intend to beat you."

"Yes." The much, much softer, she added, "Sir."

His cock throbbed with need. Whatever it was between the two of them, it was real and potent. "Whatever you need, I'll make sure you get it." Torin captured her chin firmly between his thumb and forefinger. He forced her to look at him. "Beating, flogging, spanking, punishment, humiliation, bondage..." He trailed off. "I promise you. But there are rules."

"Such as?"

She was right, and smart, to ask.

"Until we mutually agree to end this relationship, you will not go to Arthur—or anyone else. Furthermore, you are not permitted to flash your bare ass at anyone without my permission."

"Let's just have this."

"Is that what you want?" He looked deep into her eyes. "Really? Or do you want to see where it goes?"

"A few hours. Then, afterward, we can reevaluate."

Unsatisfied, he scowled.

As if sensing his restlessness and unwillingness to compromise, she relented, just a little. "For the duration of our assignment, I won't visit the Quarter without telling you."

It was as much as he could hope for. "We will debrief after this." Words they both understood, a meaning that was clear to them. A discussion, pros, cons, what worked, what didn't, and what would be different in future.

"Of course, Commander." She nodded. "Give me what I crave, Commander Carter."

"Master Torin," he corrected.

"Give me what I crave, Master Torin."

CHAPTER FOUR

HAWKEYE

"You're submitting to me?" he asked, pressing for answers so they were both clear. Consent was imperative. Without it, he wouldn't move forward. "Willingly?"

She took a breath and exhaled it in shaky measures. "Yes, Sir."

"Then, you'll wear this?" He held up the collar.

When she answered affirmatively, he secured the sturdy leather around her neck. He tightened it to the point he could get just one finger between her nape and the buckle.

She looked up momentarily. Her mouth was slightly parted, and her breaths were shortened, whether from fear or anticipation, he didn't know.

"I'm nervous," she confessed.

"I think that's what you want. Isn't it? The rush? Adrenaline? Uncertainty? Expectation? A touch of fear, maybe?"

"Is that meant to reassure me?"

"Not in the least."

"We've never played together before."

"If you think I'm playing now, think again." He placed his hands on her shoulders. "Now stand."

Since the gown was a monstrosity of length and fabric, and because her arms were still bound behind her, she struggled to comply. He made no move to help her. The usually graceful Ms. Araceli was out of her element, but to her credit, she didn't protest. When she stood in front of him, head bowed slightly, he said, "Good girl."

"I—"

"You look lovely." His cock had never been harder.

He fastened the leash to the collar's attached D-ring.

Torin liked having her at his mercy, on his leash, the black collar tight and stark against her delicate olive-toned skin.

From the beginning, Mira had fired a protective streak in him, one he'd never had for another woman. It was more than just their being partners—something much, much more.

He wrapped a hand around her upper arm to give her stability as they walked up the stairs to the private rooms. In those, there were fewer rules. The club's safe word would be honored, and DMs checked in on the scenes. Beyond that, nudity was okay, whereas it was forbidden in the rest of the dungeon.

He checked in with the DM who was in charge. "Room eight, Master Torin."

"Thank you."

When they were inside, with the door closed, he moved her to the middle of the room. "Limits?"

"What you might expect," she replied. "Bruises are okay." She smiled. "Hopefully they're more fun than the ones I received during training."

"I think you'll find them much more pleasing. Yes."

"No breaking the skin." She exhaled. "Nothing that will impair my ability to do my job."

He nodded. "Safe word?"

"Sangria."

"Sangria?"

MEANT FOR ME

"Sangria," she said. "It's red. At least traditionally, it is."

And it was a drink her country was famous for. Of course. And it fit with Ember. "What are your limits?"

"Permanent injury. Breath play. Knives. Unsafe sex."

"Nothing else?"

"No."

"You're an extreme player?" It wouldn't surprise him, with the way she approached life, as if everything was a challenge to be conquered.

"I have a safe word."

"Any problems with complete nudity?"

"Whose, Sir?" she fired back, lips quirking a little.

He grinned. The other night, she'd clearly not had any issue with him being naked. He wondered what her touch would have been like on his dick. Firm, no doubt. Araceli wasn't shy. "Yours, of course."

"I'm…" She hesitated, and he was glad.

Torin wanted her to think it through. He wouldn't be able to look without touching.

"Okay."

"Penetration?"

"With toys, fingers, yes. But… We may need to take sex as a separate subject," she said.

"Agreed." *Smart idea.* He removed the bindings from around her wrists then smoothed the red marks from her skin. Her pulse quickened. "You may want to thank me, lest I think you're ungrateful."

"Thank you," she repeated dutifully, respectfully. "Sir."

Before he got lost in her fathomless eyes, Torin unclipped the leash and curled it up on a nearby table. Then he went to work unfastening the dozens of tiny hooks and eyes that held her dress closed. He gave silent thanks that women didn't dress like this anymore. As it was, it took all his

SIERRA CARTWRIGHT

restraint not to go barbarian on her and rip her out of the yards and yards of material.

When it was most of the way open, he drew the gown off her shoulders and let it fall to her waist. "Good girl," he said when he realized she wasn't wearing a bra. His cock was hard, demanding. He reached around to cup her breasts.

"Commander…"

"Sir. Or Master Torin while we're here," he reminded her.

"Master Torin."

"Much better. Are you protesting? Needing to use a safe word?"

"No." Her response was instant. "It's…"

"You trust me with your life. Here, you need to trust me with you emotions as well as your physical wellbeing. I promised to give you what you want. In return, you have to be honest in letting me know. There's no room for lies."

"You're turning me on."

"Good." Outside of the Quarter, he wasn't sure they would have ever gotten here. There was too much between them, real-world complications, of being partners, of her being his former student. He rolled her nipples between his thumbs and forefingers.

She moaned.

Even though they were well away from the rest of the club, nearby cries reached them, as did the bass thumping from the main dungeon.

He squeezed her nipples.

She moaned ever so softly.

He increased the pressure on her nipples until he knew it was painful.

Her knees buckled, but she caught herself and stood up tall before he said anything. "I assume that means you like pain."

She didn't answer.

MEANT FOR ME

"Araceli?" Then he frowned. "Or would you prefer I call you Ember?" It might be easier for her to separate her identifies that way.

"I go by Ember when I'm here."

"Like fire?"

Her eyes were already hazy. Slowly, she nodded.

It suited her. Very much.

He squeezed her nipples even harder, then instantly backed off.

She allowed her head to tip back, and her mouth parted.

"I asked you a question a moment ago. Do you like pain?"

"Yes." It was a whisper. A confession.

"I didn't hear you."

"Yes." Her word was louder, clearer. "Yes, Sir. I like pain."

He tightened his grip on her hard flesh

Though she moaned, she didn't protest.

"Tell me what you think, what you're feeling."

"Damn. I like it," she said. "It hurts. S-s-sir!"

"Shall I stop?"

"Oh heavens. No."

Eventually, he relented and released her. She sighed and her head drooped forward. Behind his zipper, his cock throbbed. Torin wanted to be naked, buried inside her.

He unfastened the final hook and eye that secured the dress at the small of her back. The fabric pooled on the floor. Next, he untied the ridiculous layers of petticoats and let them fall, as well. "Step out of the dress and everything else." Torin's voice was scratchy, more hoarse than he intended. *This woman...*

Her motions exaggerated and delicate, she did as he said.

She stood in front of him, almost bare. Even though she couldn't have known it, her choice in lingerie was perfect. Her black lace garter belt and silky, sexy stockings were the stuff of his fantasies. Her high-heeled, fuck-me shoes were definitely not around during the Victorian era, but they sure as hell turned him on now.

If he weren't careful, she'd bring him to his knees.

He shrugged out of his jacket and tossed it on top of the table. "Remove my belt, please." Since he didn't have his toy bag with him, his options for beating her were limited.

Her eyes opened a bit wider, but she reached for the buckle. "I can't help but notice your dick is hard, Sir."

And getting harder.

She took her time drawing the leather back through its loops. Torture. Pure torture. And undoubtedly deliberate.

With both hands, she offered the leather to him. He accepted, placing it on the table near his jacket. "Now that the dress isn't in your way, you may go to the far wall." After a short paused, he added, "On your hands and knees."

Her mouth dropped open. "You want me to crawl?"

"It's not a suggestion, Ember. It's an order. Do I need to repeat myself?"

She shook her head. "My stockings—"

"Can be replaced. Please do as I say."

She sank gracefully to the floor before moving onto hands and knees, doggy-style. She moved across the floor with a flawless class that made his dick physically ache. Her pert rear swayed slightly. He admired the length of her leg muscles, and he wondered how her thighs would feel wrapped around his waist.

When she arrived at the wall, she stopped and waited for further instruction.

"Stand and face it, please. Arms above your head. I want you totally flat against the bricks. Press your breasts into them. Be sure the concrete is scratching your nipples."

She hesitated only seconds before leaning in.

"I'm going to remove your panties."

Although she tightened her muscles, she didn't protest

as he worked the wisp of material down her thighs. In turn, he lifted each of her feet to remove the thong entirely. Since he didn't want to drop her underwear on the floor, he wadded the silk and stuck it into his front pocket. "Much better."

Mira closed her legs, as if that could protect her.

"Feet shoulder width apart." While she stood there, held only in place by the force of his will and her obedience, he grabbed two sets of restraints from the pegs on the adjoining wall.

He moved in behind her. "You're exquisite, Ember."

"Thank you...Master."

Master. He liked the sound of that much better than "Sir."

He crouched to wrap the restraints around her ankles and then secure them to the hooks in the floor.

He trailed his fingers up the inside of her right thigh. Her legs trembled. "Are you damp?" He drew a finger across her tender pussy lips.

She jerked and gasped, dropping her hands beside her.

"Keep your arms above your head," he instructed her. "You are damp. Will you still be like that after I use my belt on you? Or will you be wetter?" He slid his finger back and forth then pressed the pad of his thumb against her clit.

She jerked convulsively. "I... Please. I need..."

"On second thought, lower your arms. Reach behind you and spread your ass cheeks."

Slowly, she complied with his order.

For a moment, he closed his eyes to get control of his libido. Despite the fact they'd agreed not to have sex, he wanted to plunge deep inside her, slamming her against the wall, pounding out his orgasm, and taking her with him.

Intending to arouse her to the point she couldn't think, he teased her entrance.

Arching her back, she silently asked for more. For a long

time, he played with her before plunging a finger deep inside her.

With a whimper, she jerked.

Masculine pride rushed through him. He liked having this woman respond to him so completely.

Torin drew a deep breath. He was in control of the scene, and he intended to control himself as well. "How close are you to orgasm?" he asked against her ear. He moved his finger, and her internal walls constricted around him.

"It's been a long time," she said, her breaths becoming more and more shallow as he explored her insides. "M-Master Arthur warmed me up."

Torin growled and impaled her with a second finger. The idea of Arthur taking any liberties with this woman, *his* sub, infuriated him. "You're here with me now. You'll not orgasm without my say-so."

When she didn't respond, he asked, "Am I clear?"

"Yes, Master. But…"

"Problem?"

"I come easily."

"You'll come when I say you'll come. *Keep your ass cheeks parted!*" He knelt to lick her while he finger fucked her.

"Sir!"

He stopped short of letting her orgasm.

"Master Torin, you are impossible."

He grinned but was glad she couldn't see him. She delighted him, made him want to please her. "Did you have permission to speak?"

"No," she said.

"And…?"

"The sub apologizes."

"Apology accepted." He loved the way she referred to herself in the third person. She was into the scene as deeply

MEANT FOR ME

as he was. "We'll just add another two lashes for insubordination."

She made a funny sound, somewhere between a mewl and a protest, but didn't say anything else.

He stood then pulled out his fingers from her, trying hard not to think about how badly he wanted to replace them with his cock.

He pressed a damp finger against her anus. Her muscles tightened, but instead of pressing forward and into the wall, trying to escape from him, she took a breath and pressed back in silent invitation.

Lust filled him.

He wanted her. "Bear down," he told her.

"Yes, Sir," she whispered.

As she followed his instructions, he pushed his finger in farther, past his first knuckle. She moaned and wiggled. Exactly the reaction he wanted.

"More," she begged softly.

He continued on, stretching her wider, sinking his finger all the way to the hilt.

"Mas…Master… May I come?"

"No chance." He pulled out.

She groaned in protest.

"Being impatient will prolong the amount of time until you are allowed an orgasm."

"I understand…Master."

After washing his hands in the nearby sink, he returned to her. "Arms spread, Ember. I want you properly secured."

Her shoulders rose and fell, as if she was breathing hard. Although she hadn't made anything ordinary off-limits, he knew he was pushing a boundary now. They'd never played together before, and all she had to operate on were her instincts. "I'm waiting," he said softly against her ear.

Deliberately, as if it were mind over matter, she moved her wrists higher.

Beating her was going to be a pleasure. The scent of her arousal made him that much more anxious to get on with it.

TORIN HAD BEEN RIGHT EARLIER. TO MIRA, SCENING WAS about the rush. The anticipation of knowing he intended to use his belt on her was like a drug, one she couldn't get enough of.

Realizing she was in danger of losing control, Mira called on her yoga practice and drew a breath deep into her lungs then exhaled it out in a controlled, measured way. When her nerves didn't calm, she did it again

"Right wrist first," Torin said, breaking into her thoughts.

His touch was uncompromising but surprisingly gentle as he secured her right wrist in place. Instinctively she pulled back on the tether, testing it. It was as unyielding as the Dom himself. A ripple of anticipation jolted through her body.

The wall was uncomfortably cold and the bricks scratched her tender skin. She was hyperaware of the room's chill, of the door with its window, of Torin's spicy, masculine scent.

He secured her left wrist in place, leaving her splayed and helpless.

Her pussy was still dripping, and her clit throbbed. For a moment, he traced the collar around her neck. Wildly, she wondered what it would like if it really was his, if he placed it on her as a sign of his ownership.

Scared by her own thoughts, she shoved the idea from her mind. It was ludicrous, something she didn't want.

"How many strokes with my belt?" he asked.

Uh. He wanted her to decide? A chill—part delight, part

MEANT FOR ME

dread—chased up her spine. Torin wouldn't let her abdicate her role in their play.

"Ember?"

"Eight, Sir?"

"Good place to start."

She shuddered.

"How many more for allowing Arthur to see you? And, worse, touch you?"

"When I invited him to play, I didn't realize I wasn't allowed to do that," she protested.

"That wasn't the question."

How could he arbitrarily enforce rules that she didn't know existed? It wasn't fair. Then again, nothing about their time together ever had been, starting with the training exercise at the nightclub. "Two."

"Three it is."

She opened her mouth but clamped it shut again. He'd simply add more strokes the more she argued. And since she didn't know how hard he would hit her, she figured she'd better err on the side of safety.

"How many total?"

"Eleven."

"You forgot the ones from earlier. The insubordination."

She sagged a little.

"So how many?"

"Thirteen." Quickly she added, "Sir" so he didn't add any extra for a lack of respect.

"Is your pussy still wet?"

"It was. Now I'm suddenly a little nervous," she admitted, "so I'm not as turned on as I was earlier."

He moved in behind her. Using his body, he pushed her hard against the cold, unyielding wall. She felt the scratch of denim and the hardness of his cock against her naked backside. Her breasts were flattened against the bricks. Her nipples hardened from her overwhelming arousal.

"I'm tempted to just fuck you with my hand while you're strung up here, totally helpless."

"*Now* I'm wet," she whispered. He didn't even need to touch her. He could turn her on just with words. He thrust repeatedly against her rear, simulating intercourse. She'd said no sex because it would be confusing outside of the club. But in this room, they could fuck, and maybe if they confined it just to here... More than anything she wanted his penetration, his possession. "Please," she begged. "Please fuck me."

"We need to discuss it when you're not so aroused."

His breath was warm, his body was hard, and his spicy, outdoorsy scent enveloped her.

"You'll count each stroke for me, *mo shearc*."

His use of the Irish endearment undid her. It was easy to keep herself emotionally detached from him when she thought of him as her trainer and he called her by her last name? But referring to her with tenderness, in that tantalizing brush of a brogue...? She squeezed her eyes closed, as if that could keep him at bay.

He moved away.

"Damn it," she said. "Damn you."

The bastard actually laughed.

He left her weak and needy, on the razor's edge of fulfillment.

He caught her completely off guard, unprepared.

Torin landed the first blow, right under her buttocks, with a vicious upward stroke. She gasped from shock, from sudden pain.

His punishment had been much, much harder than she'd anticipated.

"Count," he reminded her.

"One," she bit out. There'd been nothing erotic about his first smack. Maybe he wasn't as fabulous as she'd thought.

He caught her again, in the exact same spot, with the exact same pressure.

"Ember?"

"Two." She braced herself as much as she could with nothing to hold on to.

The third followed suit, and it was then that she realized his skill. His aim was exact, his timing impeccable. He was a master of beatings.

"This is meant to satisfy all the nasty things inside you that you won't give a voice to. Unless I do this, you won't be happy."

He was so fucking right that she hated him.

"How many?" he snapped.

"Three!"

He added a little more force to the fourth, and she cried out.

"Four!"

"That's my girl."

For the next few seconds nothing happened. He allowed the time and silence to stretch. The only thing she was aware of was her own frantic pulse.

"Let me know when you're ready to proceed."

He thought she was struggling to take it? That annoyed the hell out of her. "Bring it on." She waited a couple of seconds before adding, "Commander."

"You haven't learned about goading me?"

Instead of hitting her, he tormented her, moving in closer, reaching between her legs, trailing his fingertips up her thigh...making her unravel.

He pinched her clit. She cried out. It hurt, but deliciously so. She ground her hips forward, all but trying to get off against the wall.

"Stop that. Naughty hussy."

She would have stamped her foot if it hadn't been shackled.

"Where were we?"

"Four," she said.

"Are you ready to resume?"

"Yes, Sir."

"More respectful. Better." This time he caught her across the fleshy part of her butt cheeks.

Damn it! "Five." It stung so bad. *Hurt so good.*

God, she'd wanted this. She'd wanted a man who could give her everything she needed. She liked the pain he inflicted, loved the fact he gave her a few seconds to savor the sensation before moving on.

"We have an audience," he told her. "Tore has been watching for the last few minutes."

That thought turned her on.

Before she was fully ready, Torin landed the next stripe across the uppermost part of her left thigh. The tip of the belt bit into her pussy. She moaned. She groaned. She wiggled, trying to escape. But he'd confined her perfectly, exquisitely.

He moved to her other side to catch her right thigh. Again, the end of the leather monster sliced against her exposed pussy.

"I can smell your heat," he said.

"Seven…and it freaking hurt, Sir."

"Bad?"

"Bad." Miserably, she nodded.

"Is that why your pussy is so wet?"

He added the eighth on top of the last two, as if tying them together.

"Tore is gone."

Torin's next three were perfectly timed and impeccably

MEANT FOR ME

landed. Each stripe was on top of the previous one, across her butt cheeks instead of the upper part of her thighs. They hurt like hell, and he wielded the leather aggressively. He gave no quarter, and she asked for none, wanting to feel the full power of his lash.

Each of the three blows dragged a scream from her.

She'd never been beaten so soundly, never felt so overcome with pain, with emotion. And yet, a small part of her realized they weren't done yet. She still had to take the ones for her earlier insubordination.

"You remembered."

And so had he, apparently. "I'm ready."

"I'm not." Instead, he scraped the prong of his buckle along the marks he'd made, digging into her skin.

It blazed torturously, pleasurably.

Her pussy was dripping from her arousal.

No other Dom had ever turned her on this way.

"I want your ass sticking out." Torin bent to unfasten her ankles then pressed his palm against her lower belly to move her back a little. "How are the bricks on your nipples?"

Because she'd moved each time he landed a blow, her skin had been abraded. "They're not as good as nipple clamps," she confessed, not believing she was admitting this. "But hot."

"Oh, Ember. The things I intend to do to you."

She wanted to experience all of them in their short time remaining.

"Thrust your hips out from the wall."

With her body secured, it was difficult to get into the position he'd requested, but she knew better than to complain.

Before her mind could assimilate, he spanked her, his open palm landing against her already raw skin.

Unbelievably his hand hurt far worse than the bite of leather.

"How many more, Ember?"

"Two."

"Ask me for them."

She wanted to sink into the oblivion of her thoughts, absorb the pain, make sense of it, savor it. But he wouldn't allow her that luxury. "Please, Master Torin. Please spank me."

"Where do you want them?"

"On my ass, Sir."

"Not on your cunt?"

Her insides constricted. For a moment she forgot to breathe. The idea of his powerful hand landing on her pussy scared her, thrilled her. And suddenly she had to know, had to know what it felt like, had to have the experience. "Yes," she whispered.

"I didn't hear you."

"Yes," she said louder. "Punish me there."

"Where?"

"My pussy," she said.

He played with her first, stroking her labia, teasing her clit, dipping a finger inside her arousal-slickened vagina. Her body convulsed. She was so close...

The first stinging blow made her gasp, made her even wetter.

"One more."

She moved slightly, arching her back, offering him better access to her private parts.

"Good girl."

His final slap forced her onto her toes. She cried his name.

Then she felt him behind her, his strong hands forcing her butt cheeks apart even farther, making her entire body strain.

He tongued her, and she screamed. She hadn't realized

MEANT FOR ME

he'd dropped to his knees. Relentlessly he continued, forcing her to fight an orgasm. She groaned and jerked when he pressed his thumb against her anal opening. The sensations were too much, pushing her beyond her endurance capability.

Mira needed the relief from the tension clawing inside her. "Master! Ohh, Master! I need to come."

He moved away from her and pinched the inside of her right thigh, but the distraction wasn't enough.

Then, without permission, breaking his rules, she shattered, pulling against her restraints, her hips jerking uncontrollably, her entire body shuddering against the rigid wall.

The orgasm was powerful, debilitating, every bit as emotional as it was physical. She was drained, her body limp in her bondage.

His presence overwhelmed her.

Though her eyes were squeezed shut, she pictured him, tight blue jeans—made even tighter by the size of his erection—scuffed and scarred boots, a black T-shirt with short sleeves, the fabric showing his powerful arms.

His scent was consuming, spice mixed with a hint of pure male sweat and the tanginess of a heated Southern evening.

But it was the way he'd beaten her that drained her completely.

He'd been relentless, demanding.

He made her hornier than she'd been in years.

"Ember?" he said, his tone was gruff, and it cut into her fantasies. Then, against her ear, he asked, "Did you come?"

She froze. She'd seen this kind of behavior before. Other Doms she'd been with had acted the same way, feigning shock and disbelief that she'd come without permission.

She knew intuitively that Torin would have continued to eat her, tongue her, press into her anus until she came. He knew how to touch her, how to encourage the response he desired. Torin Carter had forced her into a no-win situation. Still, Mira was startled into complete silence.

"Mo shearc?"

"Yes," she whispered. "Yes, Master Torin. I came."

"Most unfortunate. Now I'm afraid you really must be punished."

CHAPTER FIVE

HAWKEYE

Torin regretted staying away from her for so long.

Mira Araceli was utterly lovely, completely captivating. He wanted to please her again and again. Her orgasm had been as loud and unrestrained as the woman herself. Her passion ran deep. She was everything he wanted. All the things that scared the hell out of him.

Worse, he planned to fuck her senseless.

Which was complete madness.

Even if they didn't plan on it, sex would cloud their working relationship. She fired a possessive streak in him. One that should bother him.

After unfastening her wrists and rubbing the skin to help restore circulation, he helped her back into her ridiculous gown and the annoying petticoats or whatever the hell they were called. He didn't, however, return her thong.

"Stand still," he said, working on the frustrating number of hooks and eyes.

"Yes, Master."

The word rocked through him. Other submissives had referred to him by the honorific, but until now, it hadn't sent a burst of possessiveness through him. He fumbled the next hook. "Who was the goddamn idiot who thought up this outfit?"

She laughed.

"I'll ignore your rudeness. And in future, I'll keep you naked." His fingers were too big for the tiny metal clasps. In frustration, he skipped a few of them. Good enough.

They needed to debrief, but when he looked at her, her deep brown eyes were clouded. She wasn't quite back all the way.

Araceli might consider herself tough, but she'd also just had a scene. No doubt endorphins were still swimming through her system.

He grabbed his jacket from the bench, then draped the soft leather bomber over her shoulders. Only then did he feed his belt back through the loops on his jeans.

Torin picked up the leash and considered attaching it. Because of her earlier reaction, he figured they should talk about it before he compelled her to wear it. He made it into a tighter loop and stuffed it in his back pocket.

Then he scooped up his little submissive and her numerous layers of clothing.

Frantically, she kicked her legs. "Sir!"

"Settle down or I'll toss you over my shoulder."

"You would, too!"

"Of course."

He carried her from the room. As he started down the stairs, she turned into him and wrapped her arms around his neck. There were ways to get her to behave without an argument.

On the second floor, he shifted her in his arms, then sat on the velvet snuggle couch.

She tried to push away, but he held her tight. He wasn't sure why she had to be tougher than anyone, never giving in

MEANT FOR ME

to human needs. As if she had something to prove. "It doesn't make you weak." She was the first recruit in the gym each morning. During training, she taped her ankle instead of having a medic check it out. She blazed forward, no matter the terrain or conditions. More recently, she'd been knocked upside of the head, and she'd refused Torin's assistance. Damn it, he wanted to protect her, make her feel cherished. He settled for, "You just had a hell of a scene."

"I'm okay."

"I'm sure you are." Then he took an emotional risk and admitted, "It takes me some time to come down too. Give me this."

She sighed. "Do you always have to win?"

"Does it really seem that way?" He turned her a little so he could study her face. "If so, I think you misread me. This isn't some move on an imaginary chessboard. It's real. It's about giving our minds and bodies to readjust to the real world." *After something so fucking sensational.*

With great reluctance, fighting his instincts, Torin relaxed his grip so she could escape if she needed to.

But that seemed to be exactly what she needed. Tension seeped from her. Her shoulders rounded, and she rested her head on him.

It was a powerful lesson. She needed to choose her own path, and her surrender was all the sweeter for it.

Hold on loosely.

He wasn't sure he was strong enough to do that.

Eventually, she splayed her fingers on his chest and closed her eyes. Mindlessly, he stroked her hair. Minutes later, their breathing synchronized. It was a powerful sensation, one he'd never shared with anyone else. "Mo shearc."

She might have dozed—but he doubted she would admit it—but some time later, she pushed herself away from him. Her absence weighed him down, a cold, physical thing.

SIERRA CARTWRIGHT

"We need to debrief."

"Do we have to?" She sat up and scooted away from him.

"Afraid so. We can talk at the bar here. Or grab a coffee. Maybe a bite to eat if you need it. Or we can soak in the hot tub."

She leveled him with a hard look. "With swimsuits."

"Of course." Her fierceness made him smile.

"I think I'll be more comfortable talking away from here. I need to find Hallie to let her know I'm leaving."

"A friend of yours?"

"We came together."

"Do you need to do that alone?"

She hesitated for a moment. "No. But I might want a private moment, if she has any concerns."

He fished the leash from his pocket as he stood. Then he offered his hand to help her.

"Is that thing really necessary, Sir?"

"I say it is." Would she defy him? He watched a struggle play out on her face. It seemed she was a little bit of a masochist, but not into something she might consider humiliating.

Her safe word hovered between them. As he thumbed open the hook, he waited for her to resist or yield to his wishes.

Though she squeezed her eyes shut, she didn't protest as he clipped it to her collar. "It's stunning on you."

She met his gaze.

"You struggle with this. Why?"

"My training, I guess. If something goes wrong, I want to be free."

"You were fine during the scene."

"It doesn't have to make sense, does it?" She curled her right hand into the fabric of her skirt. "Being restrained while I'm bottoming helps me detach from the ordinary

MEANT FOR ME

world. I don't like to play in the main dungeon where there are a lot of people."

He nodded. "I've got your six."

"You're completely trustworthy."

Those words couldn't have come easily to her, which gave them even more weight.

"It's not about you or your competence, Sir. This is who I am. My experience of the world. I look out for myself."

"Have you always?" he asked, words soft.

"Commander—"

"Curious, that's all."

"My mother died when I was four."

From her file, he knew that. What he didn't know was how it affected her.

"She was lovely, an encouraging, gentle person. My father was…" She trailed off and clamped her lips together.

He waited.

"Former military. West Point." She shrugged. "Nurturing wasn't his way, or, rather, isn't his way. Tough love. All of us being compared to each other, as well as the children of his friends and colleagues. My brothers—both older—had it tougher than I did. My oldest brother followed our dad's footsteps."

"And the other?"

"Could never measure up. He tried, but it broke him. He has a…" She exhaled. "I have no idea why I'm telling you all this."

He appreciated that she was. "Go on," he invited.

"I guess you'd say he has a gentle soul. So much like our mom." She wiped a trembling hand across her forehead. "Or what I remember of her. He has a drug problem. Sometimes, he's on the streets. Dad has disowned him."

"Jesus."

Before he could say anything else, Mira held up a hand.

"Please. I don't want your pity. Save that for someone who deserves it. It wasn't a bad upbringing. We had a nice house, food, clothing, the best schools, all the advantages."

But not the one thing she craved the most? Her father's affection, and maybe more importantly, perhaps, his approval? Torin was fortunate. He'd grown up in a family of six kids, all of whom were loved deeply and encouraged to find their own way. It was loud and boisterous, and a firm foundation from which to explore the world. Love was abundant, even when he screwed up.

He lifted the leash several inches. "If this is too much to ask, I'll remove it."

"It seems important to you." Cleverly, Mira had turned his question around.

Because she'd revealed something about herself, he gave her an honest answer. "It pleases me to have others see that you..." He paused. *Belong to me.* "Are publicly acknowledging your submission."

"Master Arthur might still be here," she surmised. "And Mistress Aviana. Tore. Everyone who witnessed the scene. And this is how you can show you've claimed me." Not needing his confirmation, she nodded. "I understand."

She fucking tilted his world off its axis.

With her leash wrapped around his hand, they descended to the halfway landing. From here, there was an excellent view of most of the club, including *Rue Sensuelle*, or as it was colloquially known, Kinky Avenue.

As she searched for her friend, she scanned the occupied settings, a schoolroom, an office, a church. "She must be in the main club."

"Any sign of her?"

"Yes! She's watching that rope bondage."

With his hand in Mira's hair, they continued down the

MEANT FOR ME

stairs, then through the back area of the club to the door leading to the main dungeon.

Without stopping, he moved her toward the area she'd indicated. An expert was demonstrating a hogtie on a model, and Torin allowed Mira to lead him to her friend.

"You're Master Hottie," Hallie said.

"I'm sorry?"

Mira elbowed Hallie. "Uhm, that's my nickname for you." She shrugged. "I've seen you here before, and I didn't know your name."

He grinned, mostly at Mira's discomfort. "I'm flattered."

"Hallie, this is Torin Carter."

Her mouth fell open as she looked from Torin back to Mira. "That Torin Carter? Like your nemesis? The guy who was standing outside your door while you were busy stroking your—"

"I apologize, Sir. My friend seems to have forgotten all protocol."

"Partner!" Hallie corrected. "You're Mir—I mean Ember's partner. Right?"

"I prefer that to nemesis, yes."

"Will you excuse me for a moment, Sir?" Mira asked.

With a grin, he unclipped the leash and wound its length around his hand while Mira dragged her friend off to one side.

He wasn't close enough to overhear anything, but Hallie glanced his direction twice, her mouth open wider each time.

Less than a minute later, they returned.

"I'll call you tomorrow," Hallie told Mira.

"I'm ready, Sir."

"Nice to meet you, Hallie."

"I definitely need a job at Hawkeye," Hallie proclaimed before returning to the demonstration.

"After you," he said to Mira.

"Did you want to put the leash back on me?"

"I'm fine."

"Really?"

"Unless you want me to?"

She shook her head ferociously.

When they were in the reception area, he used his phone to arrange for a car. Then he removed her collar.

He offered it and the leash to her. "Will you put them in a coat pocket, please?"

"I should give it back to you."

"Keep it until we get home. I gave up on a few of those hooks on the back of your dress. You may need to preserve your modesty."

She grinned. "Before we leave, I need to claim my purse."

He joined her at the coatroom, resting his fingertips in the small of her back. As she waited for belongings, she stroked her forefinger across her throat where the leather had hugged her skin. Missing it? He could hope so.

AN HOUR LATER, HE WAS IN THE HOT TUB, JETTED BUBBLES dancing around him. Movement caught his gaze, and Torin glanced up at the carriage house to see Mira descending the staircase. She wore a white robe, and her hair was secured on top of her head with a clip that sparkled beneath a light.

As she walked across flagstones, moonlight bathed her with an otherworldly glow. Though he'd seen her naked, pleasured her, made her scream, she was as much of a mystery as she'd always been.

On the decking, she dropped her robe on a chair. Her bikini was skimpy enough that she might as well be naked. Her nipples pressed against the top, and the bottom didn't completely cover her buttocks.

With her toes, she tested the water. *A metaphor for your life, mo shearc?* Until now, he wasn't sure he'd met a woman whose secrets he intended to unlock. But he wanted to know everything about her. He wouldn't stop until he did.

"It's perfect." She held on to the rail as she entered the tub.

The evening was clear, with blessedly low humidity. It was a little crisp for New Orleans, making it perfect weather to soak in the heated water.

With a sigh, she sat, sinking to her neck. Then gently, she tipped her head forward and rolled her shoulders.

"How does your body feel?"

"None the worse for wear." She smiled. But she didn't use the word *Sir.*

They'd left their scene behind at the Quarter, and she hadn't asked for help when she removed the dress.

"You're an excellent Dom, Torin. Everything I could hope." She blew out a breath.

Studying her, he scowled. "You don't sound happy about that."

"I'm not."

He waited, giving her time to sift through her thoughts, perhaps choose her words.

"The truth is…" She scooted a little farther away. "I would have preferred it if you had been awful, limp-wristed, maybe. If you hadn't pushed me a little. With most play partners, eight strokes with a belt would have been ideal, but you insisted on more…" She took a breath. "Before you say anything, I know that I have a safe word. That's not my point. You pushed for more, adding the ones for insubordination. And something inside me soared. I like to be pushed, and you know me well enough to realize it."

"It wasn't a challenge." He'd been watching her, gauging where she was at. All of his actions had been calculated to give her what she wanted.

"I know." She swirled a finger on the water's surface. "The whole experience was better than I would have imagined. You were..." She exhaled. "I'm sorry. This is difficult to admit to myself, let alone out loud." More softly, she finished, "To you."

"Take your time. But I promise you this. You are safe with me." Still, she remained quiet. So he took the first step. "You were one of the most responsive subs I've ever been with."

"It was like—I don't know how this makes any sense, or maybe it sounds ridiculous—as if it wasn't our first time."

He wouldn't have put it that way. But she made perfect sense. Everything about the scene had been natural, seamless. "I get it."

"Maybe it's because we're partners. We've worked together and expect certain things from each other?"

Suddenly, he was unaccountably annoyed. "And maybe it's because it was just fucking right."

She wove her hand in and out of bubbling water. "Okay. What if we agree on that?"

"Then we have to figure out what the hell to do next." It wasn't against Hawkeye policy for them to be lovers. And plenty of people he knew had affairs with fellow operatives. A few even fell in love and got married.

"I want to have sex with you."

Hell's fury. His erection was instantaneous.

"But we need to agree on what it is. No attachments."

That feral part of him strained forward. "Meaning?"

"We're both physical people, Commander. And we are capable of separating emotion from copulating. We can do our jobs, go about our business. And if it's convenient, we can have sex."

"You're on dangerous ground, Araceli."

Steam rose from the water, and she waved a hand to disperse it so she could look at him. "Why?"

MEANT FOR ME

"I won't agree to your damn rules." He'd been rational at the club, but he was far beyond that now. "First of all, I don't fuck without it meaning something. You may have noticed I don't share well. And if you're my…" He looked at her pointedly. What was she? Words failed him. She was more than a hookup. Less than a girlfriend, but he wouldn't stake his claim any harder if she were. Torin settled on a word that was inadequate. "Lover, then you will not be sleeping with anyone else. If you submit to me, then I will be your Dom. Your *only* Dom."

"Our assignment ends soon."

As if he needed reminding. Soon enough, he'd back at the Aiken Training Facility with a new group of recruits while she was in the field. Long-term wasn't a possibility for either of them. Once again, he was unaccountably annoyed. His life was mapped out, and he enjoyed it. But now, the idea of being alone made the future look dark, unappealing. "I'm not flexible. I want to explore you, take you inside where I can make you scream and beg as loud as you need to. But I won't do it unless you agree to my terms."

Her response took forever, long enough for a vise to clamp around his heart and threaten to consume him.

When she spoke, her words were as cautious as he would expect from her. "If I agree to your terms?"

"Then I'll ask you how hard you want it." She didn't need to answer. This time, he knew what she would say.

"Take me inside?"

She was lucky that he didn't just bend her over one of the chairs and claim her outside. If the condoms weren't inside the carriage house, he might do just that.

He climbed the steps of the tub, then offered his hand to help her. She wrapped up in her robe, and he draped a towel around his shoulders.

SIERRA CARTWRIGHT

When they reached their temporary home, he turned on a light, then locked the door behind them. "The robe, Araceli."

Her gaze fixed on him, she removed it.

"Now get rid of the swimsuit."

She sucked in a breath. "Yes, Sir."

That fast, they were back in their roles. Had she needed this from him all along?

Goose bumps dotted her skin as she reached to untie the strings behind her neck. Then she flicked open the front closure and let the top float to the floor.

Then, her gaze on him, she worked the bottom piece down. He wasn't sure if she was trying to tempt him or whether the material wasn't cooperating because it was wet. The end result was the same—it was taking her forever, and the torment made his cock so hard that his trunks could no longer contain it. "You belong to me."

Like him, she had a few scars, from the job and the rigors of training. They made her more exquisite. "Will you turn around? I want to see if your ass is still red."

Instantly, and with grace, she turned.

"All gone."

"Even the ones on my thighs?"

"Even those," he confirmed.

"I…"

"Need more?" He raised an eyebrow. "Lasting ones?"

"Yes." She took a step toward him. "I need you to fuck me."

Like oxygen, she sustained him.

"But first, do you mind if I shower? I want to wash off the chlorine."

He didn't mind at all. "I'll watch."

As if to instinctively protest, she opened her mouth. Then she closed it again, and her eyes widened with interest.

"After you," he said.

MEANT FOR ME

Mira bent to scoop her wet suit and robe from the floor, then led the way down the hallway to the bathroom. After depositing the garments in the laundry hamper, she turned on the faucets.

Since his last stay in the carriage house, the place had been remodeled. In addition to a clawfoot tub, an oversize walk-in shower had been installed. There was an overhead waterfall showerhead as well as a handheld wand.

Arms folded across his chest, he watched her stand beneath the spray.

Looking at him, she lathered the soap she must have used earlier, the one that reminded him of wildflowers. When her hands were completely covered in the bubbles, she returned the purple-colored bar to the little dish on the side.

Giving him the show he expected, she rubbed her palms over her breasts, making tiny circles, then taking turns lifting each to stroke up from the bottom.

It took all his self-control to be the stoic Dom when he really wanted his hands all over.

When she was completely covered in tiny bubbles, she reached for the handheld showerhead.

"I'll take that."

Eyes wide, she offered him the handle.

"Come closer to me." He started with her hands, then directed the spray over her chest and down her breasts before continuing lower toward her belly. "Spread your legs for me."

She sighed as he rinsed her pussy.

He could bathe her every day and not get tired of it. "I want to do your ass. Turn around and part your buttocks."

Mira swallowed deeply, but she whispered a respectful, intoxicating, "Yes, Master Torin."

Water sluiced between her ass cheeks, over her most private places. Soon, he realized his folly. Taking care of her was turning him on even more, and he was anxious to be inside her.

More quickly than before, he crisscrossed her body with the spray before replacing the showerhead and turning off the faucets. "Dry off and meet me in the living room. I'd like you naked and kneeling."

She nodded.

When she left, the wildflower scent still rich on the air, he stripped off and took a quick shower.

On his way back to the living room, wearing only a towel, he grabbed a condom.

She was waiting for him, kneeling on a small rug, head down, legs spread, and... *Fuck...* Wearing the collar. A sub had never pleased him more. "Come here."

Mira accepted his help up.

He plucked the clip from her hair, sending the long, luxurious strands tumbling around her shoulders. Then he grabbed a handful and pulled back her head.

Her eyes were hazed over. Anticipating his unspoken words, she parted her lips. Lost in her, Torin took her mouth. Her tongue met his, and he tasted the sweetness of her compliance. He was no longer capable of tenderness. Instead, he was determined to prove how much he meant his earlier words. Right now—if not forever—she belonged to him alone.

Torin thrust his tongue in and out of her mouth. With his kiss, he let her know what to expect when he fucked her.

As if she were made for him, she leaned into him, soothing all that was savage. She wrapped her arms around him and held on as if she'd never let go.

They were bare skin to bare skin. He dragged her close enough that her breasts were against him, her nipples hard, demanding nubs.

With reluctance, he ended the kiss. A hot desire for more

drove him. He dragged over a chair. "Put your palms on the seat."

Without hesitation, she did.

The air conditioner kicked on, swirling cool air over their still-damp bodies, making her nipples even harder.

When she was in position, she looked over her shoulder at him. Her eyes widened. "Damn."

He raised an eyebrow as he rolled the condom down his cock. "See something you like?"

"Ah. That's impressive. Even the other night... I... I had no idea you were *that* big."

"Problem, sub?"

She blinked alluringly. "I'll do my best. Sir."

"I've always admired your can-do attitude."

He strode toward her and placed his left palm on her shoulder. She sucked in a sharp breath. *Good.* He liked her being as affected as he was.

Torin skimmed his fingertips down her spine. Her head dropped forward, and her hair hid her features from him. She moved her body in response to his touch. He paused at the gentle curve of her spine. Then he used both of his hands to part her buttocks. "You like it hard."

"Yes," she whispered.

He slapped her right ass cheek. Instantly, he soothed the ache.

In silent invitation, Mira lifted up.

He played with her pussy, stroking her clit, sliding his finger gently in and out of her, making sure she was wet and ready.

When she whimpered, he moved in closer to place his cockhead at her entrance. She jiggled her buttocks. "Demanding, are you?"

"Dying." The word emerged on a strangled breath that he had to strain to hear. "There's a difference, Sir."

SIERRA CARTWRIGHT

A little at a time, he inserted his length into her, sliding in, then back out.

"Please."

He filled her, and her internal muscles clenched around him. He tipped back his head and closed his eyes, fighting back his imminent orgasm. He should have beat off in the shower.

Focusing on her, he reached beneath her to torment her nipples, and she gasped. "Too hard?"

"No. Just, earlier, the bricks. I'm tender, and I'm on the edge of an orgasm."

"But you're not going to, are you? Not unless I give permission?"

"No. No, Sir." She panted when he tightened his grip and simultaneously pushed her breasts together. "Oh, Sir! I'm so, so close."

Torin continued his torment until she begged. Only then did he slowly release her, making her whimper in protest.

He changed positions, wrapping her up, one arm across her rib cage, the other across her upper chest. "I want you to stand up."

"Yes." She pushed off her hands, and he appreciated how physically capable she was.

As she eased upright, his cock sank deeper into her. When he was balls-deep, she gasped. "Too much?"

"No." She arched her spine, then slid a hand behind his neck for support. "I've been fantasizing about this for years."

"Years?" Her confession caused his cock to throb with incessant demand.

"Please, Sir. Please may I come?"

The knowledge that the attraction hadn't been one-sided made him drive up into her, hard, impaling her with his thrusts. It was raw, animalistic, filled with lust, and they were consummating a heat that had burned for years. For the moment she was his, and he'd leave her no doubt about it. "Yes. Come for me, my beautiful Mira."

Her body squeezing around him, she screamed.

Mira came in convulsing waves, and he tightened his hold on her as her hand slipped to fall by her side.

Her climax pushed him over the top. In a hot stream, he ejaculated, the orgasm ripped from the deepest part of him. It was both brutal and satisfying. But it wasn't even close to filling his desperate hunger for her.

She tipped her head back to rest on his chest, and he kissed the top of her head. He'd never had an experience like that.

Her breaths were labored, and she curled her fingers into her forearm. "Are you doing okay?"

For a moment, she didn't respond, and he was content to hold her, breathing in her scent. "That was everything I imagined."

He'd never been this complete.

And it wasn't enough.

He had to know every inch of her. "I'm going to take you to the bedroom." He stroked the column of her neck.

"Yes. Please, Sir."

CHAPTER SIX

HAWKEYE

Sometime in the middle of the night, Torin awakened to an empty bed. He wasn't surprised. The shock had been that Mira had fallen asleep in his arms.

After the edge had been filed off his urgency, he'd taken her to his room, secured her to the bedposts, fucked again, and then untied her so they could make love.

In her exhaustion, she curled up in the crook of his arm, for once letting down her formidable guard. He'd never wanted to let her go.

A gentle sound drifted on the night air, and he focused his senses, listening deeper, sifting out the background noises to discern what was different. *Water?*

He glanced at the clock. 2:47 a.m.

Perhaps she was exercising. But it wasn't loud enough for that. Curious, he pulled on a pair of sleep pants and went in search of her.

The lights in the main area were off, but the bathroom was bright. Water rushed from the faucet. Then suddenly, there was silence. The door was open a crack, and he knocked on it. "Mira?" Without waiting for an invitation, he entered.

She was chest deep in the enormous clawfoot tub, resting her nape against the rim.

"Room for me?"

"Are you serious?"

He dropped his pants, and she grinned. "I'll take that as a yes, then." She sat up to pull out the drain plug.

"Stay there." Behind her, he stepped into the tub. "Damn! It's hot."

As she had no doubt guessed, the moment he sat, water sloshed over the rim.

Together, they laughed, and it occurred to him that it might have been the first time they'd done that at the same time, from pure, stupid joy. Neither their jobs nor their personalities were given to light moments. Had he always been so serious? Or had events honed him?

When enough water had drained, she replaced the plug, then scooted back, trying to find a comfortable position between his legs. "You're ginormous, Commander Carter."

"We'll fit. It will just be tight."

"I think you like it that way."

"Your deductive reasoning skills are spectacular." He grinned.

"Hallie calls it spy shit."

"Could be more accurate than either of us want to admit." He laughed. "I like your friend."

"She doesn't have a lot of filters."

"It's refreshing."

"You weren't upset?"

"Not in the least. Come closer."

Surprising him, she did. He adjusted their positions so he could fold his arms around her. "Couldn't sleep?"

MEANT FOR ME

"I drifted off, for a short while." After a few seconds, she allowed herself to relax against him. "But then... Just a little restless, I suppose."

"Want to talk about it?" When she hadn't replied after a full minute, he tried again. "Did having sex bother you? Cross boundaries?"

"That's not it." She moved a hand through the water. "Or maybe it is. I don't regret it. It was freaking sexy. But..."

This time he waited.

"It was different than ever before. *Hell.* You seem to see me differently than anyone else ever has."

"You like to keep the real you hidden deep inside?"

"I'm not unique." Maybe because of what they'd shared, what she wanted him to understand, she didn't argue. "I think we all want to protect ourselves. At least to some degree."

For a while, the silence stretched between them, with only an occasional passing car disturbing the quiet.

"Even you won't let me see your vulnerabilities," she added. "It's safer that way." She placed her fingertips on an upraised knee. "Or we like to think so, right? Things happen, but we don't talk about them. Instead, we go through our lives hiding. It's less risky that way."

And maybe because of their intimacy, he didn't argue. "You're asking about my nightmare."

"You scared the hell out of me."

It had taken him hours to throw off the disorientation and shove the combination of memories and horrific imaginings back into the deep recesses of his mind.

"Does Hawkeye know how bad it can be?"

He'd been one of the only people Torin confided in. "He does."

"Have you talked to anyone? I mean a professional."

SIERRA CARTWRIGHT

"I did. Hawkeye didn't give me a lot of choice." The dreams had been fewer and further between, less intense. Until Mira. "My partner was killed in the line of duty."

"I…" Her body went rigid, and he stroked her shoulder reassuringly. "Sorry. I had no idea."

Mira pulled away and moved to the far end of the tub. When she was as far away as possible, she turned around to face him.

Sex with her had been damn good for him too. Until he was inside her, he'd had no idea how much he craved human contact. Not just anyone. *Mira.* She hadn't needed to save him from the nightmare, then stay with him until he was out of its throes, but she had. Seeing her with Arthur had flooded him with rage, an emotion no other woman had triggered in him.

She was owed an explanation. No longer hiding, he met her beseeching gaze. "Her name was Ekaterina. We were working security at a football match—soccer to the rest of the world. In Mexico." Time hadn't diminished the memories, the colors, screams, chaos. In fact, it had sharpened each image, fine-tuning them with details he'd missed on that bright, cloudless day. "There was a duffel bag on the ground next to a trash can. Black. Canvas." He could recount the brand name, the exact dimensions.

Torin called the authorities.

He and Ekaterina were instructed to clear the area without causing undue panic. "There was a man who pushed past her. Ekaterina must have assumed he was a good guy. Instead of calling out a warning, she threw herself on the bomb. He detonated it remotely and took them both out."

Mira wrapped her arms around her knees. "Oh, Torin."

"If we had kept the perimeter like we should have…"

"That's a horrible thing to live with."

MEANT FOR ME

"There should have been something I could do to stop her."

"It might never make sense."

That was the worst thing of all. No matter how much time passed, regret and recrimination would follow him. "Come back to bed with me?"

A tiny furrow appeared between her eyebrows. How much was she willing to risk? She hesitated long enough that he straightened his back, steeling himself for her rejection.

"I'd like that." She offered a slight, half-smile. "Make it worth my while?"

"What have you got in mind?"

"I'm sure we'll think of something. Sir."

"BREAKFAST?" TORIN OFFERED, OPENING THE PASSENGER DOOR of his car.

Mira blinked, trying to moisturize her gritty eyes. It'd been a hellaciously long night. A popular starlet was getting married the following weekend, and as a last hurrah, she and seven of her bridesmaids had decided on New Orleans as stop one of their blowout bachelorette party.

They'd hopped in and out of bars, no matter how dubious they were. At three a.m., the bridal party—laden with Mardi Gras beads from flashing their breasts—had staggered into the Oubliette, a dive located off a fog-filled alley. After a round of cocktails labeled A Short Trip to Hell, they had wanted to grab food—compliments, no doubt, of the entire can of energy booster in each drink.

It had been almost six a.m. when she and Torin saw them safely onto the elevator.

"I'm not sure what I want more," she admitted when

Torin slid behind the wheel. "A shower. Sleep. Or food. That was one of the most challenging assignments ever."

"We needed more people. Who knew that eight women could be so much work?"

With a grin, she tipped her head back. Especially when one of them was so beloved and instantly recognizable.

"Some of them are going to regret the pictures on social media."

No longer their problem. And the Hawkeye team in Las Vegas would have their hands full tonight when the bridal party landed at McCarran International. "Breakfast," she decided.

He turned toward her. His blue eyes were narrowed and laced with promise, and maybe a layer of threat. Despite her exhaustion, nerve endings lit up.

"I can make sure you sleep well."

She slid a little lower in her seat. No doubt he was right. And all of a sudden, she was thinking about skipping the chicken and waffles.

"Sustenance," he decided for both of them, checking the mirrors before driving out of his parking spot. "I want you conscious when we have sex."

His words and their inflection aroused her.

"Then we can pass out for a week."

"Wouldn't that be nice?" And unlikely. Over the past week and a half, she'd realized that he slept well, but only if she was in his bed.

Torin's emotions were stoked like a furnace. He was possessive and demanding.

Consuming.

Yet she wasn't strong enough to stay away from him, even though she knew he would eventually break her heart.

After clearing an intersection, he placed his hand on her

MEANT FOR ME

knee. The gentle nonsexual touch ignited a flame that would burn until they arrived home.

Over breakfast at the Shamrock Grill, something that was becoming a tradition, they debriefed. After filing an update with Hawkeye from her cell phone, they marked themselves as unavailable for another mission for twelve hours.

When the bill came, he reached for it.

"I think it's my turn." Besides, she'd had extra chicken and juice as well as coffee.

"Oh. I insist. I wanted you to have energy, so this is all about me."

She grinned. "In that case, take me home, Commander."

The French Quarter was just waking up as they walked back to the car. The driver of a beer truck was loading cases of local brew onto a dolly. They cycle never ended, and already, some intrepid tourists were already out, making their way to Café du Monde for a plate of three perfect beignets.

Five minutes later, she and Torin were headed back to the Garden District.

He stopped in front of the estate to open the garage. "It's been too long since I've had you across my lap."

Of all the positions they used, that was her favorite.

"And enjoyed your screams."

Her mouth dried. It was as if her cries sustained him.

"Mira?"

His voice, with its hint of a rich brogue, dragged her from her reverie. While she was lost, he'd parked the car. She gave him a slight smile. "Yes, Sir."

He followed her up the stairs, then locked the door behind them when they were safely inside.

Torin swept his heated gaze over her, and her heart thundered.

He took off his jacket and tossed it over the back of the

SIERRA CARTWRIGHT

couch. Then he crooked his finger and pointed to a spot on the floor in front on him.

Her mouth dry, she stood where he indicated and remained still while he helped her out of her blazer. Taking care, he placed it on top of his.

She'd worn a slim-fitting tank top. Keeping his gaze on her, he fisted the material, then dragged it over her head.

"No bra?" Roughness gave his words a biting edge.

"It's built in."

He groaned. "Don't ever do that to me again, Araceli."

"No, Sir." *Until our next assignment.*

She toed off her boots while he unfastened her pants and lowered the zipper.

"Jesus. God. Mary and Joseph."

Normally she reserved her sexiest panties for time off, but his reaction was worth it. She lowered her head to hide her smile.

"If I'd had any idea what was beneath your clothes... All that lace?" He grabbed her pussy through her panties. "So wet for me." He squeezed hard, painfully, arousing her to the point of screaming her pleasure. "Fuck, yes."

He stripped off her panties, and she quickly undressed him. "My bedroom, Araceli."

As he customarily did, he followed her down the hallway. For fun, she gave an exaggerated butt wiggle before flashing a wicked grin over her shoulder.

"Oh, Araceli. I can't wait to have my hands on you."

She walked a little faster.

In the room, he sat on the edge of the mattress. "This is for fun. And for no other reason."

"Yes, Sir." She draped herself over his lap, then braced her hands on the floor. Without instruction, she parted her legs slightly.

MEANT FOR ME

He light strokes, he played with her clit, making her squirm.

Without giving her any warning, he slapped her pussy hard.

She gasped. "Yes." Her whole body lit on fire. With a sigh, she moved back into position.

Then he spanked her in earnest, on her buttocks, on her pussy, on her thighs. They were timed to arouse her, driving her to the brink.

Within a minute, she was begging for an orgasm. "I need..."

"You need?"

"Fuck me, Sir." Her words were breathless. "Fuck me. Please?"

"How do you want it?"

"Anal."

Torin helped her off his lap and stood her in front of him. "You're serious?"

He'd fingered her there, and a couple of times they'd used butt plugs, but she'd never asked for it. Tonight, she wanted it rough.

His eyes were narrowed, and his cock jutted forward, hard and with a drop of pre-ejaculate glistening on the tip.

"Give me a second." He grabbed a condom and a bottle of lube from a dresser drawer.

She forgot to breathe as she watched him roll the condom down the length of his impressive erection. Involuntarily, she shivered. Having that inside her tightest hole was going to be a challenge.

"On the bed," he instructed. "Facedown." He grabbed a pillow and helped her to place it beneath her belly. "Do you have any idea how red your ass is?"

"If it looks like it feels, yes, I have an idea."

"It's lovely." He spanked her again on top of a couple of

the welts, and she moved against the mattress, trying to achieve satisfaction. "Mine," he reminded her. Then, the perfect Dom, he placed a hand between her legs.

"Oh, Sir!" Desperately, she thrust her hips back. "Take me."

"Every part of you, mo shearc."

She turned her head to watch him squirt a dollop of lube onto his fingers.

"You're going to like this. Even if it's uncomfortable."

Especially then.

Slowly he inserted one slick finger into her anus, allowing her time to accommodate his touch. "Relax," he said, sweeping her hair from her neck, tangling his fingers in it.

Mira closed her eyes and concentrated on her breathing.

"Ready for more?"

"Yes." She nodded.

He inserted a second finger, followed by a third. He stretched her, holding his fingers apart. It hurt, not badly, but enough that she wanted him to back off. She was going to ask him to stop, but he leaned over and kissed her exposed nape, distracting her.

"You're doing well, Mira."

A hundred pleasurable sensations danced down her spine.

He was attuned to her reactions. The second she relaxed and surrendered, he began to move in and out, simulating sex as he lubed her channel and widened her even more.

"Yes," she finally said. "I want your cock."

With deliberation, he withdrew his fingers. He caressed her for a short while, then promised to return in a few seconds.

While he went to the bathroom to wash his fingers, her body cooled, and tension started to creep through her. She was edgy, with adrenaline flooding her veins. She'd never been more alive.

MEANT FOR ME

"On all fours," Torin instructed when he returned. The mattress sank as he knelt behind her. "Head down, and arch your back."

When she was situated, he held her ass cheeks apart and pressed the yielding firmness of his cockhead against her opening. "Bear down." He eased forward.

"God!"

Slowly, he withdrew, just a little.

It didn't give her any relief.

"Doing okay?"

"Yes," she lied. He was so hard, and this was far more intense than she'd imagined. "Just take me."

Torin proceeded at his own pace, claiming her in slow measures, starting with shallow strokes, then going deeper a little at a time.

"Will you spank my ass, please?" Anything to distract her.

He did, and the sharpness of the pain took her focus way from the way her anus burned, heightening her pleasure immeasurably.

"Stroke your clit, Araceli."

With his possession and her angle, that wasn't easy.

"Sir—"

"Do *not* tell me no," he warned.

She loved it when he was relentless with her. The fact that he'd demanded it meant it was possible.

Somehow managing to keep her balance, she toyed with her clit. He continued to spank her and occasionally reach beneath her to toy with one of her nipples.

Her vision swam, colors swirling, red and purple.

Torin drove his entire length inside her, forcing her forward. If he hadn't grabbed hold of her waist, she would have pitched forward onto her stomach.

He paused while she got back into position. "That's it."

Now that she had accommodated him, her nerve endings hummed with pleasure. "Do me," she pleaded.

"Goddamn, Araceli." He rode her hard, pulling all the way out and then surging forward, again and again, fiercely claiming her.

Faster and faster, she stroked her clit. Her legs trembled as she thrust back into him. Then her world fractured. Powerful and unexpected, an orgasm crashed into her. She screamed his name.

"Hell," he whispered, stroking her. "You're sensational."

"I want you to come."

He placed one arm beneath her hips, holding her immobile as he continued to ride her.

Even though she was sore, his pleasure nourished her.

He shortened his strokes, and his breathing changed. His grip on her tightened, as if he were a desperate man.

Inside her, his cock swelled. "Sir... Master."

His body went rigid, and he came in long pulses, and he growled with pure male satisfaction.

She wasn't sure how much time passed—seconds? A minute?—while he stroked his fingers down her spine.

When he withdrew, it was as if their emotional connection was also severed. She scoffed at her own ridiculous idea. Torin wasn't the kind of person to run or to abandon her.

"Stay right there."

"I should shower."

"You should wait," he countered. "I'll be right back."

Of course the badass alpha would insist on caring for her. She made a small attempt to smile, but she couldn't even manage that much.

He left, and she buried her face against her forearm. Even though she'd just given herself a pep talk, his absence left her bereft.

What the hell was wrong with her? She took a breath,

telling herself it was hormones after something so intense. Malfunctioning brain chemistry.

It had to be because there was nothing else between them. They worked together, scened together, and that was the nature of their agreement.

No matter what, she couldn't allow herself to get lost in Torin Carter.

CHAPTER SEVEN

HAWKEYE

"Black tie required," Mira said when she hung up the phone.

From his place on the couch in the carriage house, Torin raised an eyebrow. "As in a tuxedo?"

"Yes. Seriously. That was Ms. Inamorata herself."

He whistled. "I don't suppose you know her first name?"

She laughed. No one knew Inamorata's first name. Hawkeye's right-hand woman was damn good at everything she did, and that included keeping secrets. The office pool to guess her name had five figures in it. Whoever won would have enough money for a heck of a vacation or a down payment on a house. "If I knew, I'm not sure I'd tell you."

"So you wouldn't want to take me to Greece with you?"

"Greece?" All of a sudden, she was on a lounge chair on a white sandy beach, drinking a frappé while Torin stretched out next to her.

She shook her head to banish the image. They didn't have a future. Letting herself think about one, even momentarily, would lead to heartbreak.

"Araceli?"

SIERRA CARTWRIGHT

Torin's voice penetrated her haze. "Sorry?"

"Where are we headed?"

"The Maison Sterling. Trace and Aimee Romero have a personal security client attending a fundraiser." In addition to being recently married, they were both well-respected agents. Aimee was the younger sister of the enigmatic Ms. Inamorata. A brainiac if there ever was one, Aimee was a scientist who had recently taken up running ultramarathons. The extreme running thing made Aimee's brainpower somewhat suspect, in Mira's opinion. "In the last few minutes, there's been a credible threat against their client."

"Anyone I know?"

"Nathaniel Sinclair."

He whistled and nodded. "No wonder they're calling in backup."

The man was a media magnate. He owned newspapers, magazines, a cable network, and there was a stadium named after his family. He wasn't popular with everyone, though, and there was no shortage of people who would like to prevent him from becoming President of the United States. "Inamorata is emailing the hotel layout to us." Even though Mira had been to the hotel for happy hour, she wasn't familiar with the ballrooms. "Evidently, he refuses to be seen as weak, so he's sticking to his original plans. He'll be arriving at the front entrance, and press is expected."

"Hence the dress code."

They needed to blend in, not look like security.

"When are we due there?"

"The party starts at seven. Inamorata wants us there by five." She checked her watch. "That gives us about an hour to get ready. I think I'll take a shower."

"I'll join you."

She looked at him pointedly. "And then we'll be late."

MEANT FOR ME

He swept a gaze over her, as if calculating whether they should take the risk. "You're probably right."

Mira was glad he agreed, because all of a sudden, she was tempted.

"A hot tub and a scene after we get back?"

"I'll look forward to it all night."

He headed for his room but stopped in the doorway. Mira ordered herself to continue past him, but she didn't, because the only thing she wanted was to be in his arms. "Shower," she said aloud, reminding herself as much as him.

"Shower," he affirmed, taking hold of her shoulders.

He claimed her mouth, kissing her deeply. He tasted of coffee tempered by a hint of cream, then drizzled with sin.

She couldn't resist him.

Responding, Mira lifted up onto her tiptoes and wantonly grabbed hold of a fistful of his black T-shirt. He pressed his free hand against the small of her back, holding her tight. She wiggled about a bit, growing more and more aroused beneath his sensual assault. Torin Carter made her want to be *very* naughty.

Very slowly, he ended the kiss. Her mouth was raw and ravaged, ensuring she'd spend their night hungry for more.

Torin looked at her intently. The color of his eyes never failed to startle her, but now she read the heat of arousal in the smoky blue depths.

"Shower," he said, letting her go.

Despite the time pressing in on them, it took her a couple of minutes to shake off the effects of his dizzying kiss.

He knocked on the door. "I'm going to think you're taking so long because you want company!"

Mira quickly finished up. After she wrapped a towel around her, she opened the door.

He stood there, naked, erect.

Her mouth dried.

"Figured I'd undress to save time. Bad strategy?" His slight grin made her tummy flip over.

"You're impossible, Commander Carter." She ducked to dodge past him. When she reached her room, she closed the door.

"Araceli?" he shouted. "Skip the underwear."

She laughed. There were ways their D/s relationship crossed over to their professional life. But the truth was, it was so unobtrusive and such a turn-on that she didn't mind. In fact, she would miss it when she had a new partner.

When she didn't respond, he called out, "Excuse me?"

"I heard you!"

The shower water turned on. "And what you meant by that was, 'yes, Sir.'"

Her grin only deepened. His challenges were sexy, and she looked forward to them. "Yes, Sir!" she called out dutifully. And she skipped the underwear. She wouldn't tell him, but the dress looked better without them, anyway.

After she was ready, she transferred her identification and a credit card to her dressy handbag. She double-checked that her gun was loaded, then placed it inside a special interior compartment. Finally, she added her stun gun and her cell phone.

By the time she was in the living room, Inamorata had sent over a 3D rendering of the ballrooms and service areas, including kitchens.

Mira printed them out and placed them on the kitchen table to study them.

Moments later, he joined her, and he was adjusting one of the cuffs on his snow-white shirt.

Damn. Her heart dropped to her toes. His hair, the color of midnight, flirted with his collar. His eyes seemed all the more electric against his dark clothing. In a tuxedo, with a fresh shave, he was devastating.

MEANT FOR ME

He perused her, as if drinking in every nuance. "Show me," he said.

"Show you?"

"That you followed my command. Bend over."

"Torin..."

"Bend over, Araceli," he repeated in a tone that allowed for no argument. "And lift your dress."

Unable to deny him anything, she turned around and exposed herself to him

"Lovely."

Against her will, her pussy became slick. He walked to her, footfall firm, a staccato threat.

He stroked her, finger-fucked her, then gently spanked her vulva until she whimpered.

"That will have to hold both of us over for the foreseeable future."

He smoothed her dress back into place. After she stood, she brushed imaginary wrinkles from the fabric.

"Are those the blueprints?"

She shook her head to clear it. "Yes."

Like she had, he picked up the pages, studied from different angles, committed the schematic to memory.

He snagged the vehicle keys off a hook. "Shall we?"

"Are we driving?"

"I figured we can valet park at the hotel. We're early enough that none of the principals will be there."

"And we can expense the cost."

"There is that."

As they approached the French Quarter, Inamorata sent a text message. "We're meeting in a suite. Third floor."

When they were inside the hotel, Torin cupped her elbow and led her toward the elevators.

Inamorata responded instantly to Torin's knock and invited them in. As usual, she wore a pencil skirt, and her

SIERRA CARTWRIGHT

hair was pulled back. Surveillance equipment covered the large table. She handed each of them an earphone, and a technician secured the radios in place.

Afterward, Mira and Torin each went through a sound check.

When everything was satisfactory, Inamorata continued on, outlining the plan in her usual straightforward way. "You're a couple tonight. Aimee Romero will be arriving with Mr. Sinclair. She'll be posing as his date for the evening. Trace will be arriving in a limo at approximately the same time as Sinclair so that he's onsite without arousing suspicions."

"Got it," Mira acknowledged.

"Cocktails are in fifteen minutes. When you arrive, hotel staff and a few members of Mr. Sinclair's staff will already be onsite, including his campaign manager."

"Who's verifying the guest list?" Torin asked.

"Sinclair's executive assistant. She should know people. Laurents will be nearby in case she notices anything amiss. Barstow will be stationed at the back of the room, near the entrance. He'll be close enough to assist either you or Laurents should the need arise. Here's your official invitation."

She handed over the sturdy hand-addressed card to Mira, who tucked it into her handbag.

"Let's use the service elevator. I want to show you the kitchen and the ballrooms."

Even when blueprints were available, Hawkeye Security preferred their agents walk a venue when possible. Seeing a picture was different than being in a room that was prepped for an event. Knowing where the exits were and how to use the back of the house to move the principal if necessary could save time and lives.

"After that, I'll introduce you to Sinclair's staff. We've

MEANT FOR ME

timed it so that you'll be among the first at the event so you can watch all of the arrivals. Any questions?" At their silence, she gave a sharp nod. "In that case, come with me."

At one minute after seven, Torin placed his fingers intimately in the small of Mira's back and guided her toward a space cordoned off with velvet ropes. "Showtime, Ms. Araceli."

Sinclair's assistant pretended to look at their invitation before putting a checkmark next to their names on the official guest list. "Enjoy your evening," she said with a genuine smile.

Before they proceeded into the reception area, Torin nodded toward Laurents, their fellow Hawkeye operative.

Since party nominations were still more than a year away, Sinclair hadn't been afforded Secret Service protection. But Barstow—stationed at the back of the room— looked rather official.

Even though only one other couple was already in attendance, a live band played forties music, and champagne flowed freely. Obviously no amount of money had been spared.

Though Torin and Araceli each accepted a flute from a server, neither took a sip. Instead, they found a tall table near the entrance and watched as guests arrived. At first, it was a small trickle, but around seven thirty, crowds flooded in. Still, nothing looked unusual.

Just before eight, agent Trace Romero walked in.

Moments later, there was a buzz of activity near the door. Music ceased. Paul Kauffman, Sinclair's campaign manager, took to the stage and accepted a microphone. "Ladies and gentlemen, please welcome the next President of the United States, Nathaniel Sinclair!"

Shouts of approval and loud claps filled the room. The mogul came in with a wave, Aimee at his side.

Sinclair made his way to the stage and said a few words of thanks. He seemed completely at ease, without a care in the world.

Immediately creating a security nightmare, he left the stage and started glad-handing all the attendees. People queued up to meet him, blocking a smooth exit. Torin figured Aimee would unobtrusively move Sinclair toward safety and keep her body between him and the guests as much as possible.

"I'll be back," Mira told him.

"Araceli—"

"That man..." She leaned in closer to him so she could be heard above the din. "About six foot two. Blond. He came in after Sinclair when there were a bunch of people. I'm not sure he was cleared. He could be fine. I don't know. Check him out." Without waiting for him to respond, she walked away.

Frowning, he went to talk to Sinclair's assistant.

At the doorway, Torin looked back to see Araceli change directions, veering away from the man and toward a woman who was in line to talk to Sinclair.

He paused.

Araceli took hold of the woman's hands, as if they were old friends.

A slow alarm beating in him, he waved to Laurents. "We need to go over the guest list," he said to Sinclair's executive assistant.

Then, even though they were some distance apart, Araceli's voice rose above everyone else's.

Awareness prickled at his nape. Something was off. He keyed his mic. "Everything okay, Araceli?"

She didn't respond.

"Laurents, take over here. I want to know who Araceli's talking to. And she was interested in that blond guy." He pointed. With a nod, he started back toward Mira. He keyed his mic. "Heads-up, team. Blond male, six-two. Twenty feet from our principal. Araceli's on a brunette."

"Roger," Barstow acknowledged, making his way toward the target.

Trace also confirmed the transmission.

Looking like an attentive girlfriend, Aimee slid in closer to Sinclair.

Torin neared Araceli. Her voice was even louder now, with a fake, gushing tone woven through it. "I'm sure I've seen your picture before. You look so familiar. Are you famous? You are, right?" Mira inserted herself in front of the brunette.

Her stiff smile, obviously surgically enhanced, started to fade. "You're mistaken," she snapped. "Get your hand off me!"

"May I have your autograph?" Mira asked. "You will make me so happy. Please?"

Torin moved in next to Mira. "Everything okay, honey?"

"She's a movie star!"

"I'm sorry." Torin shrugged, as if he were a helpless male while he tried to see the world through Mira's eyes. "She's an autograph hound. If you'll humor her..."

A sheen of sweat dotted the brunette's upper lip.

"Wait! I have a pen right here," Mira said. She opened her purse. "Oh. No!" She got louder and more animated. "I don't have one. What am I going to do? Do you have one?" she asked the woman. "Can I borrow yours?"

She was drawing the attention of a lot of people, and Aimee whispered something in Sinclair's ear, then kissed him on the cheek, looking like a lover who was anxious to have her man all to herself.

"Darling, I'm so excited! She's going to sign an autograph!" Mira babbled to Torin.

The brunette snapped. "I don't have a pen."

"Just look," Mira implored. "Please?"

Her expression more a snarl than even a politely civil smile, the woman made a show of opening her pocketbook.

Mira acted. She jostled into the woman, forcing her to loosen her grip on the purse.

Metal glinted in the overhead lights

Fuck! Torin keyed his mic. "Gun!"

Pandemonium erupted, and hysterical screams rent the air.

Aimee and Trace hustled Sinclair toward a side door.

The brunette grabbed the revolver. Before he could act, Mira surged forward.

The gun discharged. The percussion deafened him, and he was helpless as the bullet ripped into Mira.

CHAPTER EIGHT

HAWKEYE

Pain shredded through Mira, glazing her vision and throwing waves of nausea through her. But they did nothing to stop her determination.

With focus borne from months of relentless training, she shoved aside survival instinct and put all of her kinetic energy into taking the brunette down. Blood dripped everywhere, and her upper arm burned, but Mira fought through it to pin the frantically struggling would-be murderer. "Fucking stay down," Mira warned.

It took forever, but it couldn't have been more than a few seconds, before Torin's reassuring voice penetrated her brain.

"It's okay, mo shearc. Laurents is here. We've got her. You can let go."

Her arms shook as she pushed herself off the brunette. She collapsed instantly, the adrenaline no longer supporting her.

She rolled onto her back, panting, not able to draw a breath.

"Take care of Araceli."

SIERRA CARTWRIGHT

That was a woman's voice. *Inamorata?* Mira blinked, staring at the ceiling, unable to see anything. Panic unfurled in the pit of her stomach.

Torin stroked her forehead. She had no doubt it was him. No one else's touch reassured her like that.

"Hang tough, Araceli. An ambulance is on the way."

She tried to nod, and fresh pain rocketed her. "Sinclair?"

"Safe. Back at his hotel, no doubt."

"And the brunette?"

"You got her. Good job, Araceli." When he spoke again, his voice cracked. "Fucking exceptional."

Over the radio, Barstow spoke, his words breathless. "The unidentified blond male is on the move. Now out the back door. I'm in pursuit."

She pushed out a breath. "He's going to get away." All the man had to do was dodge into a bar, then out the rear entrance. "Goddamn it."

"The brunette is in custody," Torin reassured her. "We'll figure out the rest."

That wasn't good enough. They needed the blond man as well.

The frustration smacked up against her pain. Then her world went black.

When she was able to open her eyes again, the room spun. It took her long seconds to realize she was strapped onto a stretcher in the hotel ballroom. An IV drip ran into a vein, and Torin stood next to her, his jaw set in a brooding, frightening line.

"You scared the shit out of me, Araceli."

Her too.

Activity buzzed around her. New Orleans's finest officers were taking statements from those who'd been close enough to witness the events.

MEANT FOR ME

"We're going to need a statement," one of the policemen said.

"It can wait," Torin snapped.

"Sir—"

"Take it up the with the mayor if you need to. She's not talking to you until she's been seen by a doctor."

"But—"

Torin snarled. "Back off, Officer."

Inamorata showed up, as if by magic. "Our man, Laurents, saw the whole thing. I suggest you interview him."

Her words were a command, not a suggestion. No doubt she would call the mayor if necessary.

While their boss was occupied with the police, Torin took her hand.

Lines of anguish were trenched between his eyebrows.

"I'll be okay," she whispered. If it had been him who had been injured, how would she have reacted?

Their jobs came with risk, and they accepted that. In the lobby at Hawkeye's main headquarters near Denver, there was a glass wall etched with names of their compatriots who'd died in the line of duty. It was impossible to enter the offices or command center without walking past the silent, stark reminder of the danger every agent faced.

But what would she do if things had been reversed tonight?

Damn it. She loved him.

"We need to get her to the hospital," one of the paramedics said.

"I'm riding along," Torin said, voice holding no compromise.

"Nice work, Araceli," Inamorata said.

"Except for the part where she got shot," Torin countered.

Inamorata ignored him. "A commendation will go in your file."

"It was my job. Following my training." It was no small feat to teach someone to move toward danger instead of fleeing from it. "I had a good commander." She glanced at Torin. He didn't smile. In fact, his blue eyes chilled, reminding her of a glacier. The earlier concern had vanished. Now he was as remote as he had been when she was his student at Aiken.

The paramedics wheeled her from the ballroom, with Inamorata and Torin flanking the stretcher. "I want to exit through the rear entrance." She didn't want to be a focus or a spectacle.

Inamorata and Torin flanked the stretcher. "Already arranged," Inamorata assured her.

Outside, Torin climbed into the ambulance alongside her.

"Commander Carter…"

His gaze was remote, and he didn't touch her. "We'll talk later."

She pressed her lips together. For the first time since her mother's death, tears threatened.

Something had happened in the ballroom, something she could never undo. It changed what was between them. "We—"

"Later, Araceli."

Her heart fractured at the harsh coldness in his tone.

"Barstow got his man," Inamorata said.

"Good." Normally, Torin would care. This morning, however, his thoughts were consumed with Araceli.

"Neither he nor the brunette are saying much. They lawyered up." She shrugged. "It's a job for the police now."

An uncomfortable silence hung between them. Narrowing his eyes, Torin stared across the kitchen table at

MEANT FOR ME

his boss. Five minutes ago, she'd arrived at the carriage house, just as he was ready to leave for the hospital. "There's something you're not saying."

"I'm sending Araceli home."

"Home?"

"As in, we've placed her on medical leave. She needs to rest, and she isn't going to do it here. She'll want to work, and you know it."

Fuck.

"Hawkeye will be giving her a commendation. She did well."

He pushed back from the table to stalked the length of the living area. He stopped in front of a window and stared out, unseeingly "She got shot." *I could have lost her.* Though Mira hadn't required surgery, she faced weeks, if not months, of rehab before she could return to duty.

"You'll have a new partner in a couple of days, three at the most."

"What?" Barely restraining his sudden anger, he pivoted. "I need to be with her."

"That's not possible. With the Memorial Day weekend coming up, we need all the coverage that we can have."

"You're not separating us."

She raised one of her eyebrows. "Something I need to know, Commander Cater?"

Damnation. Was there? *Love.* Shit. He'd fallen in love with Araceli. He hadn't meant to fall in love with her. But from the beginning, there'd been an undeniable sexual attraction. She'd been too damn young, too innocent, and his student.

And now…?

She was a perfect sub. Still with something to prove.

"Is it possible you need some time, also?"

He snarled at his boss and fought for control over his fraying temper.

SIERRA CARTWRIGHT

Mindless of the danger, much like Araceli, Inamorata continued. "After Ekaterina—"

"I'm warning you, Inamorata. Don't go there." A red haze blurred his vision.

"No?" She folded her arms over her cream-colored blazer. "How did you sleep last night?"

Unconsciously, he scrubbed a hand across his face.

More gently, she asked, "Did you sleep?"

He didn't need to answer.

The nightmare had been garish. But the reality of not knowing whether Mira was dead or alive—even for a few seconds—had been a thousand times more brutal. Blood was everywhere. And he'd stood there, paralyzed. Laurents pushed past Torin, and it had taken that jolt to make him move.

Now there were harsh truths to face.

"Risk is a hazard of the job. This is for Araceli's benefit. And yours. We need you, Commander, back at Aiken, but we need the best version of you that's possible. You're compromised...lost your edge."

She'd seen him freeze.

Inamorata was right.

Goddamn it to hell.

Ironic. When Araceli reported for training three years ago, he'd been concerned about her. In the end, he'd been the one to fail.

Inamorata stood. "One of our associates will be by in about an hour to collect her belongings."

"I'll pack them."

"That's not necessary."

"I said I'll do it." After she left, he slammed the door so hard it rattled in its casing.

Torin had always believed he was incapable of love and that his heart couldn't shatter. He was wrong.

140

CHAPTER NINE

HAWKEYE

"Let me get this straight…"

Torin looked across at Kayla Davidson Stone, the Hawkeye operative sent to replace Mira. Then he stopped to mentally correct himself. *To fill in for Mira.* No one could replace her, no matter how talented or determined.

The past few weeks had been the longest of his life.

He missed everything about Mira. Her secret smiles and stunningly submissive nature. He appreciated her wild abandon.

And, fuck it all, he even missed her feminine, wildflower scent.

When he packed up her things, he'd kept her bar of soap. Maybe a bit of a masochist himself, he'd left it in its porcelain dish where he was forced to look at it numerous times a day. Though the bar didn't really have a scent when it was dry, every time he showered, the moisture in the air seemed to release some of the fragrance, and it wrapped around him, reminding him of her. On one occasion, right after she left, the heady perfume had been so strong that he'd been convinced she'd returned.

SIERRA CARTWRIGHT

He turned off the faucet and looked around. When she wasn't there, disappointment seared his lungs, making it impossible to breathe.

Kayla took a big bite of her beignet and grinned as powdered sugar flew everywhere.

"What?" He wrapped his hands around his cup of café au lait but didn't take a drink.

"You found a woman who could actually tolerate you."

"Excuse me?"

"I know. I couldn't believe it either when you told me."

Across the table on the banks of the Mississippi River, he glared at her.

"So, back to the conversation…"

"Can we talk about something other than my love life?"

"Like what? It's the only thing about you that isn't boring."

He'd known Kayla for years, and he'd worked with her on a couple of assignments. She'd recently settled down and she wanted to share her happiness with the rest of the world. It didn't seem to matter that he'd prefer she stuff her joy in a little bag and stow it out of sight.

He wasn't sure why the hell he'd told her anything about Mira. Well, except Kayla was curious about why she'd been summoned from Colorado to work with him.

This morning, around four, he'd awakened in a cold sweat, unable to move.

In his nightmares about Ekaterina, he relived the day he'd lost her. In the ones about Mira, she was very much alive, reaching out for him, and no matter what he did, he couldn't fight through the layer that separated them in order to touch her.

After escaping the tendrils of the horror slithering through his mind this morning, he'd gone for a run and then a swim before soaking in the hot tub.

MEANT FOR ME

Of course, when he returned to the carriage house, Kayla had questions, and she'd relentlessly assaulted him with them until he agreed to talk. In that way, she was a lot like Araceli.

"Are you listening to me?" Kayla snapped her fingers in front of his face.

He shook his head.

"I was asking why you let her go." She popped the rest of the French-style donut in her mouth.

He closed his jaw so fast that his back teeth smacked together. "I didn't fucking let her go."

"Did you tell Inamorata to go to hell? Get lost?"

Putting down his cup, he regarded Kayla.

She brushed her hands together. "When Wolf decided he wanted me and Nate, he prepared letters of resignation for all of us. He told Hawkeye the terms of our continued employment, and we were all willing to walk away unless we got what we wanted. Which was each other."

"It's not that easy."

"Oh. Cuz you're special, Commander?"

"I'm returning to Aiken next month." After a solo vacation.

"And Mira?"

He shrugged while Kayla reached for a second pastry. When they placed their order, they'd agreed to share. But she was showing no signs of moving the plate to the middle of the table.

"Do you love her?"

"What the hell does that have to do with anything?" He drank half of his rapidly cooling café au lait.

Very much unlike her, she watched him in silence.

Finally, he fractured. His voice cracked with emotion as he spoke. "I froze."

"You were scared." Her tone was matter-of-fact. "That's human. I can't imagine coping if either Nate or Stone were to be wounded. But we can't let our fear get in the way of living our lives. We savor each day, maybe even more than we might otherwise, because we don't know if it will be our last."

That wasn't the way he wanted to live. Maybe he wasn't even capable of it.

"Love makes cowards of us all, Commander Carter. It's up to you what you do with that fear." She covered his hand with hers. "You may always have the nightmares. I wonder…"

He waited for her to go on. No doubt, she would.

"Not knowing where Mira is, what's she doing—will that make the future easier for you?" She released him to snatch the last beignet.

He knew the answer to that.

After he started sleeping with Araceli in his bed, curled next to him, his nightmares had abated. Now that she was gone, they were worse than ever.

"Only you can make your decisions. If I were you, I'd confront my fears. Because in the darkness, they grow."

The words haunted him long past the time they returned to the carriage house. As afternoon gave way to evening, he considered going to the Quarter.

Just as he had the past ten times he thought about it, he dismissed the idea. Araceli had ruined him for other subs. He didn't want to scene with anyone other than her. And for the first time, he had no interest in observing others.

In the darkest part of the night, he realized there was only one possible way out of this despair. He had to move through it. Acknowledge his weaknesses. Only then could he find the courage to face the risks that came with loving Araceli.

"So, I've been dying to ask…"

Mira stirred her rum punch with the tiny pink umbrella

MEANT FOR ME

the bartender had placed in it. Dreading the question, she glanced at Hallie. More than ever, she was grateful for the support and help of her friend. For the past two weekends, Hallie had driven to Mira's place in Covington, on the north shore of Lake Pontchartrain. Not only that, but she'd stayed, done some cooking, helped with the housework, and most of all, alleviated some of Mira's constant boredom.

In her entire life, she'd never been out of commission for more than a day. Two at the most. Being incapacitated was worse than she'd ever imagined. She was lonely. And worse, she couldn't turn her mind off.

Every day, she replayed the events of the time she'd spent with Torin.

Because she and Hallie were at a loud casual restaurant filled with other Saturday night partiers, Hallie had to shout to be heard. "Have you heard from Master Hottie?"

Mira exhaled a weighty sigh. "No."

Hallie sat back, taking her wineglass with her. "I don't get it."

After regaining consciousness the night she'd been shot, Mira had seen bleakness in Torin's eyes and known something had changed.

Had he been thinking about Ekaterina? Drowning in memories?

In response to Mira's questions, Inamorata had been vague, merely saying that Torin was required to finish up his assignment in New Orleans.

She'd then secured Mira's release from the hospital and sent her on her way in a limo. Since then, Hawkeye had arranged for follow-up doctor's visits, provided all the HR paperwork to ensure she received her pay without interruption. Even though she protested that it wasn't necessary, they'd provided meal delivery and a driver for two weeks.

Even when her mother passed, Mira hadn't cried.

SIERRA CARTWRIGHT

Since she left New Orleans, she hadn't stopped.

Hallie took a drink, then looked at Mira with a frown. "That night at the Quarter, he seemed like he was really into you."

Mira wasn't sure how to respond. He was. Obviously, that wasn't enough.

Hallie's eyes lit up, and she put down her glass. "You should call him!"

"Not on your life."

"Why not?"

She swirled her umbrella around and around. "Would you?" Mira countered.

"I think so." Hallie nodded.

"Really?"

"I think so. Yes. At least get some closure? Right?"

The server delivered a huge plate of nachos—Mira's favorite comfort food. Salt and warm melty cheese, with plenty of crunch. Tomorrow, she'd add a walk, maybe a short run, to her rehab program.

"Enough about me." Mira transferred a few chips onto her plate. "How're things with Master Bartholomew?"

"Well…" Hallie grinned. "Amazing. We played last night at the Quarter, and he stayed overnight. Evidently Bartholomew is his last name."

Evidently? Meaning Hallie believed so but wasn't certain?

"And yes. Before you start with your dozens of questions, he's willing to meet you. As soon as you're up for it, the three of us can go out to dinner or something."

"I want a full name."

"So you can do your spy shit?" She shook her head.

"At least give me a name."

"Nope." Hallie stabbed her fork into a jalapeno pepper. "Not happening."

"Hallie…"

"You can't give it a rest, can you?"

Mira sighed. "Of course I can. Yes."

"Tell me about the couple who just got seated."

Without glancing away, Mira replied. "They've been married about ten years, give or take. Probably a couple of kids at home. Date night. Headed to the movies after dinner. Need to get back for the babysitter by eleven."

Hallie laughed. "It couldn't be a first date?"

"Nah. They both look exhausted. Besides, he'd take her somewhere they could talk more intimately."

"I rest my case!" Hallie bit into a chip while Mira frowned.

At the end of the evening, they exchanged quick hugs in the parking lot. "Call him."

"I just need to get on with my life." There was no sense in mourning a brief fling with her former instructor. *Right?* Clearly, he was not wasting any time thinking about her. Mira shook her head. "I want to meet Master Bartholomew. Let me know what day works out for you? I can meet any day next week." She needed something on the calendar to look forward to. And poking around in Hallie's life was much more appealing than worrying about her own.

"I'll let you know."

When she was back in the car, Mira pulled her phone out of her purse.

There were no missed calls. No text messages. No emails.

Even though she hadn't expected anything different, she dropped her head onto the steering wheel as her heart splintered all over again.

CHAPTER TEN

HAWKEYE

A gunshot shredded the air. Eyes wide, reaching for him, Araceli crumpled, her blood dripping onto the white marble floor. He reached for her, and she vanished like a specter. "No!" His scream ricocheted through the room, horrifyingly useless.

In terror, he jolted awake.

Heart thundering so hard that it echoed in his ears, Torin gulped in a breath.

Shit.

The dreams were no longer random or rare occurrences. Since he'd left Araceli, they were constant and unwelcome companions.

Minutes later, when his pulse was close to normal, he crawled from the bed and headed outside.

He had no idea how many laps he'd put in, but when he hauled himself out of the swimming pool and dropped, exhausted, into a chair in the courtyard, the future was so clear that he was unsure how he hadn't recognized it before.

Mira was *his*. His to protect. To dominate.

Without her, the future loomed long and bleak, an

endless series of new recruits and lonely nights at Hawkeye's Nevada compound.

Facing his fear was easier than facing a future without her.

He needed her.

Torin sluiced water from his face.

Kayla walked down the stairs, carrying a bottle of water and mug. Without an invitation, she sat down across from him and placed the coffee in front of him.

Gratefully, he took a long drink of the thick, dark brew. "I'm going to take the rest of the day off."

"Good. I want to go and do some shopping, anyway." She picked at the label on her bottle. "New clothes."

He narrowed his eyes. No caffeine. A second order of beignets when they'd been at Café du Monde… "Are…" He proceeded with care. "Congratulations in order?"

"It's secret." She grinned. "And brand-new news. I just came here to help you get your head on straight, and then I'll be transferring to Ops for the foreseeable future

"You—"

"Inamorata and Hawkeye wanted to give you time to get past the shooting, find your footing. They figured you would refuse to take time off. And they guessed you wouldn't be sleeping."

He blinked. He and Kayla had been given relatively few assignments, and none of them involved anything dangerous. *"Fuck."*

"Are you going after your woman, Commander Carter?"

His woman. He liked the sound of that. "Yeah."

She tipped her water bottle in his direction, and he headed back upstairs.

Torin could send her a text message, but he dismissed that idea as too casual. A phone call wouldn't work either. It would be far too easy for her to send him to voicemail. Even

MEANT FOR ME

if she answered, that wouldn't be enough for him. He wanted to read her expression, look into her eyes to see the things she wanted to hide. If he was lucky enough, touch her.

Since he didn't know where she lived, he contacted Hawkeye headquarters. Not surprisingly, they denied his request for information. Next, he tried a couple of operatives and an IT guru, all of whom owed him favors. No one agreed to help.

Which left him with old-fashioned search options. He thought she had a house in Louisiana, so he began there.

Annoying the hell out of him, it took hours, much longer than it should have. Of course, Hawkeye had buried her information under several layers of security.

Once he'd programmed her address into his GPS, he sat in his vehicle for a few minutes, wondering whether she'd actually be there or not. She could be anywhere on the planet, on vacation, even on an assignment if she'd skipped out on rehab and returned to duty.

There was also the very real possibility she might not want to see him.

Still, he had to see her again. Then he would deal with the ramifications.

A LEMONADE IN FRONT OF HER, MIRA SAT IN THE WHITE wicker swing on her front porch. An overhead fan churned through the humid air but did little to dissipate June's cloying heat.

She was restless, anxious to return to work. This morning, the physical therapist said she'd be cleared for duty in another week, perhaps two.

But she was tired of television, books, magazines, online shopping, and especially her thoughts. Hallie had invited her

SIERRA CARTWRIGHT

to the Quarter, but the risk of seeing Torin was too high, and Mira wasn't strong enough for that. If he was with another submissive...

Damn. Getting involved with Torin *had* been stupid.

Mira hated that their relationship now meant she didn't want to visit her favorite club.

She took a drink from the overly tart lemonade, then rolled the glass across her forehead. Maybe she should invite Hallie and Bartholomew over for dinner this weekend. And in the meantime, maybe Mira could begin a little surreptitious research on the man. Spy shit would be a welcome distraction.

A vehicle turned onto the street.

This was what her life had been reduced to. Watching the comings and goings, wondering what was in the packages delivered by a big brown truck.

The SUV passed a couple of houses.

Her heart lurched as she saw the color of the car. Gloss white. *Like Torin's.*

Warning herself to stop the fantastical thinking, Mira slid her glass onto a nearby table. She couldn't conjure Torin. He didn't know where she lived, and there was no way Hawkeye would divulge her whereabouts.

The vehicle crawled forward, as if the driver wasn't sure exactly where to stop.

Her pulse picked up, despite the urgings of her left brain. There were hundreds, if not thousands, of gloss-white SUVs in Covington. This particular one meant nothing, no matter how much she wanted it to belong to Torin.

Two houses away, the driver parked alongside the curb.

Annoyed with herself for even the momentary lapse of judgement, she snatched up the glass and took a long drink.

The engine fell silent, leaving a mockingbird as the only sound.

MEANT FOR ME

She leaned forward for a peek, telling herself she was looking out for her neighbors, making sure things were safe while they were at work.

A man emerged, and her view was obscured by an oversize live oak tree. He had stark raven-black hair that was slightly too long.

Despite the temperature, Mira shivered.

Of course he would park down the street to allow himself time to assess the situation. *Spy shit.*

For several seconds, she considered what to do.

Go inside? Turn the dead bolt? Maybe feign surprise when she opened the door. Perhaps—to protect herself—she should ignore him entirely.

That was her preferred option, and the only one she was incapable of.

She remained where she was, threading her fingers into the material of her skirt. Then, realizing that was a betrayal of her nerves, she stood.

As he passed the magnolia tree, she studied the beautiful, harsh planes of his face. Breath vanished from her lungs.

The moment he noticed her, he stopped.

Even across the distance, she saw the worry lines trenched deeply next to his blue eyes. Torin had aged a decade since that night in the hospital.

She had no doubt he hadn't been sleeping.

Slowly he continued toward her, turning onto the path, then stopping at the bottom of the porch stairs. "I…"

Her confident, fearless former instructor ran a finger between his black T-shirt and his nape.

Because she didn't know why he was here and was too damn scared to guess, she remained where she was, saying nothing.

"I…" He took a breath.

Hurt and confusion left her unable to speak or act.

"May I...?" Torin swept his hand in front of him, indicating the stairs, the distance separating them.

Don't be here to break my heart.

He cleared his throat. "I fucked up."

Of all the words she'd dreamed of, those hadn't been among them.

"I came to apologize."

Saying nothing, she stroked a thumb across her index finger.

"I need to see how you are."

"I'm fine."

"You're pissed." He smiled, but it was the barest hint of one, and it faded fast.

Time stretched. A mockingbird zipped overhead to land in a nearby tree. The fan continued to churn.

"The truth is..."

Tears stung her eyes. Again. What was it about this man that brought emotion out in her?

"Seeing you hurt devastated me. I froze. When you blacked out, Laurents knocked me out of the way to get to you. I'm not proud. But there it is. I've never been paralyzed by fear before."

"I wasn't seriously injured."

"Logically." He shrugged. "Tell that to my heart."

She couldn't help herself. "You have one?"

Torin winced. "I deserve that."

Struggling to hide her vulnerability, she clamped her lips together.

"May I please come up the stairs?"

"If you've said what you came here for, there's no need." She had to send him away before she begged him to stay.

"Damn it, Araceli." His voice cracked. "This wasn't how this was supposed to go."

His hand trembled. Stunned, she moved her gaze to his.

"I'm screwing this up. What I mean to say is…I love you."

She blinked. It wasn't possible that she'd heard him right. "You…?"

"I love you," he repeated, voice more confident. "You can tell me to go to hell. I wouldn't blame you. But I couldn't live the rest of my life without telling you." He paused. "And asking forgiveness. I don't deserve that, God knows. And I don't expect anything from you. Tell me to get in the car and leave you the hell alone. But for the love of all things holy, say *something*."

The breath she hadn't realized she'd taken seared her lungs. Slowly, she released it. Her legs wobbled. She loved him. The crush she'd had during training had matured into something strong enough to withstand the ache of despair and the revelation of his deepest human failings.

His stark emotion melted her heart into a pool of compassion.

He was a man who needed her love to survive.

Not trusting her voice, she stepped to one side in silent invitation.

He took the two steps with great deliberation.

Now that he was close, her senses swam. His scent, of masculine determination and a moonlit night, was welcoming, inviting her home. She could more clearly read his eyes and the tiny sparks of grief in them.

"Nightmares?" she managed.

"Every time I try to sleep."

He lifted a hand as if to touch her, then dropped it to his side, perhaps realizing that spoke of an intimacy they no longer shared. "Not about Ekaterina." Pain haunted his words. "That's not why I'm here. I can deal with that." He shrugged, but it was a halfhearted attempt. "I had to come. It's selfish, maybe. Probably. But I needed to see you, look in your eyes, hear you tell me to go away. If you do, I'll respect your wishes."

The words hung between them.

"Actually. No. I won't. That's a fucking lie." He grinned ruefully and plowed a hand into his hair. "I'm going to spend the rest of my life telling you I love you and trying to make up for this. For letting fear paralyze me. For being an asshole."

The instinct for self-preservation deserted her. He was capable of hurting her more than any other person ever had, yet she couldn't tell him to leave. Every part of her craved him. "Tell me again."

He swallowed. "That I love you?"

"No." A damn tear spilled from the corner of her eye. "How bad you fucked up."

"Totally."

She swiped a hand across her face. "Completely."

"One hundred percent. Jerk."

"That'll suffice. Now tell me the other stuff again." It was all she could do not to launch herself into his arms.

"I love you, Araceli." He quirked an eyebrow. "That part?"

"You're getting there."

"I'll spend my life trying to make it up to you."

"That's better."

"I... Damn it, Araceli. If you're going to forgive me, put me out of my misery. Please?"

She took a step toward him. And that was all her Dominant lover needed. He closed the remaining distance and gently drew her toward him. "How's your arm?"

"It was superficial. I'm almost done with rehab."

"Do you love me? No. Wait." He shook his head. "You don't have to say anything. I'll be the man you deserve until you fall in love with me."

She looked at him without blinking, allowing him to see

her all of her, holding nothing back, the tears, the anguish, the depth of her emotion. "I think I fell in love with you at Aiken. I've never stopped."

"You…?"

"Yes. I love you, Torin."

The breath he released was jagged, as if dragged across the shards of his heart. "I've missed you."

She traced a finger across one of his eyebrows. Because of the vulnerability in his tone, she offered her own confession. "It's mutual, Commander Carter."

"We have a lot of talking to do."

"About?"

"The future. Marriage. How we'll make this—Hawkeye—work. Or not. Nothing, nothing is more important than being with you. If you want me to resign, I will. I don't know what we'll do, but as long as it's together, we can figure it out. Nothing is more important to me, Mira, than being with you."

"Marriage?" Of all the things he'd said, it was the only thing she'd heard.

"Maybe kids."

She swallowed hard. "What?"

"Long story. Kayla Davidson Stone is pregnant. And I started thinking."

"Kiss me?"

He did, with care and a gentleness she'd never experienced from him. "I'm not fragile."

"But you are precious." He brushed back strands of her hair, then framed her face with his hands before leaning in to give her a kiss that tasted of the promise of a thousand tomorrows.

Her toes curled, and sexual arousal rushed through her, leaving her dizzy. Desperate, she grabbed his forearms for support.

Just then, a hoot and raucous clapping snapped through her reverie. Theodore, her nosy retired next door neighbor, leaned on his porch rail, grinning.

Embarrassment flooded her. No doubt she would be the talk of his breakfast club the next morning. "I'm so sorry you saw that, Mr. Winters!"

"It's about time you stopped moping around, Mira."

"Moping?" Torin raised an eyebrow.

She rolled her eyes but gave her neighbor a half smile.

"We're getting married," Torin called out.

"Darn right you are," Mr. Winters shouted back. "Otherwise I'm going to get my shotgun."

"You didn't propose," she pointed out in a fierce whisper. "And I haven't agreed."

"You will."

Once again, she was engulfed by the sweet relentless storm that was Torin Carter.

"I think we should go inside," Torin said. "You definitely don't want him to see what I've got planned for you next."

"Oh?"

He swept her from her feet, and she placed a hand around his neck for stability.

"We have some time to make up for. And I plan to start doing that right away."

EPILOGUE

HAWKEYE

"We're going to need a different ladder," Mira said, looking up at the Christmas tree that stood over fourteen feet tall.

"We're going to need scaffolding," Torin corrected, coming up behind her to slide his arms possessively around her waist. "A crane, maybe. That is, if you still want the star on top."

She maneuvered herself around to face him. "It needs it."

"How do you know? No one can see the top."

Mira raised her eyebrows.

Her husband of three months sighed. "I figured it was worth a try." Then a sly grin sauntered across his features, sending her insides into a freefall. "It will cost you."

His eyes glittered with Dominant intent, and she was more than willing to pay his price. "You have to admit, the tree is perfect."

"Better than I imagined."

Once Mira agreed to marry him, Torin hadn't been content to wait, and they'd spent a few days away, on vacation, making plans for their future.

Since neither of them wanted to quit working for Hawkeye Security and they wanted to be together as much as possible, she'd applied for a teaching position at Aiken Training Facility.

Once she was offered the job, she and Torin started house hunting, spending hours a day poring through pictures online.

She'd fallen in love with the large space, designed to resemble a log cabin. The main living area had a soaring cathedral ceiling and numerous skylights, meaning the interior would be flooded with light even during the long northern Nevada winters.

Torin had urged her toward caution. The home needed extensive renovations, and it was impossible to tell how sound it was until they had it inspected.

But the moment they walked in the front door, the space wrapped around her, seeming to welcome her home.

Torin had been more skeptical, until their real estate agent showed them a secret room behind a bookcase in the master bedroom.

Suddenly he, too, had seen the property's potential.

"Spy shit," Hallie had said when Mira told her about it. "Of course you'd love it."

From the moment they hired the contractors, she'd known it was the perfect spot for them to build their new life together. They were on several acres of land. They were close enough to work that the commute wasn't terrible, and far enough away to have privacy after they left the training facility.

"I'll take payment in advance," he informed her.

"Will you, Commander Carter?"

All traces of teasing vanished from his eyes. "Master Torin."

Instantly she slid into a submissive mindset. If he hadn't

MEANT FOR ME

been holding her, she would have knelt.

"I'll meet you in the play room."

Even though they'd been lovers for over six months, when his tone was roughened with dominant demand, her mouth dried, making words almost impossible.

"Fifteen minutes?"

She nodded.

"Please wear a thong, fishnet stockings, a garter belt, and heels."

Slowly, he released her. "Don't be late, mo shearc."

She hurried up the stairs, and on the landing, turned to look down at him. Arms folded across his long-sleeved Henley T-shirt, he was watching her.

"You're down to fourteen minutes, sub."

"Sir." She hurried into their bedroom and pulled open the drawer of her closed built-in. One of the stockings snagged on a leather bra clasp, increasing her sense of urgency. The faster she moved, the slower she seemed to go.

In every area of her life, she was more than competent, but when it came to scening with him, she couldn't keep her thoughts straight.

She selected a red garter belt and a black thong as her mind spun through a dozen different possibilities. The Saint Andrew's cross? The spanking bench? Or the Wall of Torture designed by a friend of his in Denver?

The panties slipped from her trembling fingers.

That was her favorite thing, and he was incredibly inventive when it came to using the numerous metal rails attached to wall.

In the near distance, the door to their bedroom opened, which meant Torin had entered and her time might be running short.

She forced herself to take a few deep breaths before stripping.

161

SIERRA CARTWRIGHT

Even thought the heater had cycled recently, her nipples became hardened little beads. And they ached for his attention.

Two minutes later, she slipped into her highest heels, then walked through their bedroom and into the secret room.

Torin was in the center of the room, an acrylic paddle strapped to his side.

In the doorway, she hesitated. She hated the thing as much as she loved it. It was brutal, but each time she took it, she adored the resulting endorphins.

Though she had made peace with her need to push herself to achieve ever-greater results, she still enjoyed being taken to her limits. And it was astounding to know that he was there for her, always watching and caring.

"Oh, Mira…" He drew a breath, and his eyes became hooded as he swept his gaze over her. "Even more beautiful than this morning."

At dawn, he'd made sweet love to her, and he'd listed a dozen things he cherished about her. His constant appreciation nourished her on a soul-deep level, making her wonder how she'd managed without him.

"Please come to me."

Her shoes echoed off the hardwood flooring, the strike matching her heartbeat.

"What is tonight about?" he asked when she was in front of him.

Her tender lover from earlier had been replaced by this badass Dom.

"I want a favor from you…" She hesitated. Lowering her gaze, she finished. "Sir."

He groaned. "You're the perfect sub."

She looked up at him through her lashes.

"Your nipples are already hard."

MEANT FOR ME

In a fraction of a second, he'd once again become her Master.

"Perhaps you're anticipating having them clamped?"

Her pussy dampened.

"I didn't hear you."

"Anything you want, Sir."

"That's what I thought. Please put your hands behind your neck."

Obediently, she did as he said. He grabbed the front of her thong and pulled forward and up, forcing her onto her toes. She gasped. Mira had been sure he was going to play with her breasts, so this unexpected move hit her with double force.

The material split her in half and seared her clit.

She hissed out a breath.

"I love hurting you like this."

His grip, combined with the power of his words, sent a climax crashing through her.

"You didn't come, did you?" He made a small *tsking* sound.

"I'm sorry, Sir."

"Don't worry about apologizing."

He was a devil of a Dom. He'd work hard to give her an orgasm, then punish her for it.

No wonder she was addicted to him.

"Now your nipples." Torin released her thong but left the material scrunched uncomfortably in her crotch. He rolled each nipple, tweaking, squeezing, tugging until she was breathless and it took all of her self-control to remain in the position he'd ordered.

Then without warning, he sucked one into his mouth, applying harsh pressure and a tiny bite.

"Oh, Sir!"

With a horrid chuckle, he moved on to the other side, sucking until she cried his name over and over.

163

Without warning, he left her to select a pair of Japanese clover clamps from a drawer in the armoire he'd had built to hold their toys.

This pair had an extralong chain between them, which meant awful things for her.

Involuntarily, she shivered.

It'd been a while since they had a scene this intense. Until her whole body throbbed, she hadn't realized how badly she needed it.

He placed the clamps, then gave them a sharp tug, making her yelp.

"That didn't sound like a safe word."

"It wasn't, Sir," she assured him.

"I want you at the wall, wife."

Yes. *Yes, please.*

"But first…"

Puzzled, she looked at him.

He pulled out a pair of weights from a back pocket.

In order not to protest, she clamped her lips together. Those things would be horribly uncomfortable.

The pain-loving submissive in her soared as he wrapped her chain around one of his hands, holding it steady while he affixed the hefty teardrop-shaped pieces of metal in place.

"Should I gently let go? Or should I drop it so it yanks on you?"

They both knew it wasn't her decision. His questions were meant to stoke her fear.

"Naughty girl that you are, you'd come again if I did that." He leaned toward her and kissed her forehead. "Wouldn't you?"

"I…"

He dropped the chain. She cried out from the sudden shock. Between her legs, the weights swung back and forth.

She closed her eyes against the pain.

MEANT FOR ME

As always, he knew what she needed, and he stroked a thumb between her legs, vanquishing everything except pleasure.

"Don't you dare even consider coming."

Mira floated somewhere ethereal, where nothing existed but the moment and her man.

"Let's get you to the wall."

With his arms folded, he watched her. Each step made the weights sway, forcing her to take slow, small steps.

She hazarded a glance Torin's direction. His cock bulged against his jeans. His arousal was reward enough for her suffering.

A little more than a foot from the wall, he instructed her to stop. "Please bend over and extend your arms forward. And your feet should never cross that line."

Now she knew why he'd placed a strip of blue tape on the floor.

About waist height, he secured her wrists in place. Her back was flat, and the weights were only a couple of inches off the floor. Her bonds would prevent her from standing, and any movement would make her nipples ache.

"Comfortable?"

"Not in the least, Sir."

"Ah. In that case, let's consider it perfect."

Mira might have guessed he'd say that.

After caressing her shoulders—with a gentleness that contrasted powerfully with his sternness—he left her for a few seconds and then returned to stroke between her legs. She fought to keep still, but with the way she was already aroused, it was beyond difficult.

Despite her best intentions, she moved, trying to entice him to stroke her clit harder. He brushed aside her thong to insert a finger in her pussy. "Oh, Sir!"

"You may orgasm. But each time you do, I'll add four

strokes to your paddling."

"That's madness, Sir!"

"To the contrary, my darling bride. You're in complete control. We'll start with the eight I want to give you, and we'll go as high as you wish." Without warning, he dug his fingers into one of her buttocks and separated it from the other in order to more easily press a cold, slick plug into her anus.

"Ugh!" This was bigger than the one he usually used on her, making her struggle until she managed to control her breathing.

Torin had never demanded this much from her before, and she adored him all the more for it. He knew what drove her.

When she settled in, breathing hard to fight off an orgasm, he slipped a U-shaped vibrator into her pussy and turned it on, filling her with a slow occasional pulse.

After her first whimper, he placed the gusset of her thong over the tiny toy to hold it in.

Not knowing what to expect or when made it all the more difficult to control her reactions.

He stepped back, then used the remote control to turn up the device's intensity.

Panting for breath, Mira squirmed, trying to escape while being unyieldingly held in place.

"We're starting with eight strikes from the paddle."

The thing was a beast. Though it was much thinner than some of her wooden paddles, it hurt significantly worse. It had a little give, and if he pulled it back right away, its burn would be more significant.

Always the perfect Dominant, he warmed her up, delivering a few spanks with his hand. Because of the way the vibrator danced in her and the plug filled her ass, another orgasm was already forming.

MEANT FOR ME

She wanted to get this over with. "Sir…"

He stopped spanking her to fuck her with the toy.

Damn. No. No. "No!" The orgasm plowed into her. Arching her back, she tugged against her restraints, swinging the weights attached to her clamps.

Mira was miserable and now had to take extra strokes.

"How many orgasms since we started?"

Before answering, she hesitated. "Two, but… Well, that first one… You hadn't said I'd receive four more spanks for that one."

"I see. So you want more?"

"No! Sir." How did he always do this to her? Tie up her thoughts as surely as her body?

"Count them for me."

He delivered the first six in a precise and measured way, making them as easy to take as possible.

After the seventh, he squeezed her right nipple.

In a useless, desperate attempt to escape, she bent her knees.

"Where are we?" he asked, even though she knew he hadn't forgotten. He'd never be that careless.

"Seven. Sir."

"Meaning?"

"Five more."

He gave her another two before squeezing her left nipple. As she sidled away, he delivered two more spanks, and the sensations overcame her, pushing her over the edge again.

"Oh dear." Pleasure was threaded through his words, letting her know how much he enjoyed paddling her. "Now how many?"

From her position, the spanks, the orgasms, and the relentless whir of the vibrator, the world was turning pink.

"Seven. Sir."

SIERRA CARTWRIGHT

She was aware of the next two, then... Nothing. Just an empty, peaceful void, where she floated.

"Mira?"

Pain shot through her nipples. Then it was instantly eased as he squeezed each of them.

"Are you back?"

She blinked. Subspace? One of his arms was beneath her belly, supporting her upper body.

Then her wrists were free, and he was making broad circles on her skin to help restore circulation. She wouldn't have noticed if he hadn't since every part of her felt warm and wonderful.

Torin carried her back to the bedroom and then used a warm, damp cloth to bathe her after he removed the plug and the vibrator.

Tucked beneath the covers, in her husband's arms, Mira continued to drift.

She had no idea how long it took her to become aware of reality again, and when she did, Torin was smiling at her.

"We need to do that more often."

"Yes. Please." Scening was an amazing stress relief, and it also reconnected them. For a couple of months after she was wounded, he'd been afraid of hurting her and had refused to play with her at all. The connection, when he finally relented, had cemented their relationship as nothing else could.

Since they'd been in their home, his nightmares had stopped, and she'd let down her guard for the first time in her life.

Outside their window, the sun yielded to night. "I heard back from Hallie this afternoon," she said.

"Oh?" He moved his head so he could look at her as she spoke.

"She and Bartholomew are going to come and stay for a few days around New Year."

"Good."

Since he knew she missed her friend, he'd been the one to suggest the visit. That would give them a few weeks to finish the renovations on the guest apartment above their three-car garage.

"Did you ever do a background check on him?"

"Hallie asked me not to. Remember?"

"I noticed you didn't answer the question. Which is your way of fibbing without actually lying."

"Maybe a quick search for a criminal record."

"Mira…"

That was fair. She'd stopped short of going through his finances. "But someone named Bartholomew is automatically suspect. It's fancy, right? Like a rich name. Or a fake one."

"It's been eight months, right? If there were warning signs, you'd have seen them by now."

She wondered. It'd taken Hallie's ex-boyfriend a year to reveal his.

"Hallie's happy with him."

Which should be enough.

"She's right that you should give the spy shit a rest."

With a small smile, she snuggled back into his arms.

"I'm going to make love to you, Mira."

Happier than she had a right to be, she pulled back the blankets.

Torin stroked his fingers into her hair, then tugged back her head and held it still as he lowered his mouth to hers with purposeful intent. "You were meant for me. And I will never let you go."

Mira shivered from the husky intensity in his voice. "You are the only man I have ever loved. I've never wanted anyone but you." The she sighed, surrendering to his deep, all-consuming kiss.

HOLD ON TO *me*

USA TODAY BESTSELLING AUTHOR
SIERRA CARTWRIGHT

CHAPTER ONE

HAWKEYE

"No fucking way, Hawkeye." In case that wasn't clear enough, Jacob Walker tipped back the brim of his cowboy hat and leveled a stare at his friend and former commander across the small, rickety table that separated them.

The stench of cheap whiskey and loneliness hung in the air—as putrid as it was familiar.

Through the years, they'd held dozens of meetings at this kind of place. Didn't matter which fucked-up hellhole they were in—Central America, the Middle East, Texas, or here, a small, all but forgotten Colorado mountain town, a place with no security cameras, where neither of them were known.

As usual, Hawkeye dressed to blend in with the locals—jeans, scuffed boots, and a heavyweight canvas jacket that could be found on almost every ranch in the state. He'd added a baseball cap with a logo of a tractor company embroidered on the front. Today, he also wore a beard. No doubt it would be gone within an hour of his walking back outside into the crisp, clean air.

At one time, Jacob thrived on clandestine meetings. The anticipation alone was enough to feed adrenaline into his veins, and he lived for the vicarious thrill.

But life was different now.

After a final, fateful job in Colombia that left an American businessman's daughter dead, Jacob walked away from Hawkeye Security.

He returned to the family ranch and a world he no longer recognized. His grandfather had died, no doubt from the stress of managing the holdings by himself. Though Jacob's grandmother never uttered a critical word, he knew she was disappointed that he'd missed the funeral. He wasn't even in the same country when he was needed the most.

When she passed, he stood alone at the graveside, the only family mourner, like she'd no doubt been a few years before.

Spurred by equal measures of guilt and regret, he poured himself into managing the family's holdings as a way to redeem himself. Then, because of his loneliness and the horrible dreams after Colombia, he did it as a way to save himself.

"The op will take less than a month." Hawkeye shrugged. "Give or take. I'll give you three of our best agents—Johnson, Laurents, Mansfield. You can man the gate, rather than just utilizing the speaker box. Another on perimeter. One for relief. You have the space and a bunkhouse."

Jacob shook his head to clear it of the ever-present memories. "Is there a part of my refusal that you don't understand?" Of course there was. When Hawkeye wanted something, nothing would dissuade him. That willful determination had made him a force on the battlefield as well as in the business arena. "When I quit, I meant it." He took a swig from his longneck beer bottle. "No regrets." The words were mostly true. There were times he wanted the cama-

HOLD ON TO ME

raderie and wanted to flex his brain as well as his muscles. There was also the sweet thrill of the hunt. And making things right in the world.

Rather than argue, Hawkeye removed his cap long enough for Jacob to get a look at his former boss. Worry lines were trenched between his eyebrows. In all his years, Jacob had never seen dark despair in those eyes. "Yesterday, Inamorata received what appeared to be a birthday card from her sister."

Ms. Inamorata was Hawkeye's right-hand woman and known for her ability to remain calm under duress. She could be counted on to deal with local and federal authorities, smoothing over all the details. Rather seriously, Hawkeye said she batted cleanup better than any major leaguer.

Jacob told himself to stand up, thank Hawkeye for the drink, then get the hell out of here while he still could. Instead, he remained where he was.

"There was a white powder inside."

Jesus. "Anthrax?"

"Being tested. She took appropriate precautions and received immediate medical assistance. Antibiotics were prescribed as a precaution." Hawkeye paused. "There were no warning signs that the piece of mail was suspicious."

Meaning the postmark matched the return address. The postage amount was correct, and there was nothing protruding from the envelope.

Jacob knew Inamorata and liked her as much as he respected her. He took offense at a threat to her life. "Received at headquarters?"

"No. At her home. So whoever sent it has access to information about her and how to circumvent our protocols."

Slowly he nodded. "Any message?"

SIERRA CARTWRIGHT

"Yeah." Hawkeye paused. "Threats to take out people I care about, one at a time."

"The fuck?" Instead of sympathizing, Jacob switched to ops mode. He didn't do it on purpose—it was as immediate as it was instinctive. No doubt Hawkeye had counted on Jacob's reaction. "Anything else?"

"There was no specific request. No signature." Hawkeye paused. "I've got profilers taking a look at it. But there's not much to go on. Tech is analyzing writing and sentence structure, tracking down places the card could have come from. FBI has the powder at its lab. Profilers are trying to ascertain the type of person most likely to behave this way."

All the right things.

"But we don't have the resources to take care of our clients and have eyes on everyone who's a potential target."

At this point, there was no way to know how serious the threat was. A card was one thing, a physical attack was another.

"I don't give a fuck who comes for me."

Over the years, their line of work—cleaning up situations to keep secrets safe, protecting people and precious objects, even acting as paramilitary support operators overseas—had created a long list of enemies.

"But I can't risk the people I care about." Hawkeye reached into a pocket inside his jacket and pulled out a picture. "I need you to take care of her."

"Oh fuck no, man." Jacob could be a sounding board, analyze data, but he didn't have the time to return to babysitting services.

Undeterred, Hawkeye continued. "Her name's Elissa. Elissa Conroy. Twenty-eight. My plan was to have Agent Fagen move in with her and accompany her to work."

Makes logical sense. "And?"

"She refused. Then I decided I'd prefer for her to be away

HOLD ON TO ME

from Denver, out of her normal routine in case anyone has been watching." After a moment's hesitation, Hawkeye slid the snapshot onto the table, facedown.

Hawkeye knew every one of Jacob's weaknesses. If he glanced at Elissa's face, the job would become personal. She wouldn't be a random woman he could ignore.

Jacob looked across the expanse of the room, at the two men talking trash at the nearby pool table. Above them, a neon beer sign dangled from a tired-looking nail. The paint was peeling from the shabby wall, and the red glare from the light made the atmosphere all the more depressing.

"Her parents own a pub. Right now, she's running it on their behalf while they're back home in Ireland for a well-deserved vacation. Her father has just recovered from a bout with cancer, and they're celebrating his recovery."

Of course Hawkeye crafted a compelling narrative. He knew how to motivate people, be it through their heart-strings or sense of justice. At times, he'd stoke anger. His ability to get people to do what he wanted was his biggest strength as well as his greatest failing.

Never had his powers of persuasion been more on display than when he'd gotten his Army Ranger team out of Peru, despite the overwhelming odds.

From the beginning, the mission had been FUBAR—fucked up beyond all recognition. They sustained enough casualties to decimate even the strongest and bravest. Relentlessly Hawkeye had urged each soldier on. Despite his own injuries, Hawkeye had carried one man miles to the extraction point.

What happened immediately after that would haunt Hawkeye and Jacob to the end of their days, and it created a bond each would take to the grave.

"You've had some time on the ranch. I assume you're a hundred percent?"

Physically, yes. But part of him would always be in that South American jungle, trying to figure out what had gone so horribly fucking wrong.

Hawkeye nudged the photograph a little closer to Jacob.

"Who is she to you?"

Hawkeye hesitated long enough to capture Jacob's interest.

"Someone I used to know."

Jacob studied his friend intently. "Used to?"

Hawkeye shrugged. "It was a long time ago. Right after we got back from Peru." He stared at the photo. "She helped me through the rough patch."

Tension made Hawkeye's voice rough, and he cleared his throat.

"Shit." Jacob cursed himself for not walking out the moment Hawkeye asked for help. "It—whatever it was between you—is in the past?"

"Yeah. She's a smart woman, recognized damaged goods and was astute enough not to follow when I walked away." He shrugged. "To tell the truth, she's too damn good for me. We both knew it."

"It's over?"

"There never was anything significant. She's a friend. Nothing more. But if anyone's intent on hurting me..." With great deliberation, Hawkeye flipped over the picture.

Jacob couldn't help himself. He looked.

The woman was breathtaking. She was seated on a white-painted carousel horse, arms wrapped around its shiny brass pole. Dark, wavy hair teased her shoulders. But it was her eyes that stopped him cold.

He was a practical man more accustomed to making life-and-death decisions than indulging in fanciful poetry, but that particular shade of blue made him think of the columbines that carpeted the ranch's meadow each summer.

HOLD ON TO ME

Her smile radiated a joy that he wasn't sure he'd ever experienced. Longing—hot and swift—ripped through him. Ruthlessly he shoved the unfamiliar emotion away. He was seated across from Hawkeye, discussing a job. Nothing more. If he accepted the assignment, it would be his responsibility to keep her safe and ensure she had plenty to smile about in the future.

"After this, Commander Walker, we'll call it even."

"Even from you, that's a fucking cheap shot." Jacob didn't need the reminder of how much he owed Hawkeye. Nothing would ever be *even* after the way the man rescued Jacob's mother from the inside of a Mexican jail cell.

Unable to stop himself, Jacob picked up the photo. Hawkeye's gamble—his drive deep into the Colorado mountains—had paid off. Jacob couldn't walk away. Elissa wasn't a random client. She was a woman who'd shown compassion to Hawkeye, and that shouldn't have put her at risk.

With a silent vow that he'd care for her until the shitstorm passed, Jacob tucked the picture inside his shirt pocket.

Hawkeye lifted his shot glass, then downed his whiskey in a single swallow.

"Sir? It's closing time." Elissa summoned a false, I'm-not-exhausted smile for the cowboy sitting alone at a table for two in her mom and dad's Denver-area pub. The man had been there for hours, his back to the wall. From time to time, he'd glance at the baseball game on the television, but for the most part, he watched other customers coming and going. More than once, she was aware of his focused gaze on her as she worked.

When he arrived, he asked for a soda water with lime.

Nothing stronger. Minutes before the kitchen closed, he ordered the pub's famous fish and chips.

Throughout the evening, he hadn't engaged with her attempts at conversation, and he paid his bill—in cash, with a generous tip—before last call.

Now he was the last remaining customer, and she wanted him to leave so she could lock up, head for home. She needed a long, hot bath, doused with a generous helping of her favorite lavender Epsom salts.

If she were lucky, she'd fall asleep quickly and manage a few hours of deep sleep before the alarm shrieked, dragging her out of bed. After all, she still had to run her own business while taking care of the bar.

Over the past few days, exhaustion had made her mentally plan a vacation, far away from Colorado. Maybe a remote tropical island where she could rest and bask in the sun. A swim-up bar would be nice, and so would a beachside massage beneath a palm tree.

But she was still stuck in reality. She had to complete the closing checklist, and that meant dispensing with the final, reluctant-to-leave guest.

With a forced half smile, she tried again. "Sir?"

The man tipped the brim of his cowboy hat, allowing her to get a good look at his face.

She pressed her hand to her mouth to stifle a gasp.

He was gorgeous. Not just classically handsome, but drop-dead, movie star gorgeous.

His square jaw was shadowed with stubble, but that enhanced the sharpness of his features. And his eyes… They were bright green, reminding her of a malachite gemstone she'd seen in a tourist shop.

In a leisurely perusal, he swept his gaze up her body, starting with her sensible shoes, then moving up her thighs,

HOLD ON TO ME

taking in the curve of her hips, then the swell of her suddenly aching breasts.

When their gazes met, she was helplessly ensnared, riveted by his intensity.

The silence stretched, and she cleared her throat. She was usually a total professional, accustomed to dealing with loners, as well as groups out celebrating and being rowdy, or even the occasional customer in search of a therapist while drowning their sorrows. But this raw, physical man left her twitterpated, her pulse racing while her imagination soared on hungry, sexual wings.

Andrew, the barback, switched off some of the lights, jolting her. After shaking her head, she asserted herself. "It's closing time, sir."

"Yes, ma'am." The cowboy stood, the legs of his chair scraping against the wooden floor. "I'll be going, then."

His voice was deep and rich, resonating through her. It invited trust even as it hinted at intimacy.

An involuntary spark of need raced up her spine.

Forcing herself to ignore it, she followed him to the exit. Instead of leaving, he paused.

They stood so close that she inhaled his scent, that of untamed open spaces. She tried to move away but was rooted to the spot. She was ensnared by his masculine force field—an intoxicating mixture of raw dominance and constrained power.

Desire lay like smoke in his eyes. In a response as old as time, pheromones stampeded through her. She ached to know him, to feel his strong arms wrap around her, to have his hips grinding against hers as he claimed her hard.

Dear God, what is wrong with me?

It had been too long since she'd been with a lover, but this cowboy was the type of man who'd turn her inside out if she let him. And she was too smart for that.

"Ma'am." Finally he thumbed the brim of his hat in a casual, respectful farewell that made her wonder if she'd imagined what had just happened between them.

"Thanks for coming in." Her response was automatic.

"I'll see you soon." Conviction as well as promise laced his words, and it shocked her how much she hoped he meant it.

After locking the door behind him, she stood in place for a few moments, watching him climb into his nondescript black pickup truck. It resembled a thousand others on the road, in stark contrast to its intense, unforgettable owner.

The barback tugged the chain to turn off the Open sign, reminding her of the chores still ahead of her.

It was past time to shove away thoughts of the stranger.

She checked her watch. A few minutes after one a.m.

It had been a long day. *Another* long day. With her parents still on vacation, the responsibility for running the pub had fallen to her. That wouldn't have been so bad, but Mary, the nighttime manager, had called in sick. And Elissa's freelance graphic project was due at the end of the week. Sleep had been in short supply for the past month.

Month?

Actually, it had been more than a year. Her father's cancer diagnosis had upended her family's world. The emotional turmoil had taken its toll as they all fought through the terrifying uncertainty and fear.

After his final chemotherapy treatment, her parents had departed for a much-needed break.

Andrew continued walking through the area, switching off the neon beer signs. "Everything's done. Clean and ready for tomorrow."

"Not sure how I would have managed without you." For the first time ever, he'd ended up waiting on several customers, and he'd done a good job. "Why don't you go ahead and leave?"

HOLD ON TO ME

"I'll wait until you're done and walk you to your car."

"That's okay." She shook her head. It had been busier than usual for a Tuesday, more like she'd expect closer to the weekend. "I still have to reconcile the cash register, and that will take some time. You worked your ass off this evening. Go see your girlfriend."

"It's our one-month date-iversary. I didn't know that was a thing until this morning, and she warned me I better not screw it up." Clearly besotted, he grinned. "I don't mind staying, though, for a few more minutes."

"Go."

He glanced toward the rear exit. "If you're sure..."

"It's your date-iversary. *Go.*" She made a sweeping motion with her hand.

Grinning, she turned the deadbolt once he left.

After turning off the main dining room lights, Elissa retreated to the tiny management office. She sank into the old military-surplus style leather chair behind the metal desk. Determined to ignore the clock on the wall, she counted the cash, balanced the register, then ran the credit card settlement.

Once everything was done and the bank deposit was locked in the safe, she sighed, part in relief, part in satisfaction.

Finally.

As usual, she straightened the desktop and gave the office a final glance to be sure everything was where it needed to be.

Satisfied, she released her hair from its ponytail and fed her fingers through the strands to separate them, part of her ritual for ending the workday and easing into her off time.

Then she reached for her lightweight jacket. Even though it was summer, Colorado could still hold a chill after the sun set. Finally she slung her purse over her shoulder before plucking her keyring from a hook in the wall.

She let herself out the door, then secured the deadbolt behind her.

There were only a handful of vehicles in the parking lot, and she headed toward hers at a quick clip.

As she neared it, a figure detached itself from the adjoining building.

She struggled for calm, telling herself that the person wasn't heading toward her. But as she broke into a jog, so did the figure.

Frantically she ran, hitting the remote control to unlock the car, praying she could make it to safety before the assailant reached her. As she grasped the door handle, he crowded behind her, pressing her against the side of the vehicle.

"Get away from me!"

When he didn't, she screamed.

"Calm down."

Fuck. She recognized his gruff voice. *The cowboy.* For a moment, she went still. But when he pressed her harder against the car, fear flared, and she instinctively fought back. "Get the hell off me!"

He was unyielding, and her strength was no match for his.

"Hawkeye sent me."

Elissa froze. *Hawkeye?*

Of course he'd sent someone. She should have expected it when she refused to let him provide her with a bodyguard.

Years before, she'd met the wounded military man when he returned from an overseas mission. The first few times he'd come into the pub, he'd been quiet, drinking whiskey neat, staring at a wall while occasionally flinching.

They'd gone out a number of times, and she'd cared about

HOLD ON TO ME

him. But no matter how hard she tried, she couldn't connect with him on an emotional level. He kept more secrets than he shared. But the one thing she learned was that the need for revenge consumed his every waking thought. In the end, it had been impossible to have any kind of relationship with him.

When he informed her that he'd started Hawkeye Security, she wasn't surprised. And when he came to say goodbye, she tearfully stroked his cheek while wishing him well.

She had been stunned when he called her to tell her she was at risk. Someone from his past threatened the people he cared about. Before hanging up, she dismissed his ridiculous concerns. Their halfhearted relationship was so far in the past that no one could possibly believe that she meant anything to Hawkeye.

"You're going to need to come with me."

"Oh hell no." Her earlier attraction to the stranger had vanished, replaced by anger. She made her own choices and didn't appreciate his heavy-handed tactics. "Tell Hawkeye I said both of you should fuck off. Or better yet, I will."

"I'm not sure you understand." His breath was warm and threatening next to her ear.

And now she understood why he'd spent so many hours at that table. He'd been studying her, planning the best way to bend her to his will.

But Elissa answered to no man.

"You're in danger."

"I can take care of myself. Now get off me, you..." *What?* "Oaf."

"As soon as you give me your word that you'll get in my truck without creating a fuss."

Realizing physical resistance was futile, she allowed her body to go limp and concentrated on tamping down her adrenaline long enough to outwit him. She needed to think

SIERRA CARTWRIGHT

and escape his unbearable presence. "How about I'll go home and stay there?"

"Not happening."

"Look…" There was no way she would yield to this oversize, determined goon, even if he was pure masculine perfection. "I'll agree to have one of his employees stay with me."

"He made that offer. You turned it down."

Damn you both. Why hadn't she just agreed to Hawkeye's suggestions?

"Let me be clear, Elissa…"

Despite herself, the way he said her name, gently curled around the sibilant sound, made her nerves tingle.

"He made it my job to protect you, and he signed off on my plan."

"Care to fill me in?"

"Yeah. We'll go to my ranch until he gives the all-clear."

Unnerved, she shivered. "Ranch?" That was worse than she could have imagined, and fresh panic set in. "I demand to talk to Hawkeye this instant."

"Demand all you want, little lady."

She refused to leave town, the pub, and be somewhere remote for an indeterminate amount of time with the cowboy shadowing her twenty-four seven. "No. No." She shook her head. "It's impossible. I'm needed here. And Hawkeye knows it." Struggling for breath, she pushed back against him. "We can work something out, I'm sure."

"You can take it up with him."

"Now we're getting somewhere. Let me get my phone out of my purse." *And figure out how to get in my car and drive like hell.*

"Not until we're on the road." He looped his massive hands around her much smaller wrists and drew them behind her.

"Ouch! Release me immediately!"

HOLD ON TO ME

Though he didn't hurt her, his grip was uncompromising. "As soon as you agree to get in my truck without struggling."

"Look, Mr.—" *God. I don't know your name.* And like the asshole he was, he didn't fill in the missing information.

"We're done talking."

She stamped her foot on his instep, and he didn't even grunt, frustrating the hell out of her.

"Please get in my truck, Elissa."

Since he was immovable, she tried another approach, pleading with his better self. "I'm begging you. Don't do this. Let me go home." Elissa turned her head, trying to see him over her shoulder. Because of his hat and the darkness of the moonless and cloud-filled sky, his expression was unreadable. "You can follow me to my place." The lie easily rolled off her tongue. Anything to get away.

"Within the next five seconds, you'll be given two options, Ms. Conroy. One, you can come with me willingly."

"And the other?"

"You can come with me unwillingly."

"Option C. None of the above." With all her might, she shoved back, but he tightened his grip to the point of hurting her.

As if on cue, a big black truck—his, no doubt—pulled into view. Since he didn't react, it obviously meant Hawkeye had sent more than one person to deal with her. "This is absurd."

The vehicle, with no lights on, pulled to a stop nearby.

"I'll need your keys, Ms. Conroy."

She shook her head in defiance.

"Always going to do things the hard way?"

Since he was still holding her wrists, it was ridiculously easy for him to pry apart her fingers and take the fob from her.

"Has anyone ever told you that you're annoying as hell?"

A woman slid from the cab of the still-running pickup

187

SIERRA CARTWRIGHT

and left the driver's side door open a crack. A gentle chime echoed around them, while light spilled from the interior, allowing Elissa to make out a few of the new arrival's features.

Dressed all in black, she was about the same height and build as Elissa. She even had long dark hair.

"Perimeter is still clear." Then in a cheery voice, she went on. "I see you haven't lost your way with the ladies, Commander."

He growled, all alpha male and frustration. "You're here to help, Fagan."

"That's exactly what I'm doing."

The cowboy eased his hold a little.

"Sorry for the caveman's actions, ma'am. I'm Agent Kayla Fagan. And I'm afraid Commander Walker needs a remedial training class in diplomacy."

Walker. First name? Or last? "Diplomacy? Is that what you call an abduction?"

He remained implacable. "I have my orders, and Ms. Conroy wasn't interested in talking."

Bastard. "His behavior needs to be reported to Hawkeye."

"I'll let you do that yourself," Kayla replied. "But honestly, I'd like to listen in."

"Get out of here, Fagan." He kept his body against hers while somehow managing to toss her keys to Kayla.

"Wait! You look so much like me you could be my double."

"That's the plan. Fagan will make it appear as if you're following your normal routine this evening while we get away. When we're on the road, you can talk to Hawkeye and make a strategic plan for opening the bar." Walker's tone was uncompromising.

The infuriating men had planned out everything.

Kayla opened the car door and slid into the driver's seat.

188

HOLD ON TO ME

"Time's up, ma'am."

"Could you be any more condescending?"

"As I said, we can do this the hard way or the easy way. Your choice."

Determinedly Elissa set her chin. "I'm not going with you."

In a move so calculated and fast that she had no time to react, he took her purse from her, then yanked her around to face him. As if he'd done it a million times, he swept her off her feet, then hauled her into the air.

The Neanderthal tossed her over his shoulder, and she landed against his rigid body with so much force that breath rushed out of her lungs, stunning her into silence.

"The hard way it is."

CHAPTER TWO

HAWKEYE

"Go buy yourself a one-way ticket straight to hell." In the darkness of the truck's interior, Elissa glared at her captor. A minute ago, they'd pulled into a twenty-four-hour fuel stop, and he'd parked away from security cameras, in the shadows from the lights. Then he'd outlined his rules—rules she had no intention of following. "I mean it. There's no way —no fucking way—that you're going into the bathroom with me."

As implacable as usual, he regarded her. "In that case, we'll continue on. You can pee on the side of the road, but that won't be happening until we leave I-70." He lifted a shoulder in a small shrug, indicating he didn't give a damn whichever decision she made. "Hawkeye would prefer we limit law enforcement contact, and that's always a possibility if I pull over onto the side of the road. We should have our story straight. Could always say you're my pregnant wife who couldn't wait for the next town."

With a gasp, she folded her arms across her middle.

During the twenty minutes they'd been driving, he remained mostly silent, responding to her questions with

SIERRA CARTWRIGHT

irritating-as-hell half answers. He refused to let her have her purse or her phone. Other than saying that they were driving toward his ranch and that it was located in Colorado, he hadn't provided any further details.

"I don't want to lose time. Make a decision."

Commander Walker had already proven he was a hard-ass. Things were going to be his way or his way. Maddening.

While she didn't need the facilities right away, it was only a matter of time. And this place, on the far western side of the city, was the last reliably clean restroom for miles. "Fine."

With a tight nod, he reached into the back to grab a duffel bag. "There's some clothes in there for you."

"I'm not—"

"If you want to get out of this truck, you are."

She wasn't sure which one of them to kill first. Her kidnapper or Hawkeye. Either way, the act was going to be joyful.

"Time's ticking."

Elissa pulled out a sweatshirt and tugged it over her head. It was at least two sizes too large. The shoulder seams drooped down her arms, and the bottom would probably hit the tops of her thighs.

"Now the hat."

At least she liked the black cap with a bright purple baseball team logo on it.

Once she had it in place, he shook his head. "Can you do something with your hair?"

"Like what?"

"Stuff it under there or something."

Hurriedly she made a ponytail and threaded it through the opening in the back.

"Still too long. Recognizable."

Elissa sighed as she removed the hat. "I'm not sure what else to do." Thinking fast, she fashioned a makeshift bun and

HOLD ON TO ME

then took his advice and pulled on the hat. "No one does this. It looks ridiculous—lumpy."

"This isn't about fashion, ma'am." He cocked his head to one side to study her. "Pull the brim lower on your forehead."

"Look, Mr. Walker, I'm not cut out for this secret agent shit." Which had been one of the many reasons she and Hawkeye never had a real relationship.

"Save your breath. I'm about out of patience."

"You're almost out of patience? It isn't your life that's just been turned upside down."

"No?" The single word was quiet, but chilling. "Hawkeye gets what he wants."

Did that mean he was as reluctant as she was?

She shook her head. He was an agent—she was his mission. Nothing more.

He tucked a few loose strands of hair away, brushing her cheekbone.

Her reactions turned sluggish as his scent washed over her.

For a moment, neither spoke. Something primal—dangerous—pulsed between them.

Then, as if remembering himself, Jacob cleared his throat and glanced away from her. "There's a car pulling in on our left. Appears to have two occupants."

The abruptness edging his voice made her scoot away a little.

"We'll follow them in. Stay close. We want to make it appear we're a party of four. Got it?"

She sighed. "Is this all really necessary?"

"The boss says so. If you'd agreed to have a bodyguard when he suggested it, you could have avoided all of this."

Anger and frustration collided, making her vocal cords tight. "So it's my fault?"

Instead of responding, he kept his focus on the other

vehicle. "Be ready to move. When we're inside, head straight for the ladies' room. No stopping. Avoid the cash registers because of cameras. Don't touch anything. I've got plenty of food and water for us, enough to hold us till morning."

Are you planning to drive all night?

He kept his gaze on the car next to them. "On my mark, exit the vehicle."

Despite her insistence that this was nonsense, her heart was beating furiously, and she was even paranoid enough to check her mirrors for potential threats.

"Ready?"

Elissa nodded.

The other couple opened their doors.

"Let's roll."

Within moments, they entered the convenience store.

"Normal pace," he cautioned as they followed the signs toward the back wall. When they reached the bathroom, he held up a hand. "Wait here."

Using his foot, he pushed the door open.

As if that isn't suspicious.

After a few seconds, he returned. "Clear. Be as fast as you can."

In record time, she rejoined Commander Walker.

The woman who'd walked in before them handed a package of potato chips to her companion, then started toward the bathroom.

He nudged Elissa down a different aisle, then hurried her back outside.

In record time, he topped off the gas tank before accelerating down the on-ramp, sliding into traffic at the exact posted speed limit.

As they climbed into the mountains, leaving the metro area behind them, he looked in the rearview mirror, then

HOLD ON TO ME

loosened his grip on the steering wheel. Until that moment she hadn't realized how tense he was.

His phone rang, and Hawkeye's name appeared on the screen that had been showing a map.

Without saying anything, Commander Walker pushed the button to answer the call.

"Phase one of Operation Wildflower is underway, I presume?" Hawkeye's calm, almost cheerful voice filled the cabin.

"Operation Wildflower?" she repeated.

"I'll explain it to you later." Jacob slid her a glance before refocusing on the road and his conversation with Hawkeye. "Affirmative. Extraction complete. You already know that."

"Fagan had a couple of things to say about our client and your, ahem, lack of diplomacy."

"Stop with that word. I think you mean manhandling." Irritated, she scowled. How dare they talk about her as if she weren't there. "Actually the more appropriate term would be kidnapping."

"Hello, Elissa."

At one time, Hawkeye's voice had been as familiar as her own, until she realized he'd never allowed her to glimpse beyond a carefully constructed facade that hid his emotional pain and broken pieces.

"Commander Walker is one of the finest individuals I've ever known."

If she wasn't so annoyed, the words of praise might have meant something to her. "Is that supposed to make this all better?"

"Besides myself, he's the only one I trust with your life."

At the jagged note of emotion in his voice, her shoulders rolled forward. Whether she believed she was at risk or not, he did. "I hate this cloak-and-dagger stuff."

SIERRA CARTWRIGHT

"And I hate that you're mixed up in it. I'll never forgive myself."

Even though she wanted to be mad, she couldn't be. But that didn't give him—or anyone else—permission to upend her entire world. "You know what's going on in my life, right? Let's be reasonable."

"Yesterday you refused."

"I've changed my mind." She blew out a wisp of breath. "Kayla is welcome to stay with me. I have an extra bedroom. And that way I can go back to work—"

"No." The two men spoke in unison, making her rub her temple to ward off the growing headache.

She should have already been in bed.

"Everything is covered at the pub."

Exhaustion evaporated. *"What?"*

"I talked to your parents and apprised them of the situation. They're being provided with hourly updates."

"How dare you?" Fury, white and blinding, flashed through her. She leaned forward, and the seatbelt grabbed her, preventing further movement. "What the hell is wrong with you? My dad can't handle that kind of stress."

"Patrick is stronger than you think. His only concern is your safety, and he immediately set about providing a solution to the problem. Your manager, Mary, says she's feeling better, and she intends to return to work tomorrow."

She exhaled her relief.

"Your dad was also able to get hold of Joseph. He's agreed to take the day shifts."

That news shaved the edges off Elissa's biggest concerns. Joseph had spent a number of years working for them and occasionally still picked up a few shifts. He knew Conroy Pub almost as well as she did, and he had earned her trust. Still, she hated that Hawkeye had upended so many people's lives.

HOLD ON TO ME

As if he'd read her mind, Hawkeye spoke again, this time, more softly. "I know you're not happy. None of this would have been necessary if you'd have cooperated when I asked you to."

The same argument. Again. She sank back into the seat.

"There's a package waiting for you at the ranch. Some shoes and clothes, along with a secure cell phone—you'll be able to call your parents as soon as you arrive. You'll also be provided with a Bonds computer."

"Seriously?" Even though she wouldn't admit it, she was impressed. Because of her demanding graphic arts business, she'd lusted after one for years, but she'd never had that kind of money. Regardless, that wasn't the point. Right now, she needed her own equipment. "My software and files are on my desktop."

"You'll find everything already loaded on the new system. Bonds himself handled it."

She blinked. *"What?* Are you kidding me? You actually know Julien Bonds?" The genius of all things electronic. "And why would he do something like that?"

"We go back. And he loves getting involved in other people's lives. World-class meddler."

Even after all these years, Hawkeye still surprised her.

"Everything that was on your machine has been loaded on to your new computer."

"Wait." *God, no.* Her pulse stuttered, and when she managed to speak again, her words were a croaked whisper. *"All* of it?"

"All of it." Hawkeye cleared his throat. "Bonds said there was some kinky shit on there."

Unable to breathe, she stared straight ahead into the abyss of an endless highway.

"Kinky shit?"

She sensed that Jacob glanced at her, but she didn't look

SIERRA CARTWRIGHT

in his direction. Instead, she wished the vehicle's undercarriage would open up so she could sink through it. No one had a right to look at her personal gallery, let alone comment on the contents.

"Elissa?" Jacob asked.

Desperately she searched for an explanation. "Those pictures… It was… Uhm… A project. For a client. Sworn to secrecy." The lie was the best she could come up with. No way was she confessing—to either one of these men—that the images were created from her own line drawings and inspired by her own vivid imagination.

"Bonds said he was impressed, that you have real talent." Surprise was etched in Hawkeye's tone. Despite the time they'd spent together, there was a lot he didn't know about her. "He suggested you consider showing it."

Not even if hell freezes over and starts selling the ice. She would never reveal her most intimate self to the world.

"You're welcome to get in contact with him. He has some recommendations."

"Thanks, but no." Even if she didn't have her own hesitations, she doubted there was a gallery on the planet interested in hanging her kind of paintings. "Let's get back to the previous conversation, please."

"I'll be in touch tomorrow."

Of course the asshole of all assholes had continued talking as if she hadn't said anything.

"I assure you that every resource is committed to this situation. Follow Commander Walker's orders, and we'll have you home before you know it."

The connection ended.

"I hate him."

In the darkness, her abductor looked at her.

"I hate this."

"In your place, so would I. It takes a special person to be

HOLD ON TO ME

comfortable with this type of uncertainty."

Jacob's comments, uttered without even a ripple of emotion, intrigued her. "And you are?"

He was silent for so long that she wasn't sure he'd answer. "It comes from practice."

"Do you always speak so damn cryptically?" Like Hawkeye. Hadn't she learned a lesson about trying to communicate with military men?

"It's been safer that way."

"Well, after this is over, you'll never have to see me again, right? And it's not like I'd tell anyone anything that you said."

"The army teaches you a lot. At the time, I saw it as the only way out of a small town, the responsibilities of ranch life. I wanted adventure. You know, jumping out of helicopters, knocking down doors in a hail of gunfire."

She angled herself toward him. "You did all that?"

"Yeah." He shrugged "And more."

"Did you like it?"

"Not as much as I imagined I would. The adrenaline? That's fucking addictive. But I learned a lot that I never expected. Discipline. Patience—endless days, even weeks of waiting. Survival skills. Sleeping when I could, wherever I could. Eating even when I wasn't hungry, existing on soup for days when it was the only thing available." He adjusted one of the air-conditioning vents. "I learned how to make a plan and how to execute a new one when the first failed."

"Like throwing me over your shoulder?"

"I asked nicely."

"That's not how I remember it."

"Hmm."

They settled into silence, and she turned over the events that had unfurled since Hawkeye had called the day before. If only she had made different decisions when he said she needed protection. But at the time, she hadn't believed the threat was real. Even now, she wasn't sure it was.

Some time later, the cowboy exited the interstate. "Don't you think it's time you tell me where we're going? You have my phone, so it's not like I can contact anyone."

"The Starlight Mountain Ranch."

"It's yours?"

"Yeah." He paused for so long she wasn't sure he'd go on. "Fourth generation."

More intrigued than ever, she turned as much as she could to face him. Too bad there wasn't a little more ambient light so she could read his expressions. "And you live there with family?"

"It's just me. I'm the last one."

"I'm sorry to hear that." Her family meant everything to her. Her dad's recent health battle had only brought them closer together. She didn't like to imagine a future without them in it.

"I've had some time to get used to it."

"Is it a big place?"

"Depends on how you define that. Been added to throughout the years. The entire holding is around eight thousand acres."

"And are you ever going to tell me where it is?"

"Not far from Steamboat Springs. About twenty-five minutes south. On Trout Creek, a tributary of the Yampa River."

It was a beautiful area of the state, one she'd visited a few times. "We spent a couple of Christmases at one of the resorts near there."

"Good memories?"

They were...a reminder of a time when life was simpler, when they'd been together as a family, away from the responsibilities of running a business, and they'd played

HOLD ON TO ME

cards and board games, worked a few jigsaw puzzles, then spent evenings sipping hot chocolate in front of a crackling fire. "That's where I learned to ski and ice skate."

"You might enjoy yourself at the ranch."

"Vacations generally don't include having a jailer."

He glanced toward her. "Think of me as a protective friend."

The way she'd already responded to him made that idea laughable. "I don't even know who you are. I mean, beyond Commander Walker. Are you like Hawkeye, no first name, no last name?"

"It's Jacob."

"That's nice." Strong. It suited him. "Is it a family name?"

"No. It was one of my mother's few contributions to child-drearing before she disappeared from my life. Haven't had any contact with her since..." He paused, as if deliberating how much to reveal. When he continued, his tone was flat. "It's been a long time."

"Oh God." The more she knew about him, the more he wound his way into her emotions. To keep herself safe, she couldn't let that happen. "That had to have hurt."

"My grandparents made sure I didn't miss her much."

Was that true, though? "Is she still alive?"

"Yeah." He set his jaw and turned on the radio, telling her the conversation was over.

Over the next hour and a half, she dozed, only to be jolted awake when he drove over a cattle guard.

"Sorry about that, Sleeping Beauty."

She blinked and forced herself to sit up a little straighter. "I wish I could see the surroundings."

"I'll give you a tour tomorrow. Or, rather, later today."

Jacob stopped in front of a massive iron gate. The truck's headlights allowed her to make out an ornate *W* in the middle.

SIERRA CARTWRIGHT

He pressed a button on the dashboard, and the entrance swung open.

They continued along a dirt road for several minutes before the house came into view, fully lit. The home, constructed from beautiful pine logs, was massive, with several different wings. Numerous cozy-looking chimneys climbed toward the sky. "This is stunning."

"It's big. Too big for one person. My great-grandparents had a large family. And they took care of the ranch hands. It was a gathering place."

He pulled to a stop, and she gratefully climbed down from the passenger side. In the distance, the sun was casting its first rays, painting a few clouds pink.

Jacob grabbed his duffel bag before pressing a button on the remote to lock the vehicle. "After you."

She climbed the five steps to the porch. A swing, covered in pillows, hung near the door. Two Adirondack chairs were angled so they faced the distant mountain peak.

It appeared to be a perfect spot to sit and read.

Which she'd probably have plenty of time to do. Her stomach twisted into a sudden knot of resigned annoyance.

A loud hiss ripped through the still morning air. She glanced back at Jacob. "Uhm, do you have mountain lions or something out here?"

"Or something."

Suddenly, a massive animal leaped up the steps in a single movement, landing next to her. Screaming, she jumped sideways.

The creature crouched down, still hissing, staring at her. Contemplating if she was going to be breakfast? "Is that a lynx or something?"

"No. It's a Waffle."

"What is it, exactly?"

"A cat. Maine Coon, we think. She showed up one day as

HOLD ON TO ME

a kitten and refused to leave. We had no idea she'd get so big or be so loud. The vet says that breed vocalize more than others. Lucky us."

"Interesting name."

"Well, my housekeeper's little girl dreamed it up because of the cat's various markings. She looks like a waffle with syrup on it. And whipped cream on the nose."

"I can see it." For the first time in hours, her tension eased, and she smiled.

He shrugged. "Better than Pancake, I suppose."

"You said you have a chef?"

"I like to eat, and I don't always have time to cook."

Waffle hissed again.

"She's harmless."

Elissa crouched, and the fur on the back of Waffle's neck stood on end—then she arched her back and moved back several feet. "Harmless? Are you sure about that?"

"You could say she has an interesting personality."

The moment Jacob stepped on the porch, the feline dashed toward him, then wound herself between his legs, rubbing and purring. "At least she's got good taste in humans."

Elissa rolled her eyes as she stood. "That's up for debate."

"She's not fond of Hawkeye."

"In that case, I like her more and more."

With a grin, Jacob reached across her to enter a code on the keypad and opened the door. "Seven, six, three, nine, five, two."

"What?"

"The security code."

"You mean I'm allowed to leave?"

"Of course. Despite what you said, I'm not your jailer, Elissa."

203

SIERRA CARTWRIGHT

She frowned at him. "So I can go to Steamboat for a cappuccino? Maybe do a little shopping?"

"If I'm with you."

Remembering the ridiculous maneuvers he'd gone through to protect her identity at the fuel stop, skepticism raced through her. "And you'll take me?"

"Sure." He shrugged. "Later in the week, if things remain calm."

"That's a carrot, right?"

"Meaning?"

"You know, management techniques. Carrot and the stick. Positive versus negative reinforcement. If you promise me a reward, maybe I'll behave better."

"Yeah. That's it. You figured me out." He studied her in silence.

Annoyingly, her feminine instincts stirred again. She blamed her exhaustion as well as the night's extraordinary events.

After some sleep, she'd be herself again, back in control. There was no way her abductor could be this tempting.

"Go ahead inside."

She took a couple of steps only to have Waffle dart past her. The animal jumped onto a nearby table, looked back at Elissa, and hissed again.

"Mind your manners," Jacob told the cat before closing the door and dumping his bag on the floor. He stroked a finger between the cat's ears, and she turned her head into his hand. "Ms. Conroy will be with us for the foreseeable future."

The cat hissed, not seeming any happier with the news than Elissa was.

"I'll show you around."

At lightning speed, Waffle dashed away.

Elissa followed him to the inviting yet cozy living room

HOLD ON TO ME

with furniture arranged in a U shape. A large couch faced the flagstone patio and wide-open meadow. Another was placed in front of the oversize fireplace and television. She imagined sitting here and relaxing, maybe with a glass of wine.

Beyond it was a sliding glass door leading to the patio.

"The kitchen is through here."

Maybe because he was a bachelor and the home had been standing for so long, she expected it to be dated. Instead, it was modern, with restaurant-quality appliances and gorgeous marble countertops. "I could spend days in here. It's a chef's delight."

"Glad you approve. You're exactly right. Eric designed it himself."

"That's your chef, I assume?"

"It is. He comes in a couple of times a week." Jacob filled a bowl with cat food and placed it on the floor. From nowhere, Waffle appeared and delicately picked out a single piece of kibble. "He hopes I'll start entertaining one of these days. Maybe open the house to guests."

"Like a bed-and-breakfast type of thing?"

"I'd be the perfect host. Easygoing. Attentive as well as accommodating."

For a moment she stared at him. "You're joking, right?"

He held his neutral expression for a moment before his lips twitched.

"Was that an attempt at humor?" When he stole her away from her life, she'd seen him as a rigid, one-dimensional secret agent man. And then he'd revealed a glimpse of his childhood. The confounded cat liked him, and now this.

"Did it work?"

Elissa gave herself a mental shake. He might be more complex and vulnerable than she expected, but she was still here against her will. No way should she let her guard down.

"Help yourself to whatever you want. The housekeeper

keeps the kitchen stocked with food and plenty to drink."

Something to help take off the edge so she could fall asleep would be welcome. "Dare I hope you have wine?"

"Lady's choice. Red or white?"

"Something crisp, a little sweet. Maybe a chardonnay?"

He pulled out a bottle from a small refrigerator tucked beneath the island. "Will this work?"

Elissa recognized the label and grinned with satisfaction. As far as being kidnapped was concerned, maybe this wasn't so awful. "Do I thank you or Eric?"

"My experience with wine is limited. I've been told reds go with beef, while whites go with seafood or chicken. I have no idea about pink."

"I think you mean rosé."

"See what I mean? And then someone else told me to forget the rules and that you should drink whatever the hell you want." He extracted the cork. "I know slightly more about whiskey, and I definitely have preferences when it comes to beer." He offered her the drink.

"Thank you." She took a long, leisurely sip. Now if she had a bathtub to soak in, life would be complete.

"I'll show you to your room."

She followed him up the stairs into a large bedroom dominated by an oversize bed. The comforter was thick and fluffy, and at least ten pillows encouraged her to bury in and create a nest.

"The closet is this way."

On a shelf were two large boxes.

"As Hawkeye promised." Jacob opened one and pulled out a cell phone and offered it to her. "It's secure, and you can contact your parents at any time."

Elissa put down her wineglass to accept the device. It was fully charged, and there was already a text from her dad, letting her know they'd been updated on the situation, had

HOLD ON TO ME

things under control, and were anxious to talk to her as soon as she was able to call.

The message reassured her.

She typed a quick response, informing them she'd arrived safely and would be in touch soon.

"Obviously we'd prefer you not tell anyone else your whereabouts." Without waiting for a response, he continued the tour. "Your bathroom is over here."

Her mouth fell open. It was massive, luxurious, spa-like with a sophisticated-looking steam shower, and her greatest wish had been answered—a soaker tub. A long white robe hung from a hook on the back of the door. This was as classy as the best hotels she'd stayed at. "Are you kidding me?"

A sudden grin transformed his features, making him seem younger, somewhat less formidable. Standing this close, in intimate quarters, arousal galloped through her. "I take it you're not unhappy?"

This time, she was sure it wasn't just the lack of sleep that was affecting her hormones. It was also a result of the alcohol's slow burn.

Turning away from him, she cleared her throat. Unfortunately it didn't help to tame her heart's frantic response to his overwhelming masculinity.

She struggled to pretend this was a normal situation. "This is about the size of my entire apartment." And she wasn't sure she'd be able to return home after being cocooned in this kind of luxury. "Are you sure you haven't given me the master suite?"

"I'm downstairs. In another wing. I'll include it in tomorrow's tour of the grounds."

That sounded as dangerous as it was tempting.

"I'm sure you'll be safe here, but that button next to the light switch"—he pointed—"is for emergency situations. There's another on the nightstand. You'll find them in every room of the house. I'll be alerted twenty-four seven, no matter where I am. Don't hesitate to use it. I'd rather it be a false alarm than take a risk with your safety."

Hating the reminder of why she was here, she nodded.

"Sleep as late as you want. We're not on a time schedule."

"At this point, I might not see you until this evening."

"In that case we'll have dinner instead of breakfast. Good night."

He left, closing the door behind him.

She remained where she was, listening for his receding footsteps. They never came.

A full minute later, she toed off her shoes. She contemplated falling face-first onto the bed. But there was no way she could sleep in the clothes she'd worked in, traveled in.

A yawn overtook her, and she decided to take a shower rather than a bath since it would be faster.

Thoughtfully, a dispenser had been filled with shampoo, conditioner, and even lavender-scented soap.

After turning off the water, she wrapped her hair in a towel, then dried herself. Then, unable to resist, she snuggled into the warm, thick robe before crossing to the closet to see what Hawkeye had sent.

One box was filled with electronics, and the other contained her personal items. Cosmetics, hairbrushes, shoes, socks, jeans, shorts, tops for every possible temperature, jackets, sports bras, *panties...*

Dear God. Let it have been Kayla who'd gone through her dresser drawers.

Elissa dug to the bottom and found no pajamas.

No doubt it had been Hawkeye who selected everything. Damn it.

From somewhere close, the unmistakable rumble of Jacob's voice reached her. Curious, and hoping she could borrow a T-shirt, she left the room.

HOLD ON TO ME

Down the hallway, a light blazed, and she walked toward it. *Like a moth to a flame?*

When she found Jacob, she froze.

He was seated behind a console, and in front of him were numerous large screens split into sections that contained a video feed. Most of the images were of the outdoors—the gate, dirt road, driveway, front door, sides of the house, and the patio. Others showed pictures of the home's interior, including the kitchen, living room, entryway, and a bedroom with a king-size bed with navy blue comforter. His?

"Elissa." He spoke without looking toward her.

How did he know she was there?

He tapped an icon and removed his headset. "Is there something you need?"

"Have you been spying on me?" She dragged the robe's lapels close together, as if that would protect her. "Are you some sort of sick pervert who gets his jollies out of something like that?"

"No." He spun in his chair, but he didn't get up. "To both of your questions."

"Oh." She exhaled her flare of indignation.

"Come here."

She didn't want to. Shouldn't. "I—"

"Come here."

Because of *that* tone, uncompromising in the same way as it had been when he'd tossed her over his shoulder and kidnapped her, she moved toward him, stopping when she was in front of him.

Even though he was seated, he radiated an aura of command, and goose bumps chilled her arms.

"Your opinion of me is clear. And somewhat unfair. You have a certain degree of privacy while you're my guest."

At that, she scoffed. *"Guest?"*

"Use whatever term you prefer, Elissa. But I guarantee

you this—if you were my prisoner, things would be different."

She took a step back, but he prevented another by snagging one of her wrists with his massive hand.

"There's a room near mine. A whole lot less pleasant than the one I gave you. I spend a lot of time on the range, and I know a thing or two about ropes. It'd only take a few seconds to tie you up, maybe secure you to a bed."

Jesus. She shivered. What the hell was happening here? His words sparked fantasies, turning her insides molten.

"Or maybe you'd like that?"

Desperately she snatched her wrist away from him.

"This"—he turned toward his command post and pointed to a blank section on one of the screens—"is the feed from your room."

"Oh." What else did she say to that and her wild accusation?

"I don't spy on women, Elissa." He cocked his head to the side to look up at her.

He was close enough for her to be frighteningly fascinated by the pulse ticking at his temple. She'd either pissed him off or insulted him. Perhaps both. Maybe she should apologize, but in these extraordinary circumstances, she couldn't find the words.

"Believe it or not, I only associate with women who are willing."

And no doubt there were plenty of them. Not only was the man an alpha—he was gorgeous, protective, and apparently rich. "I shouldn't have jumped to conclusions."

"Thank you for that." The furrow between his eyebrows eased. "Apology accepted."

That was it? For two years, she'd been involved in a relationship with a man who was quick to anger, for the smallest of reasons. She'd had to earn his forgiveness. One time, he'd

HOLD ON TO ME

given her the silent treatment for days before ungenerously doling out his attention again.

Her parents and friends encouraged her to leave him. Once she did, it had taken her a long time to realize he'd used his temper to control her.

That Jacob offered forgiveness quickly and unconditionally left her reeling.

"You sought me out for a reason, presumably?"

"I…" She exhaled. The reason no longer seemed important. Needing space, she took a step away from him. "Hawkeye forgot to pack my pajamas."

"Hawkeye had nothing to do with it. The oversight was mine."

"Yours?" He'd gone through her lingerie drawer? The realization left her breathless. Had his selection been random? Or had he deliberately chosen things that appealed to him?

"Sleepwear never occurred to me."

Of course it hadn't. "Why? I mean…"

"Hawkeye sent a small team to your apartment. I gathered belongings. A technician backed up your computer after verifying there were no viruses on it."

"I guess I don't need to mention that it was password protected."

"A combination of your birthday and initials. Took about ten seconds to get in."

She sighed.

Jacob swiveled to switch to another set of videos. "This is your front door." He pointed to another screen. "And your street."

It was strangely fascinating to see a neighbor walking toward his car carrying a coffee mug.

"There's an app on your phone so that you can look anytime you want."

"Are there any cameras inside my place?"

He shook his head.

Thank God for that. "Do you or Hawkeye have any other nasty surprises in store for me?"

Once again, he turned toward her. "All of these precautions are because you matter to Hawkeye. Other clients pay premium prices for this kind of service."

"I'm supposed to be *grateful?*" Her life had become a surreal nightmare.

Rather than answer, he changed the subject. "Is there a reason you came looking for me? Did you need something? Companionship, perhaps?"

"Absolutely not." Never from him. "I was wondering if you, maybe, you know… The sleepwear you forgot to pack. Do you have a T-shirt I can borrow?"

"Yeah. Of course. In my room." He rolled his chair to the side, then turned and stood. "I'll get you one. Or you can help yourself."

Go in his room? She shook her head.

"I was heading downstairs anyway. Come with me."

It made sense. The suggestion was innocent enough. But every instinct screamed against that. He might actually have strong morals, but she'd glimpsed the wolf beneath that polished exterior.

"You're safe." He strode past her.

Her senses ignited, and in that instant she recognized the truth. She wasn't scared of him. She hungered for him. The power of her need terrified her.

When he started down the stairs, she followed, rationalizing that she was an adult. If he could behave, she could put a cage around her own attraction.

"This way."

His private wing of the house had a different aura. The woods were darker, and so were the colors. There were no

HOLD ON TO ME

pictures on the walls, and that was when she realized the ones in the entryway and living room were of landscapes, revealing nothing personal.

They passed a couple of closed doors. Was one of them protecting the room he'd threatened her with? The one she wouldn't want to stay in? "Were you kidding earlier? About ropes and such?"

"As you've noticed, I don't joke often."

She shivered.

Without hesitating, he continued through the open door of the master bedroom. After a misstep, she went in after him.

A gigantic four-poster bed barely took up any space. French doors opened to the patio, now bathed in soft morning light. Again, there were no pictures or clutter. It was stark. Sterile. As if he had no past, no present, and wanted to leave no mark on the world.

Or maybe she was being fanciful.

"All of my clothes are in the closet." He tossed his keys on top of a nightstand. "Help yourself."

That seemed really personal, but so was wearing his clothes. "You don't mind?"

"Not in the least."

Because he organized with military precision, it took no time to find exactly what she was looking for on a shelf.

Clutching a black T-shirt in front of her, she rejoined him.

He was pulling off his belt, and he stopped when he saw her.

"I, uhm… This will work." Heaven help her. Standing this close to Jacob in his room made arousal ripple through her, freezing her in place. Coming in here with him had been a horrible mistake. To save herself, she had to escape from his room. *Now.*

213

"You're welcome."

The sensual, intimate rumble in his voice short-circuited her brain cells, leaving her rooted to the spot.

As if compelled by the same madness that gripped her, he took a step toward her. "Elissa." He cupped her shoulders, his touch as gentle as it was reassuring.

She leaned into him, anticipating, hoping…

"Jesus." He took a breath and closed his eyes. When he opened them again, their gazes collided. She saw hunger in the dark green depths, combined with hesitancy and remnants of the pain she'd glimpsed earlier.

"We shouldn't."

He was right, but she thirsted too much to refuse him.

"You're my client." Possessively rather than painfully, he dug his fingers into her skin. "Mine to protect."

His words fanned a feminine response she'd never before experienced. Her heart raced, and the floor seemed to sway beneath her. Jacob Walker was as dangerous as he was irresistible. And she had to know what he tasted like. "Kiss me?" It was an invitation as much as a plea.

"Elissa…" But even as he shook his head, he continued to hold her as if he'd never let go. "These are unusual circumstances, and your emotions are likely heightened."

If the darkness of his eyes was any indication, he was not immune to her either.

"You might regret this."

"I know what I'm doing." The only thing she would regret was passing up this moment. "Kiss me."

Fire flared in his eyes. Then, with a groan, he brushed his lips across hers.

The fleeting touch wasn't enough. "Jacob…"

He drew her up onto her tiptoes and captured her mouth, seeking entrance.

This time there was nothing gentle about him. His tongue

HOLD ON TO ME

sought and found hers. Tasting of temptation, he staked a claim, feeding one hand into the strands of her hair to ease back her head.

In response to his silent demand, she opened wider, granting him the access he demanded.

As their tongues danced, her knees weakened. Desperate for the support, she reached up to entwine her hands behind his neck.

His arousal pressed against her soft belly. She was open, exposed, vulnerable in a way she never had been before, and for that moment, she was his for the taking.

The kiss went on forever yet ended too soon.

Before releasing her, he gently bit her lower lip, leaving behind a tiny sting that would remind her of this moment.

"You're beautiful, Elissa. Everything I imagined." He touched her swollen lips. "And now I need you to go to your room and lock the door. Or else I will tie you to my bed for the rest of the night."

She gasped.

"Jesus. You have to leave." He walked to the door and stood beside it purposefully.

For a shocking, horrifying moment, she considered disobeying him.

"Please." His hoarse plea sounded as if it had been dragged through gravel, promising her he'd follow through with his threat if she didn't leave.

Sleeping with her kidnapper would be insanity. She told herself it was the situation, or maybe the wine, maybe the lateness of the hour, but she'd momentarily lost her head.

Still, on her way past him, she paused.

"No matter what, don't unlock your door for me."

She shivered, as much from the threat as from the power of her own sexual response to him.

215

CHAPTER THREE

HAWKEYE

Elissa needed tea. Or really, anything infused with caffeine, hot or cold, was fine.

She dropped her forearm over her eyes.

Even though the bed was comfortable, she hadn't managed to sleep for more than a few hours. The bright Colorado sun blasted the room, despite the fact that the blinds were closed. And the deadline to get designs over to her client was only a couple of days away, creating anxiety. Not that she needed more of that.

In flashes, memories of the previous night rushed through her mind, from the strange attraction at the pub, to the hardness of his body as he'd swept her from the ground and tossed her over his shoulder. Then...the kiss. Her lower lip still tingled from Jacob's passion.

What was worse was how close she'd come to asking him to tie her up.

As long as she could remember, she'd wanted to experiment with BDSM, but she'd never had a partner willing to explore with her. Jacob, on the other hand, had read her accurately, and she had no doubt he was capable of giving her everything she desired.

Yet he was the one man she dared not play with. It would lead to nothing other than heartache.

The craziness of the situation would be over soon, maybe in a few days. She'd go back to her life. No way could she become attached either physically or emotionally to another former military man who operated in the shadows.

But still, no matter how hard she tried to shove aside thoughts of last night or the stupidity of finishing what had started in his bedroom, the stronger and more tantalizing they became.

Frustrated, she flipped onto her stomach.

Despite her efforts to control her runaway fantasies, she imagined he actually had kept her in his room and tied her to his massive bed.

First, he would strip off her clothes and trail his fingers across her needy body. Once she was aroused, he'd pick her up and place her on the mattress. Then he'd exert his masculine dominance, securing her with ropes while she writhed, captured, unable to escape his sexual determination.

She'd gasp when he played with her pussy, and she'd silently beg him to take her. And when he did, it would be as powerful as a storm.

The pictures flashing like strobe lights through her brain made her clit throb.

She needed to orgasm.

Maybe that would put a stop to the stampede of impossible, tempting thoughts. Surrendering, just for the moment, she reached a hand beneath her pelvis and pressed against her clit.

She moaned into the pillow.

Then all of a sudden she was lost…in a fever of arousal, grinding her hips, seeking release. Elissa slipped two fingers

HOLD ON TO ME

inside herself, wishing instead that it was Jacob's massive cock filling her.

Faster and faster, she moved, thinking about the sight of him holding his belt, the leather tantalizing.

Within moments, she climaxed, screaming his name, praying he didn't hear her.

For moments afterward, she lay there, her breaths disjointed as she labored to return to reality.

The climax had been as swift as it was powerful. But shockingly, she was still thinking about Jacob.

What's wrong with me?

Elissa didn't masturbate often, and when she did, she was generally satisfied for days, maybe even a week. This internal hunger for a specific man was new. And she didn't like it. She wasn't the type of woman to think about sex all the time. Or, rather, she hadn't been until the cowboy uprooted her life.

Determinedly she punched her pillow into a different shape while telling herself to focus on something else. Like work. That was always her favorite refuge. She had to decide on the colors and fonts to communicate her client's brand. He was a motivational speaker, and she wanted something engaging, a bit bold to reflect his personality, but it also needed to invite trust. Meeting planners had to be confident when booking him.

In the distance, a door closed.

Did that mean Jacob had left the house?

If so, maybe it was safe to get her tea so she could hurry back to the sanctuary of her room.

Seizing the opportunity, she turned over, then climbed out of bed.

After pulling on a pair of leggings but not changing out of his T-shirt, she headed downstairs only to freeze once she reached the kitchen.

Jacob was there, leaning against the countertop, a mug in

hand. He wore a skimpy pair of swim trunks and nothing else. His short hair was wet and slicked back, while droplets of water clung to his broad chest.

As she watched, fascinated, unable to look away, one arrowed downward, stopping right above his waistband.

The man was a living Adonis.

Every muscle was chiseled, and he didn't carry an ounce of fat anywhere. Numerous scars attested to his rough life, feeding her curiosity. As crazy as it was, she hungered to know everything about him.

"Morning."

She looked up and met his gaze, flushing when she realized she'd been caught staring at him.

As if they shared a secret, he smiled, making him even more lethal to her senses.

She would have dressed properly before coming down if she'd realized he was in the house. Self-conscious, hyperaware of his masculinity, she cleared her throat before pulling back her shoulders and pretending that this was a common experience.

"Did I wake you up?"

"No. I mean, not really. I heard a door close. I thought you'd left."

"Spent a few minutes in the hot tub, then had a swim."

She tucked wayward strands of hair behind her ears. Being in intimate quarters with a captor, especially after a sizzling kiss, was a new experience, and she had no idea how to act. She thought fast, struggling for some sort of normalcy. "I need to get some work done." If that was even possible.

"Can I get you a cup of coffee first? It's fresh."

"Tempting. But I was thinking about tea this morning." Besides, the stainless-steel carafe was on the counter next to him, and she didn't want to get that close.

"There should be some in the pantry."

HOLD ON TO ME

The shelves were well stocked, including numerous boxes of tea, and she went straight for the Earl Grey. "Yesterday, you mentioned I have a new computer here?"

"Ready to set up anywhere you wish. You could share my office."

"Uh..." She frantically thought. "The kitchen table would be fine."

"There's an apartment above the garage. Originally it was a stable and bunkhouse, but I had it converted. It has great light. There's even a small kitchen and a desk. You might enjoy the space and feel like you have a little freedom."

A small mercy. "You mean I don't have to stay in the house with you all day?" Because she wasn't sure she could survive that.

"Of course not. I want you to be comfortable."

"As if."

He inclined his head in acknowledgment. "As much as possible, then." He took a drink. "You'll find an internet connection throughout the property, so you can work almost anywhere. The hot tub and pool are at your disposal as well."

"I didn't see a swimsuit in the box."

"You don't need one."

She notched up her chin. "I don't skinny-dip."

"Pity."

The atmosphere crackled around her, supercharged, like the moment right before lightning struck.

It was then that she noticed his trunks were dry. That meant either he'd changed—which was unlikely—or he'd put them on after he exited the pool. Had he been prowling around outside naked?

Heaven help me. There was no way she would ever get that image out of her mind.

"You can always wear a bra and panties, if your modesty matters."

Not that he'd packed any underwear that covered much. He'd skipped briefs in favor of thongs and boy shorts.

"The housekeeper isn't here today, and none of the ranch hands will head this direction without my prior approval. Hawkeye has a few agents stationed nearby, but your privacy will always be respected." He refilled his mug. "For the moment, it's just the two of us."

Just the two of us. His words unnerved her. Was there anything more dangerous to her senses? "Thank you for the offer, but I'll keep my clothes on."

His quick grin disarmed her.

How many dimensions were there to this man?

"Can I get you some breakfast?"

"Uhm…"

"I want to make sure I meet all your basic needs."

She blinked. Were they talking about food?

"Thought I'd treat you to my specialty. French toast stuffed with cream cheese and covered with strawberry topping."

On cue, her stomach grumbled. "If you're serious, yes. Please." In the mornings, Elissa generally grabbed a bagel. It required no effort, and she could eat at her desk while reading her emails and catching up on the news. "Is there anything I can do to help?"

"Just worry about your tea. Not one of my specialties."

Since she was helping out at the pub and had recently been spending her time serving others, having someone take care of her needs was the ultimate luxury.

While he whipped up some eggs and added sugar and vanilla along with a generous shake of cinnamon, she placed a cup of water in the microwave to heat up. She was careful not to bump into him, something that wasn't easy. His movements were efficient, but he was so large that he dwarfed the space.

HOLD ON TO ME

Once her beverage was ready, she carried the cup to the far side of the island and slid onto one of the stools. This far apart, with an expanse of marble separating them, she shouldn't be aware of his every motion. Yet she knew exactly what he was doing, even without looking, as if her senses were supercharged.

He turned on two burners and straddled them with a griddle.

"Are you sure there's nothing I can do? Set the table, maybe?"

"That would be great. I thought we might eat on the patio. It's nice enough."

He told her where to find everything, and she once again took care to skirt by him without touching. With everything gathered on a tray, she fled from the house and her dangerous desire for him.

Outside, she released a breath, not just because she was away from him, but also because of the endless vista and the warmth of the sun on her bare skin.

The sky was a stunning shade of bright blue, and only a few wispy clouds floated by. The flagstones beneath her bare feet were warmer than she expected for so early in the summer. Numerous lounge chairs were scattered in various groupings and accented by huge potted plants and trees. Off to one side was a stone firepit with wicker furniture in front of it.

After arranging plates and silverware on the metal table, she made another trip for their beverages, and a final one for the strawberry topping. Then, since he was still cooking, she walked toward the gazebo at the edge of the patio. The lightest hint of a breeze stirred the late-morning air.

Her initial impression of the ranch hadn't prepared her for the actual experience of breathing in fresh Rocky Mountain air. In the distance, a single mountain dominated the

SIERRA CARTWRIGHT

landscape. Because she lived in suburban Denver, she rarely glimpsed an unobstructed view of anything. The landscape beckoned, making her want to explore her surroundings.

Just as quickly as the idea occurred to her, she shoved it away. Being here was temporary, and she'd never have the opportunity to return.

Inside the house, dishes clattered, signaling that Jacob was wrapping up, and she wandered to the pool area. The water rippled and reflected sunlight, making her wish he actually had packed a swimsuit for her.

When she reached the hot tub, she was unable to resist temptation, and she crouched to dip her hand into the warmth.

"You sure you don't want to get in?" he shouted from the back door.

And have him watch me walk around naked? "No." *Maybe.*

Her heart fluttering again, she met him at the table and sat down across from him. In addition to the French toast, he'd brought out a bottle of pure maple syrup and a platter of bacon. He was a man after her heart.

The meal was prepared perfectly. The bread had exactly the right amount of batter, and it was golden brown. A hint of the filling peeked out around the edges. "Looks amazing." She filled her plate, then took a bite and sighed. "Do you treat all your captives this well?"

"I prefer the term client. Or protectee." He snapped his fingers. "Wait. As I said before, guest is even better. It makes a difference to your experience. Therefore, service matters, which you know all about since your family is in the hospitality industry. We're hoping you'll leave Hawkeye a good review online and recommend us to your friends and family."

At his absurdity, she couldn't help but grin.

"I'm hoping you'll give us five stars for the Morning Star

HOLD ON TO ME

Suite here at the Starlight Mountain Ranch. I trust the bed is comfortable enough?"

Seduced by the meal, his smile, the surroundings, and his banter, she played along. "Definitely. Exceeded my expectations." Which was true. "The fluffy robe is a nice touch. If I take it home, can you add the cost to my bill?"

"It's complimentary with every five-day stay."

How different would the experience be if she really were his guest here? Everything about the place was spectacular. Over the years, she'd paid a lot of money to relax and recharge at nearby lodges and spas, but she'd never had any of them to herself.

As they ate, he informed her the distant peak was named Saddle Mountain. Then he gave her the history of the ranch, including the struggles each generation had gone through to hold on to it.

"Ranching isn't easy. And the world isn't either. My great-grandparents lost their only son in a war. There are challenges with fluctuating beef prices, drought, fights over water rights. Weather. Always the weather. One thing my grandfather was interested in was cross-breeding. Our cattle can survive the harshest winters and terrain. Because of that, we sell them all over the country, including Montana and Wyoming."

"I didn't even know that was a thing."

"It took us years to get it where it is now. Still a long way to go. But his foresight has been the thing that has helped us hold on to the property."

She sipped from her now cool tea. "You love it here."

Before answering, he looked into the distance. "I didn't always." He pushed his empty plate aside. "It took being gone to appreciate my roots."

"Did you leave to work with Hawkeye?"

SIERRA CARTWRIGHT

A red-tailed hawk screeched in the sky, then soared on a thermal.

"No. Much earlier than that. I joined the military right after college."

"So that's where the two of you met?"

"Yeah." He faced her again. "In another lifetime."

"Sometimes I think he never came back."

Jacob inclined his head to one side, watching her carefully. "You've known him a long time."

"No. I mean... As the calendar goes, yes. Years. But I don't know him at all." She shook her head. "For a little while, I thought maybe I did. Then one day he was gone. And I mean that literally. I saw him almost every day, and then...nothing."

Jacob fixed her with his intense gaze. "You were hurt?"

"Of course." A little lost. Bereft, but more than anything, confused. She'd become accustomed to Hawkeye coming into the pub late every afternoon. He'd spend hours there, staying until well after dark. They enjoyed deep conversation, and he'd taken her out for dinner on a couple of occasions. One moonless evening, after he'd walked her home, they shared a meaningful kiss on her front porch. She'd gone to bed wondering if their relationship would develop into something more substantial.

She never expected he'd leave without saying goodbye. Less than a week later, he called to say he was no longer in the state and had no plans to return. "I thought we were friends, but the truth was, he'd never let me in. He never mentioned his family or his life before the military. I know something happened in..." She paused, wondering if he'd fill in the details. "Peru or Ecuador, if I recall."

"Close enough."

So Jacob knew. Or he'd been there as well. "It was as if

HOLD ON TO ME

he'd been at the pub physically, but somewhere else mentally."

"Yeah."

Jacob was slightly different. Just as strong. Rugged. Dangerous. But last night there'd been heat in his eyes. There'd been emotion in his voice when he commanded her to leave. It made him more complex, a little more human.

"He's worried about you." He steepled his index fingers. "Clearly you mean something to him."

She hesitated before replying. "Are you fishing for information, Jacob?"

"And if I am? Wondering what you mean to each other?"

Elissa sucked in a shallow breath. Asking about her entanglements indicated either a natural curiosity or something more. Since they'd kissed, she was willing to bet he wanted to be sure her relationship with his friend wouldn't come between them. Finally she exhaled. "To be honest, nothing other than friendship. When we met, I wondered if there might be something more." She shook her head. "There wasn't."

Because he allowed the silence to engulf them, she was compelled to continue. "That's why I'm frustrated by this whole thing. You know, the way you abducted me and—"

He winced, and she stopped talking.

"You've mentioned that once or twice."

"All I'm trying to say is that Hawkeye shouldn't be concerned for my well-being at all. No one really knew about us—not that there ever was an us." She shrugged. "You have to admit I have a point, though. Right? He's overreacting." She expected to garner sympathy or at least understanding. Instead, Jacob's features hardened, and shards of jade shot through his eyes.

"Hawkeye doesn't take chances with people who matter to him."

SIERRA CARTWRIGHT

"God, Jacob. Have you listened to a single word I've said? *I don't matter to him*, and I never did."

"Someone may believe differently. And that's the only thing that matters."

With a clatter, she put her cup down. The conversation was going nowhere. Jacob was loyal to his friend rather than to her.

"I have my orders."

Like a good military man, he would follow them. Why had she hoped for anything different?

After a long pause, he finally spoke. "How much do you know about what's going on?"

"Nothing. Absolutely nothing." She exhaled her frustration. "I'm struggling with all this drama. In my place, would you take it seriously?"

"He has a right-hand woman." His tone was measured, as if deciding how much information to divulge.

"Are you talking about Ms. Inamorata?"

"So you do know her?"

Elissa desperately wanted to yank back her words. "You miss nothing."

"My life, and those of others, has depended on it."

"I swear to you, it's been a long time since I've seen Hawkeye." It was important to her that Jacob understood completely.

"And?"

Things were suddenly more complicated. They were having two different discussions. One about her relationship with his friend. Another where she was trying to convince Jacob to let her go back to her regular life. "About a year ago, Hawkeye was passing through Denver, and he stopped in the pub and ordered a whiskey, neat. I brought him the wrong brand. In the years since I'd seen him, he'd switched to some-

HOLD ON TO ME

thing smoother and much more expensive. That's when we caught up."

Without responding, Jacob nodded.

Had her explanation satisfied him?

He tapped his fingers, as if contemplating how much to reveal. "Inamorata received a birthday card at her home, and there was white powder in it. Results have confirmed it was anthrax."

A chill rocked through Elissa, and she wrapped her arms around herself to ward it off. "Is she... Someone tried to..." *Oh no.* Despite herself, the news unnerved her. "Is she okay?"

"Yes. She was immediately started on antibiotics as a precaution, and there are no ill effects. In fact, she was furious at herself for opening the envelope and refused to take any time off work." He leveled a stare at her, and his eyes were icy enough to freeze her in place. "Whoever it is has already reached the upper levels of the company. We have no idea what kind of information he—or she—has access to." He paused. "It could be someone who works for the company."

For the first time, a tendril of doubt unfurled inside her. With determination, she tamped it down. No doubt the arrogant males surrounding her were overreacting. *But were they?*

"All of Hawkeye's resources are focused on this." His tone was as cold as it was detached.

"Jacob—"

"The sooner you accept reality and make yourself comfortable here, the easier this will be." He leaned toward her and imprisoned her gaze. "You're staying in protective custody until Hawkeye says otherwise. My decision is non-negotiable."

Even though Jacob made polite conversation through the rest of breakfast, his harsh words continued to echo in her ears. How was she supposed to be comfortable out here in the middle of nowhere, alone with a stranger who'd kissed her and haunted her dreams?

"Elissa?"

Since he was looking at her quizzically, she shook her head to clear it.

"I asked if you were finished eating."

"Yes. Thanks." She nodded, then, when he pushed back his chair and stood, followed suit.

Together, they cleared the table, then straightened the kitchen.

"I'll be in my office if you need anything." He inclined his head before walking away.

Under normal circumstances, she might have enjoyed his polite, old-fashioned charms. But she already knew what lay beneath the polished exterior.

Once the sound of his footsteps had vanished and silence shrouded her, she walked to the window and stared into the distance. Just yesterday, there hadn't been enough time to get everything done that she needed to. And now, the upcoming hours seemed to loom like an unpleasant specter.

Even more restless and uncertain than she had been before breakfast, she headed upstairs, quietly passing his office on the way to her bedroom.

She closed the door and then dialed her dad's phone number.

As the call connected, she paced the confines of her temporary bedroom. When she'd first arrived, the space seemed large and luxurious. Now it was claustrophobic, the walls closing in on her.

"Elissa, love!"

At the welcome sound of his voice, an emotional lifeline like it had always been, she collapsed her shoulders against the wall.

HOLD ON TO ME

"I know you've been texting, and Hawkeye's been keeping us posted, but it's good to hear from you."

She fought for normalcy in order to reassure him. "How are things in Ireland?"

"We're at the airport."

"What? The airport?"

"Hawkeye chartered a plane for us. Can you imagine? We're waiting for our flight now."

The news shouldn't have surprised her, but it did. "There's no need to cut your trip short." They needed the break. Deserved it. "This will all be over soon." It had to be.

"It's all arranged. Hawkeye's having us picked up when we arrive at the Denver airport and assigning us a security agent."

A chill shot up her spine. "What?"

"It's out of an abundance of caution."

She exhaled a worried sigh. This was all too much. And if Hawkeye were truly that concerned, wouldn't her parents be safer if they were out of the country? "Dad. Seriously. Stay there."

"Lovey, we insisted on it. Your mother wouldn't be able to sleep otherwise."

How had her entire life been so completely turned upside down?

"They're fetching us to board the plane. We love you, Liss."

They each said a quick goodbye, promised to talk again soon, and then she was left staring at a blank screen on her phone.

Still as restless as she had been, she dialed Joseph, who was covering for her.

"I'm already at the pub so Mary can update me on new procedures. Wanted to spend a couple of hours with her while I reorient."

231

SIERRA CARTWRIGHT

"Good idea."

"Everything's under control, and yes, I promise I'll call if I need you."

Talking to him made her feel as if she were doing something useful, even though she hadn't been needed at all. Others seemed to be handling all the pieces of her life, which meant she had the time she needed to work on her graphic arts project.

After showering then dressing in jeans and a long-sleeved shirt, she searched out Jacob. She knocked on the door where she'd previously found him, and when there was no answer, she called out his name and reached for the handle.

A red light on the wall next to the door blinked, and she noticed a small touchpad there. When she placed a fingertip against it, a buzzer blasted, the sharpness ricocheting around her and making her jump back.

More surprises.

She went downstairs and, when she didn't find him, continued toward his wing of the house. "Jacob?"

"Back here!"

Near his bedroom, one of the doors stood ajar.

Still, before crossing the threshold, she knocked.

"Enter."

When she did, he turned his chair toward her. His smile was inviting, sending another little tingle through her.

"I… Uh." She tucked hair behind her ear. "I didn't realize you had two offices."

"The other is more for cameras. In an emergency, it doubles as a panic room."

"Hence the door on it?"

"Actually you'll find that type of lock in several places in the house. Anywhere I might require privacy."

"The room you don't want me to see?" Why had she blurted that out? "Unless you were joking about having one."

232

HOLD ON TO ME

"No. I assure you I wasn't."

Fear collided with excitement and turned her tummy upside down.

"And yes, it's protected…with biometrics. Do you want to see it?"

"Absolutely not." *Yes. Desperately.*

His grin was quick, evil. "So there's something else I can do for you?"

He twitterpated her so much she had to shake her head to remember why she'd sought him out. "I need to do some work. So if the offer of using the garage apartment is still open, I'd like to take you up on it." Having separate spaces was more important now than it had been an hour ago. After his teasing invitation, she'd never be able to think as long as they were under the same roof.

"I'll walk you over."

She hurried back to the living room ahead of him so their bodies didn't come into close proximity. And then she followed him out the sliding glass patio door and across to the former barn.

The upstairs space blew her away. It wasn't a tiny office—it was more like an artist's studio, with wide-open spaces and massive windows that allowed plenty of sunlight. The honey-colored wood floors were divine. There was a comfortable-looking couch, a daybed, and an anti-gravity gaming chair behind an L-shaped desk that offered her more workspace than she'd ever enjoyed before. "This is as big as my apartment."

"You're pleased?"

"It's spectacular. Really. The views…" The windows were massive, and he'd been right about the natural light that filtered in.

"There's an attached deck, through that door. Make yourself comfortable while I bring over the computer."

SIERRA CARTWRIGHT

After he left, she took his advice and explored her temporary work area. There was a small powder room and a tiny kitchenette, complete with a small refrigerator that was stocked with water bottles and splits of champagne. This apartment couldn't be any more perfect for her.

Then she walked out onto the small deck. It was only big enough for a bistro set and a single Adirondack chair, but it overlooked the meadow and Saddle Mountain. It was a perfect place to escape with a cup of tea or an evening sip of bubbly.

Jacob returned with the box containing a sleek, space-agey titanium-encased tower. It was not just functional, but a work of art with the company's famous curved lines.

Awed, she trailed her fingers down the side. "I've never seen anything this beautiful."

"Not sure I have either. I'm told it's next year's Elite Pro model. And it's been upgraded with an additional twenty thousand dollars' worth of graphics cards."

"I'm…" *Speechless.* This was the stuff of dreams. She couldn't afford the base model, let alone the upgraded pro one. "Wow."

"Apparently Bonds said that you'd appreciate something this…" He cleared his throat.

Elissa waited.

"Sensuous."

Heat seared her cheeks. The mysterious Julien Bonds knew far too much about her. "He said that? Or are you making it up?"

"I assure you—sensuous is not a word I would have associated with a computer." He tucked the unit beneath the desk. "The monitor is significantly bigger."

"Do you need help?"

"You can hold the doors."

A few minutes later, in the apartment, he opened the box.

HOLD ON TO ME

Even though he was a big, muscular man, the thing was massive.

"Bonds included these." He handed her two smaller packages with her name on them, then read the enclosed note aloud. "Gadgets he thought you'd enjoy."

"This is like Christmas." Only better. She opened the first gift. "Oh my God. Drool-worthy."

"What is it?"

"Pen tablet."

"That means something to you?"

"I can draw free hand on the pad, and the image will appear on the screen. It's a much better quality than the one I already have."

"And the other thing?"

She tore open the gift and blinked. "It's an editing console, which means I don't need a mouse or keyboard to manipulate images." With her right hand, she showed him the wheels and buttons. "For example, this one is for contrast. No clicking on anything separate."

"Time saver?"

"Huge." It was impossible to believe that Julien Bonds had put all of this together for her.

Jacob placed the monitor stand on the desk. "Want to give me a hand with the screen?"

He sliced through the cardboard with a pocketknife, and then she jiggled the foam packaging loose.

Once she caught a glimpse of the frameless monitor, she gasped. "I've only seen things like this in museum displays and when I've watched videos of the big electronics show." It took both of them to secure it in place. "I'm just flabbergasted." The screen was at least fifty-five inches. "It weighs a ton."

"Sixty pounds or thereabouts."

Within minutes, he had the entire thing put together and connected to the internet.

SIERRA CARTWRIGHT

The Bonds logo winked into view in the middle of the see-through glass, and the crispness took her breath away. "This is unbelievable."

"The tag says it displays over a billion colors."

"That shouldn't even be possible." She wrapped her arms around herself. "I can't believe I get to work on this." But she was afraid she'd never want to give it up when she returned to her real life. Even monthly payments on this would be equal to a car. "I'll leave you to enjoy your new toy." After pointing out where panic buttons were located, Jacob programmed his phone number into her new cell phone. "As I stated earlier, there are agents on the property. I have one stationed at the gate, and two on perimeter patrol. However, you're not likely to see them. Anything else?"

"I think this more than covers it. I couldn't be happier. I mean, you know…"

"Given the situation?"

"I don't want to sound ungrateful."

"Being at a safe house is always an adjustment."

And that was exactly what this was. "Thank you. Not for bringing me here, but for—"

He held up a hand. "Let's leave it at thank you. And you're welcome." With a curt, dismissive nod, he excused himself.

She paced to the window and watched him until he closed the patio door behind him.

For the first half hour, she played with the computer, learning her way around before opening her design program, then clicking on the icon for her client's collateral.

After making a few adjustments, she let her mind wander.

The new machine—combined with the surroundings— should have been enough to inspire her for weeks. Yet she couldn't concentrate.

Elissa grabbed a bottle of water from the tiny refrigerator. A loud whinny captured her attention, and she paced to

HOLD ON TO ME

the window. Seconds later, Jacob rode into view on horse-back, tall in the saddle, wearing a cowboy hat. Even though he was far away, there was no mistaking the rope attached to the saddle.

Again, unbidden, his soft threat from the night before teased the edges of her memory.

He continued on, and soon two other men galloped toward him. When they were close, each rider pulled up and formed a semicircle. Because she wanted a better view, she went out onto the deck.

The impromptu meeting lasted for at least ten minutes, and she watched every moment, shamelessly drinking in the masculine and commanding sight of him. If only they'd met under other circumstances...

At an easy canter, the party loped away, toward the open valley. Without looking back toward her, Jacob lifted a hand in a silent acknowledgment.

He'd been aware of her the whole time?

She uncapped her bottle. Of course he knew exactly where she was. No doubt he had some sort of cell phone app that was streaming images of every part of the property.

When they disappeared over a hill, she went back inside, leaving the door open.

This time, when she sat back down at her desk, she was inspired, but not to work on the project that was due at the end of the week. Instead, she accessed one of her private folders, containing the images that Julien Bonds had called kinky shit.

He might be right. No doubt plenty of people would agree.

To her, though, it was more, a pure and honest expression of sensual pleasure.

In college, she'd taken all the art classes that were offered. As part of her final grade, she'd had to display her work at a

237

small avant-garde gallery in Denver. Her drawing of a nude caught the eye of a Dominant who had then commissioned her to paint a portrait of his submissive.

When she'd arrived at their house for the initial interview, the Dom had outlined his expectations. It needed to capture emotion. While most of Lydia's body was to be bare, scarlet silk should cover her most private areas. He wanted to see just a hint of her nipples through the fabric—as if she were a precious gift to be unwrapped only by him.

And then he'd brought out heavy, thick silver chains.

Elissa had gasped at the sight. Until that moment, she'd known nothing about BDSM, and seeing the way Lydia glanced up at her Dominant with a soft smile rocked Elissa, expanding her view of the world.

Then, he'd nodded, and Lydia sank to her knees.

Belatedly Elissa grabbed her phone and snapped a dozen pictures of the sub, capturing her expression of adoring, blissful surrender.

During the weeks they worked together, Elissa received an education about Dominance, submission, what BDSM was, and what it wasn't.

The dynamic intrigued her enough to accept their invitation to attend an open house at a downtown Denver club and to eventually scene with a couple different Dominants.

Later, she'd entered that ill-fated relationship with Robby. It had taken months and endless conversations with other submissives to help Elissa realize that his need to manipulate her had nothing to do with actual Dominance.

For a while after that, she would only scene with one of the club's owners. Once she regained her bearings and learned to trust her newfound intuition, she moved on to other partners.

Because of her father's illness and the sheer number of hours she worked, Elissa hadn't been to the club since last

HOLD ON TO ME

summer. She'd missed it terribly—not just the connection with another person, but the sublime transcendence that occurred when she surrendered to an honorable Dominant.

Shoving aside the restlessness churning inside her, she opened one of her completed files and critically studied the image.

According to Hawkeye, Julien had suggested she show some of her work. She hated to disagree with a renowned genius, but clearly she didn't have enough talent. These images wouldn't be good enough even if she painted them as actual portraits—maybe because each subject reflected some part of her own personality.

Dismissing Julien's opinion as kind and nothing more, she minimized the image and opened one she'd been playing with for days.

In it, the submissive was kneeling back on her heels in front of a standing Dominant. Her head was bowed, and her dark hair fell over her face, shading her features. The backs of her hands rested lightly on her thighs. She wore a short gossamer gown, and a small collar circled her neck.

The man held a delicate chain, and he looked at his submissive with absolute adoration.

Elissa wrinkled her nose as she zoomed in on the Dom's features. Her intent was to show that he didn't need anything substantial to secure the woman's compliance. Their relationship was based on love and trust, respect, as well as consent.

The image wasn't quite what she wanted. Something was still missing.

Using the highly responsive mouse, she darkened the background to add a little more intensity. Then, still not satisfied, she changed the first layer entirely, making it dark gray so the submissive's gown appeared more ethereal.

Better.

But still not exactly what she was striving for.

Something about the man's facial features wasn't quite right. Maybe he needed to be a little more intense. With a few deft strokes, his jawline became more angular. Then she selected a deeper shade of green for his eyes.

Each alteration brought him into sharper relief, pleasing her.

Continuing on, she gave his abs slightly more definition before adding a small scar to his torso. She didn't want him to be perfect—she wanted him to be real, with flaws that made him human and gave him the capacity to care.

Then, satisfied, she enlarged the entire image to fill her screen.

In stunned fascination, she blinked.

The changes made her Dom resemble Jacob. *What in the hell?*

"Chardonnay?"

Screaming, heart pounding from sudden panic, she jumped.

"Didn't mean to frighten you."

Slowly, she spun her chair to face the door.

Jacob.

Late-afternoon sunshine silhouetting him, he stood in the entryway, holding an insulated tumbler that served as a wineglass. "I knocked. Dinner's close to being ready, and I thought you might want to unwind a bit first."

"I..." Somehow, she'd lost track of the hours. "That's thoughtful."

He stepped across the threshold and closed the door behind him.

Obviously he'd showered after his ride. The scent of summer wrapped around him, and his dark hair was still damp. He'd changed into a navy T-shirt and blue jeans. And

HOLD ON TO ME

it was everything she could do to pretend she wasn't turned on by him.

"Mind if I have a look at what you're working on?"

Horrified, she turned back to her computer to hide the image. But since the computer was slightly different from hers, the key she pushed didn't make the screen go blank.

He moved in behind her and looked at the screen over her shoulder. "That's…"

What? Had he noticed the Dom's resemblance to him? Or maybe the connection was only clear to her. She held her breath as she waited for him to speak.

"Is this what Bonds was talking about? The art he thinks should be in a gallery?"

Embarrassment raked through her, and she gave up on the lie that they were for a client. "This one is a rough draft." It shouldn't matter what the hell he thought, yet his opinion was important to her.

"It's stunning. And if you have others that are equally as good, I'm really impressed."

His warm approval sent shivers dancing up her spine.

"I'd like to have a look at all of them." His voice was soft with invitation.

She wasn't sure that was a good idea. Showing him would expose her in a way she'd never been before, making her vulnerable.

He waited in respectful silence.

Then, with a soft sigh, decision made, she opened another folder and selected the slideshow setting.

Each of her images appeared onscreen for a few seconds before vanishing.

When the final one faded and she clicked the mouse to exit, he took a step back, and she swiveled to face him.

"Bonds is right. They're spectacular."

She'd given Jacob her trust, and he'd honored it.

SIERRA CARTWRIGHT

"You should consider it."

Her hand trembled as she accepted the chardonnay. "I have line drawings of course. But painting actual portraits? It's time-consuming, and that's something that's in short supply right now. Maybe after my parents get back from Ireland." And life returned to normal. Whatever that was. "And I'm not sure any gallery would actually display them."

"Why not?"

She scowled at him. Was he dense? "In case you haven't noticed, they're more than a little risqué."

"And tasteful. There's nothing overtly sexual. In fact, they're more intimate than anything."

Her mouth fell open a little at his observation. That was exactly what she'd been hoping to convey, but that he'd gotten it made her heart soar.

"That makes them perfect for collectors and lifestyle connoisseurs. I'm sure there are online options for sales as well."

"Honestly, I'd never considered it."

"If Bonds believes there's an opportunity, there is. Or he'll create one."

"I appreciate your feedback." She took a long, fortifying sip to cover her nerves and embarrassment.

"Are they inspired by real-life events?"

She choked on her wine. Of course he was curious. But wanting to avoid this type of prying question was one of the reasons she'd never shared her art. "Let's just say I have an active imagination."

"Do you now?" He tipped his head to the side—seeing through her half answer?

He didn't pursue his line of questions, which should have relieved her. Instead, disappointment churned through her. For the first time in over a year, she wanted to be pushed.

Jacob appealed to her on so many levels, and every femi-

HOLD ON TO ME

nine instinct hummed with awareness. She longed to be in his arms, once again crumbling beneath the demand of his kisses.

"Is everything okay?"

"Fine." She shook her head to vanquish her absurd thoughts. "Yes. Of course. Why?"

"Do you have any experience?"

"Uhm…" He couldn't possibly mean what she thought he did. *Could he?* "With?"

"BDSM."

Her pulse skittered to a stop before racing on frantically. Maybe she wasn't ready for this after all.

As if he had all the time and patience in the world, he widened his stance, then folded his arms across his chest and regarded her.

His actions were so perfectly Dominant that instinctive arousal crashed through her.

The silence dragged while she squirmed.

As she'd guessed, this man knew exactly who she was, what her needs were. If she wanted, she could change the subject or refuse to answer. Or she could take a chance and see where things went. With a nervous sigh, she told him the truth. "Yes. I have some experience."

"And are you planning to ask me to give you what you want?"

Her tummy plunged into a terrifying freefall. "I'm…" Heaven save her from this man and the way he so perfectly read her. "I'm not sure what you mean."

"No? I think maybe you're deflecting, Elissa. And when you're ready, it's safe to tell me the truth about who you are."

CHAPTER FOUR

HAWKEYE

Jacob was taking a gamble. A big fucking one. But the military and life-and-death black ops situations had honed his instincts and taught him to respect his hunches.

And the beautiful woman with wide, unblinking eyes and with her mouth slightly parted in shock was a submissive. Even if instinct hadn't told him that, her stunning art would have.

Elissa was capable and resourceful, no doubt. Strong enough to live her life on her own terms. While he was at her family's pub, he'd studied her. She managed the place well, took care of the customers, and had been polite but direct when she told him it was time to leave. And then, outside, she'd been resolute in her determination not to go with him.

In addition to being attracted to her, he respected her. And there was no mistaking the fact that the male subject in the image she was working on resembled him.

The kiss last night had proven that she was interested in him. The question was, what were they going to do about it? He wasn't inclined to ignore it, but getting involved with a

SIERRA CARTWRIGHT

client was beyond stupid. He didn't take unnecessary risks. Or hadn't, until now. Elissa was no ordinary woman, and he'd never had a reaction to a woman like he did to her.

He continued to wait, wondering if she'd go on. If she didn't, that was answer enough, and he would respect her boundary.

The next move was hers entirely.

"You've already seen more than most people." Ambiguity hedged her response, and she knitted her fingers together around her glass, maybe to disguise her nervousness.

"I appreciate your belief in me." There was no gift more valuable.

"But for me, I guess the question is, who are you, Jacob? Beyond someone Hawkeye trusts with my life? A man who lives far away from the world, in his own private fortress? Someone who gets what he wants?" She tilted her head back to look up at him.

On some level, the fact she remained where she was and he stood so near, towering over her, was the first step in the dance that might culminate in a D/s experience. "Are you asking if I understand what I'd need to do to satisfy your need to submit?"

Her breath whooshed out, and her face turned a charming shade of scarlet. There was no artifice about her. Because of the life he'd lived, he appreciated that as much as a cool summer breeze. Jacob couldn't get enough of her.

"That's not exactly what I meant. I wouldn't have put it in those words."

"So how would you have put it?"

"I wanted to know about you and your experience."

It was a fair question. "On some level, I was always aware that I was a Dominant. When I was in college, I attended a club in New Orleans and mentored under the owner. Once I'd explored the dynamic, I understood why none of my

HOLD ON TO ME

attempts at dating had progressed into something more permanent. The most important thing about BDSM is the amount of honesty it requires." He studied her expression as he raised an eyebrow.

Clutching her glass even tighter, Elissa nodded.

"Would you like me to be blunt?" He waited for her nod before going on. "I think I'm right about you." He shrugged. "But that's for you to admit when you're ready. I'm interested in pursuing this conversation—and you—but only if you're willing."

"That's…" She took a sip of her wine. For courage? "You're definitely direct."

"As honest as I can be. You deserve that. So whether you tell me I'm wrong and we pretend this—and your reaction to my kiss last night—never happened is totally up to you."

"You're not wrong, but I wasn't expecting this. It feels a bit surreal."

Her soft admission meant a lot to him, but they would proceed at her pace. "We can always address this again at another time."

The wine sloshed gently against the sides of the glass, telling him her hands were shaking.

Hoping to take away some of her tension, he crossed the room and returned with a chair, then took a seat across from her. It brought them closer together, inviting trust rather than creating a disparity.

"So everything with you is safe, sane, and consensual?"

He studied her. "Of course." While he knew plenty of people who embraced RACK—Risk Aware Consensual Kink —he hadn't had a relationship that had ever developed that far. He understood the appeal. And perhaps with the right partner and enough time, he was open to the possibility. As it was, he continually communicated with his submissive to ensure her comfort and pleasure.

SIERRA CARTWRIGHT

"Without emotional manipulation?"

What the fuck? He scowled. But when he spoke, he kept his voice low. "Is there something I need to know?"

"Look…" She stood and slid her tumbler on the desk before striding to the window. A few seconds later, she turned to face him. "Maybe I'm not ready for this. Can we have this conversation somewhere else? Maybe a bit later?"

"Whenever you're ready."

"Maybe after dinner?"

"I'm cooking." He shrugged. "The one thing that's my specialty."

She gave him a small smile that told him she appreciated the reprieve. "I'll be over in a while, after I shut down my computer and straighten my desk."

"Take your time."

Forcing himself to push away thoughts of a relationship with Elissa, he strolled back to the main house, automatically scanning the area to be sure everything was quiet. So far, there'd been no reports of unusual activity on the ranch. An hour ago, he'd checked in with Hawkeye. There'd been no further attacks that the firm knew of. No one was relaxing their vigilance, but it was possible the anthrax sent to Inamorata had been an isolated incident.

Even if it was, that person needed to be found.

As he seasoned steaks, images of Elissa, and her art, filtered through his brain. And he remained enthralled by the one she'd been working on. She'd done an excellent job of capturing the Dominant's features. There was appreciation in his eyes, and he wondered if she'd seen something similar in his.

When she finally entered through the sliding glass door, he looked across at her. There was nothing more perfect. Like she belonged. A future with moments like this would work for him.

248

HOLD ON TO ME

"Hey." She slid her glass onto the counter.

"Steaks okay?"

"From your cattle?"

"And dry aged. Nothing but the best." Earlier, while she was working, he'd tossed a salad and baked some potatoes. "There's a bottle of red wine on the island. I took it out of the fridge earlier to reach room temperature. Will you grab it?"

Only their second meal together, and already they were working like a team.

"Merlot?"

"Do you like it?"

"One of my favorites. Not too heavy." After she handed the bottle to him, he uncorked it and poured them each a glass.

Once again, they agreed to eat outside, and she set the table while he fired up the grill.

When he joined her, she took a small breath, and for a moment he thought she was going to say something. But with a tiny shake of her head, she settled for thanking him.

As they dined, he decided to follow her lead. If she chose not to mention their previous conversation, he would honor that. And when she asked about his upbringing on the ranch, he ended up revealing more about his family history than he'd ever told anyone. "I mentioned my mother already. She was an only child and hated living out here. Right after she graduated from high school, she moved to Los Angeles."

"Bright lights. Big city."

"She got pregnant in her early twenties and moved back home. I never knew my father."

"That has to be tough."

He shrugged. "My grandparents did the best they could. I didn't make it easy for them. Something I'll always regret."

"And your mom. Where is she now? Still in California?"

"I'm not sure." The answer was much more complicated

than that. The truth was, he didn't know. Hawkeye had gotten her out of the hellhole that was her life in Mexico. She hadn't thanked him for the help and was furious when Jacob pulled strings to have her admitted to rehab. After a few days, she'd checked herself out and disappeared.

With Hawkeye's vast resources, there was no doubt Jacob could locate her. But she'd made it clear she didn't want to be found. "She has problems with addiction."

"I didn't mean to pry."

He wanted to know her deepest secrets. Fair was fair. "I was two or three when she left for the second time. Said the stress of dealing with a kid was too much."

"I'm sorry." Elissa placed her fingers on the back of his hand. The touch was both gentle and reassuring. And he absently wondered how long it had been since he'd experienced either. Odd. Until this moment, he hadn't missed it. And now the need for connection blasted through him like the roar of a freight train. "She abandoned you?"

"You could say that. Or that she did what she thought was best for me. Or what she needed in order to save herself."

"That's generous of you."

"Is it? Would it have been better for her to live a life she hated?"

"Did she ever come back?"

"Never. When I was little, she made an occasional attempt to stay in touch. She called a couple of times and sent birthday cards often enough that I'd be excited to get another the next year. I'd check the mailbox several times a day for weeks, looking. Hoping." His grandmother would give him a slight smile, but there'd be pain in her eyes when she saw his disappointment. "I gave up when I turned nine."

Elissa winced.

For a long time, neither spoke. Then, seeming to realize how intimate her touch was, she drew her hand away.

HOLD ON TO ME

"My grandparents did the best they could. And they were both great people. Grandad insisted I go to college so I'd be ready to inherit the ranch. At eighteen, I saw that as a curse. And maybe I have a bit of my mom in me. I wanted to see the world. There had to be something beyond these fenced-in acres. They worked from sunup to dusk and rarely took vacations. I couldn't imagine that for the rest of my life. So after I got my degree, I joined the military instead of coming home and repaying everything they'd done for me."

"I get it. Family expectations are complicated."

As he expected, she was compassionate rather than judgmental. Maybe she understood because of the way she ran her family's business.

"They didn't tell me Grandad was sick, or that they needed money because of the downturn in beef prices. They got behind on some of their loans and had to sell off parts of their holdings. Which is why I went to work for Hawkeye." The pay was beyond anything he'd imagined. It wasn't for the love of black ops. It was for the opportunity to redeem his selfish mistakes. "I wasn't there when he died. And my grandmother had to manage everything herself." Regret was his constant companion.

"You were young."

"Every day I'm grateful for what I have." In the military, he'd seen things that would haunt him forever. While working for Hawkeye, he'd done things that would haunt him forever. The world was big—that was true. But home was where he'd healed. He'd been there for his grandmother and continued the Walker legacy. "The connection with the land, the responsibility..." He glanced at Saddle Mountain, then back at Elissa with her beautiful, soulful eyes. "I've recognized it for what it is. A privilege, rather than a burden. But it's not for everyone. It can be lonely, and the winters are long."

"There are trade-offs, though. Right? The peace. I've been really creative out here." She looked into the distance for a moment. "I know you don't work for Hawkeye anymore. But it seems like a part of you. Like the biometrics and the panic room. Normal people don't live like that."

"No?"

"You mentioned the loneliness. Is there part of you that misses being an agent?"

"I've chosen to live in the present. I told him to fuck off when he first approached me about this job."

She traced a bead of condensation as it wended its way down the side of her glass. "Then why am I here? Why did you change your mind?"

"He showed me a picture of you."

She stilled.

"There was no way I could say no."

"And why the name Operation Wildflower?"

It'd been fanciful, maybe. But it fit. "Your eyes." He took a drink of his merlot. "Reminded me of columbines. They were my grandmother's favorite. I'd pick them for her, and she always pretended they were the greatest gift ever."

"My mom was the same with dandelions." She grinned. "But when you think about it, it means we wanted to give them a gift, and when you have no money, what else do you do?"

He liked the way she saw the world.

The sun moved toward the horizon, and she shivered.

"We can clean up here, then finish our wine near the firepit while we watch the sun set."

"That sounds perfect."

Within minutes, their chores were done, and they were back outside. He held a lighter to the kindling. It caught almost right away, and a soft crackle filled the air.

HOLD ON TO ME

He sat on one end of the couch, and she curled up at the other beneath a blanket he'd carried out for her.

The first hint of orange brushed the high, wispy clouds.

"It's impossibly quiet out here." She took a sip of her wine.

"You're happy in the city?"

"To be honest, I've never really thought about it. It never occurred to me to move away from my parents. I went to college, got my own place, but my parents and the pub mean the world to me."

"The constant movement."

"It's electric in a way, never silent. Kids playing. People coming and going at all hours—myself included. Parties. Even noise from televisions. But this…"

"I've grown accustomed to it. You can hear the world in a whole new way. The birds. The wind in the trees."

"Horses neighing."

"You were watching."

"I couldn't help myself."

It was an intimate confession, one he didn't respond to, choosing instead to allow the time to unfurl as she wanted.

"You had a rope on the saddle."

Jason hid his grin behind his glass. "I know how to use it."

As usual Waffle appeared from nowhere, leaping onto the couch, to land between them. She head-butted Jacob's leg before plopping down to clean herself.

"Where does she go?"

"She patrols the property, and she has a pet door entrance into the garage. She has a bed, and when it gets cold, I have a heat lamp to keep her warm." He stroked the feline's head. "We haven't had a single issue with mice or skunks since she took up residence. Even the raccoons seem to have packed up their babies and moved somewhere else."

"She earns her keep."

For a few minutes, Elissa watched as the sun sank behind

Saddle Mountain. Then she faced him and took a deep breath. "Have you ever had a submissive?"

Though the question didn't surprise him, her directness did. "As in a twenty-four-seven relationship?" When she nodded, he answered. "No." Guessing she was looking for a more detailed answer, he examined his own motivation, maybe for the first time. "My lifestyle has never been conducive to that kind of commitment. In the military, I was Special Forces, and I deployed a lot." He shrugged. "Then after Peru—"

"So you *were* there."

He didn't acknowledge her statement. "I went to work for Hawkeye. Then when we nearly lost the ranch, I knew I needed to be here for my grandmother. She deserved that."

She propped a pillow behind herself, bringing her a little closer to him. "You're a good man."

"I've done some things I'm not proud of. Bad things."

"All of us have regrets."

Some were easier to live with.

The fire crackled and hissed, and the automatic outdoor lights turned on. They weren't bright—rather they provided enough illumination to add ambience and safely maneuver around.

He'd enjoyed the patio more since she arrived than he had in the past few years. Though she hadn't been here long, she was already affecting his life.

Last night, it had taken him over an hour to fall asleep. He'd told himself it was because he heard every one of Elissa's movements and was concerned for her safety. But the truth was so much more.

As a man, as a Dominant, he noticed everything about her —feminine curves, rumpled hair, feisty attitude, talent, loyalty to her family, even her unintentional submissive air.

It'd been years since he had such an intense reaction to

HOLD ON TO ME

any woman. He'd taken a shower and jacked off while he was in there. Since that hadn't helped much, he'd masturbated a second time. The rest he eventually managed to get was light and fitful.

When he didn't go on, she placed her glass on the wicker table. "So you're not much for relationships?"

He hadn't been.

When he didn't respond, she went on. "I think they give our lives meaning."

Jacob had few friends, even fewer close ones. Maybe he was missing out.

"Have you thought about kids? Having someone to pass the ranch down to?"

"My grandparents want the land to stay in the family." But managing the holdings was a hell of an obligation, and developers had offered a lot of money for the property.

He could have a nice life somewhere else, debt free, with no responsibilities. Despite the temptation, he'd never been able to sign the papers. The work was meaningful, offering him satisfaction that couldn't be bought. And he knew his forebearers had struggled and sacrificed. It didn't seem right to turn his back.

She wrapped the blanket a little tighter around herself, and he stood to toss another couple of logs on the fire.

"What about you? As far as relationships?"

For a moment, she studied the crackling fire, as if deciding how much to reveal. "My first paying commission as an artist was from a Dominant. And that was my introduction to the lifestyle. Before we got started, both he and his submissive gave me an education. We talked about their relationship. I guess the biggest surprise for me was that they each said they received more than they gave."

He sat back down, a little closer to her than earlier, and she didn't scoot away.

"I loved being around them. It seemed as if they had their own form of communication. There was a reverence to it that I'd never seen before."

While he hadn't experienced anything like that, he, too, had witnessed it.

"I wanted something similar and was naive enough to think it was automatically part of a committed D/s relationship. You know, as if something magical happens the moment you agree to wear a Dominant's collar." She tipped her head back and stared at the moon for a long time.

Was she talking about one of her relationships? Despite an impatience that was uncustomary for him, Jacob remained silent, allowing her the space to sort through what she wanted to say.

"His name was Robby."

"Go on."

She wiggled around until she was facing him. "I met him at the club, and a couple of months later, I moved in to his apartment."

Undoubtedly she'd left a lot out.

"It was a mistake. Maybe my worst. He had rules about everything, and they changed continually. It got to the point I couldn't do anything right, and I was in trouble all the time." She looked away for a moment. "If I loved him, I'd try harder. Do better."

Anger flashed through him. She was special, to be protected and cared for. "Was it some sort of fucked-up punishment game with him?"

"Not necessarily. He was an expert at giving me the silent treatment and withholding sex and affection. He'd sleep in the guest room. Most times, he wouldn't tell me what I'd done wrong. He refused to attend my family's Christmas gathering. When I asked, he told me I knew what I'd done wrong. To this day, I still don't understand it." She shook her

HOLD ON TO ME

head and gave a helpless shrug that knocked him in the solar plexus. "His coldness would go on until I begged for forgiveness. And he never immediately granted it. I'd have to earn it a bit at a time. Cooking him special meals, sexual favors." She shifted, as if the confession had emotionally drained her. "I mean, that's part of BDSM—well, of any relationship, really. Right?"

"No." He shook his head. "There's a big difference. I get that no two relationships are the same, but there needs to be an agreement and reciprocity. Both partners need to get what they want. BDSM is not about one person's selfish need to be in control. And vanilla relationships should be the same way."

"That's what my mentors told me. It took an embarrassingly long time for me to really understand what was going on and to realize how to heal from it." She looked away for a moment.

When she refocused on him, she gave a small smile. "I guess that was my way of telling you that I don't date and that I confine my interactions to scenes at the club. And I haven't done that for a long time. Not since my dad got cancer, and I needed to take on more of their responsibilities at the pub."

He'd heard that from Hawkeye. But the pain that flitted through her eyes made Jacob's gut clench. He had an unusual —not entirely unwelcome—compulsion to soothe her.

Leaning forward, he reached for a wayward lock of her hair. "May I?"

"Uhm..." She held his gaze even as she drew in a shallow breath. "Yes."

His knuckles brushed the softness of her cheek as he tucked the strand back into place. He lowered his hand without touching her again. *Fuck.* The need to have her was a physical ache.

SIERRA CARTWRIGHT

"Earlier, you said you were interested in pursuing me if I was willing." Her voice was the barest whisper.

He waited.

"I'm willing."

Around them, the entire night became preternaturally silent. He heard the sound of his own heartbeat. His cock hardened. He'd never wanted anything more. "Tell me what you're offering. Friendship? Sex? Or do you want to submit to me?"

———

Heat seared Elissa's lungs, and it was then she realized she was holding her breath.

Admitting she was interested in him was one thing. Telling him what she really wanted was terrifying.

At the club, the Doms were vetted. And she had been going there for so long that she knew most of them, at least by reputation. This, though, was entering uncharted territory. She trusted Jacob, but it had been so long since she'd been with someone new. Though attraction sizzled, she needed walls of protection around her vulnerabilities. "There would need to be rules, as well as a safe word."

He nodded, as she expected he would. "I wouldn't have it any other way."

"I'll go with red." She appreciated that he kept distance between them while they negotiated, but it would be so much easier to have the conversation if she were in his arms.

"And yellow for slow?"

"Yes."

"And your limits?"

"Because we haven't played together, I want to go slow."

He offered a quick, disarming grin. "Rope?"

HOLD ON TO ME

Of course he'd remembered that from their earlier conversation. *"Yes."*

"Impact play?"

"Nothing too hard, at least for now." She shuddered, recalling a painful experience with Robby. "No canes or knife play, ever. Those are a hard limit. And nothing that would be permanent—I mean not that we'd have time for that, anyway."

"Agreed." He nodded. "Anything else?"

She shook her head. "If I'm gagged, I want to be sure I have a safe signal."

"Of course. As we discussed, safe, sane, consensual. I don't play dangerously, and I'd never put you at risk."

While he hadn't needed to say that, she was glad he had. It helped tamp down the tiny whispers of apprehension.

"And sex?"

Was she ready for that? The truth was, yes. She'd gone without a physical connection for so long that it consumed her. "As long as we use condoms." Robby had been awful about that. He hated the things, and he'd start with one on because she insisted, but sometimes he'd take it off during intercourse. Because of that, she ended up going on the Pill so he couldn't get her pregnant unless it was a joint decision.

In retrospect, that she'd even made that decision should have given her a clue that the relationship was in trouble. When he discovered what she'd done, fury had consumed him. He'd left for three days, and when he returned, he refused to have sex with her. Instead, he insisted on her servicing him. His anger burned for more than a month.

"And as for your rules?"

"We need to agree this is a temporary arrangement. Like we'd have at a club. It doesn't mean anything. When this is over, we'll walk away and forget each other."

"Sorry, Elissa." He shook his head. "I can't agree to that."

SIERRA CARTWRIGHT

She scooted as far away from him as possible.

"You're not some random woman I can fuck and forget."

At his raw crudeness, she flinched.

"I'm sorry you're offended. But that's not how this works." He took a breath. When he continued, his tone was low, but his words were measured and uncompromising. "You matter to me, and you have since the moment I saw your picture. I can't dictate your emotions, and if you want to detach sex from your feelings, go ahead. But don't expect the same from me."

The force of his reaction stunned her. The men she played with were happy to scene and then go back to their regular lives. She hadn't expected him to be any different.

"Those are *my* terms." He paused to study her. "Now it's up to you. Do you still want to play?"

CHAPTER FIVE

HAWKEYE

Fighting for equilibrium, Elissa took a breath. She'd never really had to negotiate in this way before. Generally she told a Dominant what her limits were and informed him of her safe words. That there wouldn't be a relationship later was understood. At the end of the scene, they each went their own way.

Until now, she'd never had to be concerned with what her Dominant wanted. She was now navigating unfamiliar territory. "Can we agree that whatever we share stays here? Let's make no promises about what happens after this is over." Why did that thought cause a pang of grief? "It doesn't need to be complicated."

"Elissa, you were a complication before I met you."

She attempted a grin but then realized he wasn't joking. "I don't know what you want here."

"Every damn thing you have to offer. Hold nothing back. I want to hear your moans. Your whimpers. Your pleas. Your screams. And I fucking want to know I'm not some random Dominant who you'll forget next week."

SIERRA CARTWRIGHT

After swallowing the sudden lump in her throat, she told him the truth. "I think you know better. Believe me when I say you're unforgettable."

"Good. Otherwise we'd be done here."

"We're getting somewhere." She exhaled a breath she hadn't realized she'd been holding. "So, can we at least agree that we'll part ways without looking back?"

"No."

"No?" She blinked.

"I respect your need for rules, but this isn't something I am flexible on. I'll always be honest with you—that's a promise. There will be no manipulation. But when the mission is over, if either of us want to discuss the possibility of continuing a relationship, we should be allowed to."

Maybe he was braver than she was. She wasn't sure she was ever capable of confessing her feelings like that. "But—"

"Maybe neither of us will want it. But I don't want to play guessing games with you. Can you at least attempt to be equally transparent with me? If you want me at the end of our time together, I need to hear it."

"I..." They were two different people from two different worlds who'd never chosen to be thrown together.

"Try."

The level of transparency he demanded was unlike anything she'd ever experienced. And it was as scary as hell.

"It's not that difficult."

Elissa always waited for a man to express his desire for a relationship first. At a club, she was different because a scene there didn't have the kind of meaning that one with Jacob would. "Terrifying."

"But you accept my terms."

Finally she nodded.

His smile was her greatest reward.

HOLD ON TO ME

"And now… Would you like to submit to me?"

"Yes." Every part of her ached for what he offered. Without conscious thought she looked away, but then dug for courage. "I want you to dominate me, Jacob."

He placed his palms on the sides of her face and tipped her head back for a gentle kiss, one that conflicted with the untamed hunger burning in his eyes.

"In that case, Elissa…" He stood and offered his hand.

Her whole being trembled as she accepted, sliding her palm against his. The blanket tumbled to the ground as he drew her against him.

"I'll be worthy of your trust."

He released her to extinguish the fire and straighten the area, gathering their wineglasses.

"Now, like a good submissive, I want you to precede me into the house."

His voice contained an unfamiliar note of command. She was no longer a client, and he'd masterfully started the scene. Adrenaline flooded her, and she took a breath to steady the onslaught of nerves.

He nodded almost imperceptibly toward the house. Obediently, now on familiar footing, she walked across the patio and into the living room. Once there, she stood patiently, head bowed, trying not to fidget as she waited for him to lock the door and load the stemware into the dishwasher.

"Very nice."

The purr of his approval flowed through her, replacing nerves with confidence.

After engaging the alarm system, he crossed the room to stand in front of her. "I'm going to kiss you again."

"Yes." She met his eyes. "Please."

He hadn't said just how passionate he'd be. He tasted of

rich red wine, and he claimed her mouth like a man dying of thirst. Her surrender wasn't enough, and he plunged deeper, one palm pressed against the middle of her back and the other cradling her head as he coaxed a response from her. He wasn't allowing her to be passive—he demanded her active participation.

At the club, no Dominant had kissed her.

Once again, Jacob proved he was no ordinary man.

He pulled away for a moment. Reeling, she blinked as she looked up at him. "Open your mouth wider for me."

When he'd said he wanted everything she had to offer, he meant it. She leaned against him, curling her hands around his neck as he devoured her.

By the time he eased back, her breathing was ragged, and the world was unsteady. He continued to hold her close; then he gently tipped back her chin.

"You're exquisite."

Ordinarily a compliment like that might have embarrassed her, but the sincerity radiating from his eyes spoke of authenticity. From him, it wasn't some meaningless platitude.

"Now I'd like you to follow me."

She nodded. Already she would follow him anywhere.

"I'd prefer to hear your answer aloud, please."

"Yes…" For a moment, she paused and frowned. "How should I address you?"

"Thank you for asking. Sir or Jacob. I'm fine with either."

"In that case, yes, Jacob."

"I like the sound of my name on your lips." He removed his finger from beneath her chin.

Quickly and effectively, he'd established a boundary, and she slipped a little deeper inside herself, to a place where the noise stopped. Sometimes that didn't happen until later in a scene, after impact play had begun.

HOLD ON TO ME

He led the way to his wing of the house and stopped outside the closed door that she'd noticed last night.

"Is this the room you were talking about? The one you said I wouldn't like?"

"My dungeon? Yes." He flashed a quick, wicked grin. "At this point, I'm thinking you'll find it to your satisfaction." After the biometrics disengaged the lock, he turned the knob, pushed open the door, then turned on the lights before looking at her.

Giving me a chance to change my mind?

"After you."

Wanting this, wanting him, she entered slowly, then turned in a slow circle, taking in the space. It was a submissive's dream, with lots of mirrors, a spanking bench with lots of rings, as well as siderails for her knees, a rather large, uncomfortable-looking straight-back leather chair fit for a Dominant, and a beautiful wood Saint Andrew's cross with a small vinyl pad in the middle to make it more comfortable. That, she would appreciate. But what captured her attention was a metal structure. It had two upright poles and another that went across the top. It made her think of a high bar used for gymnastics.

Although there was no window, there was a sink, an armoire emblazoned with the ranch symbol, and a second door, maybe to a closet. There was a fireplace with a chair and rug in front of it, along with several sturdy metal rings attached to the floor...which no doubt meant he could secure her at his feet, something she'd never experienced before. "This is..."

"Frightening? Enticing?"

She faced him.

Jacob stood with his legs wide, arms folded across his chest, all commanding and ominous. His eyes were darker than they had been earlier, and while he still looked at her

265

SIERRA CARTWRIGHT

with kindness, there was now a glint of hardness in the green depths. In his element, he was magnificent. And he was studying her closely, waiting for her answer. It was difficult to express what was happening inside her, the collision of nerves and excitement. "Both, maybe."

"What scares you?"

"The rings in the floor."

"Interesting. Why?"

"The helplessness of it." With other Doms, it had been enough to say she didn't like something. But Jacob forced her to look inside herself. "And not knowing how long I'd be there. Would I be kneeling? Sitting? Lying down? Standing?"

"Go on."

She glanced toward the fireplace setting. "But that speaks to... I don't know how to put it into words. Like, I guess, a long comfortable evening between a Dom and a submissive. He—you—might be sipping a whiskey..."

"You remembered."

"To me it represents something permanent. It seems like something that might happen in a long-term relationship— you know, between a couple who spend a lot of time enjoying each other."

"I can see that."

"A scene kind of has a natural progression—a beginning, an end—and that can be thirty minutes or a couple of hours. But you go back to your life, cooking dinner, doing the laundry."

He waited, not saying anything.

"I'm not sure I have the patience to be tethered at my Master's feet." Had she really used the word Master? Something inside her stilled. She'd never had that thought about any Dominant, even the one she'd lived with. So why Jacob?

Her breaths were frantic as she fought to control her suddenly erratic emotions. "You've got this amazing setup.

HOLD ON TO ME

Did you put it together for someone in particular?" It shouldn't matter, but she couldn't contain her curiosity.

"I have particular tastes. But no. You are the only woman—submissive or not—who has spent time in my house."

She took that in, loving that she was the first.

"I worked with a furniture designer in Denver to put the dungeon together. The cross is made with lumber from the ranch."

"It's beautiful, and I understand why you have that and the spanking bench. But I'm curious about the rings attached to the floor. Was my guess right?"

"I enjoy the flexibility they offer. And standing over a submissive who's helpless beneath me is a powerful image. For example, you could be on all fours, secured by a collar around your beautiful neck."

Unable to help herself, she pressed her palm to her chest.

"There'd be no escape as I eased a butt plug inside your ass."

His focus was relentless, and beneath his scrutiny, her pussy moistened. And he was still several feet away from her.

"You'd have no choice but to take my cock in your hot pussy as I entered you from behind." He took a step toward her, his footfall ominous on the honeyed floor planks. "You'd be full for me. And I'd show you no mercy."

Protective instincts urged her to flee, but submissive ones compelled her to stay rooted in place.

"Or maybe I'd place you on your back and require you to tug on your nipples as I dropped hot wax onto your belly."

Her knees were weak. It wasn't just from his words, but the intent beneath them. They were more than random musings. He was watching her, weighing her response.

"But I definitely like your idea—of seeing you tied at my feet while I sip whiskey in front of the fire."

Earlier, she might have put that on her limits list. But she

SIERRA CARTWRIGHT

was no longer certain of that. His scenario sounded companionable, emotional rather than sexual, and she suddenly craved that connection in a way she never had before.

"Do you know what would make this even more spectacular?"

"No." Tipping her head to one side, she looked at him. "What?"

"The image you're working on. Having the original portrait hanging on the wall above the mantel."

"Are you serious?"

"I'd like to commission the piece, if it's not too late."

Her mind reeled. *He wants it for himself?*

"Do you take requests?"

"I'm not sure what you mean."

"I'd like the submissive to have darker hair. Perhaps blue eyes as well."

He *had* seen his resemblance in the image, and he wanted the woman to look more like her? "I've never done something like that before." Of course, until today, she'd never changed an image to look like a man who was consuming her thoughts.

"Bonds recognized your talent. So do I. I'd like to purchase your art before you have a showing and the price goes up."

She laughed at the absurdity.

"I'll consider it an investment."

"Look, if you really mean it, I'll paint it and give it to you. I wouldn't feel right charging you."

"I insist. A lot of labor goes into it, not to mention supplies and the opportunity cost."

He was a businessman. Of course he'd understand that concept. While she was working on his piece, she couldn't earn money doing anything else.

Jacob named a price that made her gasp. It was twenty

HOLD ON TO ME

times anything she'd consider charging. "I want the original, along with any line drawings. No posters, giclées, or any other reproduction. It's for my private collection, and no one else can ever see it."

The offer was absurd.

There was little chance she'd ever become famous. If she wanted to pursue a career as an artist, the picture would be a crucial part of her portfolio. And being able to make copies of it would be an ongoing source of income.

Yet no one else would ever have the connection to the painting that he did, and she'd always remember his belief in her—misplaced though it may be. *"If* I finish it, it's yours. And I agree to your terms. The price doesn't include framing or potential shipping charges."

"If you're not here when you complete it, simply name the time and place, and I'll personally pick it up."

"You could hire a professional company to do that."

"I know." The huskiness in his voice traced down her spine. "It's a deal, then?"

For better or worse. "Yes." Since this was a business transaction, she didn't add the honorific that would make her feel like his submissive.

He extended his hand.

"I said *if* I finish it," she reminded him.

"Hope is eternal, fair Elissa."

When she took his hand, he surprised her by raising hers to his lips. This badass protective agent, honorable cowboy, made her swoon.

She was falling for him, hard and fast.

When he finally released her, she looked away from him, trying to put some emotional distance between them. Her reaction had to be because of the strange circumstances, being alone with him in an idyllic setting and the millions of

SIERRA CARTWRIGHT

pheromones zinging between them, creating a bubbling cauldron of sexual need.

"You told me what scared you about the room." Like a good Dominant, he brought her back to the present, but he did so in a nonthreatening way that helped her to refocus. "What pleases you?"

This, a BDSM inquiry, was familiar and not as tricky to navigate. "The spanking bench."

"Tell me why."

"Depending on the position, it supports my whole body. It's comfortable. Because I can put my head down, I find it easier to let go mentally. It helps ease my worry."

"Good to know."

"I've never seen one of those in a club." She pointed to the metal structure.

"Let me show you how it works." He crossed the room, and she followed.

Now that she was close, she noticed the notches and hooks that were in it.

"It's a variation of a suspension frame. The height is adjustable, making it suitable for Shibari rope work. I have a different plan for it." Gently he moved her so she stood beneath the overhead bar. "Unlike the Saint Andrew's cross or the spanking bench, it allows unrestricted access to a submissive's body. Of course, she won't have the same kind of support as a more physical structure, so there are times, like a sustained, sensual flogging, where something else is a better choice."

Anticipation made her pussy damp.

"This frame allows the Dominant, me, to select a number of different positions for my sub—you."

She shivered.

"I can place you on your tiptoes. Or not." He never took his gaze from hers, and she was ensnared, helpless to look

HOLD ON TO ME

away. "Your ankles can be secured to the sides so that you can't escape or try to protect your pretty cunt."

The words hung in the still air, naked, frightening, tantalizing.

"Or I can bind your legs, in a mummy effect."

"It's…" *Words.* She needed to think. But how could she when he was mere inches away, talking about what he intended to do to her? "Ah…more versatile than I realized."

"The possibilities are numerous, aren't they?"

With her imagination painting some vivid pictures that she couldn't wait to sketch out, she looked away. Now that her creativity had been unleashed, she couldn't stop the flow of ideas.

"The metal plates at the bottom are bolted to the floor, giving the structure stability. That means you will be completely safe, and you're free to turn yourself over to me."

There was nothing she wanted more.

"Take off your shoes for me, Elissa." It was part invitation, part command, and his voice was as gruff as sandpaper over pebbles. "Then strip down to your bra and panties."

Though she'd expected the soft, uncompromising order, her heart still jolted. He was a new partner, and the unexpected was as wonderful as it was scary.

Her fingers trembled slightly, and she fumbled with the buttons on her shirt. She appreciated him walking away, toward the armoire, granting her a momentary reprieve from his focus.

Once she was half naked, her clothing folded on the floor, she tried to peek at what he was doing, but his back was to her, blocking her view.

He opened a drawer and placed a few items in it.

"Music?"

"I'd like that." Anything was better than the silence, amplifying the sound of her frantic breaths.

He selected something she recognized from the club, an EDM tune that pulsed with eroticism. "Do you like it?"

It made her more aware of him, of his constrained power. "Yes."

"I was hoping you would." He bumped up the volume a little more, giving the space an audible heartbeat.

"It's intimate. Moody."

"And not so loud that I can't hear your whimpers or cries of ecstasy." He glanced over his shoulder, and she wasn't sure whether or not he was joking.

Unsure what to do, she placed her hands at the small of her back and tried not to squirm as she waited for him.

When he faced her, he was holding a leather collar. "Any objection?"

The room held a slight chill, and she told herself her sudden shiver was from that.

"Elissa?" He'd obviously noticed her reaction. "Is it a problem for you?"

"I... Uhm..."

"It's your choice entirely."

In that instant, with the way he was looking at her, she was reminded of the couple she'd painted, the one she told him about.

The moment pulsed with expectation. To her, the collar represented some kind of commitment, but she wasn't sure he meant it that way. "Is it a fetish for you, Sir?"

"Not at all. To me, it's symbolic. It will be the only thing you'll have on, and from the moment I fasten it in place until I remove it at the end of our scene, it will mean you belong to me."

Being honest would make her emotionally vulnerable to him, yet she was compelled to confess what was in her heart. "I'd be honored."

"In that case, please lift your hair out of the way."

HOLD ON TO ME

As she did so, he crossed the room. He placed a gentle kiss on her forehead, letting her know he appreciated her decision.

His touch both gentle and firm, he fastened the collar in place, then checked the fit. "Good." When she released her hair, he nodded his satisfaction. "You're mine." Possession punctuated his words. "It couldn't be more perfect if it had been custom-made for you."

Against her neck, the leather slowly warmed.

"Now finish undressing for me." This time, he watched, taking in her every movement.

When she was naked before him, she pressed her tongue to her upper lip. The club she played at had rules against nudity, and for a moment, uncertainty claimed her. She hadn't been this vulnerable since she was with Robby.

"You're even more spectacular than I dared hope." Jacob traced his thumb along the top of the collar.

Then, moving behind her, he cupped her breasts and dragged his thumbnails across her nipples.

Whimpering, she wrapped her hands around one of his wrists for support.

He leaned into her, his lips near her ear. "Do you like that, Elissa?"

She loved the way he whispered her name, the syllables laced with sensuality.

"Hmm?"

"Yes, I do. Sir."

He rewarded her by squeezing her nipples and gently tugging on them, with the right amount of exquisite pressure.

"And what do you think of floggers?"

"I love everything about them."

"Tell me."

She'd never had to explain it before, and she really hadn't

thought it through. "The way it bites. The way the falls can wrap around my body. So many points of contact. It's like a dance of pleasure and pain, and often both at the same time."

"Well said. And a violet wand?"

How could he expect her to think while he was tormenting her so exquisitely? "I've actually never played with one."

"Is it on your limits list?"

"No. I'm actually interested."

"Excellent." He released one nipple and skimmed his hand down her belly to find her heat. "Open your legs. *For me.* And keep them spread apart. Don't deny your Dominant."

Everything in her yielded to him.

He played with her pussy, teasing her to the very edge of an orgasm, and then he pulled away, leaving her shaking.

If she wasn't still holding on to him, she wasn't sure she could stand up. *"Jacob!"*

"Hmm?" He knew exactly what he was doing and seemed totally unconcerned. "Let's get you to the suspension structure so that you can earn that orgasm."

"You're such a damn Dom."

"Sounds like a complaint." This time, there was a hint of a tease in his voice, another new side of him.

Finding connection in a way she hadn't expected, she responded in kind. "It was more of an observation, Sir."

"An observation?"

"A proper submissive doesn't complain. She simply tries to please her Dominant."

"Exactly as I thought." He left her again and returned with a length of rope.

The sight of the sturdy bright-pink silk left her riveted. The color was arresting, and no doubt it would be the stuff of her future fantasies.

"Hold it for me."

HOLD ON TO ME

She accepted the strand, and then he led her to the metal structure. Then, after studying her, he raised the top bar a couple of inches.

In less than a minute, her wrists were tied together and secured above her head. Fortunately he'd been kind and allowed her to keep her feet flat on the floor.

"Now spread your legs as far apart as possible."

With speed that attested to his skill with ropes, he had her completely at his mercy in no time at all. Nervousness crashed against her arousal, leaving her reeling.

He left her for a moment while he took out a metal box, then plugged in the violet wand and tucked the conduction pad inside the waistband of his jeans, which meant he didn't need the toy. He intended to use his body to electrify hers.

When he turned on the machine and tested it, the unmistakable sparking hum made her jump. She shrank back and tugged against her bonds. Not surprisingly, he hadn't left her much room to wiggle around.

"I have it on the lowest setting. Ready?"

For a moment, she considered using her safe word. But she told herself she could try it once. If she hated it, they wouldn't have to continue.

Opting for bravery, she nodded. "I'm a little apprehensive."

"Understood." He brushed two fingers between her breasts. "How's that?"

"Like...tiny bubbles." It was so light she was barely aware of it.

He touched both of her nipples, and absolute pleasure caused them to tighten immediately.

"Oh God. That's magnificent."

"Let's try a little more intensity."

When she didn't object, he adjusted the setting. This time,

SIERRA CARTWRIGHT

when he skimmed her nipples, she cried out from pleasure. She never wanted this to stop.

Keeping contact with her, making her twitch from the little pulses, he moved behind her. He tormented her whole body—shoulders, breasts, ribs, belly. Determinedly he started over, from the top, trailing down her arms, then her sides, before zapping her buttocks, electrifying her.

Jacob crouched to electrify her legs, down to her ankles, before moving back up the insides of her thighs.

Instinctively she pulled away as he neared her most delicate spot, but the ropes caught, holding her prisoner. "Jacob…" She angled her head but couldn't make eye contact. "Sir?"

"Hmm?" But instead of stopping, he brushed his hand over her pussy.

The energy rocked through her. Instantly she became more aroused than she'd ever been. When he did it again, she whimpered. "I need…" God. She wanted sex. Had to have him.

But he was nowhere close to being finished with her.

When perspiration dotted her body, he left her only long enough to switch out the violet wand for a flogger with short falls. And he turned up the music, seeming to make the floor vibrate. Or maybe that was a residual effect of the electromagnetics.

For a few moments, Elissa allowed her eyes to close, and she was barely aware of his footsteps when he returned to stand behind her.

He swept her hair to one side and stroked a finger across her nape. "Are you doing okay, fair Elissa?"

She was. "Yes, Jacob."

"Ready for more?" He placed the strands of the flogger on her shoulder, then eased them back, igniting a promise of pleasure.

HOLD ON TO ME

"I'm already in a submissive stupor."

"Good." He kissed the side of her neck. "Should we stop?"

"No." *Not ever.*

Her body chilled when he released her. Almost instantly he was in front of her, in all his Dominant magnificence. His powerful legs were spread, and he was still fully dressed, including his hand-tooled cowboy boots. Maybe she should have asked him to release her and take her to bed.

She expected him to begin the flogging, but he didn't. Instead, he pleasured her breasts and pussy until she writhed against him.

"I love seeing you so needy."

"May…" Damn, she wanted to come, but she knew he was finding pleasure in denying her. "I'm on the edge, Sir."

"Your eyes reveal all of your reactions. You can't hide anything." He lowered his hand. "Even your frustration. You'll come when I give you my permission."

She clamped her lips together so she didn't say anything else.

"Your brains match your beauty."

Then, taking a step back, he flicked the flogger across one of her breasts. She sighed. As a Dominant, he met her every need. She'd never been with a man who intuitively read her the way he did.

In total trust, she relaxed in her bonds, turning herself over to him.

Each thuddy stroke from the thick falls was everything she could have hoped for, the pain both blunt and welcome.

He was a master. Her Master.

She had no idea how long he kissed her body with the whip; all she knew was that she was lost in the reverberation of music, of whimpers. The tears clinging to her lashes were from happiness and release, and she was soaring, dancing in a place where only pleasure existed.

He placed the handle of the flogger against her clit and rubbed hard. When he spoke, his voice reached her from a distance, compelling and commanding. "Tell me what you want. Ask for it."

Over and over, he teased her, making her beg.

An eternity later, he yielded. "That's it. You've earned it. Come for me, fair Elissa. Come."

With a scream, she spiraled, letting go as the orgasm rocked her.

She rode wave after wave as he fucked her with his hand, wringing climax after climax from her, the last so intense that she tipped back, exhausted, with nothing left to give.

Jacob moved behind her to pull her body back against his. The steel of his erection pressed against her, making her woozy, delirious with desire.

Without her consciously being aware of it, he somehow managed to unfasten her wrists. "Wrap your arms around yourself."

Once she had enough awareness, she did. And then he rubbed her biceps, helping circulation to return.

Her entire body hummed with awareness.

As he released her ankles, he instructed her to close her legs when she was ready. After he stood, he captured her face between his palms. "Are you back with me?"

"Almost. I think." Her knees were still trembly. "That was…" Because her voice was little more than a whisper, she cleared her throat to try again. "Everything." She'd yielded to him in a way she never had with any other man.

"I need to get you some water, take care of you." He held her against his powerful body, and his heartbeat was steady beneath her ear.

She snuggled in closer, knowing something had been transformed inside her. She'd never be the same again. "Jacob…"

"Anything, Elissa."

God, she couldn't let this end. "Will you take me to bed? I want you to make love to me."

Her request stoked passion in his eyes. "There's nothing I'd like more."

CHAPTER SIX

HAWKEYE

Fucking hell.

In his thirtysomething years, Jacob had experienced more than some people did in a lifetime—he'd seen plenty of horrors that he wished he never had, and he'd left part of his soul back in a hellhole. But nothing—nothing—had ever affected him as deeply as seeing Elissa's beautiful tears while they scened. A part of his heart he believed long dead was slowly healing.

And now her lower lip trembled, as if she were uncertain of his reaction.

How was that even possible?

Though he was always a considerate lover and Dom, he'd never bonded with anyone like he did her. She was the perfect submissive, willing to try what he suggested and to trust him. She'd come apart in his arms, and then she'd turned to him for comfort. Not only was he honor bound to protect her, but now he was determined to find a way to keep her with him after the job ended.

Jacob swept her from the floor and carried her to his room, where he placed her on the bed.

SIERRA CARTWRIGHT

The Dominant in him was tempted to tie her wrists to the headboard. But the need to have her arms around him while he made love to her overrode everything else.

"I've got to have you inside me."

He needed it more than his next breath.

After removing his boots, something he'd ask her—his beautiful little sub—to do in the future, he tugged off his T-shirt.

Elissa turned onto her side to watch him. He grinned.

"You're gorgeous, Sir."

Her voice was scratchy. With desire? "Not sure anyone has ever used that word in relation to me."

"They should have."

"You got the details right."

She frowned. "The details?"

"On the image you were working on."

"Oh my God. You saw?" An alluring shade of pink stained her cheeks. "It's not what you think. I mean…"

"I'm flattered. Thank you."

"Okay." She exhaled. "It wasn't intentional."

"I believe you." Neither of them were immune to the wild tug of untamed attraction. "But that's not why I bought it. There's an honesty about the piece. A yearning. A completion." And he'd think of tonight every time he looked at the finished portrait in his playroom. "I know you're wondering…" Jacob pointed to the raised bump on the far left side of his stomach. She'd replicated the jagged edges with extraordinary accuracy. And yet now, he saw the scar through new eyes. It was no longer just an ugly reminder of the past. Instead, it was a natural part of him, and a reminder that he was lucky. He'd gotten out alive. "It's from a knife." The wound had been deep, and the team medic had done his best to sew him together given the extraordinary circumstances.

HOLD ON TO ME

"It means you survived. And we get this moment."

Jacob finished undressing, and she kept her focus on him. His cock was still hard, throbbing with insistent demand.

"You're…" She met his gaze. Throughout their scene, her eyes had become a darker shade of blue, and now they were wide. "Tell me you don't expect me to… I mean, you're massive!"

"Oh, Elissa, yes. I most certainly do." He generally didn't tease, but the indignation in her voice made it irresistible. "I expect everything from you. You're my submissive."

Frantically she shook her head.

"I've got a generous nature. We'll go slow." Then everything inside him became serious. He intended to claim her in every way possible.

Honoring her wish, he grabbed a condom from the nightstand drawer and rolled it down his length before joining her on the bed. "Part your legs for me."

"But I'm ready now."

"You'll be ready when I say you are. Now do as you're told before I get my ropes."

Interest sparked in her eyes. It wasn't defiance, but rather a revelation of what she craved.

"What'll it be?" He didn't have to ask the question. Every part of him knew the answer.

She set her chin in response.

His inner alpha happily responded in kind.

Jacob prowled to the closet to fetch his sturdiest rope. Unlike the silk he'd used earlier, this was sisal, a bit ragged, something he'd bought at the hardware store, suitable for use on the range. It might chafe, and at least for a little while, it would leave his mark on her body.

Impossibly, the idea made his cock even harder.

"Come to me, Elissa."

She didn't.

SIERRA CARTWRIGHT

"Refusing to cooperate?" The more she played the game, the more ravenous he became. Whether she knew it or not, she was his.

Mine.

He'd used the word when he collared her earlier. He'd meant it, and this moment only reinforced his intention.

One way or another, Elissa Conroy was going to be his woman.

She curled into a ball, increasing the tension. He was going to fuck her so damn hard.

"Remember you asked for this," he reminded her as he picked her up and deposited her on the end of the bed.

When she immediately scooted back, he clamped on to one of her ankles and dragged her toward him. Her breath whooshed out, and her eyes darkened once more. She wanted things his way. She just wanted him to work for the victory.

Already he'd learned to recognize her expressions. He adored every aspect of her—playful, serious, emotional—and he vowed to fulfill all her fantasies.

Quickly he tied one of her ankles to prevent her from retreating again.

"Ouch! That stuff's rough!"

"Maybe that'll teach you to be a good sub and follow your Dominant's orders." *Lord, he hoped not.*

Once her other ankle was secure and she was spread before him, helpless, he crawled between her thighs, then parted her labia to devour her.

"Jacob! Don't." She thrashed her head. "I can't. It's too much."

"Would the lady like to wear a gag?"

"No!"

"In that case, I recommend you use your mouth for happy sounds. Moans, groans. Sighs. Or if you must,

HOLD ON TO ME

screaming my name." *That* would be the sweetest of all sounds.

"But—"

"Last chance." He slipped a finger inside her. "You're wet for me."

"Desperate for you."

He licked her clitoris rapidly, bringing her to the edge of an orgasm before slipping a second, then third finger inside to ensure she was fully prepared for him.

Her frantic cries were every bit as sexy as he imagined.

"Please." She curled her fingers into his hair and held him tightly. "I'm going to come."

This time, he wanted to own it.

Before she could climax, he worked his cock inside her welcoming warmth, a little bit at a time, letting her accommodate him.

"Oh…" She closed her eyes and thrashed her head from side to side.

"Yes. Take it."

Her pussy tightening around his cock, Elissa lifted her hips as much as her bonds allowed. *Fuck,* but she was so damn hot and tight.

He stroked harder and faster, meeting her demands.

When she screamed out her pleasure, he captured her mouth in a searing kiss, holding off his orgasm until she was completely satisfied.

Finally, she loosened her grip but didn't let go.

"That was spectacular, Sir."

"My pleasure, ma'am."

She smiled softly, then traced a fingertip across one of his eyebrows. "I've never experienced anything like that."

"Me either."

"Really?" She wrinkled her nose as she studied him. "Do you mean that? Or is it something you tell every woman?"

SIERRA CARTWRIGHT

"Believe me when I tell you that I've never said it before. You're one of a kind, Elissa. And sex with you isn't like with anyone else." He began to move inside her again. Need was a raw and hungry thing, demanding completion.

"Come in me." Elissa met each thrust, concentrating all her energy on his pleasure.

Yeah. She was unique, all right. Perfect for him in every way.

Wanting her to always remember this moment, he took her deeply. With a guttural moan, he ejaculated in long, hot spurts. He'd wanted to claim her as his. But now he knew the truth. He was hers.

Breath ragged, mind splintered by his realization, he collapsed on top of her, then immediately rolled to the side so he didn't crush her.

"That was amazing." Fuck. He was a goner. This woman well and truly owned him. "*You* are amazing."

As confident as if she knew that already, she smiled.

He left the bed to release her ankles, and then he massaged them to restore circulation. "You've got a mild case of rope burn."

"I was hoping I would."

"My girl."

They agreed to shower together, and as they did, he inspected her body for marks. There were none from the flogger or the electroplay.

After lathering some gel, he washed her. He could live for the sound of her soft, sweet sighs and the way she swayed toward him.

Jacob took his time rinsing her off. "How was the violet wand?"

"Spectacular. All those sensations, everywhere. It's unlike anything else, and I'd enjoy playing with it again sometime."

"I also have attachments you might enjoy."

HOLD ON TO ME

"Can I tell you something honestly? I liked that you used your body as the conduit. Your touch is what made it special."

"Anything my fair Elissa wants."

"Anything?" She curled her hand around his cock.

The whole time they'd been together in the shower, he'd become more and more aroused. And now, from her touch, he was fully erect.

She lowered herself to the tile floor and took him in her mouth and swirled her tongue around his tip, devilment dancing as she asked, "Even more sex?"

"Even more sex."

A few minutes later, they were dried off and back in bed. This time, they leisurely explored each other, and he savored every secret she revealed.

When it was over, he pulled her into his arms.

As she drifted off to sleep, she murmured something he couldn't quite make out. But she wiggled a little before settling more closely against his body.

He trailed a fingertip across her throat, then the collar he never wanted to remove.

Yeah, he'd seen a lot of ugly in his lifetime. Death. Despair. But Elissa's brightness was starting to vanquish the dark. For the first time in his life, he felt whole. And it was all thanks to her.

In gratitude, he kissed the top of her head.

"Good morning."

"Ugh. No." Elissa burrowed deeper under the covers and pulled the pillow over her head.

"I've got a surprise for you."

Next to her, the mattress dipped.

287

SIERRA CARTWRIGHT

Jacob? Suddenly she was awake. Awake and scrambling to understand what was happening.

Images, memories, flashed through her mind. The violet wand. Calling him Sir. His hands on her. Him carrying her to his room and tying her to the bed before making sweet, sensual love to her. Then falling asleep—naked—in the comfort and protection of his arms.

He tossed the pillow aside, and she blinked a couple of times, bringing him into focus.

As always, he was breathtaking. Along with faded jeans, he wore a T- shirt that clung to his broad chest. The crisp scent of the outdoors clung to him, but it was his slow, predatory smile that sent cascades of shivers through her.

He was so complex, from stern—even implacable—to reassuring, sexy, and now this. Lethal. All at once, his smile made her remember yesterday while simultaneously hinting at what was to come today.

"I'm a smart man. I brought you tea. Duke Somebody or Other."

Smart? How about perfect? "I think you mean Earl Grey."

"Whoever. I watched you make it yesterday." He shrugged "Hope you like it."

She sat up, dragging the covers with her, conscious of her nudity. "Is there a reason for your...hospitality?"

"Other than wanting to please you?"

Elissa narrowed her eyes.

"And knowing you're not much of a morning person?"

"Or the fact you're taking your life into your hands by waking me up?"

"You're ferocious, little lady. Terrifying, even."

"Hand it over, Mister."

With a grin, he gave her the peace offering. Surprisingly, the drink was still hot, and every bit as strong as she liked.

HOLD ON TO ME

"And you are correct." He waited until she'd had a second sip before speaking again. "I do have ulterior motives."

"Mmm-hmm." Over the rim of the cup, she regarded him. "I knew it."

He scooted closer to her, and every one of her synapses fired. "But first..." He brushed his lips across her forehead, then took away her beverage and kissed her mouth.

"Ohhh, yes..." The taste made her ravenous for more.

"That will have to do for now."

She scowled.

"Definitely ferocious when you don't get your way."

"You're learning, cowboy."

"Cowboy?" He lifted an eyebrow. "Rather than Commander Walker?"

"Seems fitting."

"I'm liking it. And don't think I don't want to tie you up and fuck you."

"We could start the day a little later."

His eyes darkened, and she wondered who she'd suddenly become. He brought out a naughty side of her personality she hadn't known existed.

"Except for the fact we have company, and while I enjoy your screams of delight, I'm not certain you want others overhearing them."

"Company?"

"Deborah—my housekeeper—is here with her daughter."

"I'm glad you told me. Does that also explain why you're dressed?"

"That, and the fact I wanted to get ready for our date."

"Our what?" Elissa searched his eyes for signs of teasing, but yet he'd told her he rarely joked.

"I thought you'd like to get out, take a ride out to the creek on the four-wheeler. Deborah brought us a picnic basket and filled it with food and all the other stuff she said we need to go with it. If you want, we can take a bottle of wine. We can head out around noon, assuming you want to go and your schedule permits?"

"You're serious?"

He nodded.

"You had me at wine." If she hurried, she could get in a couple of hours of work, even chat with her parents and Mary, the night manager at the pub, before leaving.

She put aside her cup and tossed back the covers.

"Oh, my lady, now we're definitely going to be late..." His eyes darkened as he moved toward her to capture one of her bare breasts.

Her nipple lengthened as he flicked a thumbnail across it, and an involuntary groan escaped from between her lips. "Jacob, please..."

"Is that a yes, continue? Or a please stop?"

Both. She wanted him to suck her nipple deep into his mouth, but she knew where that would lead. And he was definitely right about the way she'd scream when he had his wicked way with her. "Can we continue this later?"

"You can count on it." He lowered his hand, and she sighed, as much from relief as from frustration. "I'll meet you downstairs."

Once she was alone, she momentarily closed her eyes. This relationship with Jacob was unlike anything she'd ever experienced, and she needed to be careful with her emotions. Circumstances had thrown them together, and in a matter of time—hours? days? weeks?—she'd be back in her Denver apartment, working at the pub while building her business and finding rare, precious moments for her art.

No matter how much a part of her wanted this to continue, it wouldn't last. It would do no good to think about anything beyond the moment.

Resolved, she finished her tea, then hurried through her

HOLD ON TO ME

shower before dressing and going downstairs to meet the housekeeper.

Deborah was a tall, beautiful woman with a quick, welcoming smile, and she wore a T-shirt that read GOING DOWNHILL FAST. "Morning! You must be Elissa."

"It's nice to meet you."

"Jacob's been telling me all about you."

"Has he?" She scowled at Jacob, who was leaning against the counter, a cup of coffee in hand.

With a grin, he shrugged.

"I hear you're quite an artist."

"Ah…" Elissa cleared her throat. Just what had he said? Surely he hadn't mentioned her erotic images.

"You're working on a corporate logo for a motivational speaker?"

She released a breath she hadn't realized she was holding.

"I'm writing a children's book."

"Are you?"

"The main character is going to be a ski bunny."

"Your T-shirt… Obviously a skiing reference?"

"Yeah. I'm an instructor."

"Deborah is being modest." Jacob drained his cup, then slid it onto the counter. "She used to compete for the women's alpine team."

With her mouth open, Elissa looked back at Deborah. "Seriously?"

She nodded. "Until I blew out a knee one too many times. Still love it, though."

"Your celebrity will be a huge advantage."

"That's kind of you to say, but I'm sure no one remembers who I am."

Elissa's creativity was sparked. "Do you have a website?"

"No. Should I have one?"

SIERRA CARTWRIGHT

"Absolutely yes. Do you mind if I come up with a couple of ideas for you?"

"Are you kidding me right now? I mean, I can pay you a little bit, but—"

"Say no more. It's been a while since images have come to me this rapidly." And the Bonds computer would make working on them pure pleasure. "Do you have any concept drawings of your ski bunny?"

Deborah shook her head. "I don't have any talent in that area, and I haven't started looking for an illustrator yet."

"How about a color concept?"

"I was thinking along the lines of something like green or yellow."

Elissa nodded. "Bright? More muted?"

"Whatever inspires girls to go for their dreams."

"I love it."

At that moment, a young child walked in, clutching the massive, squirming Waffle against her chest.

"This is my inspiration." Deborah smiled. "My daughter, Adele."

Elissa grinned. Waffle's back was against the child's tummy, and the cat's large front paws hung over Adele's forearm.

"Honey, say hello, and put down the cat."

Rather than doing as her mother said, Adele held Waffle tighter. "But I love her, and she likes it."

Elissa was surprised Waffle tolerated being held at all.

Deborah sighed. "Do I need to repeat myself?" Though Deborah didn't raise her voice, her words were firm.

Chin set at a stubborn angle, Adele did as she was told. Shockingly, Waffle plopped her enormous body down at the girl's feet.

"And say hello to Miss Elissa," Deborah prompted again.

"Hi." She offered a tiny wave.

HOLD ON TO ME

"Nice to meet you, Adele."

"There's a teacher in-service at the preschool today, so we're driving to Steamboat for a little shopping."

Adele grinned, evidently forgetting all about the cat. "And ice cream!"

"Of course. How could I forget?" Deborah glanced at Jacob. "Picnic basket is on the table, and remember to use the ice packs I put in the freezer. Is there anything else you need before we leave?"

"That should be it," he responded. "I appreciate your stopping by."

"I'll send you some ideas for your website—and maybe even the bunny—in the next couple of days," Elissa promised.

"I'm so excited. Thank you."

After exchanging contact information, they hugged goodbye. And then Adele ran over. "Me too!"

Elissa crouched. "Of course."

For a quick second, Adele wrapped her arms around Elissa's neck before hurrying away to chase Waffle into the living room.

"I guess we'll be going for real now." Deborah grinned.

Jacob said he was going to walk them to the car and promised to be right back.

When the door closed, the house was suddenly silent, and Elissa stood there, staring, a dozen different thoughts and feelings racing through her.

Her days were consumed with work, and it had been a long time since she'd dated or even thought about the future.

But seeing Deborah and Adele together had made her . wonder what she was missing.

The love between the mother and daughter reminded Elissa of what she shared with her own mom. And would she ever feel that with her own child?

Fortunately Jacob returned, interrupting her musings.

SIERRA CARTWRIGHT

"Deborah liked you."

"It's mutual." To keep herself busy, Elissa turned on the kettle. "How did she become your housekeeper?"

"She's the sister of one of my ranch hands. Left a bad relationship right before Adele was born, and we put her in one of the property's cabins while she got back on her feet. She refused to accept what she called charity, so she insisted on doing some work around here. At this point, I'm not sure how I'd manage without her."

"Adele is wonderful. And even Waffle seems to like her."

"That says something." He grinned. "She's smart for her age, too. And she shows an aptitude for skiing, like her mother." He placed his cup in the sink. "Can you be ready to leave around twelve?"

"That's perfect." Even if he wanted to head out in ten minutes, she'd make sure she was ready.

"I'll meet you back here then."

She nodded.

Once again she was aware of how big the house was, and for the first time in her life, a pang of loneliness assailed her.

The strange emotions had to be a result of the even stranger circumstances, she reached for the box of pastries sitting on the counter. Bypassing the apple fritter and several eclairs, she grabbed a chocolate-covered chocolate doughnut, complete with sprinkles.

After she'd devoured it and brushed off her hands, she finished brewing her tea, then carried it outside.

She paused for a second to take in the view from the patio, refusing to admit the truth to herself—that she was hoping to catch a glimpse of Jacob in the distance.

With the drink cooling, she continued toward the garage apartment. Waffle darted in front of her, nearly tripping her as she opened the door.

HOLD ON TO ME

The cat wound her way between Elissa's legs before racing up the stairs. "I see you're joining me."

Inside, Waffle found a patch of sunshine and dropped down to groom herself.

Before starting work, Elissa made calls home to talk to her parents and to check in with the bar.

Once she'd powered up the computer and settled into her chair, her creative energy flowed. The previous day, she'd been stifled, but now, inspiration danced from her fingertips.

It took only a couple of minutes to decide on her final choices for the motivational speaker's color palette. It was a shade darker than she'd been working with, and the change made the logo pop.

Less than two hours later, she'd added a couple of finishing flourishes to the logo and drafted a mock-up of his website's landing page. Finally satisfied, she sent the files to her client for his approval.

Then, captivated by Deborah's excitement about the ski bunny, Elissa spent another hour sketching out a couple of versions of the cartoon bunny.

She was deep in concentration when a notification skittered across the bottom of her screen, signaling an email from her client. Curious to know if he was pleased, she clicked through to find he was more than happy. *"Yes!"* She fist-bumped the air, and Waffle shot her a narrowed-eye sleepy glare. "Oh. Sorry. Didn't mean to disturb Your Majesty." Elissa had never had pets, and she was enjoying the feline's companionship.

Elissa promised the vector file to her client within twenty-four hours and asked him to supply pictures and videos, along with text to populate the actual website. Elissa shut down the computer and headed back outside, Waffle trailing behind her.

SIERRA CARTWRIGHT

A noise captured Elissa's attention, and she paused. Moments later, Jacob drove up in a red all-terrain vehicle.

Instead of continuing on inside, she waited for him, admiring the way sunlight glinted off his dark hair. Even across the distance, she was aware of his gaze, and shivered anew at the way she'd come undone for him.

When he reached her side, he shut off the loud, rumbling beast and climbed out of the bucket seat. "Your ride, ma'am."

"I'm impressed." The machine had half doors, and the front part had a cover over it. "I imagined it would be a little more rugged than that."

"In what way?"

"I thought I'd be sitting behind you."

"You're thinking of a quad—all-terrain vehicle. Generally carries one person. This is a UTV—a utility task vehicle. It hauls cargo and can pull a small trailer. The seats are actually comfortable. Has heat and air-conditioning. Even a sound system." He cocked his head to one side. "But the idea of you straddling me and holding on tight has me rethinking my decision."

The image made her squirm, just as he'd no doubt intended. "This one's fine. Great even." Her tone was somewhere between prim and squeaky, and she cleared her throat.

He grinned. "Of course, we can save that for this evening."

For a moment, her heart skittered. She'd hated the idea of coming to his ranch, and yet all of a sudden she didn't want to leave. Denver and the outside world seemed so far away.

"I'll grab the picnic basket if you want to get a couple of towels from the hall closet."

"Why do we need towels?"

"So you can dry off after you get out of the water." He grinned.

"You might remember I don't have a swimsuit."

"Yeah. That's right." His grin turned feral. "There's a

HOLD ON TO ME

camping blanket in there too. Something for us to sit on. Or for me to ravish you on."

She shivered. His words excited her more than she could ever admit. "Oh no. No no no. *No.* Nuh-uh. There shall be no public ravishing, Cowboy."

His eyes narrowed. "Challenge accepted."

"That's not what I meant." Or was it? She cleared her throat. God. The way he looked at her... It might be impossible to deny him anything.

"You may want a hat. Or something to keep the hair out of your face."

She nodded, then hurried inside. While she was there, she changed into a pair of shorts, telling herself it wasn't because they'd be easier to get out of than her jeans were. As she'd already told him, she wasn't the type of woman who skinny-dipped or who made love outside—not ever.

Within minutes, carrying the items he'd requested, she rejoined him.

Very slowly, very thoroughly, very approvingly, he swept his gaze over her, lingering on her bare legs. "You're a beautiful woman, Elissa."

His words were laced with conviction. She'd never seen herself as anything other than ordinary, but she had no doubt he meant what he said, and for the first time in her life, she saw herself the way he did.

"You ready?"

"Yes. I'm excited."

He placed the picnic basket and a bottle of wine inside a storage box, then stacked the blanket and towels on top. After that, he added a folding table and a couple of collapsible chairs to the cargo area.

"I see we really don't need the blanket." Elissa propped one hand on her hip.

This time, there was no trace of a tease in his eyes.

SIERRA CARTWRIGHT

Instead, his gaze was as dangerous as it was predatory. "Oh I assure you, we do."

Her pulse picked up a few extra beats. Silently she cursed her very feminine reaction to him. The more determined he was, the more she was attracted to him.

He helped her into the vehicle. "Buckle up, Elissa."

Was that a warning?

After donning a ball cap that had been on the floorboards, Jacob climbed in next to her. Then he grabbed his cell phone and activated a button on its side. "Wildflower on the move. And we'd like some privacy."

"Roger that."

Without another word, he slid the device into a plastic holder attached to the dash.

"For a minute, I actually forgot why I was here."

"Good. I want you to relax."

Even though she honestly believed there was no real threat, there were constant reminders.

"We're doing our best to keep the intrusions to a minimum." He started the vehicle and headed down a narrow dirt road, in the direction of the distant Saddle Mountain.

"So who were you talking to?"

"Lifeguard."

She waited for him to go on. Instead, he focused on the road in front of him, features inscrutable. "Are you going to tell me anything more?"

"He's a coordinator, of sorts."

"Is this part of you trying to keep the intrusions to a minimum?"

After sparing her a quick glance, he nodded. "It's a balancing act. There's a lot of activity in the background that you don't see. And you have a right to the information you want to receive."

HOLD ON TO ME

She was more curious than ever. "You said the man on the phone is a coordinator, of sorts. What does that mean?"

"When we're running ops, he oversees them. No one knows more about the nitty-gritty details of how Hawkeye is organized than he does. He works out of a control center where he monitors everything and provides us with any assistance required."

As much as the safety belt would allow, she angled her body toward him. "Go on."

"He has our backs—handles any emergency call from anywhere on the planet and dispatches appropriate resources. Police. Fire. EMT. FBI." Jacob paused. He appeared to want to go on but didn't.

"And other people?"

He didn't respond. Instead, he deftly changed the conversation. "He was injured in combat, and he lost the use of his legs."

"Is he a friend of yours?"

He kept his gaze trained on the road ahead. "Yeah."

"And Hawkeye's?"

"We go way back."

"To the service? Peru?"

"Astute guess. When you go through something like that, it changes you. Those of us who made it out are still close. Well, except for one guy."

She remained quiet, studying him. A line furrowed between his eyebrows, and his lips were set. Lost in the past? "I'm sorry. I shouldn't pry."

"It was a long time ago."

"But you still never talk about it."

"No. I don't."

What must it be like to have seen so many horrors and to continue on? Jacob found solace in the land, while Hawkeye

SIERRA CARTWRIGHT

still sought refuge in his work. "And you don't forget." It was more of an insight than a question.

Just when she thought Jacob might ignore her, he reengaged in the conversation. "I moved on. That's the best I can hope for. Hawkeye is as loyal as they come, never forgets his men or their capabilities. He believes in people, even when they've lost faith in themselves. And Lifeguard? Taking care of us—protecting us—is his purpose. It drives him."

"What kind of phone is that?"

"Designed by—"

"Bonds?" It was a guess, but no doubt a good one.

"It has a few extra features that are useful in an emergency. He has one that allows him to see holograms."

"That—*what?* Like in the movies?"

"Entertaining as hell, but I'm not sure how useful it is. I generally like to keep my discussions more private."

"From what I've read, he's constantly dreaming up new ideas. Some of them are just for his amusement."

"Probably accurate."

A minute later, he stopped the UTV to point out a mule deer. As if realizing she was being watched, the animal froze, staring back with enormous eyes.

When they remained in the vehicle, she eventually looked away and began grazing again.

"Thank you. That was amazing."

"I thought you might like it."

A few minutes later, he hit a big bump, tossing her around, and she grinned. "This is fun."

"Fun? In that case, I'll let you drive us back."

"I'd like that." She took in the endless expanse of sky and a few puffy clouds. Because of their speed, the breeze managed to whip a few errant strands of hair across her cheeks.

Less than half an hour later, he braked to a stop in a small clearing.

HOLD ON TO ME

After unbuckling, she joined him at the back of the vehicle. The ground was carpeted in green, and a few shrubs sprang from the earth. "This is a wonderful spot. So beautiful, peaceful."

"I couldn't agree more."

While he set up the table and chairs, she wandered down to the river. Because it was only a tributary, it wasn't wide, and it was shallower than she expected. Colorful river rocks adorned the bed, and water burbled along invitingly. She crouched to test the temperature, then pulled her hand back against the bite of the chill. "It's freezing!"

"When the sun heats you up, you won't be able to resist the temptation of getting naked," he called back.

"You *are* persistent."

"I haven't even started turning on the charm yet."

Shaking her head, she returned to the makeshift campsite. He'd covered the table with a red-and-white-checkered cloth, and the picnic basket sat on top.

"Are you ready to eat?"

"I can wait for a little while."

"Good. That's what I was hoping to hear."

She shivered. "Do you ever stop?"

"Tell me honestly…" He thumbed back the bill of his baseball cap. "Do you want me to?"

The world went silent for a moment, and she found the courage to admit her truth. "No."

"Then we're in agreement." Gently, he captured her chin.

Her heart fluttered like a butterfly's wings. Even though she'd known him only a short amount of time, she craved him.

The intensity of his kiss shocked her. Rather than relaxed, it was urgent, and she responded to his passion, meeting each thrust of his tongue with a parry of her own.

He made her heart hammer and her thoughts swoon.

When her knees buckled, he caught her and pulled her tight against his chest.

"I've got you, Elissa."

Recognizing the inevitable, she surrendered. *"Yes."*

Jacob captured her mouth a second time. He slid his palm against her buttocks, pressing her against his pelvis. His cock was already hard, and the knowledge he wanted her turned her on. Response flooded through her, and she wrapped her arms around his neck, silently giving more than he asked.

He released her momentarily, long enough to search her features and to thread his fingers into her ponytail. His grip firm, he held her in place as he sought her lips once again, devouring her moans and whimpered pleas.

Desperate for more, she wrapped her arms around his neck and lifted her heels so she could move her hips against his.

He needed no other hints. "I'm going to make love to you."

Shocked that she needed his possession more than her next breath, she nodded and reached for his belt.

Within seconds, he'd taken over, pulling her shirt off over her head and unhooking her bra, seemingly all in the same sweeping move.

In the breeze, her nipples instantly hardened.

"Nice." He bent his head to suck one into his mouth, and desire plowed through her.

"Tell me you have condoms." She had to ask before common sense fled entirely.

"Always. I consider that essential equipment now that you're around, fair Elissa."

Thank God.

He removed his shirt and draped it around her shoulders, then left her only long enough to spread out the blanket and

HOLD ON TO ME

grab his cell phone. Something else he obviously considered essential.

Then he opened the metal button at her waistband. Looking in her eyes, he lowered the zipper. Instead of pulling her shorts off, he slid his hand inside, then brushed aside the gusset of her panties to stroke her clit.

At his light touch, she moaned.

"You're already wet, aren't you?"

"Mmm." He coaxed responses from her that she didn't know she was capable of.

As he continued to work his magic, she clamped her hands on his biceps for support and allowed her eyes to drift closed.

"Come for me, Elissa. No holding back."

His rough command melded with his masterful touch, lighting a fire deep in her. Within seconds, whimpering and crying, she climaxed, giving him what he demanded, as if it could be any other way.

Finally, when her breathing returned to normal and the brain fog cleared, she looked at him.

Maybe it was a trick of the sunlight, but she read purposeful intent in his dark green eyes.

"I need to be inside you, Elissa."

She nodded. Rather than satiating her, the orgasm had only made her crave him more.

After he guided her to the blanket, he tossed aside his hat. She reclined onto her elbows to watch as he shrugged off his lightweight jacket to reveal a gun holster.

He's carrying?

She shook her head. Of course he was. How could she think otherwise?

He covered the handgun with a towel, then tugged his T-shirt up, revealing the honed planes of his stomach. A shiver of arousal chased through her as he finished tugging the material over his head.

"See something you like?"

Elissa blushed. "I'll be honest, I've never been so fascinated by a male body before."

Showing zero embarrassment beneath her steady gaze, he gave her a quick grin. "And I meet your approval?"

A shiver tracing through her, she met his eyes. "You know you do." And she ached to explore every part of him with her fingers as well as her mouth.

He toed off his work boots and socks, then unfastened his belt before removing his jeans. His tight gray boxer briefs showcased his enormous erection. "You're ready for me, aren't you? Tell me you are."

"I always want you."

Jacob removed his underwear before stripping off her remaining garments. Within seconds he'd taken total control. He was lying on his back, and he captured her wrists to guide her on top of him.

"Couldn't get over the image of you like this, sitting up, wide open."

Being in nature, naked, straddling him, should have made her shy. Instead, his approval emboldened her.

He toyed with her pussy to ensure she was lubricated, allowing her to set the pace.

Since her insides were a little tender, she took him in small, measured strokes.

When he was all the way inside, he groaned. "My God, woman." He cradled her breasts, then tweaked her nipples.

The sensation—tenderness and pain in one—caused her to pitch forward. As she'd known he would, he caught her, protectively cradling her against him.

Then he grabbed hold of her ankles and tucked her feet

HOLD ON TO ME

inside his thighs, forcing her knees even farther apart, seating himself even deeper inside her.

"I..." She whimpered.

"You can." After taking hold of her chin, he kissed her deeply and for so long that her senses were overwhelmed, and she no longer noticed the discomfort of him filling her. "Touch yourself for me."

With as tight as he was holding her, it took some maneuvering for her to slide a finger across her swollen clit.

"That's it, Elissa."

He grasped her waist, steadying her as his powerful hips pistoned and he fucked her hard, seemingly with no restraint —not that she would deny him anything.

She was rising and falling on him, finding her climax when he moaned. How incredible this was, knowing he was on the verge.

Elissa lifted her head enough to watch him in fascination, adoring the way his lips pressed together and his jaw tightened.

His breaths were shallow, and he bit out her name, along with a soft curse.

The forceful way he came in her sent her over the edge, but he was there for her, clasping her again, murmuring reassuring words in her ear.

It wasn't until long minutes later that she became aware of the sounds around her—the burbling water, the cry of a hawk. She managed to slow her breathing and regain her bearings long enough to press a palm against his chest in order to sit up. She blinked against the sunlight and saw his triumphant smile.

"I think you liked that."

"More than a little." The admission was easier than she imagined it might be.

"Then I think you'll also enjoy my next suggestion." Using

SIERRA CARTWRIGHT

his superior strength, he managed to roll them over, leaving her pinned helplessly beneath him.

"Oh?" Skeptically, she raised her eyebrows.

"Skinny-dipping."

"I… Uh." She drew a breath. "We've had that discussion before. I don't do that kind of thing."

"Until five minutes ago, you didn't have sex outside either."

"But…"

"You have to admit, it will feel nice after being hot and sweaty."

No doubt he was right about that. Because there were no clouds, her skin was warm.

Unabashed, he stood and crossed to the four-wheeler. She sat up and watched as he discarded the condom, then grabbed two towels. He tossed one to her. "You can preserve your modesty with this."

"It's a little late for that."

"That's not a bad thing." He strode to the water and stepped in. "Cold, but not frigid." He crouched to pour a handful of the pure Rocky Mountain water over his chest and half-hard cock. "You'll love it."

"I don't know about that." Despite her reservations, she was tempted.

"Have I led you astray?"

"Not *yet*."

As if conceding her point, he grinned. "Never know when you will get another chance." He extended a hand toward her. "Live a little. Promise I'll keep you warm."

CHAPTER SEVEN

HAWKEYE

Clutching the towel closed, Elissa walked to the water's edge.

"So very brave."

She still wasn't convinced.

"It's okay once you get used to it." Eyes dancing with a wicked gleam, he scooped up a handful of water and flicked it in her direction.

That was the motivation she needed.

After dropping the towel, she waded in, gritting her teeth against the temperature shock. "Look, Mister…" She crouched to return the favor, splashing him hard enough to drench him.

He took it like a man, standing there grinning even as droplets raced down his chest and thighs. "Do it again. Only this time come closer."

Was that a threat? Or an invitation?

Either way, she couldn't resist him.

After taking two tentative steps toward him, she bent over. His reactions were lightning fast. He swept her up and dragged her against him, holding her close, pressing one palm against her buttocks and the other between her shoulder blades.

"Your nipples are hard."

"You said you'd warm me up."

His eyes telegraphed his intent, and she obediently tipped her head back to accept his kiss.

He claimed her, plundered, then silently promised her more. And she wanted everything he offered.

By the time he pulled back, she was shaking from a fresh wave of desire. And even though she expected him to release her, his grip was firm.

"Admit it. I was right. It's better than you thought it would be."

Against her, his cock began to harden again.

"Yes." Everything was. *The sex. His kiss. Skinny-dipping.* "Much better."

He brushed his lips across her forehead before letting her go.

Now that they weren't playing, the chill crept back in. She made her way to the river's edge to pick up her towel and wrap it around her before finding a large, warm rock to sit on.

"I think we have a bottle of chardonnay in the picnic basket. Shall I pour you a glass?"

"Please." She should help, but she was so comfortable that she didn't want to leave her spot.

A few minutes later, he joined her. He'd pulled on a pair of shorts but hadn't bothered to dry off. Was he immune to the cold, as well as everything else that bothered mere mortals?

"Scoot over."

She wiggled over a few inches, enough to give him a little room. Then she accepted the plastic tumbler he offered her.

HOLD ON TO ME

After sitting next to her, he tipped his glass toward hers. "Not a bad way to spend an afternoon."

They clinked their rims together.

"Actually I can't think of anything better."

He raised an eyebrow. "Still feeling like a prisoner?"

There were reminders, constant ones. But they'd faded into the background. "Not as much. I really needed this."

"Good. I have other ideas on how to keep you occupied."

So did she.

"Food."

She blinked. *"Food?"*

"What did you think I was talking about?" Jacob's voice held a light tease.

Right now, he was so different from the serious cowboy who'd kidnapped her and the implacable Dom who'd tied her up and sent shockwaves of orgasms through her body.

She liked every side of him and marveled at how much more emotionally revealing he was than any other man she'd ever been with.

"I'll set out the picnic, and you can join me when you're ready."

Once she'd finished her wine, she shimmied back into her clothes. No way would she ever be as comfortable with near nudity as he was.

Deborah had provided everything they might need, including utensils, plates, and napkins. The feast included fresh guacamole and tortilla chips, sandwiches on thick, crusty bread, olives, and a brick of cheese with apple slices as an accompaniment. There was also a delicious-looking assortment of cookies and brownies—not that Elissa needed them after this morning's doughnut. "This looks amazing."

After filling their plates, they sat in the chairs to enjoy the meal.

SIERRA CARTWRIGHT

"Are you really going to come up with an idea for Deborah's ski bunny? Or were you being polite?"

"I already have. But if she wants me to illustrate the children's book? I'll need a pseudonym."

"Because of the work you're doing on the portrait for me?"

"I never said I'd complete it."

"Then why else would you need a pseudonym?" With a triumphant grin, he stood, then offered to take her empty plate.

He'd won. And they both knew it.

An hour or so later, he dressed and loaded up the UTV. "Still want to drive it?"

"Really? You meant it?"

Once she was behind the wheel, he gave her a few quick instructions.

She accelerated and was shocked by the responsiveness. Quickly she backed off the throttle, then looked in his direction with her mouth parted from shock.

"Top speed is about sixty miles an hour."

That seemed really fast for this machine. "Am I scaring you?"

"It would take a whole lot more than that, Elissa."

She set a comfortable pace while he updated Lifeguard on their status.

While she drove, he scrolled through his phone before finally sliding it back into the compartment on the dash. "How many kids do you want?"

"Me?" Elissa took her eyes off the makeshift road long enough to glance at him again. "Why are you asking?"

"You asked me."

"But that was related to the ranch. Passing the land to the next generation."

"You're working with Deborah, and Adele really liked

you." He adjusted his ball cap. "Seemed like a logical extension to me."

"I've been so busy with life that I hadn't given a lot of consideration to being a mom." And this discussion would be easier if she wasn't sitting so close to a man she could suddenly picture as the father of her children.

"Hypothetically, then. Would you like to have kids?"

She flexed her fingers on the steering wheel. "I guess so. Yes."

"How many?"

For a moment, she considered her answer. "Two? Maybe three."

"I was thinking the same thing."

The summer air was suddenly too hot to breathe. *"What?"*

"I gave your question some more thought. Four sounds like a good number. Close in age. What do you think?"

They were having two separate conversations, weren't they? He couldn't possibly be talking about—thinking about—having babies with her. "Four?" The pitch of her voice was high and squeaky.

"Hypothetical children. Four's a good number, don't you agree?"

Heat, warm and liquid, flowed through her at the idea of having his children.

"This is hypothetical, right?"

"Until it's not."

He reached over to steady the steering wheel, and that's when she realized she was dangerously skirting the edge of the road.

"We can start with two and figure it out from there."

"Jacob…"

His phone rang. Without apology, he answered it. For minutes, while she sat there, thoughts swirling, he discussed ranch business.

As she braked to a stop near the house, he ended the call, with a promise to get back to the person he was talking to.

She exited the vehicle, and he joined her at the front of it. "I've got some work to do. Sorry. How about I join you for dinner in an hour or two? I'll cook."

A little time alone suited her fine.

Jacob paused for a second to trace her jawbone before striding into the house. She opted for a quick shower after being outdoors all afternoon...and having sex with him in the wide open.

When she returned to the main level, there was no sign of Jacob, and she was restless. After pouring a glass of wine, she headed back to her office, Waffle darting ahead, constantly underfoot.

Pulled by creative energy, she opened the image she was creating for him. Who was she trying to fool? From the moment he'd asked for it, it belonged to him, much like she did.

Chardonnay pushed to the side, she went back to work, darkening the submissive's hair and changing her eyes to blue.

She realized what had been confounding her—it was the muted emotion in the picture. While there was some, she wanted people who saw it to gasp at the realness of what was happening between the Dominant and his submissive.

But after surrendering to Jacob last night, and what they'd shared today, she was different. More open. More vulnerable. Maybe a little apprehensive. And she intended to infuse the image with the depth of her feelings.

Determined, she began her edits, dramatically changing the scene. She moved the woman's hair aside to expose her face. Then she altered the tilt of her chin. And now, instead of having her gaze cast down, the submissive looked up at

HOLD ON TO ME

her Dom through a fringe of lashes. Adoration melded with trust to create... Love.

Time stood still as she made hundreds of tiny corrections to the draft. Then, once she was satisfied, she pushed back from the desk and exhaled.

"Jesus." Jacob's single whispered word was heartfelt, and she knew the changes she'd made were the right ones.

She hadn't consciously heard him enter the apartment, but she'd known he was there. Every part of her recognized his presence and responded to it. She'd drawn inspiration from his comforting, commanding presence, even though he hadn't said a word.

Slowly she spun her chair to face him. He stood near the bar area, arms folded. His eyes were dark, radiating his approval.

"May I?"

"It's not the image you asked for. So if you'd like me to work on the other, I can. I still have the original saved."

As he crossed the room, she turned back to the monitor.

He stood behind her, hands tight on her shoulders. "It's even better than the previous version."

"I'm glad you're pleased." Now all she needed to do was translate it onto canvas, which would be a painstaking process—and worth every minute.

"But I want to see that expression in your eyes this evening."

She tipped her head back to meet his gaze.

"After dinner, I want you to present yourself to me in the dungeon. You'll wear my collar. This time, you'll ask me to put it on you."

His voice was confident, as if he didn't question her compliance.

"Be mine, Elissa."

That word again—*mine.*

SIERRA CARTWRIGHT

Every time he said it, it became truer for her.

———

For the fifth time in as many minutes, Jacob took his gaze off the camera feed in front of him and checked his watch. Eight o'clock couldn't come soon enough.

Earlier, they'd eaten dinner together, but Elissa had mostly pushed food around her plate. She'd been jumpy, as if nervous about their upcoming evening together.

Rather than soothing her, he'd slipped into Dom mode, telling her what time to meet him, and asking her to wear nothing other than his T-shirt when she arrived. Though he preferred her naked, until she was more comfortable, that was too big of a request.

After sending her upstairs to get ready for their evening ahead, he'd taken a shower, then headed to his command center to call Hawkeye. Of course the man hadn't answered, and now Jacob was reviewing tape from the day and glancing through the notes provided by the security team.

Nothing out of the ordinary. John Mansfield, the agent occupying the temporary guard shack near the ranch's gated entrance, reported the arrival of a delivery van at one thirty-seven p.m. The driver proceeded to the house and dropped off several boxes that Jacob had ordered. The van was logged back off the property fourteen minutes later.

All perimeter reports filed by Laurents and Johnson were clear.

The phone trilled with Hawkeye's ringtone. "Walker."

As expected, Hawkeye skipped ordinary pleasantries. "How's Wildflower?"

Though he knew his friend was hoping for a detailed answer, Jacob had no intention of revealing anything that wasn't necessary. "Adapting."

HOLD ON TO ME

"That sounds promising."

Before Hawkeye dug for more information, Jacob seized control of the conversation. "What have you found out?"

"Not fucking enough."

The response was more honest than Jacob had expected.

"The list of my enemies is long."

"Narrowed it down?"

"According to the profilers we've got working on it, we're most likely looking for a man, though a woman can't be ruled out."

"Because of the anthrax."

"And the UNSUB is targeting people I care about."

Jacob nodded. In general, certain patterns of behavior were perpetrated by men. But women were known to use poisons. So the unknown subject could be either sex.

"We're looking at protective services cases where one of our clients got hurt or lost someone close to them."

"Or something from our ops overseas." Over the years, there'd been plenty of casualties, intentional as well as unfortunate, unintentional ones. "And there was a training accident at the compound."

"As I said, the list is long." Hawkeye's voice held a weary note. "We're assigning investigators to the targets that seem most likely."

It had to be asked. "Including Colombia?"

"Yeah."

Maybe if they'd been called in earlier, the Hawkeye team could have provided more help and had a better outcome. As it was, Melvin Rollins thought he could pay the hefty ransom and secure his daughter's release. Thirty-six hours after the money drop, there had been no sign of her. Frantic, Rollins had hired Hawkeye. But by the time Jacob and the rest of the team located her, she'd been dead—for less than two hours.

The abject horror and disappointment had killed his desire for any further involvement with security.

On the day of his daughter's funeral, Rollins had given a grief-stricken press conference, unfairly blaming Hawkeye Security for failing to mobilize faster.

"Rollins is supposedly out of the country at the moment."

Which didn't mean he was innocent, but it made him less likely a suspect.

"We're working twenty-four seven."

Which meant they were consuming a lot of resources.

"Keep Wildflower safe."

The idea of anyone harming her sent raw anger and fury surging in him. *They'd have to go through me first.*

He ended the call, then left his command center. In the hallway, he paused. Water was running, and the soft scent of lavender filled the air. That was all it took for him to be ravenous, his whole body demanding he possess her.

To steady himself, he dragged a hand through his hair.

He'd never been in love before, never understood why men did stupid things—wrote poetry, sent flowers, bought stupidly expensive rings, forgot common sense—when it came to women.

And now. Now he knew.

Because he was in danger of thinking about nothing other than her and the future he wanted them to create together.

Earlier, they'd talked about children. Until now, it had been little more than an abstract idea. His grandparents had wanted him to keep the ranch in the family, passing it on to their heirs. This afternoon, though, the idea took hold, and he couldn't shake it. He imagined spilling his hot seed inside Elissa's slick pussy, then seeing her pregnant with his baby.

He pictured their kids learning to ride horses, playing in the river, ice skating on a pond, traversing every inch of the land, then, as they were older, heading out on snowmobiles to find the perfect Christmas tree.

For a man who'd lived only for the present, this was a hell of a departure for him.

The house fell silent, and then the sound of a soft splash reached him.

Since less than an hour remained before she would join him, he jogged down the stairs. Unnecessarily he double-checked that all locks were engaged, and he informed the team they were in for the night.

Then he entered the dungeon to prepare it for her arrival.

He adjusted the room temperature so it was a little on the warm side. Since he intended to have her bare before him, he wanted her to be comfortable. He placed a couple of bottles of water in the refrigerator to chill, and he draped a light-weight blanket over the back of the chair. Even though it was summer, she might want to snuggle for comfort after the scene.

He checked the equipment he intended to use, making certain everything was in working order. Finally he completed two circuits around the space and stopped with his back to the fireplace, waiting.

Right on time, she arrived, pausing in the open doorway.

Her perfection took his breath away.

His T-shirt reached the middle of her thighs, and her hair brushed her shoulders. She looked at him with a mixture of trust and apprehension.

"I've been waiting for you."

Yesterday, their scene had progressed naturally, starting with a kiss. Tonight, he wanted to create something a little more formal, hoping to nudge her into a submissive head-space before they began. If his plan worked, tonight's experience would be even more pleasurable. "I'd like you to undress before entering."

SIERRA CARTWRIGHT

Though she hesitated, she didn't protest.

In a single move, she pulled the material off and allowed it to fall to the floor.

Her nipples blossomed into tight buds, and she clasped her hands in front of her for a brief second before evidently realizing what she'd done. With a deep inhalation, she lowered her arms to her sides.

"Come to me, Elissa."

Nodding, she crossed to him, her bare feet silent on the floor. He'd decided against music. He wanted to hear her breaths, every sigh, moan, whimper.

"Uhm…"

"Kneel, my fair Elissa."

Her motions were perfect, artistry mixed with grace. "Open yourself. Your hands behind your neck with your shoulders and elbows turned back."

Once she did, he uttered words of praise. "Perfection. It's as if you're offering your breasts to me."

"Yes…Sir."

Generally when they spoke, her voice was strong. But here, there was a quiet submissive respect that he adored. She was still the confident woman he had fallen for, but she was willing to reveal a side she hid from the world. That was heady indeed, and he vowed to honor that trust. "Now spread your knees as far apart as you can."

Because she couldn't use her hands for balance, she made a couple of adjustments before settling in.

"Exactly as I like. This is what I mean when I ask you to open yourself."

"I'll remember."

He left her long enough to fetch a thin collar and a delicate leash. While the pieces weren't an exact match for the ones in the image she was working on for him, they were close enough. "Ask me."

HOLD ON TO ME

Her voice wavered, barely above a whisper. "Please put your collar on me, Sir." Mouth slightly parted, she stared up at him while he fastened it in place.

He could repeat this act every day for the rest of his life and never tire of it.

Her breath caught when he attached the leash.

Holding the end, he took a step back, instantly recognizing that her picture had captured this moment in advance.

Her wildflower-blue eyes were wide with adoration. Though she'd never professed her love, he saw it in her gaze.

And he had no doubt the same was reflected in his.

More than ever, he was anxious for her to get on with the painting so he could have the portrait here where it belonged. "I'd like you on the top of the spanking bench."

"Of course, Sir."

Jacob offered no assistance while she stood, preferring to watch her sensual movements. "Go ahead. I'll follow you."

He remained where he was until the leash tightened, and she froze to look back at him.

Having her at his mercy like this made his cock hot and heavy, throbbing with need. "A perversion," he offered by way of apology. "I wanted to see what you would do." With enough force, the leash would snap. His control over her was not much more than an illusion, and without her permission, he held no power.

"And?" She tipped her head quizzically. "Is this a game? If so—"

"No." He held up a hand. "I promise you, it's not. We're simply exploring this part of our relationship. Continue."

This time, he followed her, close enough that the lead remained loose.

When she arrived at the bench, she placed a knee onto one of the siderails.

"I want you on your back, not your belly."

She looked over her shoulder. "Sir?"

"I have a few things in mind before I begin to torture you."

Her gulp of fear thrilled him. "Up you go. Then scoot to the end and part your thighs."

Once she was in place, he removed her leash and fastened it to one of his belt loops, then stood at the far end of the bench.

"I'm confused."

"I think what you mean is that you're being patient while awaiting your Dominant's next instruction."

"Yes. That's exactly what I meant. Sir."

Perfectly trusting. Perfectly compliant. Perfectly his. "There's a mirror on the wall to your right. Look at yourself."

Though she turned her head, it was his gaze she sought.

"Watch us."

As if to ask a question, she opened her mouth. A scant second later, she closed it again.

"Very good." He smiled, and in response she wriggled around a little before resettling. "Now, remembering my command to watch us, I want you to get yourself off."

She went rigid.

Rather than chastise her, he gently cupped her breasts, then squeezed them. In reaction, she moaned and arched her back.

Exerting a tiny bit more pressure, he leaned over to capture her mouth.

He took every bit of her sweetness and demanded more. When her tender mouth was swollen, he reluctantly ended the kiss.

While she watched, he pinched her sensitive nipples, and she gasped. "You're driving me mad."

"Good."

Without further prompting, she began to masturbate,

HOLD ON TO ME

using her left hand to spread her labia while using her right index finger to stroke her clit.

Watching her get off while he played with her tits made his cock ache. Jacob had never been driven by lust, until she blazed into his life.

"Jacob... Sir..."

"Hold off a little longer."

She bit into her lower lip, and she moved her finger off her clit.

"I didn't give you permission to stop."

"But—"

"Or to argue. You may want to do as you're told before I change my mind about letting you have an orgasm at all."

In the mirror, her eyes pleaded with him. Delighting in the power of her obedience, he shook his head.

"It's pleasure." She whimpered. "And pain."

Jacob severed the connection of their gazes to look in the mirror attached to the wall in front of him. "You've allowed your thighs to close."

When she moaned instead of correcting her error, he tugged on her nipples harshly before releasing them.

"Oh! *Oh!* I'm going to come."

"My wonderful little sub enjoys a little nipple play? Good to know." His use of the mirrors provided an added dimension. She was compelled to stare at him, but he was looking at her pussy. She couldn't see him clearly enough to read his reactions. "But no orgasm yet."

"Ja-*cob!*"

"You may want to do as I said. Show me your clit. Let me see how swollen it is, how needy it is. And did I say you could stop playing with it?"

Elissa hiccupped a tiny cry. There was no artifice here, just pure feminine response to his dominance. Her abdominal muscles quivered as she parted her legs, then pulled back her pussy lips.

"Move your right hand to your tummy and keep that pretty cunt on display."

Her clit was as swollen as he'd hoped. That she'd held off her orgasm as long as she had was probably nothing short of a miracle.

Like a wolf, though, he was hungry for more. "It doesn't look at all like you need to climax."

"What?"

"You may continue."

She tore her gaze away from the mirror to look up at him. "Question, sub?"

Color fled from her face, as if she realized what she'd done. "No! I mean, no, Sir."

Because she didn't immediately correct her mistake, he slowly walked around to the far end of the bench. "Perhaps you need a little assistance."

"I'm sorry, Jacob." Misery dripped from her words.

"Nothing to apologize for."

"Does this mean… Are you going to let me come?"

"If you were the Dominant, what would you do?"

"That's not a fair question."

"Is it not?" He slipped his forefinger inside her, then brushed her clit with the moisture. "Nevertheless, it's one I'd like an answer to."

She curled her right hand into a tight fist.

"Waiting." Enjoying her ever-more frantic movements, he flattened the pad of his finger on her clit.

"Fuck. Fuck, fuck, *fuck.*"

"Elissa? If you were me, what would you do to a submissive who can't control herself?"

"I guess…" She jerked her pelvis toward him, silently

HOLD ON TO ME

begging him to get her off. "I'd make her come multiple times."

"Forced orgasms until she couldn't stand up or think?" *Wily.* He fought to suppress his grin. "You wouldn't deny her entirely and keep her on the edge?"

"No." She panted. "Absolutely not."

"So you'd do this…" He inserted two fingers inside her.

"Yes. Yes. That's it."

"And this?" He eased out, then slid forward again with three digits, stretching her. "Are you watching in the mirror?"

At his prompting, she turned her head to do as he said.

"I want you to see my fingers in your pussy."

Her muscles began to clamp down on him. Helplessly she struggled to press herself against his hand as she sought relief. "Please, Sir. Please?"

"You beg so pretty." He moved, then teased the entrance to her tightest hole with one of his pussy-slickened fingers. "You're getting so close to being rewarded."

"Oh God. I can't, Jacob." She jerked her hips in desperation. "I mean it. This is too much. Too, too much."

"You can. You can do this for me."

Tiny beads of sweat glistened on her chest. Had he ever pushed a submissive this far? And how much more could she —would she—take? Fuck, she was hot. Beyond amazing.

"I'm going to come."

"Of course." In the mirror, he captured her gaze. "In about a minute. Maybe two."

She squeezed her eyes shut. This time, he let her get lost in her head. "Count, breathe, anything to distract yourself from what I'm going to do next." Her body convulsed as he slowly finished inserting his finger into her ass.

Elissa cried his name over and over. The sound echoed

around the room, bringing him pure Dominant satisfaction. "Keep your labia spread, Elissa."

Her mouth parted, the only acknowledgment of his demand.

Still finger-fucking both of her holes, he bent to eat her pussy.

He filled her, consumed her.

Then she screamed as her entire body went rigid and her juices drenched his hand.

Before opening her eyes, she drank in long gulps of air. He eased his fingers out of her and helped her to move back a little on the bench so she could prop her feet on the siderail for support.

"You're even more beautiful when you come, Elissa."

She struggled to sit up, and he offered his forearm for leverage.

"That was…" With a sigh, she wrapped her arms around her. "I'm actually no longer sure what day it is."

"Then my job here is done."

Her eyes widened. "Really?"

He laughed. "Fear not. We haven't gotten started yet." A fact his cock was insistently reminding him of.

"That's a little frightening."

"Then, fair Elissa, you should be terrified." He left her long enough to wash his hands and grab her a bottle of water.

Since she was still a little shaky, he uncapped it for her before asking, "How much of a break do you need?"

After taking a sip, she offered the water back to him. "What do you have in mind, Sir?"

Pride in her surged through him. A sub who could keep up with his pace was priceless. "There's the small detail of your failure to keep your gaze on us while I was being generous enough to give you an orgasm."

HOLD ON TO ME

Her breaths were shallow. "But wait." She glanced up at him, with hunger in her expression. "I can explain."

"Unnecessary."

"I'm throwing myself on your mercy, and your understanding nature."

He scoffed.

She blinked several times in quick succession.

"Did you just bat your eyelashes at me, submissive? Trying to manipulate me into going easier on you?"

"Me?" She pressed a hand to her heart in mock surprise. "I'd never do such a thing. Perhaps Sir is mistaken."

"Mmm. Not convinced, Elissa."

She shivered, more from anticipation than fear, he surmised. "Let's attach you to the bench in a more conventional way, shall we?"

He relished the sight of her as she straddled the top, then settled in. After she was in place, he grabbed some ties to hold her securely. "What's the appropriate punishment?"

"Forced orgasms, Sir."

Jacob laughed. Her response had been too quick, as if she'd prepared in advance. "Try again."

"Uhm…" She moved around until she could see him. "A spanking?"

"And you'll watch from beginning to end?"

"I'll keep my eyes open this time, Sir."

If she became as lost in pleasure as he intended, there would be no way for her to do as she promised. He strode across the room to select a small leather flogger.

When he returned to the bench, her body was supple with relaxation, despite her bonds. In fact, they seemed to free her. "Gorgeous."

"Touch me?"

As if he could refuse her anything. Gently he rubbed her back and shoulders.

SIERRA CARTWRIGHT

Her breaths became deeper, and she sighed. "Could we do this all night?"

"We could. Maybe a little oil and candlelight?"

"Sounds nice. But I'd prefer something a little different."

Their gazes met in the mirror, and she gave him a soft, serene smile he would never forget.

"I can get a massage at any spa. But I've never had another experience like this. I'd rather scene with you."

With long, slow motions, Jacob moved lower until he reached her buttocks. Then he increased the pressure to warm her up.

He continued, until even the backs of her thighs were light pink color.

Only when he was sure she was ready did he pick up the flogger.

For the first few minutes, she was able to keep her vow. Then as he heightened the intensity, she rested her cheek on the vinyl pad and seemed to fall into a light sleep. "Are you with me, Elissa?"

"Mmm-hmm."

He was flogging her in earnest now, leaving small welts on her skin. The more intense his strokes, the more approving her feminine little sounds.

Slowly he eased off, bringing her back to reality.

"Elissa?" He brushed strands of hair back so he could read her expression.

"Will you fuck me, Sir?"

Consumed by desire, he released her from bondage. "Please situate yourself at the end of the bench."

"Yes, Sir."

While she got into position, he undressed and rolled a condom down his cock. One day, in the not-too distant future, they'd be making babies instead of worrying about contraception.

HOLD ON TO ME

Her buttocks were still hot from his spanking, making him groan. This woman would be his undoing.

"I need you in me."

Instead of taking her as he wanted, he fingered her clit, just to be sure she was ready. The little bundle of nerves hardened, and she moaned, arching her back as she offered herself to him.

The scent of her arousal was an aphrodisiac, and his need could no longer be contained.

Jacob eased his cock into her and began to stroke.

"This…" She tightened her buttocks as she rocked back and forth. "Yes…"

"Elissa…" He dug his fingertips into her hipbones and dragged her back, allowing him even deeper inside her.

"Oh Jacob! Sir!"

"Press your breasts against the bench, then come for me."

He forced himself to hold back while she ground out a screaming climax. Over and over, she called his name. Her sounds and their friction were potent and primal, and he went rigid, gritting his teeth as he orgasmed in a long, hot stream.

She was breathing heavy, and she didn't move even as he withdrew.

"Stay where you are."

"Don't worry, Sir. I don't think I can stand up on my own."

He grinned, her comment making him stupidly happy.

After throwing away the condom, he crossed back to her, picking up the blanket on the way.

He wrapped it around her before helping her down.

When her feet were on the floor, her knees wobbled, so he scooped her up and carried her toward the chair in front of the fireplace.

"You sweeping me off my feet seems to be a bit of a habit."

"Objections?"

She pressed a hand to his chest. "Not even one."

"I kind of like it myself." He managed to sit while still holding her.

"So strong."

"Flattery, Elissa?"

"An observation, Sir."

Maybe. Regardless, her approval mattered, feeding the hungry wolf inside him. His woman was proud of him.

She snuggled against him, and he inhaled the subtle scent of her shampoo.

"When I have fantasies about BDSM, they're like this."

"In what way?"

"The aftercare. Well, and during care, too. I felt safe, which allowed me to completely let go. You don't seem impatient to get rid of me and get back to your real life."

Maybe he'd be able to make her understand that she *was* his real life.

"Honestly I've never had a scene like this before. Like you're genuinely concerned about me enjoying it, and you're not just going through the motions."

He'd likely been guilty of that when he was younger, and he cursed the insensitive bastard he'd been. Now his focus was Elissa, and her enjoyment was paramount.

"There's something different about being in a relationship with—" She broke off before sitting up and attempting to escape. "Not that we do. I mean, we're not, and you're not—"

"Stop." He tightened his arms around her waist, keeping her close, determined to nurture her emotions with the same ferocity that he'd protect her physical body. "We do have a relationship. When this is over, we'll figure it out. But I'm not prepared for you to walk out of my life without a backward glance." If necessary, he'd follow her to the ends of the earth.

"Jacob…" She placed a hand on her throat.

"How does your ass feel?"

As he'd hoped, her eyes darkened.

"Are you trying to distract me?"

"No more so than you were with me earlier." He grinned. "Answer my question, subbie."

"Fine. I guess." She wrinkled her nose. "What do you have in mind?"

His cock stirred.

"Oh." She bounced a little, making him even harder.

With her in his arms, he stood and carried her to his bedroom. "We've got a long night ahead of us, Elissa."

"Let's get started, Sir."

CHAPTER EIGHT

HAWKEYE

Consciousness teased the edges of her sleep, but Elissa didn't want to wake up. Instead, she pulled the comforter tighter around her and tried to drift off again. But clattering sounds continued to disturb her. And then there was the scent. Coffee. Even though it wasn't her preference, there was no denying its enticement.

Not inclined to give up, she opened her eyes long enough to find a pillow; then she pulled it over her head. As had been a habit since she'd arrived a week ago, she was in Jacob's bed. Protected in the comfort of his arms, she slept better than she ever had before. And waking up and having leisurely sex in the middle of the night was amazing.

He didn't need as much rest as she did, and most mornings he let her stay in bed as long as she wanted.

Even though she'd protested mightily at being kidnapped, the experience had been amazing.

Her creative energy had been higher than ever. She'd met the deadline for her client, and she'd started painting the piece Jacob had commissioned. Additionally she'd kept in

SIERRA CARTWRIGHT

contact with her parents at the pub. Joseph was still helping out, and they seemed happy, if a little tired.

Not only that, but her evenings were spent with Jacob, watching television, talking in front of the outdoor fire, or scening. Still, she couldn't get enough of him.

Without knocking, he entered the bedroom. "I brought you tea."

His bribe was almost enough to tempt her to remove the pillow. *Almost.* But after the intensity of last night's sex, she wanted rest more than anything.

"It's your favorite."

"Hmm."

"Earl Matcha, or somebody like that. Not sure who he is."

He was impossible, and every day he came up with innovative names for her drink. With a laugh, she tossed aside the pillow, then sat up and aimed it at him.

He ducked, avoiding contact, all without rattling the cup. "Stop with the missiles! I know the difference, honest. You drink Earl Grey in the morning because of the caffeine. Matcha is what you prefer in the afternoon. And it gets made in a whole different way. It's a lot more complicated and makes a green mess all over the counter."

For a moment, she lost her voice. Like that first morning, he was wearing nothing but shorts, and her reaction was visceral. Every time she saw him, he was even more breathtaking.

Already, they were building a history together, layers of memory, making him more complex. In addition to his stunning looks, he was infinitely gentle and patient with her. He cared for her during and after a scene and always, always made certain her needs were met.

How was she going to manage when this crisis was over and she was back at home, alone, and he was no longer part of her life? Though he'd reserved the right to talk about a

HOLD ON TO ME

future, one was impossible. His life was here, and hers was with her parents in Denver.

Trying to restore her equilibrium, she pretended everything was okay by saying the first thing that popped into her mind. "So what do I have to do to earn it?"

He looked at the drink, then back at her. "Well, considering it's the Earl with a splash of whole milk, I'd say the bar is pretty high."

"I have an idea."

"Do you, indeed?"

"Why don't you put the cup down, Sir?"

"As I've said before…anything for the lady." He placed it on the nightstand.

"Grab a condom while you're there." She'd never been the initiator before, and judging by the way he angled his head to one side, he liked her boldness. "Then bring your beautiful cock back to bed."

He grinned.

But not for long. Once he was lying on the bed, she stroked and licked him to hardness, sucking his length down her throat.

Digging his hands into her hair, he moaned. "Jesus, Elissa."

He began to pump harder. When she realized he was getting close to coming, she stopped what she was doing.

"You're a fucking goddess at that."

She couldn't help her triumphant grin.

"I had no idea you had that skill."

She didn't either. Until him, she had no interest in even trying. And she'd had no idea how thrilling it was to turn him on like that.

Somehow, even with her hand trembling, she managed to unwrap the condom, then sheathed him in it.

While he watched, she slid a finger inside herself, then

SIERRA CARTWRIGHT

pulled it out to show him how much he aroused her. "You do this to me, Jacob."

"That's enough." He captured her hand to lick the glistening drop from her, then dragged her on top of him.

She leaned forward to brush a kiss against his mouth. His jaw was tight, showing his restraint.

Elissa adjusted her position, lifting herself up to guide his cockhead toward her pussy.

He was enormous, filling her completely, and she took a few breaths to relax while her body adjusted to the depth of his penetration. Because they had sex so often, her insides were still sore, but her need for his possession was too powerful to ask him to stop.

For the first couple of minutes, he allowed her to be in charge, and she rode him with slow, sexy, rhythmic undulations.

But then, inevitably, he growled. "You're fucking killing me, Elissa."

With that, he dug his fingers into her buttocks and lifted her higher with the next stroke, changing the pace, becoming more frenetic, hotter. Her breasts bounced, and her hair wildly swung back and forth. Every part of her was on fire from his possession.

She was lost in him.

Her orgasm loomed just beyond reach. As if knowing that, he moved one of his hands from her ass, licked a finger, then pressed it against her anal whorl. The pressure, combined with their motions, made her splinter. She came hard, and her body shattered beneath his relentless sensual assault.

Screaming, she pitched forward. As always, always, he caught her, wrapping her tight while she recovered. This time, however, he continued to rock his hips, sliding just the tip of his cock in and out.

HOLD ON TO ME

The sensation was different, tingling, ratcheting her tension again.

Like the generous lover he was, Jacob brought her to a second climax before he unleashed his powerful control.

"Fuck. *Fuck.*" His body went rigid, and muscles and sinews contracted.

Watching him orgasm—seeing the result of their joining taking him apart—sent a rocket of feminine satisfaction arrowing down her spine.

They held on to each other until their breathing returned to normal, and she savored the moment.

Before she was ready—not that she ever really would be—he helped her to climb off him.

He rolled to his side and wrapped a lock of her hair around his hand. "That'll have to hold us."

"Can it be evening yet?"

"You, me, the dungeon at seven?"

"It's a date."

After pressing his thumbpad against her chin in a motion that was both affectionate and possessive, he climbed out of bed and headed for the bathroom. In the doorway, he stopped and looked back at her. "Oh, Elissa?"

"Hmm?"

"Your tea is cold."

"It was worth it." She grinned. "Most definitely worth it, Sir."

"WOOT!" ELISSA PUSHED SEND ON THE EMAIL TO HER CLIENT, letting him know the final touches on his website were done, which meant the entire project was now complete. Online, the speaker's branding was consistent across all platforms, from social media to business card, making him appear

SIERRA CARTWRIGHT

professional as well as polished. She took a few minutes to finalize his invoice, which was almost as rewarding as finishing the actual work.

Right now, everything was perfect with the world—well, except for the fact that she could use a hot bath to ease the tension from her muscles, and it wasn't just from sitting in front of a computer for hours. It mostly had to do with the way Jacob had attached her to the Saint Andrew's cross and spent an hour having his wicked—and delicious—way with her last night—not that she was complaining.

The last two weeks with Jacob at his ranch had been amazing. Relaxing. Though she talked or video chatted with her parents at least once a day, the disconnect from her regular life had allowed her to see things differently and be more attuned to the wonders of nature around her.

Because of the mountain darkness, the number of stars at night was breathtaking. She'd downloaded an app so she could figure out which constellations and planets were visible, and she was starting to recognize them. A couple of times, she and Jacob had sat quietly near the firepit and watched the moonrise. She was enjoying it so much she was considering buying a telescope. Which she might actually do once her client paid his bill.

With a smile of satisfaction, she closed all of her client's files, then decided to take a quick break to celebrate and reset before working on Jacob's portrait.

That morning, he said he needed to work on some ranch business and provide guidance on some projects and help repair fence line. She'd walked him out to the UTV, and he'd promised to return midafternoon, and informed her that Hawkeye's agents were close.

One was stationed at the gate. Another was in proximity to the house. A third was patrolling the grounds a little farther out. They had a drone in the air, and it would patrol

HOLD ON TO ME

the grounds in segments. Jacob had a link to all the cameras on his cell phone. Radio checks would occur every thirty minutes, and Lifeguard was periodically monitoring the feeds.

Then, unmindful of anyone who might be watching, he'd given her a kiss so deep, coaxing a response so immediate and powerful that she had no doubt that he was the only man for her.

A peek out the window showed that Deborah was still at the main house, and Elissa looked forward to visiting with her for a few minutes. And a cup of matcha would be perfect to help her switch into a different frame of mind.

"Kettle's already turned on," Deborah said when Elissa slid open the patio door. "I saw you walking across."

"However much Jacob's paying you, you deserve a raise."

Deborah grinned. "I'll tell him you said so."

Outside, Waffle raised up on her haunches and pressed her front paws on the door. "She's a pest." Deborah sighed. "If she's inside, she wants to be out. If she's outside, she wants to be in."

"I can sort of relate," Elissa admitted. "Relaxing in the hot tub is always appealing when I'm cooped up in my office." Funny how she'd already claimed the garage apartment as hers. "But when I'm out there, I get all these ideas that make me want to be back at my computer."

Once she opened the door, the cat dashed in. In a blur, she ran past Elissa and jumped up on the counter to steal a piece of bacon.

"Shoo!" Deborah waved her arm, but Waffle was already running out of the room in a flurry of fur.

Elissa laughed. "She won that one."

"She has no manners at all. If she wasn't so darn lovable..." The kettle beeped, and steam escaped the spout.

SIERRA CARTWRIGHT

Deborah used some of the boiling water to warm the inside of the ceramic teapot before starting to brew the matcha.

While waiting, Elissa perched on a barstool. "How's the book coming?"

"Slow. Every word is an effort, and I second-guess every one of them. Does it convey the right tone? Is it entertaining enough?" She sighed. "I always have three files open. The document, a dictionary, and a thesaurus. Every day I seem to remove more words than I add. I honestly had no idea how long this would take or how hard it would be to concentrate. Sometimes I think I'm my own worst enemy."

"Do you make up stories for Adele?"

Deborah nodded. "That's where the idea came from."

"Have you tried recording one and transcribing it? I mean, just doing it without judging it as you go?"

"As if." Deborah rolled her eyes, and Elissa laughed.

"How about a transcription service? You send the voice file, and they send you back text?"

"That's an interesting idea." Deborah leaned against the counter "When I'm at the computer, I think differently than when I'm just entertaining my kid, you know? And then I'm always second-guessing myself."

"It's an idea. I had a client who couldn't provide any of the verbiage he needed to complete his website, so he employed that technique. It hadn't been perfect, but at least they'd had something to edit." She shrugged.

"Might be worth a try."

"I've been playing with your website. Of course, I'd prefer everything to be in your voice, but I found some articles about you online, so I came up with a rough draft of your bio. I understand you're modest about your accomplishments, but that's the thing you'll need to stand out."

Deborah poured a cup of tea and slid it across the counter. "I'm not comfortable talking about myself."

HOLD ON TO ME

"That's why I'm working on it for you." Elissa grinned. "And we need to start talking about social media, and you posting pictures from around the Steamboat area since you'll be using it for inspiration for your series of books."

Deborah gulped. "Series? I haven't finished one yet."

"Marketing. And you went right past me saying we need to get your social media in order."

She wagged a finger at Elissa. "That was tricky."

"Did you find an illustrator yet?"

"I'm still talking to a couple of artists."

"Let me know when you make a decision. I'll be happy to send over the files that you like."

"You know…" She picked up a dish towel and studied Elissa. "You've already done a lot of the work. I'm thinking about hiring you. I mean, you know my concept, and—"

"Wait." Elissa put down her cup. "Me? No. I can't."

"Now who's being modest?"

"You don't understand." She shook her head. "I love your ski bunny, but definitely don't think you want me working with you."

"You're talented."

"But…" How did she confess this? "I assume that Jacob hasn't told you what I'm painting for him?"

Deborah waited.

Would she have to get used to admitting this in the future? "Adult in nature."

"Oh?" The other woman blinked. *"Oh."*

"I'm honored that you'd think of me, but believe me when I tell you that I'm not the right person for a children's book."

"Could you use a different name? I mean, no one would have to know, right?"

Elissa and Jacob had jokingly tossed that idea around, but the truth was, she was happy with the direction her creativity was headed. "I'm happy to help you in any way, but…" She

SIERRA CARTWRIGHT

cleared her throat. "Anyway, I can always have a look at the project and give you some advice."

"So when do I get to see some of this other art of yours?"

"Are you serious?"

"Oh, shit yes. I spend so much time with my kiddo that I've forgotten what it's like to be a grown-up."

"In that case, I'll give you a peek when I have something I'm willing to share." This first one was so personal, an evolving reflection of what she shared with Jacob, that she wanted to keep it private.

"I can't wait." Deborah refilled Elissa's cup.

"Thanks."

"I always enjoy the break. It's nice having you here."

As far as Elissa knew, Deborah didn't know the whole story, and she hadn't asked.

"I'm going to finish up here since I need to pick up Adele from school."

"I'll let you get back to work. Give Adele a hug from me?"

"She can't wait to come see you again."

Maybe because they'd spent an hour coloring together at the kitchen table last week.

"And she misses Waffle too."

Now that Elissa had enjoyed a short break, she was reenergized.

"Tell Jacob I'll be back next week. Since Eric's on vacation, I brought over some groceries for you two. I also made a lasagna. It's in the fridge with some baking instructions. As you saw, I also fried some bacon—not that there are as many pieces as there were." She scowled at the cat, who didn't look up from bathing her paw after devouring her treat. "Anyway, I figured you could eat it with breakfast or make BLT sandwiches tomorrow. There are also a few meals in the freezer that Eric made, but if you need anything before I'm back, just

HOLD ON TO ME

give me a call. Other than avoiding my book, I don't have a lot going on this week."

Elissa laughed. "I've dealt with that with some of my design projects, so I totally understand." She slid off the barstool, then grabbed her cup.

"The pot's more than half full. Do you want to take it with you? There's a serving tray in the pantry."

"Good idea." Elissa located the lacquered piece, and once she had it loaded up, she said goodbye before opening the patio door. Waffle darted across the room, then dashed between Elissa's legs. She had to do a fancy sidestep to keep her balance.

"Be careful! That darn cat is going to end up tripping someone."

"She's definitely fast." And somehow managed to be everywhere at once.

When they were outside, Waffle raced toward one of the lounge chairs on the patio and jumped onto it. By the time Elissa reached the garage, the feline was already curled up and appeared to be sleeping.

Elissa topped off her tea and was about to wake up her computer when the sound of an approaching vehicle captured her attention.

Curious, she walked to the window that faced the house.

A large white panel van bearing the name of a well-known delivery company ambled up the driveway and parked.

The driver slowly exited, and she absently noted he wasn't carrying anything as he started up the path toward the porch. Then the vehicle's rear door exploded open, and another person—appearing to be a man, tall, dressed in black, with a ball cap pulled low to disguise his features —jumped out.

341

SIERRA CARTWRIGHT

The delivery guy looked over his shoulder and hurried a little faster.

Sudden, hot fear slammed her heart into overdrive.

She told herself she was being ridiculous. All of Jacob and Hawkeye's fears had made her paranoid, and she was overreacting.

It was just a delivery.

But then the second man moved faster and appeared to stick something against the driver's spine and forced him up the steps.

Elissa jumped back, away from the window.

Think. She had to think.

Deborah was all alone in the house, and even if she didn't open the door, the men could get in through the patio. That would only take another minute or two.

And Jacob wasn't expected to return for another couple of hours. She wrapped her arms around her middle, silently assuring herself there were plenty of agents around. No doubt they were already aware of the situation and had it under control. In fact, maybe the man she'd seen was one of Hawkeye's men.

But what if he wasn't?

She remembered Jacob's admonishment to reach out to him for any reason. He'd rather it be a false alarm than to take any chances.

Hurriedly she rushed to the light switch and pushed the panic button.

She expected an alarm to ring—something, anything—but nothing happened. Was it even working?

Elissa returned to the window in time to see the door open. Then a shot rang out, the delivery driver crumpled, and the man dressed in black shoved his way into the house.

CHAPTER NINE

HAWKEYE

An alarm shrieked on Jacob's phone, splitting the silence. It wasn't an ordinary tone. It meant a panic button had been pushed somewhere. Cold fucking dread ripped through him.

He released the wire tightener he'd been using on the fencing and grabbed his phone from his belt clip to check the display. In neon green, the words GARAGE APARTMENT were flashing.

His training kicked in at the same time that anger flattened his heart rate.

Immediately he opened the video feed app even as he strode back toward the grouping of vehicles. He'd driven his utility vehicle, but one of the ranch hands had arrived on a tricked-out ATV that was significantly faster than his.

Though he didn't stop moving, he exhaled his relief when he saw Elissa staring out a window. He selected an option that would allow him to talk to her over the room's speaker system. "Elissa?"

"Jacob!" Her voice was wobbly. She looked around

SIERRA CARTWRIGHT

instinctively, as if seeking him out. "He's in the house, and the delivery driver…" She gulped. "I…think he's dead."

He tried to understand what she meant, but he needed her safe while he did so. He took less than a second to brush the key on the side of his phone, alerting Lifeguard he was needed. "I need you to breathe. Stay calm. You've got information we need in order to end this situation. Do you understand?" He took a breath of his own and forced a note of calmness into his tone.

On the screen, he saw her nod.

"Is there anyone outside?"

"No. He's in the house, with Deborah."

Shoving away tendrils of panic, he focused himself on staying in the moment. This wasn't Peru or the attacked convoy in Colombia. He could and would get Elissa and Deborah through this safely. "Move away from the window and close the blinds, then walk over to the door and lock it."

There was no response, and she remained where she was, as if frozen to the spot.

"Elissa." He kept his words measured, reassuring but uncompromising. "Pay attention to the sound of my voice. Close the blinds." She was safer if no one knew she was in there. "Elissa?"

"Okay." She nodded as she pulled on the correct string.

"Good. Now I need you to lock the door. Do it for me. Do it *now*."

Finally she moved and threw the bolt home. He exhaled his relief. "Help's coming. I'm on the way." He signaled to the ranch hand who'd been riding the ATV. "Need your keys."

"Sure, boss."

Jacob caught them with one hand, then straddled the beast and fired it up before sliding the cell phone into a holder. Jacob gunned the throttle and raced toward the house.

344

HOLD ON TO ME

Trying to stay in control of the four-wheeler, he pressed a key on the side of his cell phone that immediately connected him with Lifeguard. "Operation Wildflower. Got a situation at the ranch house. Need to know what I'm dealing with. Delivery person down? My housekeeper is inside with the UNSUB." Unknown subject. "And I'm on a fucking ATV."

"Roger that." As always, Lifeguard was unflappable.

"Get me a damn sitrep."

"Mansfield at the guard shack is down."

Goddamn fuck it to hell. Of course he was—he had to be. Deliveries were common enough, and Mansfield would have recognized the driver as someone who belonged on the premises, which left him vulnerable.

On the feed to the office apartment, he heard Elissa's soft, rapid breaths. "You're doing good, Elissa." To Lifeguard, he was abrupt. "Intel from the drone?"

"Redirecting. Johnson inbound from perimeter on ATV. No response from Laurents."

He prayed they were only dealing with one UNSUB.

"Jacob?"

Elissa's soft, frightened voice reached him, going straight to his soul. "I'm here, baby. I've got you." He would die before breaking his vow. "Stay with me. I need you to take a breath and tell me what you saw—in great detail. Don't leave out anything even if you think it's unimportant." He pressed the key to connect Lifeguard so he could overhear the details she was providing.

"A delivery van arrived, the same one that always comes, and the driver wasn't carrying any packages."

"Go on."

"There was a man behind him, and it looked as if he shoved something into the delivery guy's back. And I heard a shot. Oh God. Oh God. Oh God. He's inside, Jacob." Her voice caught on a sob.

SIERRA CARTWRIGHT

He disconnected from Lifeguard. "Stay in the apartment unless I tell you otherwise. Promise me? I mean it."

After she agreed, he reopened the channel to Lifeguard. "You got eyes on the garage apartment?" Minutes seemed to drag on, while in reality, he knew no more than a few seconds had passed.

"She's clear. All around."

Jacob pushed out a ragged breath.

"We've got drone footage. Laurents is down. Could have been hit by the delivery van."

"Goddamn it."

"Unmoving male on the front porch. Replaying front door cam to see if we can get a hit on the person's image. House camera showing armed male in the kitchen. Woman tied to a chair. Crying. Appears to have red marks on her face."

Fucking fuck.

Jacob resisted barking orders. He'd seen Lifeguard in action. Even though he was relaying information in a measured tone, he was summing up the situation, entering information in a computer that would summon help, link in others, including Inamorata and Hawkeye. The entire strength of the organization was being harnessed.

Rationally, Jacob knew all that—the primal part of his brain had been activated. Nothing—nothing—was happening fast enough. Rather than following the road, he was making a straight line toward the ranch house, and there were still more than four miles to go. But in this moment, he was completely, terrifyingly useless to Deborah as well as the woman he loved.

"Johnson's inbound on an ATV. Was doing the outer perimeter check. ETA five minutes."

Adrenaline compelled Jacob to gun the engine even

HOLD ON TO ME

harder, pushing the tricked-out machine to eighty miles per hour, despite the danger from the uneven terrain.

"Laurents here," a man broke in, breathing heavily. "On foot. Fucking delivery truck hit me. Vehicle's useless."

Thank God he was still alive.

Jacob switched back to the woman he loved, pretending a calm he didn't feel. "Still there, Elissa?"

"Yes."

"You're doing great."

Lifeguard broke in. "UNSUB is moving through the lower level of the house. Now upstairs, clearing the rooms."

Life was happening between a series of his heartbeats.

"UNSUB back downstairs. Moving through the living room."

Time was running out.

"UNSUB out the back patio door. Headed for the garage."

"Jacob? Someone is calling my name."

"Don't respond." He edged the ATV to eighty-five. "Fuck it to hell."

"At the garage door."

"Elissa, I'm going to keep silent so that no one hears us, okay? Help is less than two minutes away." He'd never been more helpless. "We'll keep you safe. Hang in there, baby."

"UNSUB in the garage."

At least the sonofabitch hadn't headed straight for the stairs, and that bought him a few more precious seconds.

"Back outside."

"I hear footsteps, Jacob."

"A minute, minute and a half, baby. I'm right here." Jacob focused on his destination, calculating his response. The assailant likely had no interest in killing Elissa. She was a better weapon against Hawkeye if she was alive. But harming her? That was a possibility. But not on his watch. Not ever

SIERRA CARTWRIGHT

fucking again. "When Johnson arrives, I want her to disable the van and my truck. I don't want him to be able to escape with Elissa."

"Roger that."

"Jacob!" Her whisper was frantic and breathless. "I don't know if I can do this."

"Sixty seconds, Elissa. Stay calm for one more minute. Don't say anything more. But I'll stay on the line. I'm here with you."

The ensuing silence was more awful than anything he could imagine.

"UNSUB outside the apartment door."

Knowing he was now close enough to be picked up on Lifeguard's video, Jacob clipped his phone back into place.

The moment he neared the garage, he cut the engine, jumping from the ATV before it completely stopped moving.

Fear sharpening his senses, he started to run.

An unholy shriek ripped through the air, followed by a crash and a thud.

Then a shot rang out, echoing in his ears.

Shouting her name, gun palmed, events unfolding in horrific slow motion, Jacob raced up the stairs.

When he arrived at the doorway, he took in the scene. The assailant was lying facedown on the floor, his gun in hand, aimed in Elissa's direction. Liquid oozed around him, and shards of pottery—some large, some small—were splintered like arrows.

She was huddled in the far corner, her knees upraised, clothing damp, staring straight ahead with blood dripping down one of her arms. His fury spiked. "You okay?"

She nodded, her body trembling.

Instead of going to her like instinct demanded, he focused on his training. He had to secure the scene.

He stepped over the hissing and spitting cat that was

HOLD ON TO ME

somehow in the room and kicked the intruder's hand hard enough to break his grip on the gun. Uncaring whether or not he'd shattered bone, Jacob flipped the man over. *Christ.* "Rollins."

"Fuck off, Walker." Rollins lunged for Jacob's gun, and Jacob lashed out with his steel-toe boot, connecting with the man's jaw.

Jacob's effort was rewarded with a satisfying crunch.

And he wanted to do so much more. But his priorities were Elissa and Deborah. "You're lucky I don't fucking take you out."

"Like you murdered my little girl?"

He channeled his anger into a cold, calculating strike. "You killed her yourself, you motherfucker, with your swagger and your refusal to call in law enforcement. You waited until it was too late, then blamed everyone else. You deserve to go down. Sins of the father."

Rollins sneered. "Fuck you."

"You'll live with Shayley's death for the rest of your life. And you can be sure you'll be in a hellhole of a prison for your attack on Inamorata and Deborah." He crouched. "And Elissa." *The woman I love.* "You didn't get revenge on Hawkeye —you sealed your place in hell."

Gun drawn, Johnson arrived and silently took in the situation.

"I want this sonofabitch out of here."

She nodded. "Yes, sir."

Happily he flipped Rollins over again while Johnson wrenched cuffs onto the assailant.

"Emergency medical is en route. Inamorata in the air." Lifeguard's reassuring voice filled the room.

"Send Laurents directly to the main house to take care of Deborah."

"Roger that."

"Get up, you lowlife bastard." With Johnson's assistance, Jacob dragged Rollins to his feet. Then he looked at Johnson. "I don't care what you do with him, but don't let me ever see his face ever again."

"Yes, Commander."

Lifeguard spoke one more time. "Bird is inbound."

Everyone knew where the landing pad was. Things were as under control as they could be. "Walker out." He hit the switch to reset the panic button system, giving them privacy. "Elissa."

Elissa was still in the corner, and he crossed to her then sat next to her. "You did good."

The cat stopped her hissing and dancing and slunk toward them.

"I never believed it was real."

"Let me see your arm." Jacob had to repeat the request before she complied. Fortunately it seemed superficial, but the trauma from the day would last a long time. And for the rest of his life, he'd regret that he'd been away from the house when Rollins showed up.

No doubt she was in shock, and he applied direct pressure to the wound, praying EMTs would arrive soon. "Tell me what happened?"

"I… He forced open the door. I don't know how, since it was locked." Waffle wiggled in close to Elissa, and she absently stroked the cat's head. "The only thing that was close was the teapot. I was behind the door, and I hit him with it. Then I got as far away from him as I could."

She was damn brave. "You sacrificed your afternoon matcha?"

He was happy when she rewarded him with a half smile.

"He tried to come after me."

Even after she'd brained Rollins hard enough to break the ceramic? "So what happened?"

HOLD ON TO ME

"Waffle."

"Waffle?"

"She attacked him and ended up tripping him."

"In that case, we'll get her all the bacon she ever wants."

"I think she earned it."

Then, seemingly annoyed with the attention, Waffle stood, stretched, then sauntered off.

In the distance, the unmistakable whir from the helo signaled that Hawkeye's A-team had arrived to deal with the authorities and clean up the mess. "I'm so proud of you."

She leaned into him. "I was so scared. Especially... The gun. My ears are still ringing. I think maybe they will be forever."

He didn't bother with platitudes. She'd go on, and she'd get better. The events would fade, but she'd never be entirely the same again. He regretted she'd ever gotten wrapped up with Hawkeye. Her biggest sin was a compassionate heart.

"I guess it's safe to go home now."

"Yeah. But you don't have to. And I'd prefer you never did."

"Jacob..."

Any further conversation was interrupted by a sharp staccato beat on the stairs. Inamorata—no doubt. If she had a first name, no one knew it. But there was a large office pool with bets. Always cool and composed, she was the best fixer he'd ever met.

Without announcing herself, she entered the apartment and glanced around, taking in every detail. "Commander Walker." She nodded.

As usual, her blonde hair was pulled up, and she wore a slim-fitting pencil skirt and stiletto heels. "Medical technician is right behind me."

"Good." The sooner they were here and gone, the better.

She walked across the room and crouched near them.

351

SIERRA CARTWRIGHT

"Ms. Conroy, I'm Inamorata. Hawkeye speaks highly of you. And with good reason. I saw the feed. If you're ever looking for a job—"

Jacob's protective instincts flared. "You can fuck the hell right off, Inamorata. And take Hawkeye with you. Go do what you're paid to do."

For the briefest fraction of time, he thought she might smile.

Instead she pushed to a standing position and left without another word.

As promised, two emergency technicians strode in, carrying bags. They checked Elissa's vitals and bandaged her up.

"You can take over-the-counter pain reliever if needed."

Since discretion was of utmost importance to Hawkeye, the firm kept an assortment of professionals on call, meaning employees and clients rarely visited a hospital.

"Rest and hydrate, and don't do any more than necessary."

When they were alone, he stroked back her hair. "You ready to get back to the main house? Or we can stay here as long as you want."

"Is Deborah okay?"

"Let's go see." He kept his arm around her as they walked back to his home.

Deborah was still there, and the two women fell into each other's arms and held on tight.

Agent Kayla Fagan took a step toward them, and he held up a hand to wave her off. Fagan nodded and leaned against the counter to wait.

"Agent Fagan was going to take me home, but I couldn't leave until I saw you."

"Me? I'm concerned about you. What happened to your cheek? Are you okay?"

HOLD ON TO ME

"He hit me when I wouldn't tell him where you were."

"Oh my God." Elissa reached out her hand as if to touch Deborah's face, but then didn't. "I'm so, so sorry."

"Don't be. I'm told I might get a black eye. And it will make a great addition to a Ski Bunny story one day."

Elissa shook her head. "If you don't find an illustrator, let me know. I can never repay you for what you did today."

"You'd have done it for me."

"You were really brave. Thank you." Elissa pressed her palms together. "Did someone go to get Adele?"

If he hadn't already been in love with Elissa, it would have happened at that moment. After all she'd been through, she was concerned for his housekeeper's daughter.

"My sister went to the school." A river of tears washed down Deborah's cheeks. "I was so scared for you."

"No need. Waffle tripped him and took him down."

Deborah wiped her face with the back of her hand. "Are you kidding me?"

"Swear to God." Elissa crossed her heart with her index finger.

"What a good kitty! I always knew she was perfect."

Elissa grinned.

"But what about you? Is your arm okay?"

"This?" Elissa brushed two fingers over the bandage. "It's superficial."

Jacob knew she was lying. From experience, he knew it hurt like hell. "Take some time off," he told Deborah. "As long as you need. A month. Two. You'll get your full paycheck." And a big juicy bonus, even if she opted never to come back. He wouldn't blame her for that.

"I can't." She shook her head. "You need me."

"I'll have Hawkeye send someone until you're ready to come back."

"Do you really mean it?"

"He does." Fagan made the promise as she moved forward. "If you're ready, I'll drive you home. Someone else will bring your car."

Fagan was a skilled professional, and she was easy to talk to. There was no one better to debrief a victim of a horrific experience.

"Maybe I'll finish writing the Ski Bunny story."

"The first Ski Bunny story," Elissa corrected.

They both laughed.

After the two women hugged again, Fagan took control, offering plenty of reassuring words and helping Deborah find her purse before ushering her out the patio door.

No doubt the scene on the front porch was still being secured, and Fagan would do her best to ensure Deborah didn't witness it.

"Can you give me a few minutes?" He filled the kettle and turned it on. "Agent Johnson will stay with you. I want to wrap up a couple of things with Inamorata. Then I'll be back. And I'll be yours as long as you want me."

She nodded and took a seat on a barstool.

He walked to the small circle of people surrounding Inamorata. When she saw him, she nodded, then detached herself from the group.

"Status?"

"Mansfield didn't make it. GSW."

Gunshot wound. "Fuck."

"Appears he leaned past the driver. Had his gun in hand, but not fast enough."

He raked his hand through his hair wishing he'd sent Rollins to hell while he had the chance. "Delivery driver?"

"Deceased."

A total, complete goat fuck. "Need this place cleaned up. And the cat taken care of. Bacon every day."

HOLD ON TO ME

"Excuse me?"

"You heard me. I'm getting Elissa the hell away from here. I'll file my report later."

"The job is done, Commander."

"It's just started. And it's Jacob."

She smiled. "Good wishes for all your happiness in the future."

"If you're a praying woman, pray she'll have me."

"I'll do that."

A man from the group called out her name. "If you'll excuse me." With a nod, she strode off.

Jacob returned to the house, waved Nan Johnson away with a silent thanks, then slid onto the stool next to Elissa. An untouched cup of Earl Grey sat in front of her. "How about we get out of here for a few days?"

She tilted her head quizzically to one side.

"Are you serious?"

He grabbed his phone and pressed the key on the side. "Hey, Lifeguard. Gonna need reservations for two at a cabin in Steamboat Springs. Plenty of privacy."

"Not my specialty, Commander."

"I'm sure you can find someone who can help."

"Believe I can."

And then he remembered that he'd ordered his truck to be disabled. "And a vehicle. Tell Hawkeye not to be a cheap bastard this time."

"Already have one ordered—for Inamorata."

"I'm sure she won't mind me taking it."

"Roger that."

When he slid his phone onto the countertop, Elissa looked at him. "Steamboat?"

"We need to get away. Rest. Maybe have a bottle of wine. On Hawkeye's tab."

"A nice bottle?"

355

SIERRA CARTWRIGHT

"Very nice." He nodded. He was ready to have her alone, to confess his love, and pray she didn't turn him down and walk out of his life. "How soon can you be ready?"

CHAPTER TEN

HAWKEYE

"This is luxurious." Elissa turned a slow circle.

Jacob hadn't just procured a cabin—this was a high-end house, no doubt for world's elite who traveled to Steamboat to ski.

"I hope you're pleased."

As he'd promised, a nice bottle of wine—bubbly, even—was chilling in a silver ice bucket. Nearby was a charcuterie board and plenty of fresh fruits. It was more a honeymoon than an impromptu escape.

"Shall I pour you a glass?"

"Yes. Please." *Or just uncork the bottle and pass it over.*

The afternoon had been surreal. From the attacker, to being injured, to watching the Hawkeye Security team in action.

She'd had no idea what she'd been swept up in.

After she video chatted with her parents to prove she was okay, Elissa and Jacob had left the ranch. For most of the drive, she'd been quiet, hardly noticing the scenery as she replayed every single event of the day, and the biggest thing for her was the fear that she might never see Jacob or her

SIERRA CARTWRIGHT

parents again. Determinedly she'd refused to allow that to happen. Though she wasn't a fighter, she summoned the strength that had helped her to leave her ex and the determination that helped her deal with her dad's cancer, and she'd channeled them into determination to fight back.

After opening the champagne, a label even Jacob said he recognized, he looked across at her. "Are you doing okay?"

"I am now."

"Now?"

"That we're here." *With you.*

Even though it was summer, Jacob had lit the electric fireplace when they arrived. Despite the size of the place, the atmosphere was cozy. And she had his assurances that it was safe.

The threat was over. Rationally she knew that, but it would take time for life to return to normal.

Jacob had allowed her to listen in to all of his conversation with the Hawkeye team. Rollins had hired hackers to get the information he needed, and the FBI was now working the case. From what Inamorata had learned, Rollins had two of his employees observing the ranch. They knew what time deliveries were made, and noted the frequency of the drone passing overhead. The attack on Mansfield had occurred within sixty seconds of his last-ever radio check-in.

He brought her drink to her. "You really did a phenomenal job, Elissa. I'm damn proud of you."

"Really?" She accepted the glass.

"Yeah. Really."

They tapped the rims of their glasses together.

"Look, I know my timing sucks, but relationships aren't my strong suit—"

"You're ready for me to leave." Despite what he'd said over the past few days, in her heart, she knew it would end. Unusual circumstances had thrown them together, and it had

HOLD ON TO ME

upended both of their lives. Having some sort of affair had been predictable.

But just as predictable, they had separate lives. He was a man of the land, and she had a full life in the city with her parents.

"What?" He dragged his free hand through his hair. "Jesus, Elissa. What the fuck? No. How could you think that?"

Dumbfounded, she stared at him.

"It's the opposite. Entirely." He put down his glass, untouched. "I started to fall in love with you the first night we scened, when you offered your trust. I didn't recognize it at first. But this afternoon—" He broke off and looked away.

"Love?"

When he met her gaze again, his face was haunted. "I was scared as fuck that I wouldn't make it back in time. And I didn't know how I'd live without you. I've found peace with you, in bed, in the way we laugh together. Nothing gives me more joy than your happiness. And then... You asked Deborah about Adele."

Gently, oh so very gently, he captured her shoulders, taking care with her injury.

"For the first time in my life, I'm thinking about a future, about passing the ranch on to future generations. You're the only woman I've ever wanted as a wife."

Unable to fathom his meaning, scared that she was misunderstanding, she remained silent.

"I'm messing this up. Elissa Conroy, I want you to marry me. To spend our lives together. To be the mother of our children."

Everything he said was making her wildest dreams come true. Then he dropped to one knee, completing the fantasy.

"Will you say yes?" He captured her hand. "Tell me you love me and that you'll be mine, Elissa." His voice held an entreaty. "Will you make me the happiest man in the world?

Will you allow me to spend every day trying to make you happy?"

"Jacob, I…" Everything they'd gone through was pushed aside. All that mattered was this moment. "Yes. I love you. Being married to you is my dream. I can't imagine anything more perfect. I want to be your wife. I want us to have kids."

He grinned. "Four?"

Her heart was racing, and she was giddy from excitement. "No. Two."

"To start."

"I thought you were kidding about having that many." Frantically she shook her head.

"Having babies with you is not something I joke about. We can get started whenever you want. I'll let you set the pace in case you need time to recover."

Her mouth fell open when he stood and plucked her glass from her hand. He placed the delicate flute on the mantel before sweeping her into his arms and turning toward the stairs.

"Hold on to me, Elissa."

For the rest of her life. "Always." She grabbed his shirt for stability. "This is getting to be a habit I like."

"I've got a few more habits I'd like to establish with you, Ms. Conroy."

"Do you indeed, Mr. Walker?" She snuggled against the strength of his chest. "Would you like to talk about them?"

"I do believe I'd rather show you."

"In that case, Sir…" She gave him her cheekiest grin. "What are you waiting for?"

When they reached the master bedroom, he carried her inside, kicked the door closed, then proceeded to show her exactly how he intended to keep her happy for the rest of her life.

HOLD ON TO ME

For the first time since they'd been together, Elissa was up before Jacob. She turned over in the bed of their borrowed home and watched him sleep.

Yesterday, when he'd stormed into the garage apartment, tension and fury had channeled deep lines beside his eyes. Afterward, when he sat next to her on the floor, he'd offered a reassuring smile, but concern for her had darkened his green eyes.

Last night, their lovemaking had been incredible, but he'd been gentler than she wanted. When she asked for a scene, he said she'd gone through an ordeal and he wanted her wound to heal first.

The only thing she'd wanted was to forget the horrible fear when that man, Rollins, crashed through the door and the terror that rocked when she was afraid she might never see Jacob again.

If she'd had any doubts about her love and devotion to him, they'd vanished in that moment. She was committed to spending forever with him, no matter the sacrifices.

Sometime around two, Jacob had dragged her against him and muttered soothing words until she responded by turning over and blinking her eyes open. Screams from her nightmare had awakened him.

For an hour they'd sat up, and he listened while she talked about the experience she'd been through. He hadn't dismissed anything she said, and instead reassured her that processing it would help her move beyond it faster.

Comforted, she'd drifted off in the security of his arms.

This morning, in the soft, filtered light of dawn, he looked a decade younger. Gently she smoothed back a lock of his dark hair before sliding from beneath the covers and silently walking to the closet to find a pair of jeans and a T-

361

shirt. Then she slipped into the plaid shirt he'd lent her when they took a moonlit stroll after dinner.

In the kitchen, she found a jar containing an assortment of teas, and she selected a calming one. Today, she didn't need caffeine.

And since he always took such good care of her, she made a pot of coffee for him before going out onto the deck to enjoy the new day, and the first one of their future together.

She'd just taken the first sip from her cup when he joined her, the waistband of his jeans seductively hanging open, his denim shirt unbuttoned to reveal the lean lines of his abs and the sleeves turned back to show off his biceps. "I don't think there's a better-looking man on the planet."

"No?" Holding an oversize mug, he took a seat across from her. "Then we have something in common. I don't think there's a more beautiful woman in the universe."

Elissa angled her head. "It seems we're charter members of our very own fan club."

"Membership does have its advantages."

"Such as."

His grin was wolfish. "Exclusive access to other members."

"I'm interested in hearing more about that."

"Oh. You will. Without a doubt." He took a drink, then skimmed his gaze down her body. "How are you feeling today?"

"A million times better. Physically as well as emotionally."

"I'm glad to hear that."

"Thank you for letting me sort through it last night."

"In every way, Liss, I will be here for you."

The nickname was new, intimate. No one else had ever called her that, and she smiled at him, liking it.

"After your bath, I'll change your bandage. And we can go into town for brunch, maybe do some shopping."

HOLD ON TO ME

"If it looks as if it's healing, can we do something else with our day?"

"Hmm." He stared into his mug, pretending to ponder her meaning. "Like what?"

His perplexed expression was so comical she had to laugh. "I want to have my wicked way with you. Reverse cowgirl so you can spank my ass while we have sex."

He arched his eyebrows. "That was specific."

"And even if my arm is hurting, we can still manage that."

"I'll be the judge of that."

"Come on, it has to be better than lugging shopping bags around for me. Right?"

"Woman, at what point will you realize I won't compromise your health? I'll carry a thousand bags before I let that wound get infected." He placed his cup down, clanging it onto the metal table. "The reverse cowgirl while I slap your sexy little butt will definitely happen. When I say."

She scowled.

"Give up the fight. I'm the Dominant."

"And you have my permission to say so." Her words were carefully selected, provocative and cheeky.

He grinned then, something more feral than playful, and her stomach took a nosedive. "Okay, subbie. Off your ass and up the stairs. I'll have a look at your injury and then decide what kind of punishment is in order."

His words thrilled her too much to even pretend to apologize.

He was the man she wanted, the Dominant she needed. No manipulation. No games. Nothing but love and understanding.

"I have one question, Liss."

She gulped. "Sir?"

"Why are you still sitting there?"

Immediately, happier than she'd ever been, she pushed back from the table. "Just on my way inside, Sir."

"The faster the better."

Laughing, she raced across the living room and dashed up the stairs, with him close behind her.

When he reached the bedroom, he slammed the door, then stripped her before backing her onto the bed and spread her legs wide, devouring her with his masterful tongue even as he slipped his fingers inside her.

If this was a glimpse of what awaited her, she never wanted it to end...

EPILOGUE

HAWKEYE

"I can't believe this is happening."

Jacob grinned at his beautiful bride-to-be as their driver eased to the curb in front of the Gallery Royale in New Orleans's French Quarter for Elissa's first-ever opening. Immediately cars started honking, and a bicyclist darted around them.

"I'll be standing by, Mr. Walker. With tonight's traffic, give me a few minutes' heads-up."

"Thank you." After exiting the car, Jacob rounded the hood to offer his hand to Elissa. She stepped out in strappy high-heeled sandals and a formfitting red cocktail dress, alluringly cinched at her waist with a sparkling silver belt. A stylist had done her hair, scooping some of it up and allowing a few long, curly tendrils to tease the sides of her face. Her scent was that of success with an undertone of sweet vanilla. To complete the look, she'd added red lipstick, and the shade had to be Tempting Torment. It took all of his restraint not to suggest that they get back in the vehicle and return to their suite at the Maison Sterling. As it was, he had

SIERRA CARTWRIGHT

to be content with the knowledge that she'd be beneath him, surrendering, within a few hours.

Earlier in the day, they'd met Claire Richardson, the gallery's owner, and walked around to double-check that everything was hung the way Elissa wanted and that the placards were with the correct piece.

And now, the gallery was closed to the public. Fairy lights danced around the windows, and music from a live jazz band beckoned.

A tuxedoed woman opened the door for them. "Good evening, Ms. Conroy. Mr. Walker."

Once they were inside, Elissa leaned in closer. "Am I supposed to pretend I'm not awestruck?"

He laughed. "You'll do fine." He plucked two glasses of champagne from the tray of a passing server. After giving her one, he raised his drink to her. "You deserve every moment."

"You made it happen."

"I had nothing to do with it. The talent is yours. And you got the paintings together to do it." She'd worked her ass off, day and night, to make it happen, and he did his best to be the supportive man she needed in her life. When she forgot to eat, he took food over to her. And he welcomed her to bed when she finally joined him each night.

After their time in Steamboat Springs, they'd taken a trip to Denver so he could meet her parents, and she could inform them of her decision to marry him.

Mr. and Mrs. Conroy had shocked Elissa into silence by announcing they were selling the pub. They no longer wanted to work so hard, and their time in Ireland had shown them they wanted to travel while they still had the energy.

Elissa had been nervous that she would be letting her parents down by moving away, but they reassured her that they had no plans to stay in Denver. In fact, they were planning to sell the business to Joseph.

366

HOLD ON TO ME

Then her mother had said they may want to purchase a cabin in Steamboat so they could be near Elissa when she finally decided to have children.

Though Patrick had sipped a whiskey and leaned back to stay out of the conversation, Ann had agreed that four children would be perfect.

Seeing Elissa happy made Jacob's life complete. Well, almost.

There was the little detail of getting her down the aisle. She wore his engagement ring, and they'd decided to start trying to have a baby after the opening. Which gave him some ideas for the upcoming evening when they returned to their suite. All he had to do was control his ravenous hunger for a few more hours.

Her portraits were hung in the far end, past the final arch. The room was constructed with half-round faux art deco pillars attached to the walls, creating secondary framing for the paintings.

He understood why Julien Bonds had selected this gallery. It was elegant, high-end, and most definitely catered to a clientele with eclectic tastes. "Shall we?" He offered his arm.

"Look at me. All confident and everything."

Accepting her invitation, he swept his hungry gaze over her. Excitement radiated from her. "Most definitely confident."

"Right." She nodded. "Confident. I belong here."

He laughed. "You wouldn't be here if you didn't."

"Right. Right again."

The back door was open to a private patio, and that was where the band was playing. A full-service bar was set up near them.

The gallery was large, and the lighting was perfect to bring out the deep, rich colors of her oils.

"I can do this."

SIERRA CARTWRIGHT

"There's no doubt."

They mingled for a few minutes with the crowd that was larger than expected. One woman raved about how much she loved *Waiting for Him*, and Jacob went to greet a Hawkeye trainer—Torin Carter. The man had met his wife on a mission in the Crescent City and had fond memories of the Big Easy. When Hawkeye mentioned he intended to don a suit and attend the opening, Torin had opted to join him.

"I'm thinking of buying one for Mira. I think it would be a perfect present to give her when the baby's born. One of the subjects bears a resemblance to her."

"Excellent choice. I'm sure she'll love it." He glanced over at Elissa to be sure she was okay. He'd stayed nearby in case she needed him, but far enough away that she could talk to the invited guests. And as he expected, being in the spotlight made her shine.

The gallery owner walked over to Elissa to shake her hand, and Elissa beckoned Jacob to join them. He immediately excused himself to stand next to her while Torin searched out an assistant to complete his purchase.

"Congratulations. We've already sold one of your paintings."

Elissa's mouth parted. "I… I don't know what to say. You mean a print, right?"

"No. An original. *His Pleasure.*"

"Oh my God, that's amazing. Surreal. I'm not dreaming, am I? Should I pinch myself?"

He couldn't be prouder. At Bonds's urging, she'd priced her paintings considerably higher than she was comfortable with. "I think you've just sold another." He nodded toward Torin, and Elissa clasped the heart-shaped pendant Jacob'd recently bought for her.

"You're certainly one of the hottest artists around right now, Ms. Conroy. And I'll do a formal welcome and intro-

HOLD ON TO ME

duce you in a few minutes, if that's comfortable for you? We're waiting for a couple more guests."

Including Hawkeye. And maybe Bonds would grace them with an appearance.

"Of course." Elissa nodded. "That's totally fine."

With a nod, Claire moved on to speak to other people.

Elissa was going to say something, but before she could, a woman approached, holding her handwritten invitation to the event. "Do you mind autographing this for me, Ms. Conroy?"

She blinked but recovered the instant the woman offered a pen. "I'd be happy to."

He accepted the champagne flute she asked him to hold. It seemed Elissa was stepping into the shoes of stardom as if they had been custom fit for her.

After returning the stemware to a server, he wandered outside and got caught up on the latest Hawkeye cases with Torin. Jacob was glad for the time—it reaffirmed he didn't miss the job one bit.

About thirty minutes later, the music trailed off, and Claire asked for everyone's attention. She gave rave reviews about Elissa's talent and suggested she was someone to watch. "You know how you all wish you'd have bought Bonds stock when it was under a thousand dollars a share? You know how you promised yourself you wouldn't ever miss an opportunity like that again? Well, tonight is your chance. By tomorrow, with all the press coverage and reviews, Elissa will be a household name, and if you want to add a Conroy to your collection before you need to take a second mortgage to pay for it, this is your one and only chance."

As if for reassurance, Elissa reached for her pendant and touched it, but instead of pausing, she continued to raise her hand, and she gave a friendly wave.

A lightbulb flashed as a photographer captured the moment forever.

"Do you mind saying a few words, Ms. Conroy?"

Elissa smiled. "Thank you for being here, and I hope to have the chance to talk to every one of you personally." Her words sounded natural even though she'd practiced at least a dozen times. "I appreciate the way you've reacted to the pieces of my heart and soul that you see on the canvas. Every painting has meaning, and I'm grateful to share it with you."

Of course, the first picture she'd ever finished, *His*, was on the mantel in their dungeon, in the room he'd built for her. Of course he hadn't known it at the time, but he'd created the space with the idea of having a cherished submissive, and he wanted a private place for them to explore all the nuances of that type of relationship. He'd had no idea how multifaceted their dynamic would be or that it would change, evolve, become even more meaningful.

The first night he took her into the room, they had a conversation about the rings he'd attached to the floor. She'd mentioned being chained to them while they were in front of a fire, with him sipping whiskey while a gentle snow drifted down. She'd trusted him enough to do that.

He'd shared a fantasy of his own—her being on all fours, secured by a collar around her beautiful neck, having no escape as he slid a plug inside her ass, then took her pussy from behind.

He'd watched her press her hand to her heart as he talked, and he'd sworn to show no mercy. And he hadn't.

And his beautiful Elissa—his beautiful submissive—had begged for more. Last week, she'd even brought a collar to him while he was working on his accounting program. She'd knelt at his side, looking up at him, and asked him to fasten it in place.

HOLD ON TO ME

He could never have asked for anyone more perfect for him.

"I'd also like to acknowledge my future husband, Jacob. Without him, I would have never met the deadline for this showing."

Jacob bowed to her.

"And to a good friend..." She glanced in Hawkeye's direction but didn't call out his name. "Thank you for setting all of this in motion."

He and Torin both looked toward the corner. Jacob hadn't been aware his friend had even entered. Like everyone else, he was wearing a tux, and no doubt he'd walk away tonight with a few more clients. There was no better place than New Orleans to meet people who needed to protect their secrets.

"To Julien Bonds, connoisseur of everything significant—"

People looked around for the Genius, but he wasn't in the room.

"Thank you for the wonderful equipment that I use when I'm creating." More photos were snapped.

"And most of all, I'd like to thank Claire Richardson and the entire staff at Gallery Royale for your belief in me and for hosting this exquisite event."

The guests applauded, the music struck up again, and the waitstaff moved into motion with canapés and other appetizers.

Elissa returned to his side and slid her palm against his. He was leaning over to kiss her when Claire swooped in. "I'm stealing her away. I have a social media influencer who wants to meet her."

He had no idea what that was. "I assume that's a good thing?"

SIERRA CARTWRIGHT

Claire ignored him and beckoned to a young woman with bright pink hair.

At a loose end, he sought out Hawkeye.

"I'm glad to see Elissa happy."

"She's happy you came."

"Hell, after what Bonds said—kinky shit—" Hawkeye smiled. "I wouldn't have missed it. Looks like she's quite a success."

"Two of her portraits have already sold."

"I'm sure it will be more by the end of the night. Claire has a great eye for up-and-coming talent. And her opinion matters. When she tells people to buy, they listen."

Right then, the lights flashed.

"Pardon the interruption..." A bigger-than-life-size holographic image of Julien Bonds appeared in the middle of the room.

A gasp rocked the air as patrons automatically stepped back to make room for the tech rock star. The music abruptly ceased, and silence echoed off the walls.

"He likes to make an entrance."

Jacob looked at Hawkeye. "He does indeed."

Though his image was comprised of a million shimmering parts, Bonds was both a presence and an enigma. He wore a white collared shirt, a thin bright-yellow tie, a gray jacket, blue jeans, and horrifyingly garish hot-pink shoes with glowing green laces. When he moved, the Bonds logo on his athletic shoes lit up.

"Where are you, Elissa?"

"Uhm..." Even as Claire nudged her forward, Elissa looked around for Jacob.

More than half the gathered attendees whipped out their cell phones for pictures and videos. Since Bonds was a notoriously private person, banning cameras when he attended events, this was a once-in-a-lifetime occurrence.

HOLD ON TO ME

Elissa found Jacob's gaze and shrugged. He grinned and gave her a thumbs-up. With his gesture, Bonds had ensured she'd be catapulted to the upper levels of the art world.

She neared the hologram and stopped.

"Ah. There you are." He waved his hand through the air. "It's the hour, and you are the woman of it."

"I… Am I?" She shook her head and laughed. "What I meant to say is thank you for being here."

"From the moment I saw your kinky shit—"

"Snooped through my hard drive is what I think you mean."

Go, Elissa. Jacob grinned.

"Well." Bonds cleared his throat. "Hmm. Well, then. The data had been delivered into my possession at the time, and it was a simple procedure of transferring it to your machine that is totally safe from any prying eyes."

Hawkeye cleared his throat as he'd been the one to authorize said transfer.

"At any rate, I needed to have something for my personal collection. Which is your most expensive offering?"

"Forever." Claire supplied the answer, pointing toward the gilt-framed portrait occupying prime space on an oversize easel. It was as if she'd been prepared for the moment.

And maybe she had been.

"It's a hundred and twenty thousand dollars."

Bonds staggered back a step.

Eyes wide with shock, Elissa spun to face Claire, who was grinning beatifically.

"I'm sure we must have a bad connection." At Bonds's absurd comment, people laughed. The transmission was flawless. "Did you say…" The leader of the first company in history to be valued at a trillion dollars took a breath, as if unable to comprehend that figure, wringing drama from the moment. "One hundred thousand dollars?"

SIERRA CARTWRIGHT

"No." All eyes were on Claire who was clearly playing her hand well. "I believe I said a hundred and fifty thousand dollars."

Jacob wouldn't have missed this moment for anything.

"Does that include shipping and handling?"

Claire arched an eyebrow. "Are you haggling, Mr. Bonds?"

"Well, a dollar is a dollar."

"Not only does it not include shipping or taxes—it doesn't include my handling fee."

Elissa looked back and forth between the two, and Jacob wasn't sure he'd ever seen a paid production that was this compelling.

Bonds grinned. "A bargain at thrice the price. I'll arrange for shipping—and handling—myself. Elissa, a pleasure meeting you. I look forward to adding more of your creations to my curation." With that misspeak—intentional or not, no one ever knew—Bonds vanished with sparkling fanfare.

Stunned, silent reverie hung in the air before everyone began speaking at once.

One of the assistants draped a purple SOLD sash around the painting.

Jacob said his goodbyes to Hawkeye and sought out Elissa. She appeared shell-shocked, and he leaned down to whisper in her ear. "You've arrived."

"Over a hundred thousand dollars?"

"I'm glad I got in when I did." Though she hadn't wanted to take money from him, he insisted that a deal was a deal. And now, in a matter of months, his investment had soared in value. Not that he'd ever part with it. To him, it was priceless.

The band resumed playing, this time at a louder volume that continued to feed the electric buzz that Bonds had sparked.

374

HOLD ON TO ME

Champagne flowed freely, Claire spoke to the woman who'd requested Elissa's autograph, and the gallery's assistants moved about the space with their Bonds tablets, quickly writing orders and taking payments.

"This whole experience has been crazy."

He lifted her hand and kissed it. "And well deserved."

"Since I met you, all my wildest dreams have come true."

"All of them?"

"Well..." Seductively she bit her lower lip before placing her hands on his shoulders and rising onto her tiptoes to create intimacy. "Maybe not all of them."

Hunger and desire flooded him. "Shall we get to work on them?"

"How soon do you think we can escape?"

He glanced around the room. "You've got a legion of fans hoping for a moment of your time."

"Okay." She nodded. "An hour?"

"Meet me in the courtyard. There's a gate we can use. I'll have the car waiting back there."

"One hour?" She checked her watch, then brushed a kiss across his lips. "Don't be late. We have babies to make..." She paused and straightened his lapels. "Sir."

"We have...?" For the first time ever, she'd made him tongue-tied.

She smiled. "If you're ready, so am I."

"Are you sure? I know we talked about waiting until your opening, but I didn't know you meant it immediately after."

"I've never been more sure of anything."

Love and lust collided, forcing a rush of primal need through him. He needed to possess her, be in her. Holding that passion momentarily in check, he held her, cherished her, and pressed a gentle kiss to the top of her head.

"So we're agreed, you'll be on time?"

SIERRA CARTWRIGHT

He was considering summoning the car right this moment. "My Liss. You can bet everything I own on it."

"Good. I can't wait to have your children."

Grinning stupidly, he watched her sashay back into the crowd. He couldn't wait, either. Months ago, he'd been alone, a broken shell of a person, and now... Now? Her love had breathed air into his life.

He'd do anything, everything to make her happy.

Even though she was talking to a young couple, she looked over her shoulder to find him. She blew him a kiss and mouthed "Soon."

For him, it wasn't soon enough.

He waited fifty minutes, which was all he could tolerate, then called the driver. Then when she was alone, he strode across the room, swept her up and over his shoulder.

She squealed as the air rushed out of her lungs. "Jacob!"

"Tell me to stop acting like a Neanderthal, and I will."

"No way." She grabbed his tuxedo jacket. "When I talked to you about making babies, I suspected you'd do something like this."

The stunned crowd parted for them as he strode through the courtyard.

In the car, he told the driver to put up the privacy screen; then he captured her mouth in a hungry, demanding kiss. It was enough—barely enough—to sustain him for the few minutes it would take for them to reach the hotel and ride the elevator to their suite.

"Is this how it's going to be, Sir?"

"Oh yes. From this day forward."

"Promise?"

"Yeah." He tugged her head back so she could see the pure honesty in his eyes. "I promise."

She leaned forward, and he took her mouth again, sealing his vow forever.

HOLD ON TO ME

◊ ◊ ◊ ◊ ◊

Thank you for reading Beg For Me! I've loved the men of Hawkeye for years. To make me happy, just give me a determined, protective alpha male any day of the week. :::shivers:::

I invite you to continue your Hawkeye adventure with Initiation…

Hawkeye agent Logan Powell does the women of the world a favor by avoiding emotional entanglements. They deserve to be loved and cherished, something he's not capable of.

But when he meets the beautiful and innocent Jennifer Berklee, not even his military training will be enough to keep his jaded heart safe…

DISCOVER INITIATION

If you enjoyed Trace and Mira's trip to the Quarter in New Orleans, I think you'll really love His to Claim. It was only supposed to be for a weekend. Now the overwhelming billionaire Dominant is demanding Hannah's heart forever. ★★★★★ Full of real, raw, beautiful emotions with vibrant characters. ~Amazon Reviewer

DISCOVER HIS TO CLAIM

Continue reading for an excerpt from INITIATION

INITIATION
CHAPTER ONE

*F*uck.

Ever since he'd been unceremoniously dumped on his ass three years ago, Logan Powell had done the world a favor by avoiding the fairer sex. Women had very real needs, emotional as well as physical. They deserved to be involved with someone who was a better person than he was.

So what the hell was he doing in the dungeon of his friend's home, at a BDSM play party, staring at the petite blonde on the other side of the room?

It wasn't just her strong, athletic build that attracted him, but also the short blonde hair that framed her face, fuck-me boots, tight black T-shirt and skimpy leather skirt. But what did him in was the way she tugged on the hem of her skirt in a betrayal of nerves.

He propped a foot against the wall behind him and watched her exhale as he considered his next move.

It had been months since he'd scened. And on the rare occasions when he did play, he preferred to engage with experienced submissives. If his tingling detective senses were

SIERRA CARTWRIGHT

anything to go by, the woman in question had never been dominated.

Double fuck.

He shouldn't ache to be the one to give her the first taste of the exquisite pleasure that came from submitting. *Shouldn't.* But he did.

Joe Montrose, the house's owner and tonight's host, walked over and stood next to Logan. "Jennifer…"

"What?" Logan cupped his ear to indicate he was having difficulty hearing over the thundering pulse of a Nine Inch Nails song.

Joe repeated himself. "Her name's Jennifer Berklee. She works with Noelle. It's Jennifer's first time at one of these events."

"I'm not interested." Logan shook his head, wondering when he'd become a liar.

"You don't miss it?"

"Playing with a newbie?" Teaching her about her own responses? Driving her to the edge of distraction, keeping her there, then shoving her over it so he could catch her and care for her? "No."

"Not at all?"

Despite himself, Logan watched as Jennifer squared her shoulders and moved toward Simon, a Dom who attended a number of events in the area. Her hips swayed alluringly, and Logan adored the way she all but strutted in those booted heels. For a stupid, but thankfully brief second, he wished she was walking in his direction. "Is Simon still looking for someone to collar?" Logan asked. Simple Simon, as Logan thought of him, though it probably wasn't a fair nickname. But from what Logan had seen, the man had a single approach to women, and a boring one at that. He never seemed to drive a sub to the very edges of endurance and

BEG FOR ME

give her amazing completion. The man wasn't a bad Top, just an uninspired one.

"Yeah," Joe replied. "He's been looking since Lisa ditched him."

Shouldn't matter. Nope. Not a bit.

Joe said something that Logan missed. Even though he clearly knew he was being ignored, Joe kept running his mouth. "So, are you?"

Logan dragged his attention away from Jennifer. "Am I what?"

"Coming to Noelle's surprise birthday party? She's turning thirty."

"When is it?"

"Three weeks."

Logan turned and narrowed his gaze at the man who'd been a friend since basic training. Later, after they'd left the service, they'd returned to the Middle East as civilian contractors. They'd survived two years of skin-searing heat and an explosion where most of their team had died.

Now they worked together again, based out of the Denver office of Hawkeye Security. They still had each other's backs. Because of what they'd shared and how well they knew each other, Logan's vague answer meant he was hedging. "What date?" Logan asked. "Specifically."

"Ah. February fourteenth."

Logan scowled. "I fucking hate Valentine's Day. You know that." It wasn't just the cloying expectations but the still-raw memories he preferred to leave buried. Being among happy, loving couples only made it worse.

"Missing the party will make you a bigger asshole than you already are."

"Fuck off."

Joe grinned. Not much bothered the man.

SIERRA CARTWRIGHT

In silence, they watched the exchange between Jennifer and Master Simon.

"If you're interested in playing with her, either Noelle or I can arrange it." Without waiting for a reply, Joe moved off, leaving Logan in blessed, voyeuristic peace.

Dom and sub spoke for a few moments and eventually Master Simon nodded at the St. Andrew's cross.

A blaze of unwelcome and unwanted possession arced through Logan as she closed the distance toward the X-shaped BDSM equipment.

As if sensing his attention, she glanced over at him.

He folded his arms across his chest as their gazes locked.

Even across the distance, he saw her shiver.

Smart girl, recognizing his danger.

After a few seconds, she shook her head and turned away.

Simple Simon took a step in her direction.

Suddenly Logan realized he did want to be the man behind her, pressing her against the wood, instructing her to lift her arms high so he could affix her wrists to a pair of cuffs.

Instead, another man had that honor.

The man secured her in place, and she immediately pulled her right wrist free. If Logan were in charge, that wouldn't have happened. Even if all she wanted was a taste of his dominance, he'd make sure she would never forget the experience.

After putting her wrist back in place, Master Simon rubbed her buttocks through her skirt.

Logan's cock thickened.

Because he needed human contact to maintain his sanity, he showed up at Joe and Noelle's events several times a year. While watching others scene interested him, he'd rarely gotten aroused from it.

382

BEG FOR ME

Then again, he'd rarely had this kind of visceral reaction to a woman.

Master Simon selected a sturdy leather paddle. It wasn't a bad decision, Logan mused. The toy was intimate, but not overly so. And since her delectable derriere was covered by her skirt, the impact would be minimal. Good choice for a neophyte.

Master Simon gave the sub three swats.

The third made her move her body to one side—something she did easily since her ankles weren't secured.

Another mistake Logan wouldn't make.

He wanted his subs to feel every damn thing he did to them. He wanted them aware, aroused, interested, committed, and he wanted them to stay in place while it was happening.

Without any change to the rhythm, Master Simon delivered two more swats.

Then the man put down the paddle on a nearby bench, and she freed herself from the restraints.

Logan blinked. Was the scene already over?

Jennifer turned toward Simon, adjusted her skirt, then smiled politely before scurrying up the staircase.

With a curse, Logan pushed away from the wall and followed. If she had scened with him, there would have been no bland, polite smiles afterward. At the very least, he would have talked to her and asked questions instead of allowing her to walk away.

When he found her, she was near the front door, reaching to take her coat from a rack.

"May I?" he asked.

"I…" She dropped her hand and turned toward him before meeting his gaze.

Until they were this close, he hadn't known her eyes were blue, bright, wide, and vibrant.

383

He wanted to see them widen with shock, darken with desire. "Logan Powell," he said by way of introduction as he grabbed her coat and held it for her.

"Thank you." She settled into it, then knotted the belt around her waist as she faced him.

"I watched your scene with Master Simon."

Her shoulders stiffened.

"You didn't seem all that into it."

Her mouth was pressed into a firm line, making him realize he wasn't any more adept than Simon had been. Bulldozing on, Logan took a business card from his wallet and offered it to her.

She hesitated, and he wasn't sure she'd accept it.

"Feel free to call me if you want to experience a real scene."

"That felt real to me." She rubbed her behind.

"Perhaps I'm mistaken," he allowed. "But it seemed as if you might have wanted something more. BDSM is not just about impact. There's a mental and emotional component as well. Trust is involved, and so is getting exactly what you're looking for. I think you know that."

She glanced at his contact information before taking his card and stuffing it into her pocket.

"Joe and Noelle can vouch for me."

After saying good night but not responding to his offer, she left, closing the door behind her with a decisive click.

"You crashed and burned," Joe observed.

"How long have you been lurking?" Logan pivoted to level a glare at his friend.

"Lurking? I prefer to think of it as making sure my guests find their way out safely."

Noelle joined them. "Ignore my husband. He's being nosy." She lightly pressed her fingertips to her husband/Dominant's forearm.

BEG FOR ME

Logan didn't miss the sign of deference and affection. Until this moment, he hadn't envied the pair their hard-won relationship. Tonight, though, he felt a twinge of regret for the life choices he'd made.

"I was hoping Jennifer would talk to you." Noelle sighed. "She needs someone."

"Maybe if Logan had more tact than your average gorilla, he might have had a chance."

Noelle frowned at Joe.

"She took my card." Logan needed to advocate for himself. Maybe, maybe, she'd contact him.

"YOU SHOULD CALL HIM," NOELLE SAID.

Jennifer feigned ignorance. "Call who?"

Noelle snagged a garlic bread stick from a basket and wagged it at Jennifer.

"Who are you talking about?" asked Ella, another member of the infamous Carpe Diem Divas.

To avoid the unwelcome question—and her startling responses to the unforgettable Dominant—Jennifer reached for the bottle of Chianti and topped off the wineglasses of the four other women gathered around her kitchen table.

The small group had started meeting two years ago when they were all going through relationship challenges. They decided they'd seize life, no matter what it tossed at them. Over a pitcher of margaritas at Fiesta Olé, their favorite Mexican restaurant in South Denver, the Carpe Diem Divas had been formed.

Even though Noelle was now happily married to Joe, she still attended. Jennifer couldn't blame her. The evenings were fun, filled with laughter, support, and shared secrets.

Tonight, they were gathered in her somewhat-renovated

SIERRA CARTWRIGHT

Highlands bungalow for the first time. To save money, she was doing most of the work herself, which meant some things were almost finished and others were nowhere close, including the dining room walls that were still a shocking shade of canary yellow.

"We're talking about Logan Powell." With a smile, Noelle answered Ella. "He's a hunky Dom." She folded her arms triumphantly. "And he's interested in Jennifer."

"What?" Ella demanded, turning to face Jennifer. "Details. Now. All of them."

Hyperaware that she was the focus of everyone's attention, she took a sip of wine and stalled. "There's nothing to tell. Really."

Undaunted, Ella leaned forward. "Where did you meet him?"

Noelle supplied the information with a smile. "At a play party at my house."

"Do you mind?" Jennifer scowled. "What if I wanted it to be a secret?"

She expected her best friend to show some sympathy, but Morgan defected to the other side. "No secrets in this group."

Noelle grinned in triumph.

"You went to a party?" Ella prompted. "About time."

About a year ago, she and a few members of the Carpe Diem Divas had gone to see a movie about BDSM. Of course Jennifer had heard about BDSM, but seeing it played out, larger than life, with one of her favorite actors in the leading role as a Dom, had fascinated her.

She'd watched, unblinkingly, as the man had removed his shirt and flogged his helpless submissive. She'd imagined herself in the heroine's role, helpless beneath a man's sensuous lash.

At a bar afterward, she'd pestered Noelle with dozens of questions. But it had taken Jennifer a number of months to

BEG FOR ME

work up the courage to accept an invitation to experience it for herself.

Ella was nothing if not persistent. "Did you play with this Logan guy?"

"No." Jennifer shook her head. "With someone else."

"And what did he do to you?"

"He, um"—she ran her finger over the base of the wine-glass—"gave me a few swats."

"A few swats? Is that all?"

"What did he use?" Amelia asked.

"A paddle," Jennifer admitted.

Noelle sat back, sipping her wine, following the conversation as if it were a tennis match.

"Wait a minute." Morgan scowled. "I thought you had a thing for floggers."

Definitely, there were no secrets with this group of friends.

She and Morgan had recently gone shopping for a bachelorette party that Morgan was hosting. They'd ended up at an adult book store. And, encouraging each other, they'd ended up in the shop's dungeon area. Maybe because of the movie, she hadn't been able to get the idea of floggers out of her mind. Fortified by the mojito she'd had at dinner, she'd allowed the sales guy to show her the expensive leather pieces. Morgan had encouraged her to buy one. Before the end of the night, she was the owner of a still-unused flogger that had cost her half a paycheck.

"Back to the story." Ella drummed her fingers on the tabletop. "What kind of paddle was it? A wooden one like in the movie?"

"It was leather."

"How was it?" Amelia asked.

Jennifer wrinkled her nose.

"You didn't like it?" Ella demanded.

SIERRA CARTWRIGHT

"It was a bit disappointing. I was dressed, so…" She shrugged. "I didn't really feel much."

"That's why you should call Logan." Noelle finally rejoined the conversation. "He'd give you a paddling you'll never forget. Better yet, a flogging."

Jennifer squirmed as her whole body heated.

"You *have* been thinking about him." Noelle narrowed her eyes.

All week. Jennifer had remembered the way Logan had held her coat and the way he'd skimmed his strong hands across her shoulders. He'd ignited nerve endings as well as her imagination.

At six-foot-something, he towered over her and was impossibly broad. His raven-colored hair fell in place with military precision. When he spoke, respect and command lace his baritone.

No one had ever studied her as intently as he had. His piercing jade-colored eyes had unnerved her. It was as though he'd seen beyond her polite veneer and wanted to excavate beneath the surface until he revealed her every last secret. "He's not my type." Was she hoping to convince herself or her friends?

"Why not?" Noelle demanded.

"He's…" Jennifer paused. She didn't have to struggle to remember details. No matter how hard she'd tried, she'd been unable to erase details of their exchange from her thoughts. But how did she describe his disturbing effect on her? With a sigh, she settled for, "Dangerous." Too masculine. Too intent. If she hadn't refused him, he would have over-whelmed her.

"You have to admit his scar's sexy as hell."

Scary, as well. It meant they were from different worlds, and she likely didn't understand his.

BEG FOR ME

"He has a scar?" Ella asked, looking between the two of them. "What kind of scar? Where?"

Without giving Jennifer a chance to answer, Noelle supplied he information. "A big, jagged one. It runs from the corner of his eye up into his hairline." Noelle gave a delicious shudder. "When I asked him about it one time, he changed the subject. And Joe told me to leave it alone."

Jennifer didn't want to be intrigued, but she was. More than she wanted to admit, she thirsted for details. "He and Logan have been friends forever, since they were in the service. Then they went to the Middle East together, but Joe doesn't talk about that much. I'm guessing that's where it happened."

Ella asked the question that Jennifer wanted answered. "What does he do now?"

"Works for Hawkeye, of course. Just like Joe." Noelle sighed. "I guess once a warrior, always a warrior."

Amelia shivered dramatically. "Logan sounds yummy."

"He is." Jennifer had noticed him the moment he'd entered the basement, and her core temperature had shot up. And his scar had tantalized her, continually drawn her attention, despite her intention not to stare.

When she'd gone home after the party, she'd masturbated. But instead of remembering the paddling, she'd imagined that Logan had been standing behind her. Rather than swatting her through the skirt, she'd fantasized that he'd bared her skin and given her hard, deliberate smacks.

And now...the image of him wielding a flogger was all but etched in her mind.

"So why haven't you called him?" Ella asked.

Her blood went sluggish. "Because I'm a coward."

"No you're not," Amelia countered. "You did go to the party after all."

Jennifer appreciated her friend's loyalty.

SIERRA CARTWRIGHT

Noelle smiled at Jennifer. "Here's your chance to live a little. Let go of your past."

She'd always done the right thing. In school, she'd worked hard so she could get into the college her parents had selected for her. She'd graduated near the top of her class, become a CPA, and joined her father's firm, exactly as expected. Even so, she was still figuring out what *she* wanted.

"I think he's trustworthy," Noelle went on. "Joe considers him a friend. He doesn't say that about many people. Very few, in fact. And…" She slid her glass onto the table as she mysteriously trailed off."

Despite herself, Jennifer scooted forward on her chair.

Noelle glanced around, heightening the tension. "I've spoken to a couple of the subs he's played with…"

"Quit teasing!" Ella laughed. "You're driving us crazy."

"They say he's an exceptional Dom. Unrelenting, demanding, but patient."

Amelia and Morgan fanned themselves. Jennifer was tempted to do the same.

"As good as the guy in the movie?" Morgan asked.

"Better." Noelle sighed.

Amelia shook her head. "No way!"

"He's a pretty wonderful guy." Noelle leveled a look at Jennifer. "You could do worse."

Ella gave a gentle smile. "I'm with the others. You deserve to be happy with a man who's worthy. You're far too amazing and wonderful to let the Cheating Asshole ruin your future."

"Brett," Jennifer supplied. And Ella was right. The man had occupied far too many of her thoughts. It was time to stop letting her past hurt define who she was.

"Maybe you should let this Logan guy flog you," Amelia said. "See how you like it, at least."

"*Master* Logan." Noelle grinned.

Jennifer met her friend's gaze.

"Well, if he were swinging a flogger at my naked body, I'd call him Master Logan."

No matter how hard Jennifer tried to shove that image from her mind, it wouldn't budge.

After a few giggles, the conversation moved on, thankfully away from her and a fictional scene with Logan.

Amelia mentioned the new guy who'd been hired at her firm. She said he dressed in suits and seemed aloof. "I saw him last weekend while I was running in Washington Park."

"You were running?" Morgan asked, eyes wide.

Amelia shrugged. "So, fine. I might have been walking, but he was like a world-class marathoner. It was so warm that day." She fanned herself. "And he was wearing short-shorts, and a mesh-like sleeveless shirt, and his arms are all tattooed."

"Mr. Professional has an intriguing side." Morgan took a drink of wine.

"Did you talk to him?" Ella asked.

"Maybe trip him?" Morgan supplied with a laugh.

Amelia shook her head.

"You should go for it," Noelle encouraged. "Ask him to coffee or something. What can it hurt?"

Though she tried to participate in the conversation and nodded at what she hoped were appropriate intervals, Jennifer's mind once again returned to thought of Logan, even though she tried to shove them away. But a tantalizing fantasy unwound, one in which he might demand she call him Master...

Once her guests had gone home for the evening, images of the breathtakingly handsome man became brighter, more vivid, and completely persistent. More than ever, she wished she had been brave enough to take him up on his offer at Noelle's party.

She retrieved his business card from her coat pocket

where it had rested, undisturbed, for more than a week.

His name was listed directly beneath the words Hawkeye Security. There was nothing else other than an email address and office phone number.

She traced her fingers across the raised lettering, and a dragon seemed to roar to life in her stomach. It wasn't butterflies, but something fire-breathing, threatening to consume her.

As much as she wanted to have the courage to take her friends' advice, she couldn't find the courage.

Instead, she dropped the card back into the pocket. At some point, she'd see him at a future event. If he invited her to scene again, she'd accept his offer. She wouldn't give into her fear a second time. After all, Noelle had said he was a good Dom. And that made him a safe choice.

A chill skated up her spine and caused a cold feeling to seep into her head.

There was no way Logan Powell—Master Logan—was safe, no matter how much she wanted to believe he was.

As Noelle had noted, he was a warrior, had seen combat. And Jennifer knew that Joe's job at Hawkeye was all sorts of dangerous.

But that realization didn't stop her from walking into her closet and taking her flogger down from its hook.

She traced one of the strands. The leather was firm and thick.

For a frightening, dizzying second, she pictured the handle in Logan's hand as he took a purposeful step toward her.

Her breath froze. More than anything, she wanted him…

DISCOVER INITIATION

Continue reading for an excerpt from HIS TO CLAIM

HIS TO CLAIM

CHAPTER ONE EXCERPT

There were a hell of a lot better ways Mason could be spending his Friday night. Watching a documentary on television, for example. Doing woodwork in his shop. Putting together ideas for his upcoming pitch to a home and garden network for a renovation show.

Instead, not looking forward to the evening, Mason pushed through the door that led from the stairs to the reception area of the Quarter, New Orleans' most exclusive BDSM club.

Because of the large number of guests arriving for tonight's charity slave auction, Aviana, the owner, was helping the receptionist check people in. When she spotted him, she smiled. A moment later, she excused herself and rounded the podium to greet him. "Mason!"

"Milady." He raised her hand to his lips. "Radiant, as always."

Tonight, the tall, willowy woman looked fierce, every bit the Mistress she was. Her boots snuggled her thighs, and the heels sent her soaring past six feet tall. Her two-piece outfit was sensational. The skirt and cropped jacket-type top were

HIS TO CLAIM

brown leather armor and adorned with hundreds of metal pyramid spikes. Her long hair was piled on top of her head, and silver pins were stabbed into it, making sure none of the strands dared attempt an escape.

"You look dashing," she said, smoothing one of his lapels.

"It's rented."

"Your secret is safe with me."

It wasn't a secret. Mason spent his days in blue jeans, well-worn boots, and T-shirts as he visited his job sites. When he had the chance, he swung the hammer himself.

"I didn't expect to see you."

"You..." He cleared his throat. *Coerced.* "Convinced me."

She smiled with obvious triumph.

To be fair, he owed her the show of support. They both served on the board of a charity his father had started, rehabilitating homes for the city's elderly population. And once a year, Aviana hosted a fundraiser that helped make their work possible. He'd skipped last year's event, and she'd made a point of mentioning that fact at each of their monthly meetings ever since.

Still, this was the last place he wanted to be. He preferred to visit the Quarter on those rare occasions when he desired the connection with a submissive.

"Program?" Aviana offered, taking one of the folded pieces of paper from the top of the podium.

He shook his head. "That won't be necessary. Thanks." Mason had no intention of bidding on any of the women participating in the slave auction.

"Who knows? Perhaps you might be tempted."

To spend an entire weekend with a woman he'd purchased? Not likely. It had been more than two years since he'd invited anyone to share his bed. He checked his watch. "What time can I escape?"

"The festivities should end around midnight."

HIS TO CLAIM

"Drinks being served?"

"The bar is closed until the auction ends."

He generally appreciated her rules. Right now? Not so much. The next few hours would be much easier with a nice bourbon.

A crowd entered the foyer, filling the space with laughter.

"We'll catch up later?" she suggested. "Perhaps lunch within the next couple of weeks?"

"As long as it's friendly, with no written agenda."

"Of course."

He eyed her suspiciously, unsure whether she was telling the truth.

Aviana turned away, then stopped to look back over her shoulder. "I'm glad you came."

He gave her a half smile. It was the best he could manage. Until he picked up the tux a few hours ago, he hadn't been sure he'd actually attend.

Mason pushed through the frosted-glass door leading to the dungeon that was filled with loud, thumping music, no doubt meant to excite the crowd.

The first thing he noticed was Aviana's throne, placed on a raised dais off to one side where she could lord over the event.

All the usual play equipment had been removed from the area. The Saint Andrew's crosses were lined up against the walls, with spanking benches placed in front of them.

A stage had been erected at the far end of the room. Never one to do things by half measures, Aviana had hired lighting and camera crews and had positioned two large screens at angles so that all attendees would have a good view.

Comfortable padded chairs had been arranged in precise rows for the bidders and gawkers who'd paid Aviana's exorbitant admission fee. He knew exactly how much it was,

HIS TO CLAIM

since she'd billed his ticket to the credit card the club kept on file for his incidental expenses.

Numerous gilded cages hung from the ceiling, all containing at least one person, several containing two. The entertainers moved in time to the music, some holding on to a wire in the top, others grabbing the bars, a few sliding up and down. The atmosphere seethed with energy.

For twenty minutes, he talked to a few people he knew and thanked them for attending and supporting the charity.

Suddenly the lights dimmed. Music shut off, and as if on cue, performers froze in place in their cages.

"Welcome to the Quarter!" The words reverberated through the dungeon, loud and commanding.

On the stage, a flash exploded, and a stunning couple appeared near the edge. They were tall, exceedingly thin, and they looked so much alike he guessed they were twins, though one appeared to be female, the other male.

They were dressed identically in stark-white pantsuits. Each had enormous eyes, with long, feathery lashes. Stunningly, they also sported dark hair, cut in a long bob, accented by angular bangs. Aviana was providing her guests with a spectacle. Despite himself, Mason was intrigued.

The twins clapped in unison, then spoke as one. "Ladies and gentlemen, your seats, please."

Dungeon monitors urged attendees toward the chairs. Mason remained where he was, back pressed against the wall. Tore, Aviana's massive bearded chief dungeon monitor, nodded his permission to allow Mason to stay where he was.

As soon as everyone was in place, the twins spoke again. "Please rise for Mistress Aviana."

The doors were thrown open, and Aviana stalked into the room. Two beautiful male submissives trailed behind her, their leashes attached to her epaulets.

She made her way down the center aisle. With each step,

HIS TO CLAIM

the gold in her outfit shimmered beneath the spotlights that were turned on her. When she neared the front of the room, Tore fell in step next to her, then offered his hand as she climbed onto her dais.

After waving to acknowledge her adoring crowd, she took her seat on the throne. It had been commissioned years before by an admiring sub, and Aviana's likeness was carved into the top. The rounded arm ends were custom-made from a plaster cast of her grip. As befitting her stature, the upholstery was the finest maroon-colored velvet. It had been crafted with hooks in strategic places where she could attach a slave or submissive.

Once her subs were settled, curled at her feet and chained in place, the twins invited the audience to return to their chairs.

Aviana didn't put on many displays of her dominance, but when she did, the power of her command was as impressive as hell. His gaze strayed to the men at her feet.

At one time, he'd had a submissive who showed him the same kind of deference. But behaving well during a scene hadn't meant a flying fuck outside of it. When she finally left him—at the worst possible time—part of him had been relieved. Since then, he'd avoided personal entanglements.

Until this moment, he hadn't missed having a sub.

Maybe Aviana had been right to encourage him to visit the Quarter more often.

The twins introduced the evening's emcee, Jaxon Mills, a renowned—and at times polarizing—internet marketing superstar. The man had in excess of a million followers on his social media platforms, people who hung on his every video and podcast. He'd started giving speeches to rapt audiences, and since his recent marriage, he'd evidently stepped up his volunteer work as well.

A spotlight hit Jax as he all but leaped onto the stage. He

HIS TO CLAIM

pointed a finger, then swept it wide, indicating everyone in the crowd. "Get your checkbooks out and your credit cards ready. We have the world's most stunning subs available for you tonight. And it's all for a good cause. You've heard of Reclamation, a charity that benefits seniors living in our great city." On the screens, a video started, showing volunteers scraping paint, hammering shingles into place, installing windows, working on plumbing, replacing furniture and appliances. Everyone was dressed in T-shirts bearing the charity's logo. Volunteers were dirty, sweaty, but smiling, often pictured with the residents they were helping.

Surprising Mason, several of the images included a picture of him.

Without losing a beat, Jaxon continued. "This is what your contribution does. As you know, the need in our community is great. Because of your abundant contributions, last year we restored more than two hundred homes. If you were one of the heroes who made that possible, thank you." He pushed his palms together and bowed. "But let's be honest, shall we?" His voice was low and intimate.

The man's charisma had the room spellbound.

"You know damn good and well that you're fortunate sons of bitches. You can do a fuckpile more than you do. You can dig deeper. If you don't help out tonight, you're a loser, and I'm calling you out on it. We're here for a purpose, and that isn't just to leer at some gorgeous humans. It's to leer *and* make our city proud."

"Hear, hear!" a woman called out.

The video ended, and he stood there in a shimmering pool of light.

When the raucous clapping ended, Jax reached inside his tuxedo jacket, pulled out his wallet, and extracted a check. "Can I get a close-up, please?" Jax held up the piece of paper.

The audience gasped, and Mason nodded approvingly. A

HIS TO CLAIM

hundred grand. Not a bad way to start the evening. There was a stunning amount of good they could do with that kind of money.

"I have a confession." Jaxon folded the check and used a thumbnail to make the crease sharp. "I'd budgeted fifty thousand for this event. But my wife watched this video. After seeing it, she volunteered for the charity."

A spotlight found a woman who was at the front of the room. She wore a long gold gown, formfitting and glittering with sequins.

"In case you don't know, this is my wife, Willow Mills."

People cheered for her, and Mason knew, firsthand, it was deserved. Despite being a submissive, she was next to her husband, and he credited her with helping him become a better man.

"Tell them what you said to me, honey."

"I told *you* not to be a cheapskate"—a close-up image of her face was being projected on the screen, and her eyes danced with laughter that showed the love between them— "Sir."

The crowd exploded with laughter and more applause.

"All right, all right!" He grinned. When the attendees settled again, he went on. "So I'm passing along her words. Don't be a damn cheapskate. Our seniors have given so much over the years. It's time to give back. And hey, if you're not bidding, or you miss out on your favorite slave, you aren't off the hook."

More hoots and cheers greeted his words.

"There are silent auction items in the bar and reception areas. I know you want to hear some of the highlights. How about a week on a private island in the Caribbean? Griffin Lahey has made the donation, and your stay there includes a chef and an outdoor massage for two." Images scrolled across the screens, of a couple snorkeling among tiny bright-

HIS TO CLAIM

colored fish, then lounging on chairs beneath an umbrella, a cocktail in hand. A sunset was shown next, with kayaks seemingly being rowed out toward it.

How long had it been since Mason had taken a vacation? *Shit.* He dragged his hand through his hair. Not since his dad had passed. The year before that, Mason had been swamped with trying to keep the business running by himself. Maybe that explained his soul-deep exhaustion.

"If that's not your style, how about a high-roller weekend at the Royal Sterling Hotel in Las Vegas?" The resort was pictured, soaring from the Strip with its glass sparkling against the desert sun.

Though Mason wasn't a gambler, the restaurants were legendary, and the pool was the stuff of fantasies. He could sleep there for a week. *Jesus.* He really did need to get away.

"Perhaps you'd like to fall in love with New York this autumn with a package that includes tickets to the hottest performances"—the pictures showed Broadway, then Grand Central Station—"a horse-drawn carriage ride through Central Park, and three nights and unlimited possibilities in the penthouse suite at Le Noble."

Even though he had no one to invite along, Mason was tempted to bid on every damn one of the escapes.

"We have something for every taste. How about a signed giclée by Flahey?"

A few people gasped at the sight of the bold colors and staggering lines slashed across the canvas. Mason knew the artist was well respected. He just didn't understand why. The image was supposed to be of a rock star. If he squinted and turned his head to the side, he could make out a guitar. Maybe. Still, the man commanded a fortune from collectors. The cynic in Mason would definitely prefer that money go to Reclamation.

"If you don't win a weekend with one of the Quarter's

HIS TO CLAIM

amazing subs or one of our spectacular prizes, we'll still accept your more than generous contribution at the end of the evening. There will be boxes throughout the space, at the coat check, at the exit, and a bunch at the bar. Oh, and one last thing—free drinks for anyone who donates more than five grand." He paused for dramatic effect. "I hope you were prepared for me giving away your booze, Mistress Aviana!"

The camera flashed to her. She gave a half smile and a very regal nod.

"Ah, and finally, anyone who donates over ten thousand dollars will get an exclusive half-day consultation with me."

That was reportedly worth a lot more than ten grand. Jax was gifted at studying a business, branding it, focusing on its strengths, and positioning it for success.

"And if you don't contribute something, your name is going on my shitlist."

His statement was met with laughter—some genuine, some nervous.

"In case this is your first auction, I'll give you a little background on how the evening will proceed. We have a total of fifteen slaves. Yes, fifteen gorgeous, well-behaved individuals"—he looked directly into the camera—"who want to spend the weekend with *you.*"

"Get on with it!" someone shouted.

"They will be presented for your inspection in groups of five. After all the introductions have been made, we will have a brief intermission, and then the bidding will start. Now... who's ready to begin?"

The dungeon plunged into darkness. Moments later, strategic lights hit the stage and the overhead cages with their writhing occupants. Cheers rocked the room, and music again blasted through the air, a thumping, arousing sound that penetrated even Mason's jaded senses.

Behind Jaxon, a black curtain parted to reveal a large

HIS TO CLAIM

rectangular acrylic platform with two steps leading up to it. There were other round see-through pedestals fanned out in a semicircle.

Jax moved to one side, and Tore strode onto the stage. As usual, he wore a vest. Tonight, however, instead of the customary one with fleur-de-lis, this was crafted from the same brown leather as Mistress Aviana's, and it hung open to show off his honed abs.

Over his shoulder was a long, thick chain, with the first five volunteer slaves attached to it. The group was eclectic. Tall and short. Male and female. Of various ages and ethnicities. Men wore only a scrap of stark-white material, not much more than a pouch that left little to the imagination. The women were dressed in string bikinis beneath sheer sarongs.

The twins floated onto the stage. Together, they unclipped the first slave from the chain and assisted her onto one of the platforms. The camera followed each of her flawless moves.

They repeated the process for each participant. When they were finished, they stepped aside while the camera panned the semicircle. Most of the slaves were relaxed, and one of the men was flexing his biceps, trying to draw attention.

"There you are!" Jaxon called. "It's going to be an extraordinary night!"

Adrenaline fired through the room in the form of claps and appreciative whistles. As much as Mason wanted to be immune, he wasn't. It was a hell of a spectacle.

"Ladies and gentlemen, I present slave number one," Jaxon said when the audience settled down.

The twins helped the first sub from her platform and escorted her to the front of the stage where she stood in the spotlight.

HIS TO CLAIM

She lowered her gaze, then gave a quick peep through her lashes. It was seductive. Judging by the way one member of the audience sucked in a sharp breath, it was also effective.

"Fiona is looking for a top who is firm but fair. And fortunately for you, she's happy to be won by either a man or a woman." He went on to list her limits and then asked her to turn around so the bidders could study her from every angle. "The minimum bid will be five thousand dollars."

Several people used lights from their cell phones to scribble notes into the margins of their programs. The woman, as beautiful and obviously well trained as she was, didn't stir Mason.

After she'd turned around and presented herself in a variety of poses, the twins returned her to Tore, then escorted the second slave, a man, to the spotlight.

The process was repeated until all the slaves had been introduced. Once they were led away, the next set was brought on. Mason checked his watch. As he'd tried to tell Aviana, this wasn't his kind of event. He either came to scene or he stayed away.

After an interminable amount of time, Tore led the final group in for viewing.

And the woman who was second in line snared his interest.

She was at least half a foot shorter than he was, with impossibly large, wide-open eyes, and brunette hair that tumbled over her shoulders. The gauzy film that covered her couldn't disguise her small, beautiful figure. The building's air-conditioning hardened her nipples. To him, she was a tiny wisp of feminine perfection.

Repeating the same process as with the other participants, the twins unclipped her from Tore's chain. As she walked toward her acrylic platform, she missed a step and stumbled slightly. The twins reached for her upper arms to

HIS TO CLAIM

steady her. All the other slaves had appeared to be veterans and enjoying themselves, but her actions betrayed her as a novice.

Mason was torn, his dominant urges stirred. Part of him wanted to protect her. The other, more primal part of his nature urged him to make her his.

What the fuck was wrong with him?

He wasn't given to wild fantasies. Or, maybe he had been, once upon a time. But that had been before Deborah.

The slave gave a quick smile of gratitude before stepping up onto her display platform.

The twins moved aside, and the spotlight moved on to the next contestant. But he looked toward the shadowed part of the stage to watch number twelve. Her shoulders shook, and she curled one hand around the small collar she wore.

He was consumed with a need to know more about her. Why the hell hadn't he accepted one of the programs?

Mason checked his watch again, but for a different reason this time. He was anxious for the pomp and circumstance to be over with so he could have a better look at her.

After the other subs were in place, the first sub was brought forward. His impatience soared. He was interested in only one woman.

Finally, the twins led her to the front of the stage where she stood next to Jax. Her image was projected onto the big screens, making her larger than life. Confounding him, she kept her head lowered, shading her expression.

"Hannah joins us this weekend from Austin, Texas."

When she wobbled a little, Jaxon steadied her, and she grabbed on to him.

Even though he covered his mic to ask if she was all right, the words whispered through the dungeon. "Bend your knees a little. It will help."

She nodded and did what he said.

HIS TO CLAIM

"Do you want to continue?"

She dropped her hand to her side and nodded several times. "Just nerves."

After Jax studied her for a few seconds, he continued. "Hannah prefers a male Dom who is patient but unyielding. Her limits list includes canes, humiliation, isolation, being shared."

Suited Mason fine. He didn't like to share.

"Let's see your face," Jax encouraged softly, but firmly, part host, part reassuring Dominant.

In the glare of the spotlight, she turned to him, but he nodded toward the audience.

Hannah drew a deep breath before tipping back her chin. Her eyes were unblinking, and a bit wild. They were a rich shade of amber, ringed with a bright gold, speaking of riches. He shook his head. That was a trick of the light and his over-tired imagination.

"Turn around so your potential Doms can inspect you better."

The slave obeyed, and when she faced the front again, she seemed to seek Mason out. That wasn't possible. The lights would prevent her from seeing the back of the room, and the idea of her picking him out from the crowd was ludicrous.

"After the intermission, you'll have the chance to bid on our lovely Hannah. If you're making notes, she's number twelve in your program."

The twins collected her.

Several men grabbed pens. A couple more typed notes into their cell phones, pissing Mason off. *The fuck?* It might be irrational, but Mason decided no Dom but him was spending the weekend with her.

She was his. And within the hour, he intended to claim her.

As if she knew that, she once again glanced in his direction.

The auction continued, but Mason refused to take his gaze or his fantasies from the brunette who'd awakened something inside him that he'd been sure was dead.

DISCOVER HIS TO CLAIM

ABOUT THE AUTHOR

I invite you to be the very first to know all the news by subscribing to my very special VIP Reader newsletter! You'll find exclusive excerpts, bonus reads, and insider information.

https://www.sierracartwright.com/subscribe

For tons of fun and to join with other awesome people like you, join my reader group here:

https://www.facebook.com/groups/SierrasSuperStars

And for a current booklist, please visit my website.

https://www.sierracartwright.com

USA Today bestselling author Sierra Cartwright was born in England, and she spent her early childhood traipsing through castles and dreaming of happily-ever afters. She has two wonderful kids and four amazing grand-kitties. She now calls Galveston, Texas home and loves to connect with her readers. Please do drop her a note.

ALSO BY SIERRA CARTWRIGHT

Titans

Sexiest Billionaire

Billionaire's Matchmaker

Billionaire's Christmas

Determined Billionaire

Scandalous Billionaire

Relentless Billionaire

Titans Quarter

His to Claim

His to Love

His to Cherish

Titans Sin City

Hard Hand

Slow Burn

All-In

Hawkeye

Come to Me

Trust in Me

Meant For Me

Hold On To Me

Believe in Me

Master Class

Initiation

Determination

Temptation

Bonds

Crave

Claim

Command

Donovan Dynasty

Bind

Brand

Boss

Mastered

With This Collar

On His Terms

Over The Line

In His Cuffs

For The Sub

In The Den

Collections

Titans Series

Titans Billionaires: Firsts

Titans Billionaires: Volume 1

Hawkeye Series

Here for Me: Volume One

Beg For Me: Volume Two

Printed in Great Britain
by Amazon